The Nature of Demons

J.D. Carmicle

Demon Mythos

For my family

The mind is its own place, and in itself can make a heaven of hell, a hell of heaven.

John Milton, Paradise Lost

Chapter 1

Prelude

Humans are riddled with contradictions and insecurities, messy. Demons don't have that problem. They're pure.

The Last Day

Jacob tapped his phone to check the time. Quarter after midnight. He poured another glass of bourbon, leaned back into the leather of his favorite chair, and closed his eyes. Scriabin's tenth piano sonata moved around him like a phantom, its claws of dissonance plucking at his spine. Reality itself cracked along the music's contours. He caught a glimpse of another world, a place of mystery and dark beauty.

Tomorrow would bring court proceedings, settlement negotiations, trial preparations—all the games he had been playing for over a decade. If everything went well, another of his firm's clients would end up a step or two closer to freedom from whatever legal entanglement they had gotten themselves into. If things went poorly, he'd be in for a long night of crisis management.

Jacob took a sip of whisky to clear his head. This wasn't the time to worry about work, not while dreams of a life altogether different swirled through his mind.

Two o'clock had come and gone before he got to bed. Regardless of how anyone felt about it, a new day soon arrived, bearing lessons about drinking into the wee hours on a work night. A bleary-eyed wreck in rumpled pajamas, unshaven, his hair a riot of dark swirls, Jacob shuffled through the house to find his wife standing in a hellishly bright kitchen. She might as well have stepped out of a hospital advertisement, with her lab coat neatly buttoned over blue scrubs, a stethoscope slung around her neck, and her chestnut hair pulled into a no-nonsense bun.

"Breakfast?" Rebecca asked.

"No time, early meeting at the courthouse."

She gave him a look of low-grade concern. "Are you sure? I can pour you a bowl of cereal. It'll only take a minute."

"The meeting shouldn't take long. I'll grab something after."

Rebecca's weighted glances had become more frequent over the past several years. At thirty-eight, Jacob wasn't getting any younger. If he moved up at the firm, which seemed all but inevitable, he'd need to act more responsibly. And, of course, there was his health to consider. As a doctor, Rebecca's idea of a healthy lifestyle left precious few opportunities for late-night bourbon binges.

With a sigh, she went back to reviewing her schedule. She was most likely planning to leave work early to squeeze in some quality time with Micah, so everything needed to go like clockwork.

"Still picking M up at school today?" Jacob asked as he fumbled with the coffeemaker.

"Yeah. I'll see patients in the morning, then look over lab results and catch up on paperwork during lunch. Whatever I don't get done by two—"

Micah burst into the kitchen, an explosion of blonde hair and skinny limbs dressed in a plaid skirt and a black t-shirt emblazoned with an anarchy symbol. Jacob had given her the shirt a couple months earlier for her tenth birthday, despite Rebecca's insistence that a kid wouldn't know what to make of it. Laughing like a lunatic, Micah bounced off Rebecca, almost spilling her coffee, and careened toward her dad.

Jacob's morning sluggishness vanished in an instant. He caught her in an embrace that lifted her off her feet. Between wild fits of giggling, she yelled in what she took to be an English accent: "'Cause I wanna be *an-ar-chy!*"

"Is there really time for this, Jacob?" Rebecca snapped. "Aren't you supposed to be downtown?" She shifted her gaze to Micah. "And you know you can't wear that to school. Go upstairs and change. We're leaving in ten minutes."

Micah ran off, Jacob's jolt of energy fading with her receding laughter. Deflated, he returned to his morning routine.

The meeting at the courthouse was about a lawsuit filed against a local plastic surgeon. Allegedly, the plaintiff had lost all sensation in her cheeks after a facelift. The presiding judge had summoned the attorneys for both sides to discuss a procedural matter. Hopefully, it wouldn't take long. Mike Stevens, opposing council in the lawsuit, wasn't someone Jacob wanted to deal with first thing in the morning.

A brazen asshole of the type that relished the role, Mike's already bloated ego had swollen to monstrous proportions since he had joined the local outpost of McConnell & Barth, a prestigious firm out of New York. Now he did nothing but feign annoyance at having to travel to "the city" and complain about the dearth of Salvadoran restaurants in Cincinnati.

As Jacob made his way through the courthouse's bustling main hall, one of the elevators opened and Mike stepped out. After making some minor adjustments to his slick blond hair, he graced Jacob with a nod of acknowledgment.

Mike imagined himself something of a ladies' man and looked the part. With his boyish good looks and impeccable taste in suits, he appealed to a certain type of older woman having a certain type of midlife crisis. He welcomed the attention whenever it furthered his professional or social ambitions. How often things went beyond flirtatious banter was a matter of furious debate among the upper echelons of Cincinnati's legal community.

"Freeman!" Mike called. "Good of you to make an appearance, and without a minute to spare."

Jacob paused to allow Mike to close in on him. "You're going the wrong way. Forget something?"

"No, no, nothing like that. Judge Stock called in sick today. They taped a note to her door. A *note*. Can you believe it? This is the twenty-first century, isn't it? Am I wrong?" Mike took his phone out of his pocket and began flicking through messages.

"That's too bad," Jacob said, his mind already on the coffee shop he'd visit instead of going back to the office—as well as the pretty Asian barista who worked there most mornings. "Well, I'll see you—"

"Congrats on the NanoMite dismissal, by the way," Mike said as though Jacob hadn't been speaking. "You got them off the hook on that one. Dupree wouldn't shut up about it over drinks at The Palms. To hear him tell it, the plaintiffs ran from the negotiating table with their tails between their legs."

Jacob nodded. "Thanks. A lot of work went into that case."

"You know, Freeman, McConnell & Barth is always looking for talent. If you ever feel underappreciated at AVM, I can put in a good word for you."

"Thanks for thinking of me, Mike, but I'm happy where I am."

"Suit yourself. It's an open-ended offer. Keep us in mind."

"Will do."

Mike thrust his phone into his jacket pocket and pivoted toward the exit. "Duty calls," he said over his shoulder. "Catch you later, Freeman."

Jacob hated people like Mike, of whom he knew many—poised, ambitious, always looking to scramble one rung higher up the ladder. He almost wished the lawsuit would go to trial, despite all the work that would entail. He'd love to destroy that little prick in court.

Ten minutes later, Jacob stepped out of a sticky, summer day into the coffee shop's cool embrace. Pleased to find his favorite barista behind the counter, he ordered a macchiato and chatted with her as she worked. For the last time, he smiled at her in a way that fell into the gray area between friendly and flirtatious. He couldn't have known it was the last time, but it was.

Sipping his coffee and watching the world pass by, Jacob pushed the lawsuit from his mind. He wouldn't give it another thought for as long as he lived. There would be no more late nights in his den or hectic mornings getting ready for work. Never again would he stand outside a courtroom wondering if he could be the person everyone inside expected him to be.

That was the day the world ended.

Fractured Memories

It started as Micah was getting ready for bed. After brushing her teeth, she flashed an impish grin then bolted from the bathroom, giggling madly.

"Oh no you don't!" Jacob bellowed as he chased her into the living room, where she launched herself into a cushy chair in the corner. "*Nobody* escapes bedtime!" He picked her up and nuzzled her squealing face. "*Nobody!*"

That's when it took him. Everything froze, like a video had paused. Their comfortable living room seen through a golden web of Micah's hair—it was an image he would never forget: home.

The world went dark.

Time passed; how much, it was impossible to say, an instant and an eternity. Jacob awoke to a universe born anew. Lamps had become tiny suns, bearing down on him. The air conditioner blasted arctic fury. His mind spun, a scrambled mess of terror and confusion—and something else, something that didn't belong. Inexplicably still standing, he held his daughter before him like a sacrificial offering, fingers digging into her shoulder and thigh. With a stiff jerk, he lurched forward and dropped her onto the couch.

Micah sprang to her feet, gaping at him in horror. "Mom!"

Time skipped again. Rebecca's panicked face now hung over him. She was yelling, but without any sound. Micah stood off to the side, her ashen cheeks streaked with tears.

"She can't see this. She..." Jacob reached for his daughter.

He tried to sit up, but his muscles didn't respond. The light throbbed, excruciatingly bright. His vision broke down into an angry haze. Rebecca shook him, but he couldn't make out her face. He needed to speak, to tell her they'd get through whatever this was. His mouth opened, closed, and opened again, but words failed to come.

She raced back to her office where she must have left her phone. A pale ghost lost in light, Micah let out a shocked cry.

Jacob blacked out.

He woke up in the front yard under a black, empty sky. White and red lights flashed against the house. Sirens, alarms, shouting—noise all around.

His head rolled to the side, which brought the street into view. People were mobbing an ambulance parked in the road, breaking windows, pulling at its doors, jumping on the roof.

Red...white...red. Twisted, inhuman faces snarled in the crazy lights.

The hot-metal taste of blood in his mouth, Jacob lay face-down on a hard, rough surface slick with a viscous fluid. Everything hurt. He opened his eyes. A basement...*his* basement. Blood spread across the concrete around him, glistening black in the moonlight shining through the small window over the dryer. Outside, insects sang.

A futile effort to call out produced only a raspy wheeze. After clearing a fistful of bloody mucus from his throat, Jacob croaked, "H-hello?"

A tiny yelp shot out from the direction of the stairs.

"Micah? Is that you?" Pain and nausea drowned out his words. He clawed at the ground to drag himself forward. "Help...please."

Shapes formed in the shadows, thick and fluid, like black streams of oil swirling in the air. They hesitated a moment, then converged on him. No escape. A thing that both did and didn't have substance—darkness given form and a terrible will—enveloped him.

From under the stairs, impossibly far away, an anguished cry reached for him but couldn't reach far enough.

Energy like Jacob had never before experienced thrust him back into the real world. Power, raw and hot, coursed through his body. Consumed by a bloody purpose, he tore through the moonlit living room like a bullet and bounded up the stairs toward the second floor. He needed to find the intruder.

Halfway up the stairs, a makeshift barricade of furniture and household objects blocked his path. Without breaking stride, he plowed through, plunging into the pool of shadows on the second-floor landing. A short hallway to his right led to several closed doors. To his left, a hint of light leaked out from underneath another door. There! Jacob lunged forward and burst into his bedroom.

A predator, he strained his ears for any hint of life. On top of the dresser, a cluster of candles in a variety of colors and scents lit the room. Drawers hung open, vomiting clothes. Empty soda bottles and snack wrappers littered the floor. Soiled sheets clumped together at the head of the bed, exposing a dark stain on the mattress. The candles' cloying sweetness mixed with the stench of piss, sweat, and semen. Revolting.

Click. That small sound, a lock snapping into place, might as well have been fireworks in the otherwise silent house. It came from a door on the other side of the room. *Got you*, Jacob thought in a voice that both was and was not his.

Keeping an eye out for traps, he stepped up to the door then gave it a hard shove. Its jamb splintered as though a sledgehammer had hit it, sending it crashing into a small bathroom. Jacob's shadow cut across the white tile floor as candlelight poured in around him. In the bathtub, a shapeless mound of flesh quivered with fright. The intruder.

Jacob's murderous expression relaxed into a sardonic smirk. "Ah, what's this? A greedy pig rooting around in my garden?"

A child's whimper escaped the great mass of the intruder's body. After a few moments of sniveling, an arm draped with folds of fat raised above the bathtub's rim. The intruder held up a stuffed lion. Jacob recognized it as something the girl downstairs had once treasured. She wouldn't want it now though, not with a hole in its throat and its mane caked with filth.

That girl, don't I know her? The thought that had wandered into Jacob's mind wandered back out again.

"A peace offering?" he asked. "No thanks. I brought toys of my own." A box cutter emerged from his hip pocket. The blade snapped into place.

Fire raged all around, lashing at the night sky. Jacob stood among a smattering of abandoned cars in a vast parking lot, surrounded on three sides by a horseshoe-shaped wall of flames. In a different world, it had been a shopping center.

The sky loomed overhead, as heavy and dark as the bottom of an ocean. Ash swirled across the black sea of asphalt around Jacob, carried on waves of heat to pile up against his new boots. The boots had come from one of the burning stores. Black leather, supple yet strong, they pleased him.

He stroked a scrap of silky fabric in his left hand and raised the half-gallon of vodka held in his right for another swig. Alcohol took the edge off his too-keen senses, keeping overstimulation at bay. Something unfinished bubbled up in his mind. The piece of cloth had come from a nightgown worn by a gibbering idiot out of her mind with the night's energies. Jacob had trapped her in one of the stores before the fire caught up with them. Such a pretty thing, slender and quick.

In the grip of a mania all her own, she had only half-realized what had happened when he seized her. Her eyes jumped from place to place, landing everywhere except on the man wrestling her to the ground. Kicking, spitting, and gnashing her teeth, she fought viciously but without focus. All the while, a flood of disjointed nonsense poured from her mouth—on and on she went, rambling about dream worlds and monsters of the mind.

Jacob was getting used to that sort of thing. It had been a long and eventful night.

As the flames closed in on them, he considered wrapping himself around the squirming lunatic to see what the inferno would do to them. Instead, he let her go.

Some time later, as he stood in the parking lot watching the world burn, a restless hunger grew in him. Savage howls sounded in the distance. Their urgency inflamed his passion. Adventure awaited. His thoughts returned to the wild thing who had slipped from his grasp. Where had she scurried off to?

In a soft hiss, he said, "Ready or not, here I come."

"Dad!"

Jacob's eyes twitched under their lids. He had been lost in...what? This thing in him didn't have a name. Darkness.

"Wake up!"

From the other side of a thick fog, a girl's voice lashed at him. Unbearable. He needed rest. Hoping the noise would stop on its own, he lay still. It crested to a wail, then fell into weepy murmuring. Not ideal, but he could tune it out.

"Dad!"

Abrupt and sharp, the voice jerked him back into consciousness.

"Wake up. Please, we need you."

Small hands grabbed him by the shoulders and shook. At her touch, every muscle in his body cramped. Nausea welled up in his gut as though someone had shoved rancid meat down his throat. Frantic, he lashed out at the girl.

A crack, a thud, then nothing. Too exhausted to move, heart pounding, he sunk into the floor. Quiet, a blessed moment of peace.

From a distance, he heard a muffled groan, barely a sound at all. Then it exploded into a scream that shattered the universe. Like a crazed animal, it tore into Jacob, ripping layer after layer of Darkness away, exposing parts of him best forgotten.

He knew that girl's voice! His mind boiled over—horror, revulsion, rage. Too much. He'd die if this didn't stop. An image blasted through the black wall that had formed between who Jacob was and who he had once been: a child, a beautiful girl with golden hair. A feeble, very human cry escaped from some hidden depths he didn't know he possessed.

Flung into a roiling sea of madness, visions flashed through his mind. Flames dancing across an obsidian sky—deranged cries pregnant with de-sire—a wolf's grin resting easy on his face, his voice a dagger sheathed in velvet, *Ready or not, here I come.*

No, it couldn't have been real. He didn't do those things! The thought rang hollow in Jacob's head. Those hadn't been tricks or illusions, but memories. The fiendish presence lording over the chaos outside, the preda-tor in the ruins, the thing that had just hit that girl—him.

The girl. Wasn't he supposed to protect her? Despite everything, hadn't he tried to keep her safe? Tried and failed. Darkness had changed him. Against his monstrous strength, her body would be spun glass. He had killed her. The woman who lived here with them might be dead too. If not, she wouldn't last much longer. Once Darkness regained control, she'd be next.

Woman, girl, they seemed so familiar. The girl and her...mother? The girl and—

Everything stopped. Mentally and physically, Jacob locked up as pres-sure built in a place Darkness hadn't yet corrupted. Memories erupted with the force of a supernova. The first time he had held Micah, his daughter. How beautiful Rebecca had looked on their wedding day. Never in his life had he been in such awe. First day of school, family vacations, the restaurant he had taken Rebecca to for her birthday only weeks ago. So much more, the entirety of his life—the joy, the shame, everything he did both in darkness and light.

"Get out!" he screamed at the thing that had taken him.

It recoiled like a wounded snake, twisting around itself in shock. Jacob's universe ignited as he tore himself apart.

Sunlight filtered through a pale blue sheet hanging over the basement window high overhead. Covered in filth, Jacob lay on the floor, staring up at the light. How long had he been awake? Minutes? Hours?

That sheet didn't use to be there. Rebecca had been after him for years to replace the basement windows with glass blocks, but he had never gotten around to it. He always meant to at least cover them so no one could look inside to scope the place out for a break-in, but he had never gotten around to that either. She must have put those sheets over them.

Rebecca. He remembered her now. Micah too. His memories were back, all of them except for most of what had happened over the past few days. But he had paid a price. Darkness still wove through him, sinking its roots deep, distorting each thought that passed through his head. There was no way to unravel man from monster anymore.

Only by giving up had he ultimately found a way to reclaim some semblance of freedom. The last of his energy spent, all hope stripped away, he had threatened to destroy himself before allowing Darkness to take him again. A risky gambit, but one he knew would work. He had learned something about his adversary: it wanted to live, and without him it couldn't. Faced with death, it yielded. They made a deal, a compromise. Something new, neither man nor Darkness, came into being.

For a second, Jacob thought of stirring the new power within him. It was right there, ready any time. But no, not now.

"Hello?" he called. No response, although he sensed their presence. With a flood of relief, he realized they were *both* there.

"It's okay. I'm...I'm all right."

Rebecca's Account

Day One, 7:45 p.m.

Jacob came home late, but that was to be expected. He had a court date the following week and needed to prepare. Nothing about his appearance or behavior struck Rebecca as unusual. He reheated his lasagna dinner, chatted with her while he ate, then went into the living room to see what Micah was watching on TV. Rebecca sat at her desk to catch up on some reading.

Just after nine, she heard the TV turn off, and Jacob ushered Micah into the bathroom to make sure she did a good job of brushing her teeth. (If left unsupervised, she wouldn't do it for the full two minutes Rebecca's dentist friend had recommended.) The two of them were engaged in a heated discussion about a vampire girl with a weird name and a king of ice, whatever that meant. Looking up from her book, Rebecca sighed. If Jacob showed as much enthusiasm for court proceedings as he did for Micah's cartoons, he'd already be a partner at the firm.

A short time later, Micah burst into laughter and ran out of the bathroom. Annoyed by the disruption to her daughter's bedtime routine, Rebecca took a deep breath to settle her nerves. She wouldn't say anything. Not yet.

After a minute or two of giggling, the living room fell silent. That was weird. Once those two got started, the silliness usually lasted until Jacob had tucked Micah in and kissed her goodnight. Quiet seconds ticked by. Concerned, Rebecca set her book down. Something didn't feel right. Just as she got up to check on things, a sharp cry cut through the house.

"Mom!" Micah screamed.

A firebomb of terror ignited in Rebecca's chest. She raced to the living room. Micah stood on the couch, pointing at Jacob, who was curled up on the floor. After quickly verifying her daughter was okay, Rebecca's medical training took over, and she swung into action. A first assessment didn't reveal any obvious injuries, but Jacob was unresponsive. Shallow, rapid breathing. Alarmingly high heart rate. Dilated pupils. A heart attack? Stroke? She ran into the hallway to call 911.

Fifteen minutes passed as they waited for help. Not knowing what else to do for Jacob, Rebecca took Micah into her arms. "Don't worry, honey. It'll be all right."

Finally, the ambulance arrived. Amid a flurry of shouting and hectic activity, two paramedics loaded Jacob onto a stretcher and wheeled him outside. Rebecca followed close behind, holding Micah's hand.

Halfway across the front lawn, pandemonium erupted. The paramedic at the rear of Jacob's stretcher fell to the ground in what appeared to be a seizure. His partner rushed over to help.

Meanwhile, a middle-aged woman staggered down the sidewalk toward them. When she reached the ambulance, she stopped to gawk at the unfolding emergency. Her blank stare morphed into a mask of animal rage. She tilted her head back, let out a shrill cry, then charged at the paramedics. Before the one crouched over his stricken partner could react, the woman leaped onto his back and sunk her teeth into his neck. Almost simultaneously, a group of people howling like maniacs came out of nowhere and attacked the ambulance.

Rebecca let go of Micah's hand, yelling for her to go inside. Driven by panic, she ran to her husband, pulled him free of the stretcher, and dragged him back toward the house. She wanted to help the paramedics, but needed to make sure her family was safe first. Trying not to hit Jacob's head on the porch steps, she pulled him into the house and locked the front door. After fumbling with her phone, nearly dropping it, she managed to dial.

A robot voice picked up. "911 service is currently unavailable in—"

"God damn it!" Rebecca cried, hung up, and tried again. Unavailable.

In hopes of seeing an emergency announcement that would tell her what to do, she clicked the TV on. Live footage from Fountain Square, the central plaza downtown, showed an enraged mob kicking over garbage cans, upending benches, and banging on storefront windows. Most of them were dressed in business clothes or looked like they had come from one of the trendy restaurants around the square. A riot? Involving office workers and people out for a night on the town? The crowd wasn't lashing out at the city, though, but rather attacking itself. A fat man in a gray suit tackled a teenage boy who had been wildly swinging a backpack at anyone who approached. Instantly, a half-dozen other people swarmed them both like a pack of starved jackals. As Rebecca's shock morphed into horror, she saw a man in a security guard unform laughing uncontrollably as he attempted to kiss a young woman pummeling him with her fists.

The camera cut to the square's namesake: a large bronze fountain capped with a sculpture of a woman holding out her arms. At the fountain's base, a naked woman with impossibly long, black hair danced in the falling water.

Rebecca switched the channel and Fountain Square became Times Square in New York seen through a broken window several stories up. Huge video screens embedded into the surrounding skyscrapers flashed cheery, colorful advertisements as utter chaos played out below. Thousands of people ran in every direction, some trying to escape while others assaulted whoever they could catch. Pockets of violence flared up throughout the crowd. Across the square, smoke billowed from a row of windows near the top of a building. Behind the camera operator, a man shouted incoherently...and the video feed cut off. Static.

Rebecca's forgotten phone finally connected to 911. Before she could say anything, a female voice blared into her ear. "Buzz, buzz, buzz! That all you got? Devils is what you are. Devils!"

Nothing made any sense. Rebecca put her phone away. Forcing herself to think of nothing but the right here and right now, she pulled Jacob into the living room, collected her sobbing daughter, and turned off all the lights. They'd wait this out, whatever it was. Screaming, crashes, and explosions rocked the night.

Day Two, 10:30 a.m.

Morning came at the wrong time. It was past ten o'clock before a sickly greenish light that didn't seem to have a source uniformly filled the sky.

It looked more like a world-size computer monitor slowly powering on than a sunrise. Rebecca didn't have time to worry about solar phenomena though. She was in the middle of a crisis.

The electricity had gone out at some point during the night. Although it would have made sense to preserve her phone's battery, she couldn't stop herself from checking the internet one more time. Most of the sites she tried were either down or hadn't been updated since all hell broke loose. CNN's homepage displayed a crude drawing of a grinning penis. Scrawled underneath were the words, *Cock-a-doodle-doo! Good morning to you!*

"Goddamn it," Rebecca muttered. She went to the window and peeked through a gap in the curtains. One of the paramedics lay dead in the front yard, nothing left of his head but a pile of gore. There was no sign of his partner.

The battered ambulance sat in the road like a relic from a long-forgotten civilization. A teenage girl with an open wound on the back of her head had spent most of the night before carving intricate patterns of interlocking circles into its paint with a pocketknife. She didn't seem to notice the blood matting her hair and staining the shoulders of her t-shirt.

As far as Rebecca could tell, there hadn't been any sort of meaningful emergency response. How was that possible? Insane teenagers weren't supposed to wander the streets. Headless corpses weren't supposed to stay in front yards indefinitely. Where were the police? Why hadn't the National Guard shown up to restore order? What the hell was going on?

Just then, a skinny Black man wearing only boxer shorts groggily stumbled out from behind the ambulance. Long dreadlocks hung over his face, swinging perilously close to the four lit cigarettes that dangled from his lips. After giving the wounded girl's handiwork a cursory look and failing to notice the dead paramedic, he moved on. Rebecca held her breath as he made his way down the street then disappeared around a bend.

With a relieved sigh, she returned to where Jacob lay on the floor. When she knelt beside him to check his vitals, his eyes snapped open and he gasped for air.

"Oh my God! Jacob, are you all right?"

His face frozen in an expression of mute agony, he stared at her.

She found he could move despite his obvious discomfort. Rebecca had been hoping for an opportunity like this. Although she had pulled the curtains, someone looking closely from outside could still see into the house. Given what she had witnessed the night before, it wouldn't be good to be noticed. The basement seemed a safer place to wait for help. She helped Jacob to his feet and began walking him toward the door in the kitchen that led to the basement stairs. Every few steps, he tensed up and became completely immobile. No matter how much force Rebecca applied, he wouldn't budge.

While they inched their way through the house, Micah laid out a pile of blankets on the basement floor for her dad to lie on. After a grueling journey down the stairs, Jacob collapsed onto his makeshift bed.

Exhausted, Rebecca slumped against the dryer to consider her next steps. She hadn't anticipated ever being trapped in her house for an extended period of time, but her family wasn't entirely unprepared. Thank God for her dad's paranoid streak! He had insisted she maintain an emergency stockpile of food and supplies in case...well, in case something like this happened. Every time he came over, he found some excuse to poke around downstairs so he could scan the shelves of canned food and bottles of water for expired goods. Micah would complain about eating cold soup and beef jerky, but they could go weeks without needing to resupply, over a month if they needed to. The crisis wouldn't nearly last that long.

Day Two, 4:45 p.m.

Every hour or so, Rebecca snuck upstairs in hopes of finding a rescue operation moving down her street or at least seeing sane people outside. On her way back through the kitchen after yet another fruitless trip to the front window, something caught her attention. A sound in the back yard. Laughter? She walked to the window over the sink and peeked outside.

A little girl—maybe seven years old—wearing a frilly dress that could have been a costume for a Victorian period piece was skipping around Micah's swing set, happily talking to a hairy lump on the ground between the two swings. A pet? It didn't look alive though. A stuffed animal, Rebecca guessed.

The girl picked up her toy, balanced it on a swing, then took a seat on the other one. Lazily swaying back and forth, she resumed her conversation with—

Rebecca dropped into a crouch. Her hand flew to her mouth, both in horror and as a reflex against vomiting. A head. The girl had a severed human head.

Day Two, 7:45 p.m.

Sunset had been as wrong as sunrise. After only six hours of daylight, the sky faded from yellow-green to green-gray to black. Had the mass psychosis or whatever happened last night affected Rebecca? The sun couldn't really be broken.

Jacob grew more active as the night wore on. He groaned, coughed, and clawed at his bedding, but didn't speak. With each passing hour, his movements became more violent and the sounds he made more animalistic. At one point, he rolled off his blankets and lay on the bare concrete. Rebecca tried to push him back into a more comfortable position, but couldn't move him despite putting all her weight into the effort. It was as though his body had turned to stone.

Somehow Micah slept through it all. She had been complaining about sore muscles and a headache, so Rebecca piled blankets in the space under the stairs for her to lie down on. She fell asleep within minutes of nightfall. Rebecca was jealous. She doubted she'd be able get any rest with Jacob panting and grunting only a few feet away.

Day Two, 11:45 p.m.

Strained, mucus-laden coughing echoed through the basement. Micah sat bolt upright under the stairs, her eyes wide.

"Hello?" Jacob called.

Rebecca knew she should go to him; it didn't make sense not to. Her legs turned to jelly though. She could barely breathe. Flashes of the things she had witnessed over the past twenty-four hours flickered through her head: the girl on the swing, the crazed woman tearing into the paramedic's neck, the mob violence on TV. What if Jacob was like that?

He tried to speak again, but his words crumbled into a long, miserable groan. A moment later, sounds of cloth dragging across concrete made their way through the basement. Seconds stretched into an endless expanse of time as Jacob dragged himself toward them. He groaned again then stopped moving. Silence returned.

Micah buried her face in her mother's chest and cried.

Day Three, 10:15 a.m.

Despite everything, Rebecca had managed to sleep for a few hours curled up beside Micah in the nest under the stairs. Somewhere in the distance, Jacob made soft snuffling noises, a marked improvement over the terrifying sounds she had heard the night before. Micah lay quiet and still, not yet awake.

They couldn't leave the house until the authorities had restored order. There were plenty of supplies, so staying put was their best option. Or rather, it would be as long as Jacob didn't wake up as a violent psychopath. Rebecca hated to think like that but knew she needed to. If he suffered from the same condition as the people she had seen outside, he was dangerous.

A plan germinated in her mind. The chaos outside seemed to slow down during the daylight hours. She could take the opportunity to cover every window upstairs and secure a place for her and Micah to rest. It would be easier to sleep out of earshot of the awful noises Jacob made, and they'd be safer if he had some sort of violent episode. They'd get to work as soon as Micah woke up. In the meantime, she should check on Jacob. That needed to be done at some point, and she didn't want any distractions on the way upstairs.

After pulling a blanket over Micah, she crawled out of the nest and straight into a fresh nightmare. Blood covered the floor where Jacob had been lying. A thick red-brown smear led to the dryer, where he lay in the fetal position. Rebecca rushed to him and attempted to uncoil his body from itself so she could do a proper evaluation. It was like trying to dismantle a wrought-iron fence by hand. She crouched over him, calling his name as calmly as she could manage.

Blood covered the dress shirt he had worn to work the day all of this started, but she didn't find any indications of an injury. It looked like his clothes had gotten stained from the blood on the floor. But where had *that* come from? Jacob clutched his head in both hands, so Rebecca shifted her attention there. Maybe he had fallen and hit it on the floor.

With a gasp, she jumped to her feet. Something was wrong with Jacobs's head, but not anything a fall could account for. Bone protruded through his scalp in two symmetrical spots where his forehead crested into the crown of his skull. Less than an inch tall and about two inches in diameter, the circular masses appeared to be organic growth rather than broken fragments that had ruptured the skin. They looked like—

No, that was insane. Her husband wasn't growing horns.

Rebecca closed her eyes then opened them again. Nothing changed. *Get it together! There's a rational explanation, you're just not finding it.*

"Mom?" a frightened voice called from under the stairs.

Her heart nearly jumped into her throat. "Stay in bed, sweetheart. I'll be right there."

Trying to reassure her daughter with awkwardly upbeat small talk, Rebecca broke down a large box and placed it over the blood on the floor. She couldn't let Micah see that. After a final check to make sure the worst bits were covered, she returned to the nest.

"Hi, honey," she said, hoping her voice didn't indicate how close she was to full-blown panic. "You feel okay?"

"My head hurts."

"Mine too." Rebecca settled down next to the sleepy child. "I have an idea. Let's go upstairs and get some medicine. I think it'll be safe during the day if we're really sneaky. We can get a snack too. You must be starving."

Micah stared at her own toes. "I'm not hungry. Is Dad okay?"

Rebecca took a second to collect herself. "Let's let him rest. He had a rough night."

She helped Micah crawl out of the nest and led her around the stairs, attempting to avert her attention from both Jacob and the mess on the floor.

"Wait, Mom. I want to see Dad."

Micah's voice trembled but carried a steely edge. Rebecca knew that voice, and it was the last thing she wanted to hear just then. When Micah set her mind on something, no one could dissuade her. Ignoring the request, she took her daughter's hand and guided her toward the stairs. The girl had barely said a word since all of this had begun; surely shock and fear would keep her stubborn streak in check for another ten seconds.

"Mom, you're pulling!" Micah planted her feet and yanked her hand free.

"So much for quick and easy," Rebecca muttered to herself.

"I want to see Dad."

"Your father isn't well. He needs to rest."

"He's not sleeping. I hear noises. And look! He's not even under his covers." Micah's eyes scanned the basement floor. "Where's Dad's bed?"

Rebecca rubbed her forehead and said a silent prayer for patience. "He rolled out of it last night. Maybe he was too hot."

Tears pooled in the corners of Micah's eyes. "No he wasn't! He called for us, and you didn't help him."

"Micah...sweetheart, your dad is sick. You saw those people outside. He might be like them."

She considered this for a moment. "Is he?"

"I wish I knew. But until we find out, we need to be careful."

Micah glared at her with eyes like blue flames.

"Fine," Rebecca said. Might as well get this over with; she couldn't hide Jacob forever. "You can see him, but you have to promise to stand behind me."

"I will."

They walked across the cardboard together and stood in front of Jacob. Micah peered around Rebecca's back. "He's... Oh, Mom." She started to cry.

Rebecca thought Micah would run away, but she didn't. Instead, she gathered her courage and stepped forward to face Jacob directly. "Don't give up, Dad. You have to get better." Choking back a heavy sob, she heaved a final burst of words. "I love you!"

She flew across the cardboard and collapsed at the base of the stairs. "Come back, Dad," she wailed. The words came again and again, like a mantra: "Come back. Come back. Come back."

Day Three, 11:30 a.m.

After spending the better part of an hour consoling Micah, Rebecca pressed on with her plan. There was a lot of work to do and precious few daylight hours to do it in. She took Micah's hand, climbed the stairs, and opened the door to the kitchen. Splotches of color floated across her eyes as they adjusted to the relative brightness. It was the same weird, muted light that reached the basement, but the kitchen's larger windows allowed it to fill the room. Weird or not, the light was a welcome contrast to the gloom downstairs.

"Does your head still hurt, Micah?"

"Uh huh."

"Let's get some medicine first. The sooner you take it, the sooner it'll work."

Micah nodded and took her hand.

"Remember, stay away from windows and be very, very quiet. Super sneaky."

"Okay."

They kept medicine upstairs, in the bathroom off the master bedroom. Rebecca led Micah through the living room to the house's entryway, stopping to give the front door a nervous tug. Still locked. There were other ways into the house though. Sunlight gave way to shadow as they headed up the stairs. A foul odor hung in the air, sour and sickly sweet.

Rebecca paused on the second-floor landing. Something didn't feel right. After surveying the scene for a moment, she noticed a barely perceptible light flickering through the gaps around the door to her left, the master bedroom. She glanced down at Micah, whose eyes were fixed on the same sliver of light.

To their right, on the other side of the landing, a soft click broke the silence. Rebecca's entire body lit up with alarm as the door to Micah's bedroom swung open. Grey light seeped onto the landing from inside the room. A high-pitched male voice hummed a nonsense melody, sending its broken notes skittering through the darkened house. Shadows stirred around the doorway.

Rebecca gripped Micah's hand and held a finger to her lips. *Shh.*

A naked man, grossly obese and completely hairless, stepped out of the bedroom. His skin had a dull yellow pallor in the half-light. He carried a bundle of toys and some of Micah's clothes pressed against his sagging belly. Still humming, the intruder turned his back to Rebecca and Micah and walked down the short hallway that led to the guest bedroom. He hadn't seen them! After shifting his load to free up a hand, he opened the door and went inside.

Sweat trickled down Rebecca's forehead. She willed the intruder to shut the door and close himself in the bedroom. Micah stood on the stair behind her, digging her fingers into her mother's forearm. She leaned forward to get as close as she could.

No! Rebecca thought. *For God's sake, don't move.* It was an old house. The smallest pressure on the wrong part of the stairs and—

Creak

With the slow inevitability of a glacier moving to the sea, the man pivoted. He didn't speak or hide his nudity, just stood staring across the landing at Rebecca and Micah. Gradually, a leering grin unfurled across his face. A dark, hungry menace rose in him, then abruptly collapsed into idiotic glee. He burst into guffawing laughter, dropped the things he had been carrying, and started toward the stairs.

Rebecca's paralysis broke. She grabbed Micah by the shoulders and drove her back down the stairs. They hesitated at the bottom as Rebecca cast a desperate glance toward the front door. The man pursuing them didn't look like much of an athlete; they could lose him outside. But what if there were more crazy people out there? And they couldn't just leave Jacob lying in the basement with a maniac in the house.

Heavy footsteps pounded the stairs above. Rebecca yanked Micah toward the kitchen. There was a crowbar on a shelf in the basement. She'd grab that and hit his legs as he came down the stairs after them. He'd surely lose his balance and tumble down headfirst. If necessary, she'd then bash his head in. Whatever happened, that creep was not going to lay a finger on Micah.

With the man barreling through the living room behind them, Micah sprinted ahead and flung open the basement door. Rebecca, whose mind was on the crowbar and what she had to do next, nearly plowed into her. Rooted on the second step with a death grip on the handrail, Micah stared into the shadows below.

Jacob stood at the foot of the stairs, streaks of blood running down his face. Taut and poised, he wasn't anything like the wreckage they had left just a few minutes ago.

No time for shock. Rebecca picked Micah up and ran down the stairs. As they reached the midpoint, the intruder paused in the doorway, giggling and panting. At the bottom, they brushed past Jacob, who didn't react.

Rebecca put Micah down behind some boxes and told her to stay hidden. Not at all sure it was a safe choice, she grabbed the crowbar and took a position next to her husband.

The intruder stood motionless in the doorway above, his eyes fixed on Jacob. His entire body shivered as if caught in a blast of frigid air. Everything about him said he wanted to flee, but for some reason he couldn't. He just stood there—naked, helpless, and consumed by fear.

In a low, clear voice saturated with disgust, Jacob uttered a single syllable: "Go."

The man yelped like a wounded dog and stumbled backward. Tripping over his own feet, he fell into the kitchen with a slap of flesh on tile. In a clumsy jumble of limbs, he scrambled forward and slapped at the door a couple times before managing to slam it shut. The lock clicked. Footsteps thumped across the floor overhead.

Jacob stood motionless until the house was quiet, then slumped into a seated position on the bottom stair. Rebecca started to say something, but he waved her off.

Unsure what to do, she called Micah out from her hiding place. They crawled into their nest. Micah wanted to talk to her dad, but Rebecca wouldn't allow it. She had sensed something in Jacob as they stood together, something she didn't want Micah to feel: a cold malevolence that sent a jolt of terror up her spine. He had changed, and not in a good way.

Day Three, 7:30 p.m.

All day and into the night, Jacob sat on the stairs, leaning heavily against the wall. If he hadn't moaned every now and then, Rebecca would have thought he was dead.

Exhausted, Micah fell asleep as soon as it got dark. Rebecca sat beside her in the nest, gripping the crowbar. Her body ached. Her mind was a pulsing field of white noise. When the weight of everything that had happened fell on her, she wept in raw, heaving sobs that felt more like vomiting than crying.

Several hours after dark, Jacob finally stirred. The stairs complained as he shifted his weight. After a moment, a jeering voice barely recognizable as his drifted through the basement like poison gas. "Are you afraid, little lambs?"

Panic electrified Rebecca's already-frayed nerves. Holding her breath, she clung to her weapon. The basement fell quiet. A full minute passed as she wondered if Jacob had fallen asleep. Did he call them lambs? But that voice...it hadn't been his.

"That revolting creature is still here, you know," the voice called again. "He's rooting around upstairs. Despite his fear, his need won't let him leave. So he waits, dreaming of a world where nothing stands between him and his vulgar pleasures."

Jacob laughed—a smooth, sinister sound that chilled Rebecca to the core. "Such desperate, reckless hope," he continued. "It's admirable in its way. But alas, the time has come to relieve our guest of his delusions."

The stairs creaked. Light footsteps tapped above the nest, followed by a sharp crack as Jacob broke the basement door's lock. He moved through the kitchen then the dining room at an amazing speed.

Rebecca didn't budge. She had no idea if he would come back. Maybe it would be better if he didn't.

Day Three, 11:15 p.m.

Jacob did return. He walked down the stairs, then disappeared into the quiet and the dark. A few seconds later, footsteps approached the nest. Rebecca had nailed up a sheet as an impromptu door, so she didn't see him, but he was close.

She held up the crowbar. If he meant to hurt them, she might not be able to stop him, but she'd damn well try. Only a few feet away, with nothing but a bit of cotton between them, he stopped. Rebecca heard him breathing.

The bottom edge of the sheet covering the nest rose just enough for Jacob to slide a small box under it. Ibuprofen.

Day Four, 1:30 p.m.

Rebecca felt much better the next morning. The intruder was gone. The medicine had helped Micah's headache and eliminated her own. She had even managed to get some sleep. All things considered, their situation could have been much worse. The more she thought about it, the more she wondered if she had been hasty in considering Jacob a threat. His behavior was unsettling—no doubt about it—but so far, he had only tried to help.

She and Micah spent most of the day cleaning and securing the basement. Rebecca swapped the blood-soaked cardboard on the floor for freshly broken-down boxes. She then covered the windows by nailing sheets to their wooden frames, cursing Jacob for never getting around to having glass block windows installed. A search for more nails uncovered a bolt lock someone had bought for a forgotten purpose. Micah helped install it on their side of the kitchen door.

The night before, Jacob had pushed the washer and dryer together, presumably to serve as a bed. He lay on top of them all day, out of the way. From time to time, Micah stole a glance at him but kept her distance. The protrusions on his head both scared and fascinated her. Over four inches long now (a growth rate that shouldn't have been possible) and porcelain-white, they curved back along the ridges of his skull just above his hair. Micah constantly pestered her mother for a "doctor's opinion" on how they'd grow: curly like a ram's horns, straight out like a bull's, or branched like antlers? Rebecca wished they'd fall off.

After she had coerced Micah into eating a bowl of dry cereal for dinner, which the stubborn girl made a grand spectacle of not enjoying, they prepared the nest under the stairs for another long night.

Once the basement had slipped into darkness, Jacob moved to a remote corner, where he sat on the floor, gazing at a window high up on the wall. The moon rose, and his shadowy spot became a pool of liquid silver.

Knowing her dad was awake, Micah couldn't fall asleep. Despite Rebecca's increasingly pointed commands not to, she kept calling out to him.

"Dad? Can you hear me?"

"Micah! I told you not to bother him."

"But he's just sitting there. Why doesn't he want to come in here with us?"

"He's still sick. He needs to be alone for a while."

"Dad?" she called again.

In a bid to stop her from worrying, Rebecca agreed to check on Jacob. She crawled out of the nest and cautiously approached him, stopping a good ten feet away. He was still sitting in the corner, staring at the window.

"Jacob?"

He turned his gaze to her. A blur of conflicting emotions flashed across his face: pain, anger, fear, spite, confusion, desperation. Finally, his expression settled into a groove that ran between irritation and distaste. His eyes drifted back to the window, and he waved a dismissive hand in her direction.

Rebecca told Micah he wasn't ready to talk yet. They both tried to get some rest.

Day Five, 1:15 a.m.

Footsteps on the basement stairs woke Rebecca. Jacob walked up, released the new lock, and entered the kitchen. She strained her ears to track his movement through the house. He went back and forth between the first and second floors, moving with an easy gait she took to be a sign of mental stability. Cabinet doors opened and closed in the kitchen.

Roughly an hour later, he returned to the basement and sat in his spot under the window. Rebecca decided to check on him again, imagining he might be in a better frame of mind after his calm tour of the house.

He had washed up, his body no longer covered with blood and grime. The filthy clothes he had worn to work the day everything changed had been swapped for a pair of black jeans and a white t-shirt. On his head, the freshly cleaned growths glowed lunar white. As Rebecca neared, Jacob looked directly at her. His eyes were dark and full of malice. A crooked sneer twisted his face, daring her to come even an inch closer.

Without saying a word, she returned to the nest.

Day Five, 11:30 a.m.

They slept well past dawn on the fifth day. Rebecca expected to find Jacob tossing and moaning in a corner, as was the case most mornings. Instead, he sat cross-legged on top of the dryer with his face downcast and his eyes closed, as if in meditation. He didn't acknowledge her repeated inquiries. She and Micah passed the day double-checking their subterranean lair's new security features and playing card games. Jacob didn't move a muscle all day.

About an hour before nightfall, Rebecca instructed Micah to stay in the nest while she went upstairs to look out the living room window. It was something she did every day before locking the basement door for the night, one final check to make sure the authorities hadn't shown up.

Nothing had changed outside. The neighboring houses seemed vacant. The ambulance, which had become a magnet for insane graffiti, hadn't been disturbed. There was still a dead paramedic decomposing in her front yard. No sign of rescue. With a heavy sigh, Rebecca headed back down-stairs.

As soon as she opened the basement door, she knew something was wrong. Micah sat on the floor near the bottom of the stairs, cradling her head in her hands. In a panic, Rebecca flew to her daughter.

"Micah! Are you all right?" A frantic assessment revealed no injuries.

Micah made a feeble attempt to push her away. "Ugh...fine. Nothing."

"You're *not* fine. Tell me what happened. Did you hurt yourself?"

"No," she said, still holding her head. "Sorry. I didn't mean to."

"What is it, honey? What happened?"

"I didn't do what you said. I tried to talk to Dad. He wouldn't answer, so—"

"Did he hurt you?" Rebecca asked, a hot streak of rage in her voice.

"No. I...I touched his arm. For some reason, I felt yucky all of a sudden, like I was going to throw up. Then an invisible hand pushed me down."

"Invisible hand?"

"Yeah. Dad didn't do anything. I promise."

Rebecca stood in stunned silence. She didn't know what to make of that.

"Mom, I feel sick. Can we lie down?"

"Yeah...yeah, sure. Let me carry you to bed."

Day Five, 4:00 p.m.

"Mom?"

Rebecca looked up from the notebook where she had been recording her observations on Jacob's condition. Someday science would need to make sense of all this, and her notes might provide unique insights. "Huh? Want more soup?"

"No. It's gross."

Micah, who sat on the other side of a flipped-over box they used as a table, hadn't touched her food. Rebecca gave her a stern look. Split pea soup straight out of the can wasn't very appetizing, but they needed to eat *something*. At least it wasn't the condensed kind.

Refusing to meet Rebecca's gaze, Micah stirred her soup. "Will I ever go back to school?"

"I hope so, honey. I really do."

"What about the other kids?" Micah looked up from her bowl. Desperation lurked just below the worry on her face. "Do you think my friends are okay? And what about Mrs. Turner? Will she still be our home room teacher? There's something wrong with her back, so she has to use the elevators at school. She wouldn't be as good at hiding in basements as we are."

"Micah, please..." Rebecca said. She hoped her daughter hadn't heard the cracks in her voice. She couldn't break down. Not now. Not in front of Micah.

"I got in a fight with Sandy in gym class," Micah continued. "She hit me with the ball on accident. It was so stupid! I meant to give her a friendship bracelet on Monday, so she'd know she didn't have to say sorry as long as I didn't either."

The wall Micah had built to restrain her emotions buckled. Tears filled her eyes and a gush of words spilled from her. "But what if there's nobody like Dad at Sandy's house to scare bad guys away?"

Then Rebecca did break down. She couldn't help it. The box between them scooted aside, and she wrapped her arms around Micah. Together, they wept.

Day Five, 5:15 p.m.

The first rays of moonlight trickled through the makeshift curtains. The moon always came up at this exact time, always in the same spot and always full. Once again, Jacob climbed the stairs overhead and let himself out. Rebecca waited. Minutes turned to hours. Still nothing, not even the sound of him walking around upstairs.

After forcing herself to lie still for half the night, she got up and paced in the dark. At one point, she pulled a ladder to one of the windows to peek through a corner of the sheet covering it. To the west, the sky glowed an angry orange. Something big was burning.

Finally, a few hours before dawn, plodding footsteps made their way down the stairs. Half-expecting another intruder, she crept out of the nest to find Jacob collapsed on the floor in front of the dryer. Relief swept over her, washing away the excruciating anxiety. She knew she should be angry, furious even. The bastard had run off to God knew where, leaving them alone all night in this hell. Maybe that would matter in the morning, but right now she thanked God he hadn't abandoned them. All Rebecca could feel was gratitude, and she hated herself for it.

He lay on his back, his face set in a pained grimace. The t-shirt he had changed into earlier was blackened with what appeared to be ash. He reeked of alcohol. And where had he gotten those boots?

Rebecca wanted to help him but didn't know how. Thoroughly exhausted, she crawled into the nest.

Day Six, 7:45 a.m.

A sharp cry rang through the basement, wrenching Rebecca from a dreamless sleep. She reached for Micah. Empty blankets. Gone? That scream! She burst from the nest, ran to where Jacob had been lying, and found Micah writhing on the floor with her hands pressed to her face. "Oh, God," Rebecca gasped. "No!"

Micah's entire body clenched then exploded in another scream—a raw, bloody sound torn from deep within. Rebecca knelt beside her and pulled Micah's hands away from her face. The world warped, then became a blur as Rebecca's mind rejected what it saw. Not real. It couldn't be real. Half of Micah's face had been crushed, her right temple and cheekbone a deformed mass of bloodied tissue. It wasn't clear if she still had an eye. Her jaw hung loose and uneven. Micah grabbed her mom's arm in a feeble attempt to pull herself up into a sitting position, making pitiful gurgling sounds.

There were no words for the depths of shock Rebecca fell into. She couldn't look away from Micah's pleading, ruined face. Her girl, her beautiful girl. She had known Jacob was dangerous; she had fucking *known* it! This was her fault.

In a blind rage, Rebecca ran to the shelves by the stairs and grabbed the crowbar. She charged back to Jacob and swung it hard at his head.

Micah clawed the floor in a futile effort to do something—anything—to end the nightmare. An anguished moan escaped her useless mouth.

There was no crack of metal breaking bone, no splatter of blood. The crowbar recoiled as if it had struck a steel plate except without any sound. Rebecca's arm stung from the force of the impact. She raised the crowbar again and brought it crashing down on Jacob's chest. Blocked. Out of her mind with grief and rage, she kicked him. Her foot slammed painfully into something unseen an inch from his body, an invisible shell.

A sudden whoosh of air blew past Rebecca; an instant later, something shoved her chest, and she stumbled backward. Except nothing had pushed her—at least nothing she could see. Terrified, she swept Micah up into her arms and ran upstairs. More than anything, she wanted to keep running—out of the house, down the street, to a different city, however far she needed to go to escape.

One arm reaching for the front door, the other holding Micah, Rebecca paused. Nothing awaited them out there but death; she knew it with absolute certainty. All that chaos and violence—they'd meet a brutal, ugly, utterly pointless end.

No. If she and Micah were going to die, it would be at home, fighting for the things they had lived for. Rebecca walked back into the living room. She had work to do.

Day Six, 9:15 a.m.

Rebecca stood by the sliding glass door that separated the kitchen from the patio, secured with a board in its runner after that intruder had broken the lock. Until a few minutes ago, an old blanket had covered the door to keep anyone from looking in. Taking down the blanket hadn't been smart, but being smart wasn't Rebecca's highest priority anymore. She needed to stay sane, at least for a little while longer. Watching the moon sink below the horizon helped. Soon, this horrific night would end. When light returned to the world, she wanted it to flood the house.

The last hour had passed in a pointless flurry of action. She had done her best to clean the wreckage of Micah's face and bandage her wounds. Without access to a hospital, it was all she could do. Thankfully, Micah had been unconscious since they came upstairs.

The sliding door's cool glass felt good against Rebecca's skin. It was solid, real. It made sense. In a few minutes, she'd move Micah from the kitchen floor to the couch in the living room. It was a more comfortable, dignified place to die.

Day Six, 3:30 p.m.

A miracle occurred. There was no other way to describe it. Micah's injuries healed. As she slept on the couch, fractured bones reformed and torn skin knitted itself back together. Unbelievable. Rebecca *didn't* believe it. Convinced she had slipped into delusion, she poked and prodded Micah's injuries over and over.

Only hours before, the damage had been catastrophic. A portion of her skull had collapsed, making brain damage a foregone conclusion. Her eye socket had been destroyed, crushing the delicate organ within. Both her nose and jaw were broken. In medical school, Rebecca had seen her fair share of head trauma cases. Wounds like that should be fatal or leave a person in a vegetative state. At best, the patient could hope for a partial recovery after reconstructive surgeries and years of physical therapy. Even then, there would be permanent neurological problems.

Yet Micah's condition had completely changed over the course of a single day with no medical intervention whatsoever. Rebecca revised her diagnosis to bruising, swelling, and a possible concussion. Micah still looked awful, like someone had savagely beaten her, but it was a drastic improvement over the night before. The divot in her skull had mended. A new eye formed in the gory pit where her old one used to be. Even the teeth Jacob had knocked out grew back. "Miracle" was the only word for what happened that day.

When night returned, Rebecca moved Micah to a bed of towels on the floor in the first-floor bathroom. It would be easier to protect her there. Holding a chef's knife she had taken from the kitchen, she kept watch throughout the night.

Day Seven, 10:00 a.m.

Although Micah's recovery stalled for a time, it resumed at dawn, which came hours later than it had a week ago. By one o'clock, the only remaining evidence of the assault was a black eye. There weren't even any scars.

Rebecca had never given much thought to miracles, but she understood they were gifts. They should be accepted with gratitude, humility, and a renewed faith in the power of God. Still, a dark specter of worry lurked behind her immeasurable gratitude. Micah's recovery wasn't the only un-natural phenomena she had witnessed over the past few days, and none of the others had been good.

That afternoon, Micah woke up. She could speak, her memory seemed unaffected, everything was normal. A miracle. Within a couple hours of regaining consciousness, she started to badger Rebecca about checking on Jacob. Even after what had happened, she wanted to make sure he was okay. *Unbelievable.*

Knowing Micah would eventually sneak downstairs on her own, Rebecca gave up on arguing. Jacob usually slept through the day; if they had to see him, this was as good a time as any. Gripping the chef's knife in white-knuckled hands, she opened the basement door and started down the stairs.

They found Jacob lying under a window in a pool of what smelled like whiskey vomit, shivering and groaning. Micah gasped but didn't cry or look away. Mother and daughter sat on the stairs. It was all they could do for him, bear witness. He looked so alone, such a small and wretched thing. Minutes passed in silence. Rebecca knew they should go back upstairs, but she didn't have the heart to make Micah leave. Lost in thought, the two of them bowed their heads. Time slipped by. Their welfare check had become a vigil.

"Hello?"

Micah and Rebecca snapped to attention. They knew that voice. It wasn't a cruel imitation of Jacob—it *was* Jacob.

"It's okay. I'm...I'm all right."

Micah's Rules for a Better World

Be brave. Even when your body shakes and your blood turns to ice, be brave.

Chapter 2

Prelude

Alone, the only spark of life in a dead world, you call into the Darkness, needing any answer at all—anything but the stillness of death. Just as fear tips into despair, darkness itself whispers to you.

All Right

Jacob put his pencil down. Dawn had come at last.

Bursts of wild energy, crazy thoughts flashing like fireworks, uncontrollable impulses—that was how his nights passed. And the nights were so very long. Morning arrived like a cool breeze on a summer day, clearing his head. He became almost human. *Almost.*

The paper on his desk was a horror show of crudely drawn skulls and thick black slashes. Jacob had never been much of an artist, but drawing helped burn off the manic energy that built up each night. Averting his eyes from the paper, he took it to an old file cabinet and slipped it in the top drawer. It was an artifact of the night before. Although he kept it, he never wanted to see it again. Someday he'd burn that file cabinet.

"All right" is a subjective term. Whether it applied to Jacob was a point of contention. As days stretched into weeks, he began to feel all right, but Rebecca disagreed. She didn't think he existed in the same universe as "all right." No matter how hard he tried, how far he came, she would always see him as the monster who had attacked Micah. She wouldn't even tell him what had happened that night. All he remembered was the attack itself. It had been a solid hit, the kind he knew his new body could use to smash bricks or dent steel. Yet Micah didn't have a scratch on her. How was that possible?

Guilt writhed through Jacob's insides like a snake, sinking its fangs into his heart. For days after his recovery, he wallowed in a pit of misery. Again and again, he begged Micah to forgive him, which she did each time. If only it were so easy to forgive himself.

Micah refused to talk about what he had done to her. She said she was okay, but the hurt in her eyes told a different story. Jacob didn't know how to fix that. He didn't know what to do about her nightmares, the tears that came out of nowhere, or the way she flinched if he moved too quickly. He couldn't find the magic words to cleanse her mind of the pain and fear that had settled into the places trust used to be. There was nothing he could do.

So much had changed over the past few weeks. Jacob didn't know if "change" was even the right word for it. When it came to his body, "metamorphosis" seemed more appropriate. He felt fine. Better than fine—strong, healthy, full of life and vigor. He couldn't remember ever feeling so at one with his physical self. Other than the horns sprouting from his head, he appeared normal. Nothing could be further from the truth though. Eating and drinking were now optional. He had only eaten once since his recovery and found the experience somewhat disgusting. Apparently, he now subsisted on air alone, and he wasn't entirely sure he needed that. He didn't sleep, and as far as he could tell, he didn't need to. Injuries healed in minutes. He was stronger and faster than any human should be. Jacob had been completely remade.

He must have grown used to the horns while he was sick, as they didn't bother him. Curving back from his temples, they ran along the ridge of his skull before wrapping around his ears and tapering off into blunt points in the style of rams' horns. Ivory-white and harder than steel, they were remarkable. Despite them being the most obvious effect of whatever had happened to him, Jacob couldn't help but grin whenever he looked himself over in a mirror, which he did often. Horns suited him.

One evening, he stood gazing at his reflection in the large mirror mounted over the dresser in his bedroom. The collection of candles arrayed along the dresser's top lent his horns an orange glow. Occasionally, he wondered if black might not have been a better color for the horns, but when they picked up ambient light like this he appreciated their bone-like color. Black would stand out more in sunlight, but sunny days seemed to be a thing of the past.

"What are you doing?" Rebecca asked as she stepped into the room. It came out as an accusation rather than a question.

"Just wondering if I need a haircut. What do you think?"

She scowled at him.

Stroking his chin, Jacob said, "Did you know I don't have to shave anymore? If I cut my hair, would it grow back or stay how I cut it forever? Hey...what if it grew back overnight like in this vampire movie I saw one time?"

"Are you done cleaning?" Rebecca asked.

He gestured at the empty room behind him. He had removed all the furniture except the dresser and dumped it in a neighbor's yard. Everything in the bedroom stunk from when that revolting lunatic had taken up residence there. "I'll tear out the carpet tomorrow," he said.

"Forgot something." Rebecca pointed to a wadded-up sheet in a corner.

With a put-upon sigh, Jacob turned from the mirror. The sheet rose from the ground and floated across the room like a grimy ghost. After waiting for the bedroom window to open itself, the sheet flew outside and dropped.

"Done," he said.

Rebecca left without further comment.

Jacob's change had brought him another gift: he could move things with his mind. The new power also allowed him to create invisible objects of various shapes and sizes. A moment ago, when he had heard Rebecca coming up the stairs, he had considered blocking the bedroom door with an invisible wall. She hated it when he did that.

Different footsteps made their way up the stairs, and Micah took her mother's place in the bedroom doorway. She looked half-asleep. "You're up late. Going to bed?" Jacob asked, trying to make it sound like a normal thing to do at 6:30 p.m.

She yawned dramatically and shuffled toward him. Without thinking, she reached out for a goodnight hug. Force of habit. A wave of sickness hit the instant her fingertip brushed against Jacob's forearm. Panic streaked across her face, and she pulled her hand back as if it had touched a live wire.

Jacob felt it too—an eruption of nausea and an intense feeling of dread. He stumbled back a step. In an unsteady voice, he said, "Careful, M."

Micah recovered quickly, as she always did. "Sorry, Dad." A mournful expression came over her and she left.

The final change Jacob had undergone was the only one he would unreservedly give up. He could no longer touch his daughter. Physical contact made them both suddenly and violently ill. Even being near her sent jolts of terror up his spine. He couldn't hug her, hold her hand, or place a comforting arm around troubled shoulders. Only words could pass between them.

Days were dull, which was a blessing. There weren't any good kinds of excitement anymore. The family had a month's supply of food and water, along with other essentials, thanks to Rebecca's dad, who had been preparing for doomsday since the Cold War. The supplies should last even longer since Jacob didn't eat. For the foreseeable future, there was no need to leave the house.

Rebecca took advantage of the relative calm the daylight hours offered to catch up on sleep and scan through the static on the radio in hopes of picking up an emergency broadcast. Jacob and Micah settled into a routine of storytelling, board games, and collaborative drawing. Piece by piece, the two of them worked on rebuilding their relationship. It wouldn't be the same as before, but to Jacob's eternal gratitude, Micah wanted to see what it could be.

Things changed at night. Everyone retreated to the basement, which became a pressure cooker of anxiety and tension. The alien energy that fueled Jacob's new abilities—a thing he called Darkness, for lack of a better word—swelled in him until he felt he'd burst. His face stretched into a diabolical grin, and his voice became smooth and venomous. Restraint, compassion, and patience fell by the wayside as far less-agreeable characteristics rose in their place. He was still Jacob, but a different Jacob.

Micah slept through her father's nightly reign of terror. As soon as the moon began to rise, she crawled into the nest under the basement stairs and didn't reemerge until dawn. Although her parents worried about her sleeping through two-thirds of the day, they were glad she didn't have to witness Jacob's nocturnal behavior.

Rebecca wasn't so lucky. He tried not to bother her—he really did—but his boiling restlessness often overcame his resolve. Overflowing with strange and beautiful ideas, new perceptions, and fascinating observations that needed to be shared, Jacob would seek her out. Before he realized what was happening, he'd find himself whispering ominous nonsense to Rebecca, shoving a paper into her hands with nothing but red and black smears on it, or doing other things that left her shaken. It didn't take long for her to decide nighttime Jacob was as crazy as the people she heard screaming and howling outside.

One night, his madness took a coltish turn. He decided to lighten the mood in the basement with a game. Giggling like a little boy, he hid behind a storage cabinet, waiting for Rebecca to walk by. When she did, he threw a blanket over her and swept her off her feet. It was a game he used to play with Micah when she was little; they called it "Capture the Princess." Drunk on his own energy and more gin than anyone should consume in a single evening, he thought Rebecca might want to play.

She didn't. Bucking and kicking, she freed her arm from the blanket and began punching blindly behind her. She hit a horn, then his cheekbone, before finally connecting with his left eye.

A burst of white erased half of Jacob's vision. He dropped her, his hands flying to the injury. "Ow! Damn it, Rebecca. Why—"

Silver flashed in the dark. A searing pain shot through his arm. She had sunk the kitchen knife she carried around into his shoulder, then extracted it with a vicious slashing move, extending the wound several inches down his bicep. He staggered backward, gaping at her. Silently, Rebecca stood her ground, brandishing the knife. Her eyes were ice.

It only took an hour for the wound to heal, but the hurt lingered. It had been a childish prank, no doubt about it, but did he deserve to get stabbed? That seemed excessive.

Another night, he called Rebecca over to the workbench in the basement, his voice glistening with danger and excitement. He held a hammer in his right hand. His left lay in a pool of candlelight on the workbench. Before she could say a word, he swung the hammer up then brought it down hard on his prone index finger.

Rebecca jumped back with a shocked gasp. "What the hell? Are you out of your goddamned mind?"

"Come closer," he said through gritted teeth. When she refused to comply, he picked up the candle from the table and held his bloodied finger up for inspection. "Look!" As they watched, crushed muscles mended themselves and skin crept back into place. As far as he could tell, the bone hadn't even broken. "Medical opinion?" he asked with a dark sneer.

Rebecca didn't have one.

One especially awful night, Jacob went upstairs in a futile effort to escape from himself. An angry wraith bound to the mundane world, he paced through the darkened bedrooms wishing the walls would fall away so the sweet air of freedom could fill his lungs.

Rebecca and Micah rarely went upstairs, even after he had cleaned up the mess left by that filthy squatter. A couple of mice hiding in their hole, certain every shadow—even the memory of a shadow—was a hawk. What did they have to fear? Jacob the Dutiful shooed away every crazy who came near the house. All he needed to do was make his presence known and they ran like the devil himself were at their heels.

For lack of anything else to do, he reached one of his telekinetic arms into Micah's room and snatched a doll from the floor. It was one of the plastic ones with big eyes and a vacant smile, a knockoff Barbie named Mindy or

Trixie or whatever-the-fuck. Jacob's sister always sent Micah crap like that for her birthday even though Micah didn't play with dolls.

Jacob practiced his telekinetic fine motor skills by levitating the doll a few feet in front of him while swinging its legs, rotating its arms, and twisting its head around *Exorcist*-style. Bored again, he popped the doll's head off. A stray moonbeam caught its platinum hair, which coarsened the magical light into something as cheap and soulless as the toy itself. He tossed the decapitated doll back into the bedroom and went downstairs.

After checking on Micah, who was fast asleep under the basement stairs, he turned his attention to Rebecca on the other side of the room. She was sitting at a card table, reading by the light of a battery powered lantern. So composed. So brave. Two reactions coiled around each other in Jacob's gut like battling serpents: affection and seething contempt. The dissonance made him nauseous.

A thin band of telekinetic energy glided across the floor, climbed the back of Rebecca's chair, and tapped her on the shoulder.

She spun around so violently her chair nearly toppled over. "Don't touch me!"

Jacob's laughter, as slick as oil and just as black, filled the basement. "Relax, Becky, just showing a little affection. I hear that's part of a healthy conjugal relationship."

"What do you know about marriage?" she snapped.

He circled the table, his hungry grin shifting in and out of the shadows cast by the lamp. "There's no need for you to stay up all night worrying yourself into an early grave, not when you have such a loyal husband to watch over you. How about we go upstairs and find you a proper bed? I'll tuck you in." He positioned himself behind Rebecca's chair and laid a hand on her shoulder. "And if you can't sleep, there are other things husbands and wives do to pass the time."

With a slow, deliberate movement, Rebecca reached under the table to take the kitchen knife from her lap. "I said don't touch me."

Jacob let out a long sigh. "So cruel, Becky." He pulled a chair to the table and took a seat. "Can we at least talk for a while? I'm bored."

"Talk about what?"

"I don't know..." He gestured vaguely. "What does marriage mean to you?"

"Support. Trust. Understanding. The man I married knew I hated to be called 'Becky.' Not once in all the years I knew him did he call me that. He never said anything he knew would hurt me."

"Oh? And what else didn't he say? What secret thoughts never escaped his regrettably horn-less head?"

"Shut up!" Rebecca yelled, her face bursting scarlet. "You don't speak for him. You're the disease that took him from me, the thing that tried to kill his daughter."

Jacob redirected the gush of pain her words unleashed into a hollow place where it wouldn't trouble him for a while, not until his Darkness receded in the morning. "So, are you asking for a divorce? In the unlikely event that the courts ever resume business, I can recommend a few good attorneys."

"I'm not asking you for anything," Rebecca said. "I don't have a husband anymore."

Jacob's laughter once again echoed through the basement. "Husband, monster, guard dog—think of me however you like. But make no mistake about it, you and I aren't finished." He got up from the table and disappeared into the wall of darkness beyond the lamp's light. "Good night, Becky. Sleep well."

***

"Damn it," Jacob muttered as he rummaged through the liquor cabinet in his den one night. He had just consolidated the household's dwindling supply of alcohol, and there was less than he had thought. Drinking blunted the impact of the storm that raged inside him every night. Drawing helped, but he needed alcohol too.

Before he had changed, drinking half this much would have taken its toll, but he had a feeling it wouldn't hurt him now—at least not physically. If he could smash his finger with a hammer and take a stab wound or two, his upgraded liver should be able to take a beating as well. He grabbed a couple bottles of wine. That might be enough to get him through the night if he paced himself.

Jacob was torn, split in two. The cycle of day and night felt like dying and being reborn, only he didn't know which side was life and which death.

Later that night, while bending spoons to practice his telekinesis, an idea struck him. He would start a journal. A written record of his ups and downs might help him keep track of who he was and who he wanted to be, prevent him from flying off the rails. Context and perspective—that's what he needed. And if he ultimately lost his mind, at least there would be evidence he had tried to keep it together.

But how to begin?

Dear diary: Last night I trapped my wife in an invisible bubble just for kicks. Now I feel bad.

Dear diary: This morning, my daughter accidentally touched me, and I felt sick for an hour afterward. I recover from stab wounds faster.

Dear diary: I have a secret! Sometimes I want to run away from home and play with the crazies outside.

There, that last one. If ever a problem needed context and perspective, that was it. While the urge to escape might be understandable, he had a family to protect. Determined to sort things out, Jacob sat at his desk and put pen to paper. Hours later, he had produced a dreadful poem about wolves and several doodles depicting houses on fire. Maybe journaling wasn't such a great idea after all.

From there, the night got rough. He tried to read in the basement but couldn't stand the sounds of life—Micah breathing, Rebecca shifting in her chair. Both of them were so...*there*, two cinder blocks tied to the ankles of a drowning man.

Days passed. Creepy drawings and the occasional practical joke no longer satisfied Jacob's Darkness. It wanted more. Much, much more. He worried someone might get hurt if he didn't find ways to allow it to express itself, breathe a little. That meant leaving the house.

As luck would have it, the family's supply of food and water was finally running low. Thanks to the fact that Jacob had eaten exactly one third of a can of black bean chili in the weeks since his recovery, it had lasted longer than expected, but within a week Micah and Rebecca would go hungry. As the only Freeman with superpowers, Jacob volunteered to go outside to gather supplies.

Rebecca put up a token resistance, more out of a general suspicion of any idea that sprang from Jacob's corrupted head than any rational objection. It didn't take long, though, for her to come around. She needed a break from him as badly as he needed a break from the house. Her only stipulations were that he look for help—a refugee center, a military outpost, a rag-tag group of survivors, anything at all—and that he gather information on what had happened. Jacob promised to try, but never said he'd try all that hard. He had other priorities.

Leaving the house unprotected after dark was out of the question, so he would do whatever he needed to do during the daylight hours. That meant being apart from Micah during the only part of the day when she could keep her eyes open. She didn't like that one bit. As good as it made Jacob feel to know she wanted him around, he insisted. If he lost his mind, he'd be a threat to her. Eventually, Micah relented. Even stubborn kids understand the need for fresh water. The prospect of finding a safe place where there might be other kids also swayed her.

In the end, Jacob agreed to go exploring every third day, to always be back before dark, and to bring Micah new books and toys. The girl drove a hard bargain.

Notes on the New World

Twenty-Seven Days Post-Transformation

This was it, the big day. The front door clicked shut behind Jacob. His Darkness, which was usually quiet during the day, bounced around like an excited puppy. He and it stood alone with the entire world stretched out before them.

Birds chirped. Cicadas hummed. If he closed his eyes, he could almost imagine a lazy summer afternoon with nothing to do but lounge around and enjoy being alive. Almost, but not quite. The stomach-turning stench rising from the long-dead paramedic on his lawn was a hard-to-miss clue that things weren't right. It only got worse when he opened his eyes. The light, which didn't appear to come from anywhere in particular, held a green tinge, as though the sky were choked with toxic smog. A derelict ambulance sat in front of their house, covered in cryptic graffiti and a web of meticulously carved scratch marks. Across the street, an improvised rope fashioned from tied-together bed sheets hung from a second-floor window. Dwelling on who had made it and why seemed like a bad idea.

For a second, Jacob's human half panicked. Everything was wrong. The entire world, reality itself—wrong. And his Darkness's hunger for the wrongness scared him. He took a deep breath, the weight of Rebecca's gaze through the front window urging him forward. She tried to hide it, but she had been looking forward to this time apart. Turning back now would have all sorts of unpleasant repercussions. So off he went.

The outside world was stranger and more horrifying than he had imagined. Dead bodies littered the neighborhood—puffing up like balloons in the street, spilling out of houses, dangling from trees, everywhere. There were no discernible patterns to the slaughter, no common cause or purpose that linked the killings. The neighborhood wasn't a war zone or the site of a massacre, but the scene of countless individual murders. Each corpse told a unique story of brutality and degradation. The only analogy that came to mind were medieval depictions of hell: crowds of people crying out in agony as demons gnawed on their limbs, roasted them alive, pulled out their entrails, and enacted other unspeakable horrors.

At the intersection where Micah used to wait for the school bus, an orgy of violence had taken place. Gore covered the road like confetti after a parade: severed limbs, a few heads, unidentifiable viscera. In an open garage, the bodies of two women lay bent over toppled garbage cans. Naked, their decaying faces ground into the cement floor, their genitals obscenely exposed, they must have suffered in ways no one should.

People couldn't have done these things; it must have been demons. That was the only way Jacob could process what he saw. Hell had come to the human world. Inside him, his Darkness recoiled from the carnage as well, although in disgust rather than horror. This wasn't to its taste.

Less than a mile from home, he came across a body that had been burned at the stake in a school playground. Chained to the tetherball pole, a mound of charred books at its feet, the body slumped into its bonds. And gathered in neat concentric circles around the pole—

No. This must be a nightmare, the worst Jacob had ever had. He closed his eyes, but the image refused to fade from his mind. Butchered bodies woven around one another in chains of flesh—lifeless eyes, gray tongues lolling out of gaping mouths, limbless trunks. *Children.* They were all children.

Jacob's mind shut down. In a daze, he walked home. More scenes of torture and death passed before his eyes, but he only saw that playground.

Thirty Days Post-Transformation

Ignorance is weakness, and Jacob couldn't afford to be weak. He was the only thing that stood between his family and the sadistic fucks who had killed their neighbors. To better protect Micah and Rebecca, he needed to understand the threats they faced. That meant forcing himself back into hell when the next exploration day came around.

Murder can mean a million things, many of which had played out around Jacob's house while he and his family hid like rats in a hole. Some of the deaths appeared to have been convenience killings, the casual removal of someone in the way. Others were quick and savage, explosions of rage perhaps. Still others bore signs of some sick passion indulged at the expense of the deceased. Then there were the special cases. Jacob came across a few scenes so bizarre, so meticulously crafted, he could only call them death art.

The first installation he found was a man and a woman wearing Victorian formal wear whose bodies had been propped up against each other in a shop window as though they had chosen that spot for a dance. A sword pierced their chests, skewering them together as they rotted into each other.

A few blocks from the entangled couple, a man wearing the leather jacket and white t-shirt of a fifties greaser was splayed out on the hood of a vintage sports car. Lightning bolts, skillfully painted in a bold yellow, shot out from his body across the car. Someone had screwed lightbulbs into the man's eye sockets.

Already in a daze, Jacob stopped by Rebecca's friend Michelle Cramer's house, hoping to find her family hiding in their basement. Maybe one of them had grown horns too. Finding no one in the house, which had been ransacked, he wandered into the back yard.

The Cramers had always been proud of their custom-designed pool and the expansive patio surrounding it, complete with all the amenities. The sounds of children playing and smells of grilled meat emanated from behind their fence almost every weekend during the summer. Rebecca often brought the pool-deprived Micah to Michelle's house so she could splash around with the Cramer kids while the ladies sipped cocktails at the poolside bar. Jacob had joined them for a few cookouts, engaging in shallow guy-talk with Jim Cramer over the grill.

And there was Jim now, hanging from a nylon cord fashioned into a noose and affixed to a ceiling beam in the shelter over the bar. His naked body was still recognizable, although nowhere near freshly dead.

Weeds had defiled the formerly pristine patio, poking up between the pavers in ugly clumps. Slimy, neon-green algae covered the pool. An inflatable flamingo the size of a loveseat, its pink body splattered with muck, slowly drifted.

As Jacob braved the smell to approach Jim's corpse, he noticed black bruises and shallow cuts on and around the dead man's genitals. A notebook left open on the bar in front of Jim had the words *Make it stop* scrawled across one page in black marker.

Michelle, Rebecca's friend, and the family's two children—a girl a little older than Micah and a boy about seven years old whose names Jacob couldn't remember—were nowhere to be found. An uneasy feeling made him grateful the algae hid the bottom of the pool though.

That was enough for one day. Numb inside, Jacob went home.

Thirty-One Days Post-Transformation

Moonlight poured down on Jacob's house. He sat on the roof, lost in thought. Those children on the playground, the Cramers, all the other horrific things he had seen—how much of it could he have prevented if he hadn't spent a month holed up in his house? Could he have saved the entire city?

He rubbed his aching head and lay down to gaze up at the starless but moon-bright sky. There was no way to know.

Thirty-Three Days Post-Transformation

Instead of exploring, Jacob focused on collecting the canned food and bottled water he had promised to get a week ago. Fortunately, the local grocery store appeared to have undergone only sporadic looting. Crazies looking for a quick snack probably.

After bringing home enough supplies to last Rebecca and Micah another month, he decided to finally get rid of the dead paramedic in his front yard. A landscaping project at a house a couple blocks away had been cut short by the end of the world, leaving bags of topsoil and mulch piled up in the yard. Dumping that on the body would spare him the ordeal of moving it, likely seeing the thing fall apart in the process.

As Jacob walked down the street with a dozen bags of dirt floating in the air behind him like a bunch of helium balloons, it struck him how little physical damage had been done to the neighborhood. With a few notable exceptions, there wasn't the kind of mass destruction one would expect. Crazies seemed to prefer violence against people over property crimes.

After setting the bags down in the road, Jacob created a dome-shaped barrier around himself to keep out the stench of rot. It helped, but he found he couldn't move the bags through the barrier. Apparently, there couldn't be anything between him and an object he wanted to manipulate, not even one of his own invisible walls.

Cursing the limitations of his power, he dismissed the barrier and got to work.

Thirty-Nine Days Post-Transformation

Like so many other things, atrocities become less remarkable with frequent exposure. In Jacob's case, every third day was frequent enough. Dead bodies became an unsightly part of the urban landscape like litter. Even the elaborate corpse-themed installation pieces were mere curiosities, only the most creative of them worth noticing. However, he occasionally still came across something that struck a nerve.

Late in the day, he found a recently deceased woman sitting on a park bench. She was leaned against a board painted with flames that framed her body. Ropes of braided copper wire threaded through holes in the board to fasten her to it and keep her centered.

Although Jacob couldn't say what, something about the scene pierced his calloused indifference. The woman was young, mid-twenties perhaps, with delicate features and strawberry-blonde hair pulled back into an elegant chignon, giving her the look of a Greek goddess. She must have been beautiful in life.

Two hunting knives stuck out the sides of her head, buried to their hilts in her skull. Polished wooden handles protruded like horns. Other than a trickle of blood seeping from the knife wounds and running down her neck, there was no mess. She could have been made of stone.

Icy fingers of dread gripped Jacob's heart. Blood rushed to his head in a thundering flood. He desperately wanted to look away, but couldn't. Blue lips…skin just starting to turn gray…milky eyes. How could anyone do *that* to her?

His paralysis broke, and he ran as fast as his new body would go.

Forty-Five Days Post-Transformation

Sickly, post-apocalyptic light leaked through the canopy of leaves over a trail through the woods. Poets used to compare sunlight to honey. This stuff looked more like phlegm. Every now and then, Jacob walked this trail to escape the incessant depravity on display in the streets. Winding through a hillside park near his house, it offered views of the Ohio River and Kentucky's rolling hills beyond.

The trees around him seemed confused by the recent changes to their environment. Who could blame them? After millions of years of adaptation to certain conditions, one day the sun disappeared and plants were left with a measly six hours a day of snot-light to work with. Some trees had turned orange, red, or gold in anticipation of fall. Others remained green. Still others had given up and dropped their leaves.

What would happen if all the plants died and the food chain collapsed? Jacob didn't need to eat. After the canned food was gone and the last corpse had been picked clean, would he be the only thing left alive?

It still rained, though, so nature would probably find a way. Not that the weather behaved in anything like a normal way. Every day except Sundays was a constant eighty-four degrees with fifty percent humidity, day and night. Each Sunday, a gray mass of clouds covered the sky and it drizzled until dawn Monday morning.

Jacob came to an abrupt stop, derailing his musings on the miracles of nature. Someone had placed a Barbie doll in the middle of the trail, binding her to a tent stake to keep her standing. Splashes of red stained her frilly white dress. Her hands had been replaced with severed cat paws. Careful not to disturb the tiny sentinel, he stepped over her and continued down the path.

Fifty-Three Days Post-Transformation

The basement door flew open, and Micah burst into the kitchen. "Halloween!" she squealed. "It's Halloween!"

Jacob had prepared for this. Before the woman with knives in her head spooked him, he had looted a huge amount of candy from the grocery store and stashed it in a cabinet. As he sat at the kitchen table watching Micah hop around, chanting, "Hall-o-ween! Hall-o-ween!" he opened the cabinet door with invisible hands, scooped up one of the bags of candy, and levitated it across the ceiling.

"Watch out, M!" he yelled in mock alarm. "There's a ghost over your head!"

Her eyes darted up and her jaw dropped. "Yes!" she said, doing a fist pump of victory. "I'll go get my witch costume from last year. We're doing Halloween!"

Jacob followed her upstairs to put on his own costume. Since he already had horns, the devil seemed an obvious choice. A black suit, some red face paint, a bit of hair gel, and he was ready.

After Micah got dressed, they set up "houses" for all her stuffed animals and gave each a pile of candy. Then they got busy trick-or-treating. Micah had so much fun, she hardly noticed when it got dark. The moon found her still busy sorting candy, chatting about which kinds she liked best.

Jacob felt good. He had done something right. If only Rebecca could have shared the experience, the day would have been perfect. His costume had been too much for her, so she spent the entire day in the basement.

Fifty-Seven Days Post-Transformation

As Jacob rummaged through yet another abandoned house, it occurred to him that there weren't enough dead people. There were plenty, just not as many as there should be. Hyde Park, the comfortably affluent neighborhood his family called home, had been fairly densely populated. Many of the residents must have become crazies and were hiding or doing whatever crazies did during the daytime, but there couldn't be that many crazies. Maybe there had been an evacuation after all. Rebecca would kill him if she found out people were being evacuated while he had spent the past few weeks screwing around and scavenging candy.

He'd make an honest effort to search for survivors, but not just yet. Other priorities took precedence this day, namely the worrisome state of his liquor cabinet.

Slipping past a wrecked car partially blocking the door, Jacob stepped into his favorite neighborhood bar. A carpet of glass crunched under his feet. It appeared to be mostly from the front window and a huge mirror that used to hang behind the bar rather than from broken bottles. The bottles were gone. Apparently, crazies had a taste for liquor.

He ran a telekinetic hand down the length of the bar, watching a streak appear in the dust as if a ghost were gliding over it. A few weeks ago, he had done the same thing on the flour-covered floor of an aisle in the grocery store to see how far he could reach. Thirty-six feet. At the time, the number had struck him as oddly significant, but now it was just a number.

Jacob had done a lot of measuring that day. He discovered he could lift at least three thousand pounds with telekinesis and about four hundred the old-fashioned way, run fifteen miles an hour at full sprint (a pace he could maintain for a half-mile), and jog laps around the entire neighborhood without tiring. But he wasn't interested in his monster stats at the moment. He needed to find a bottle of liquor before dark, or he'd be in for a rough night.

A commotion outside grabbed his attention. "Back! Get back!" a thin, cracked voice screeched.

As quietly as he could, Jacob snuck to the broken front window and peeked out. An elderly Black woman stood in the road, facing off against a boy whose pale complexion, nearly round shape, and complete lack of clothes made him look like a miniature moon. Crazies up past their bedtime?

The woman shakily brandished a fire poker. In her other hand, she carried a paper grocery bag. "Back!"

"You got somethin' good?" the boy asked. Although his crisp, piping voice was that of a child, it carried the leering menace of a seasoned predator.

"Pretties, pretties..." the woman said, seemingly to herself.

Eyes fixed on the bag, the boy said, "I smell treats. Whatcha got? Cupcakes? Cookies? I smell 'em!" He lunged at the woman.

Surprisingly agile for her age, she sidestepped his attack, swatting his fleshy bottom with her poker as he stumbled past. "Got what was comin' to you! After my pretties like that."

The boy let out a howl, half temper tantrum and half enraged animal, and launched himself at her again. His full weight slammed into her frail body, knocking her off her feet. Both fell hard. The bag flew out of the old woman's hand and landed a few feet away. Dozens of porcelain figurines spilled onto the road.

Both boy and the woman scrambled toward the bag on their hands and knees. No longer fighting, they sifted through the figurines.

"Pretties!" the old woman wailed.

Fat tears rolled down the boy's cheeks. "Where's the treats?"

It was as if each had forgotten the other existed. The world was nothing but broken pretties and absent treats.

Sixty Days Post-Transformation

Hyde Park Square was a narrow, park-like space that ran down the center of a divided road. Lined with stately oak trees and surrounded by boutiques and restaurants catering to the refined if somewhat conservative tastes of Cincinnati's old-money elite, it had always been the focal point of the neighborhood. Apparently, it still was. Every time Jacob visited, he found evidence that crazies had been enjoying the square—garbage cans tipped over, seemingly random objects arranged in weird configurations, the occasional dead body. He always made a point of tidying up. It was his neighborhood too, after all.

As Jacob approached the square one morning, an anxious feeling came over him. He ducked behind an abandoned car, pulled a pair of binoculars out of his backpack, and peered through the wall of trees that shielded the square from the road. He had an excellent view of the fountain that served as the square's centerpiece, a rectangular stone pedestal with bronze lions' heads sticking out of each side. Water once poured from the lions' mouths into four large basins attached to the pedestal. A sculpture of a nude woman holding a cloth, which partially protected her modesty, stood on top of the fountain.

Below the statue, Jacob was surprised to see an actual woman sitting in one of the basins, a lion head glaring down at her. Her arms were stretched out to the sides as if she were mimicking the top half of a crucifix. Young and fit, dressed in a gray tank top over a sports bra, she looked like she should have been out for a morning jog, not sitting in a dry fountain.

Upon closer inspection, he saw her wrists were tied to a rope that looped around the fountain's central pedestal behind her, pulling her arms up and out. A second rope formed a noose around her neck. Its tail draped over the edge of the basin and disappeared behind a knee-high concrete wall around the fountain's base. Jacob couldn't see if it attached to anything on the ground.

Someone came into view from the other side of the fountain: a burly, heavily bearded man with a duffel bag slung over one shoulder. Dressed in a white bathrobe, he looked supremely pleased with himself and the world in general. Beaming a wide grin, he set his bag on the ground then said something to the bound woman.

She screamed. There were no words, only a piercing wail. Thrashing against her bonds, she attempted to stand up but immediately fell back into a seated position. The rope around her neck had gone taut, causing the noose to tighten.

Chuckling at the futility of his captive's struggles, the man in the robe unpacked his bag. Hacksaw. Pliers. Rags. Assorted knives.

"Damn it," Jacob muttered. Stumbling upon a murder in progress wasn't something he had mentally prepared himself for when he left home. Assuming Bathrobe Guy was a crazy, which seemed a safe bet, he would probably run away if Jacob made an appearance, but "probably" didn't seem certain enough when dealing with a man carrying a bag of dismemberment tools.

The woman could be crazy too. If Jacob rescued her, she might very well return the favor by following him home and attacking his family. He pressed the binoculars to his face, straining for a closer look. Clean and well groomed. No open wounds, do-it-yourself tattoos, or foul substances smeared on her body. She didn't look crazy. His gaze retraced its path over her body, slower this time. Neatly bobbed auburn hair that confidently straddled the line between sassy and serious. A slim, athletic build. Healthy skin, rosy pink from all the screaming. A long, graceful neck. Not bad-looking...not bad at all. More cute than sexy, but—

What the hell? The binoculars fell from his face. That woman was about to be killed, and he was eyeing her like he would the prettiest girl at a cocktail party. That must have been his Darkness acting up; it had to have been.

An unpleasant idea wormed into Jacob's mind: there wouldn't be a problem if a man were sitting in that basin, or a less attractive woman. He'd walk away, patting himself on the back for having avoided a dangerous situation. This woman was different; her beauty made her matter. Thinking about why that might be made his head spin. There wasn't time for self-reflection anyway. Bathrobe Guy had completed his preparations.

"Fuck it," Jacob said. Saving someone's life for dubious reasons had to be better than letting them die in the name of moral consistency. He broke cover and ran for the square.

Bathrobe Guy stood facing the fountain, so he didn't see Jacob striding down the path behind him. The woman saw though. Her terror shifted from screaming panic to mute shock. She stared, her eyes widening pools of dread. It must have been the horns.

Jacob raised his index finger to his lips in a *shh* gesture. The uncertainty he had felt seconds before melted away. Darkness coursed through him, charging every cell in his body. A mischievous grin crept across his face.

In true mad-genius fashion, Bathrobe Guy was busy explaining the intricacies of his plan to its intended victim. Overflowing with enthusiasm and oblivious to the world outside his own head, he had no idea someone was sneaking up on him. "Magnificent!" he bellowed. "When silver falls from heaven above, my work will greet the night. There's precious little time, but I'll be ready."

Jacob paused to mouth *Blah, blah, blah* for the petrified woman's benefit.

Bathrobe Guy gestured toward the statue on top of the fountain. "Behold! Our Lady of the Waters, high on her pedestal. And below, sunken in shadows, my most ambitious work to date! Fruit of the Earth, peeled and sliced, served in a bowl of her own juices!"

By the time the man had finished his monologue, Jacob was standing right behind him, close enough to whisper in his ear. He chose not to whisper.

"Boo!"

Bathrobe Guy nearly jumped out of his bathrobe. In a graceless maneuver, which nearly landed him on his ass, he hopped away from Jacob while simultaneously twirling to face him. Rage flared in the insane man's eyes, then shifted to horror as he noticed Jacob's horns. Bathrobe Guy stared in disbelief, his mouth comically agape.

Jacob reveled in the moment. He didn't know why crazies had a visceral fear of him. He didn't understand much of anything, but in that moment, he was profoundly happy with what he was. "What do have we here?" he asked in a slick voice that usually only came out at night.

The crazy didn't respond. Surprisingly, he didn't run away, although he clearly wanted to. Jacob gave him some time to reconsider any notion he might have about becoming a martyr to his art. Bathrobe Guy snatched a knife from his duffel bag and assumed a theatrical dueling pose. Knees knocking, sweat pouring down his hairy face, robe coming undone, he looked utterly ridiculous. "Not this day!" he yelled.

Jacob's smile grew. "Are you sure about this, big guy?"

With a shrill shriek, Bathrobe Guy charged. Jacob easily dodged him, sending the clumsy combatant stumbling away from the fountain. After pivoting, he charged again. Once again, his blade met empty space.

Jacob broke into a fit of laughter, a sinister sound that made the captive woman sink down into her basin. Why had he been worried about confronting this crazy? It was like playing tag with a toddler. After a couple more futile charges, Bathrobe Guy resorted to wildly swinging his knife at nothing in particular. Jacob grabbed him around the middle with invisible hands and hoisted him a dozen feet into the air. In a berserk rage, the crazy kicked and flailed his arms.

"You seem upset," Jacob said, now wearing a full smirk. "I think you need some alone time."

Pulling Bathrobe Guy behind him like a kite, he walked across the street and deposited him on the roof of a three-story building. "That should keep you busy for a while," Jacob said mostly to himself. He turned his attention back to the fountain and the woman, who would undoubtedly be grateful if someone set her free.

A piercing scream rang out from above. Jacob looked up to see Bathrobe Guy charge over the edge of the roof and plunge toward the sidewalk. As though it were happening in slow motion, he fell—legs churning, knife swinging, bathrobe fluttering around him like absurdly ineffectual wings. Then he twisted into a dive and hit the ground headfirst. Bathrobe Guy was no more.

For a moment, Jacob wondered if he had an obligation to feel bad, but decided he didn't. Choosing to feel good instead, he turned away from the grisly scene and headed back to the square. No one gave Bathrobe Guy another thought ever again.

"Hello?" Jacob called to the woman as he approached. "Don't be scared. I won't hurt you."

After a few seconds, a trembling voice rose from her basin. "Go away."

"But you're tied up. Don't you want me to help you?"

"No. You can only hurt."

Jacob stepped closer, holding out his hands in an attempt to appear harmless. "But you don't even know me. How about we talk for a bit? I'm sure we'll be friends in no time."

"Demons don't talk. They hurt. Their words hurt."

"Demon? I'm not a—"

"Whispers that burn your life away. Silent voices screaming in your head. They hurt...they hurt so much."

Crazy or traumatized? Jacob couldn't tell. Either way, he was enjoying the conversation in ways he knew he shouldn't. "I might look scary, but I'm no demon. I'm just—"

"Shut up! I won't let you in!" The woman pulled at the ropes binding her arms.

"Shh... Take it easy," Jacob said. "We don't have to talk. It would be a shame not to get better acquainted though. I think you'd find being my friend has certain advantages. For starters, I could make sure this sort of thing doesn't happen to you again." He stepped over the short wall around the fountain. "But if you'd rather go it alone, I'll just cut you free and be on my way."

The rope tied around the woman's neck wound through a pair of cinder blocks on the ground under the basin she sat in. If she stood up, their weight would tighten the noose around her neck in an inverted variation on being hanged. She could have freed herself if her arms weren't restrained, but as things were, she was stuck. Clever. Sick, but clever.

Carefully peeking into the basin, Jacob found her crouched down as low as she could get. The rope tied to her wrists pulled her arms up into a painful imitation of a bird in flight. Tears squeezed through her tightly shut eyelids. He picked up a serrated knife that had fallen near the cinder blocks and sawed at the strangling rope.

The instant it broke, the woman sprang backward onto a narrow ledge where the metal basins attached to the fountain's stone core. With her arms still tied to the rope that looped around the fountain, there was nowhere for her to go but around the square ledge where she precariously stood. It was at least a four-foot drop from the ledge to the ground. If she tried to jump, the rope would catch on the basins, and she'd be left suspended by her arms with a couple of dislocated shoulders for her trouble.

Crouching under the lion's head that had once filled her basin, she stared at Jacob. Her fear was so pure, so simple, that it brought a smile to his face. Then she bolted. In a blind panic, she ran around the ledge, deftly dodging the lion-head spouts above each basin.

Like tiny bubbles streaking through freshly poured champagne, a giddy malevolence rose in Jacob as he watched her futile bid to escape. "What a quick little bunny you are! But where are you going?"

He chased her around the fountain, sometimes dashing ahead to make her reverse direction. It was a game, predator and prey. After a minute or so, she finally missed a dodge and smacked her hip into a lion's head. Somehow managing not to fall, she crumpled into a whimpering ball on the ledge.

"All done?" Jacob asked. "Pity. I was rather enjoying that."

"Do it," the woman gasped. "Whatever you're going to do, just do it."

Jacob approached her. After taking a moment to savor her surrender, he leaned in close and whispered, "Were you playing a game, little bunny? Why else would you run around like an idiot on a leash?" He stroked her sweat-soaked hair, deeply inhaling the smell of her fear.

She cringed.

"Do you like games?" he continued. "There are other games we could play." His eyes lingered on the curve of her neck; a scrap of the strangling rope still hung there, a macabre necklace. The surrounding skin was raw and bleeding. What a shame—she had such lovely skin.

Abandoning her hair for the time being, he ran a fingertip lightly down her neck and across her shoulders. "Are you hurt? I know where we can find a doctor. We should have her examine you." His finger swirled around the ridges of her spine. The muscles there quivered under his touch. Exhilarating.

"Maybe I should have a look first though," he said. "You might require immediate attention." His hand slipped under the back of the woman's tank top, exploring her shoulder blade. Strong and lean. Perfect.

He'd help her down from that ledge and take her to one of the park benches. They'd both be more comfortable there. Then, after his new friend had calmed down—

With no warning, the woman's will to fight came roaring back. She whipped her head up and lunged at Jacob. The ropes didn't allow her to grab, so she bit. Snarling, eyes flashing, she tore into his neck.

He yelped like a kicked dog and stumbled backward, tripping over the short wall around the fountain. With a crack of horns on concrete, he landed hard on the other side. He scrambled to his feet and clamped a hand over the wound on his neck. Blood...there was a lot of blood.

Growling and spitting, the woman pulled at her bonds, straining to get at him again. She was like a rabid dog.

Something shifted in Jacob's mind. Nothing that had just happened made sense. Why had he said those things? He was supposed to have cut her free and gone home. Why wasn't he at home? He snatched a hatchet from the ground, sprinted around to the other side of the fountain, and chopped the rope binding the woman. Her arms flopped down to her sides. After growling at him one last time, she hopped down and ran away.

Jacob walked home more troubled than he had been since his recovery. That night his Darkness raged as it never had before.

Sixty-Six Days Post-Transformation

Jacob figured he wouldn't be much of an investigator if he didn't talk to a few crazies. They were, after all, the ones who had wrecked the world. Well, maybe they didn't do it all themselves. They probably didn't mess up the sun or make people grow horns, but they were definitely suspicious. The odds of a crazy having anything useful to say were negligible, but it didn't hurt to check. If nothing else, they were more entertaining than corpses.

Finding where crazies hid during the day turned out to be surprisingly easy. Anywhere dark, sheltered from the weekly rain, and hidden from other crazies was a good place to look. Basements and attics were popular choices.

By the time Jacob entered his second month as a post-apocalyptic explorer, he found one or two crazies most times he went out. After dutifully asking if they knew why the world had ended and if they had happened to run across any refugee centers during their adventures, he got to the real business at hand: having fun.

There was no reason to hurt them. He derived no pleasure from inflicting pain, and they weren't a threat to him. He did, however, occasionally get a little carried away. Once, he launched a man fifty feet into the air then caught him in a telekinetic bubble as he fell. It was so much fun, he did it again. Another time he conducted a strip search of a young woman he had accused of hiding information regarding the secret refugee center. That was way out of line. And who could forget the crazy who had pulled a gun on him? Jacob took the gun and stuffed the man under a car. That guy might have gotten a little hurt.

One incident proved a perfect illustration of the dangers Darkness-tainted thinking presented. Worried Micah might be lonely, Jacob thanked his lucky stars when he happened across a girl about her age in the grocery store. He swept the child up in a telekinetic bubble and set off for home. Fortunately, he came to his senses and let her go. Micah probably wouldn't want to play with a kid he had found singing "Happy Birthday to Me" as she cut a diamond ring from a bloated corpse's finger.

Over time, playing with crazies became a critical component of Jacob's Darkness appeasement program. He had to be careful though. Keeping his Darkness satisfied but not letting it get so worked up it overwhelmed him was a delicate balance. In the interest of preserving his humanity, he came up with a few ground rules to guide his interactions with crazies.

- No touching

- Walk away if they get violent

- Never take them home

- Everyone keeps their clothes on

  - In cases where a crazy wasn't wearing clothes to begin with, he or she was exempt

One final rule went unsaid, because Jacob didn't want to acknowledge it. His Darkness must be appeased. Every time. No exceptions. If that meant one or two of the other rules fell by the wayside now and then, that was the way it had to be.

Micah's Rules for a Better World

Find good things in the world. Even if it looks like everything is as bad as it can be, there's something good you can find.

Chapter 3

Prelude

Other people don't see the world in the same way you do. That's a problem when you're what's being looking at.

The Ghoul

Before the world ended, Jacob had loved spending his lunch breaks wandering through the patchwork of old and new that made up Cincinnati's core. Glass-and-steel skyscrapers huddling up to gilded art deco office buildings. Blocks of Italianate architecture colliding with stark masses of modernism. Crumbling relics of throwaway, mid-century culture popping up here and there like scars. Even the blight, surging and receding with the tides of prosperity, was interesting in its way.

The intersection of Eighth and Plum held a special fascination for him. A cluster of imposing structures on three of the four corners dominated the eastern edge of downtown. Equally grand in scale, the buildings' striking differences in design generated an uneasy tension as though they were rival gods squaring off against each other.

City hall occupied the northwest corner. Its dark, heavy stones and commanding profile projected indelible power. A sturdy clock tower rose from its body as a bulwark against disorder.

The Greek revival St. Peter in Chains Cathedral stood on the southwest corner. With its pure white facade, classic lines, and rows of Corinthian columns, it carried an air of nobility and grace. Its narrow, sharply pointed steeple pierced the sky to tap into heaven's glory.

Elegant and refined, the Isaac M. Wise synagogue held court on the southeast corner. Subtly Moorish, with intricate detailing and a magnificent rose window, it spoke of things beautiful and mysterious. Twin minaret-like towers crowned the temple, beacons of light in a dark world.

That left the northeast corner, where a drab auto shop sat like a wart. Notable only for its plainness, it should have been embarrassed to appear in such exalted company. But there it was, representing all things dull and utilitarian. It didn't have a tower.

When his daytime explorations brought him downtown, which didn't happen often as it was six miles from home, Jacob never failed to check on the old buildings at Eighth and Plum. Someday, after nature and neglect had taken their toll, they'd make spectacular ruins. It would be a shame if a crazy blew them up before then.

As he sat in front of city hall one day, he noticed the auto shop's garage door was halfway open. He crossed the street to investigate. Warm, stale air smelling of grease seeped out from under the wide opening. Stooping down to peek inside, Jacob could make out a dark figure barely visible in the gloom. Someone was squatting on the floor with their back to him, working on something on the ground. *Probably a crazy*, he thought. Still, there must be other people like Rebecca and Micah, people who hadn't lost their minds. He ought to check it out.

As Jacob ducked under the garage door, the entire world changed in a subtle yet fundamental way. It was like stepping through a portal into an alternate universe. A hushed stillness weighed on the garage's interior, giving it a feeling of timeless significance. Dust hung in the air, lazily drifting through the sparse light. Tools, spare parts, the usual clutter of a garage, except everything was imbued with gravity and mystery. This was a place apart, a sacred place.

An old man's voice rose from the center of the room. "Welcome."

Jacob froze. His Darkness surged, ready to defend him.

Without turning to face his visitor, the man on the floor asked, "What can I do for you, stranger?" His voice carried a slurred, moist quality, as though he were salivating over each word. He wore a bulky black sweatshirt. Tangled ropes of greasy gray hair dropped down his back. An unseen candle flickered in front of him, its warm light playing across a pool of dark liquid on the floor.

The thing the man had been working on was a human body. A pair of pale legs, all knobby knees and ankles, stretched off to his right. To his left, a toolbox with its lid open blocked the top half of the body from Jacob's view.

"Do you need something?" the man asked. "Or are you just stopping by to say hello?" Calm and patient, he didn't sound like a crazy.

Panic clawed at Jacob's insides. A powerful instinct demanded he run, but reason said no. He was supposed to be finding out what had happened to the world. What kind of investigator would he be if he didn't investigate this? After clearing his throat, he spoke. "I didn't mean to disturb you. I saw the door open and got curious."

"Curious? Tell me then, have you seen enough? Are you satisfied?"

"Far from it," Jacob replied, still talking to the man's back. "I assumed there was a crazy person in here. Unless I'm mistaken, I've found...uh, something else."

With a dry, brittle chuckle like rustling sticks, the man said, "Oh, stranger, you don't know the half of it."

Jacob struggled to find his next words. Something about this place made it difficult to frame his thoughts. The garage's tranquility moved around him like warm water, enveloping him, soaking in. The longer he stayed, the more comfortable he grew. He wanted to sit down and just *be* here.

No! What had gotten into him? Now more than ever, he needed to stay sharp. Learn what he could from the old man, then go home. That was the plan. But he found it so difficult to focus. This place...

A heavy silence settled over the garage, the kind that feels like it would be a sin to break. A quiet corner in a library, a cemetery on an autumn evening, snowy woods under a full moon. Jacob reflected on the mysteries of his new life, remembered how ordinary the world had once been, dreamed. Although he remained aware of his host, there was no need to talk. They were two ships drifting in calm waters. At some point, the old man's arms went into motion. He had returned to his work.

A sharp crack ripped through the garage, and the body's legs gave a limp flop. Startled from his daze, Jacob scrambled for words. "I'm…I'm looking for—"

"Tell me, stranger, did you come to ruin my meal?" the old man asked. "Or maybe you want to steal it?"

Jacob's stomach convulsed, forcing a gush of hot acid up to the back of his throat. *Meal?* "I… Uh, no. Like I said, I didn't mean to disturb you."

"Glad to hear it."

A wet pop and the body on the floor shuddered. What seemed like days passed as the old man slurped, sucked, and chewed. Ghoul. That was the only word for this thing, a ghoul.

Even as Jacob conjured nightmare images of fairy-tale monsters made real, he had an almost irresistible urge to sit down and allow himself to become lost in thought again. Barely noticeable currents of energy flowed through the garage, an insidious influence that lulled him into a false sense of ease.

No, it wasn't the garage; it was the Ghoul himself. He emanated an aura of well-being, a relaxed feeling of contentment. Despite his ghastly appearance and the fact that he was happily consuming a corpse, being near him felt like curling up in a soft bed with a good book. A realization broke through the opiate fog clouding Jacob's mind: The Ghoul was using Darkness. It couldn't be perceived in any normal way, but he sensed it—warm and expansive, nothing like the thick fluidity of his own power, but Darkness nonetheless.

He pumped the imaginary muscle that controlled his telekinesis. A surge of familiar energy cleared his mind and sharpened his focus like a stimulant to counteract the Ghoul's calming effect. As long as he kept this up, he'd probably be okay. Probably.

Still with his back to Jacob, the Ghoul asked, "What brings a guy like you out in the bright light of day, hmm? Must be important."

Jacob didn't know what to say.

The Ghoul bent low and slurped at what must have been the body's belly, then sat back up with a contented sigh. The light from the candle in front of him danced, then settled again. Speaking in a friendly way, he said, "If you're here to chat, you might as well make yourself comfortable. There's a stool under the window. Pull it over. I wouldn't mind a little company."

Without consciously deciding to, Jacob found himself doing as the Ghoul had suggested. Only after getting to the stool did he wonder if it might not be a better idea to run for the door. Darkness was dangerous; being around another person infected with it couldn't be safe. On the other hand, this man might have insights into how Darkness worked, where it came from, how to control it. Jacob couldn't pass up the opportunity to compare notes with another of whatever he was. He grabbed the stool and wheeled it around the pool of blood. For the first time, he faced his host and the body before him. There was a lot to process.

From the front, the Ghoul was ugly beyond description. An enormous mouth protruded from his bony face, giving him a canine appearance. Loose, thin lips weren't enough to cover his pointed teeth. Black beady eyes peered at Jacob through a curtain of tangled hair wet with gore.

A dead girl not much older than Micah—eleven, maybe—lay on the ground between the two men. Her clothes had been removed, carefully folded, and piled on a nearby shelf next to a car battery. A long, jagged cut stretched from just below her breastbone to her sex, splitting her open. Blood slicked her midsection, dripping down to feed the ever-expanding pool around her. A neat braid of black hair rested on her chest to keep it out of the mess. Despite the violence her body had suffered, the girl appeared to be at rest. Her face was set in an expression of sorrowful resignation, like a marble angel watching over a grave. Her glassy green eyes contemplated the monster hovering over her without casting judgement.

Jacob placed his stool on the other side of the corpse from the Ghoul, next to an overturned bucket where the candle sat.

"Ah, that's better," the Ghoul said. "You can't get to know someone properly unless you can look them in the eye."

He extended two skeletal fingers capped with thick, talon-like nails toward the dead girl. With a deft plucking motion, he extracted a nugget of flesh from the gouge in her abdomen. Struggling not to lose the slippery thing, he placed it on a hideously long blue-black tongue. It disappeared into the creature's maw.

Jacob sat in silent horror as the Ghoul chewed.

"What's the matter, stranger?" he asked as he reached for another bite. "You look a little green around the gills. Squeamish?"

Speechless, Jacob stared.

The Ghoul's dark eyes narrowed. "I hope there isn't a fight brewing in that horned head of yours. This might not be your cup of tea, but it's nothing to get all bent out of shape over."

"No, nothing like that," Jacob said, finally overcoming his shock. "I don't want any trouble."

"Good. Too many of us like trouble. Can't help themselves, I suppose; it's their nature."

"Nature?" Jacob asked, his interest piqued by the weight the other man had added to the word.

The Ghoul plucked stringy bits of meat from his dagger-like teeth, then licked his claws clean. "Nature," he repeated. "What makes you *you*."

Jacob's face went blank. He could think of something to say in almost any situation, but words repeatedly failed him here. What was the old man going on about?

"Don't get out much, do you, friend?" the Ghoul asked. "Take a walk around these streets after dark, and it'll be as plain as the nose on my face. People like us are driven by our nature. For some, that means killing; for others, it might mean screwing or collecting fancy jewelry, any damned thing. It's the thing you've got to do. More than horns or teeth, we are our nature."

Not sure how to handle himself around a dog-faced cannibal with supernatural abilities, Jacob fell into cross-examination mode. "You're justifying *this* by claiming to be compelled by nature?"

The Ghoul waved a hand to dismiss the question. "Justify to who? No offense, but I don't give a rat's ass what you think of my dining habits."

Lulls in the conversation didn't seem to bother his host, so Jacob allowed himself a minute to mull things over. Could that be what Darkness was? Desire, an irresistible impulse? Thinking of it that way explained a few things.

The Ghoul took another scoop from the girl's belly. "So, what are you into?" he asked. "For your sake, I hope it's something more interesting than pestering people while they're trying to eat." He cackled at himself, allowing his long tongue to slip out of his mouth.

Distracted, Jacob kept returning his gaze to the dead girl's face. Although pale from loss of blood, her skin showed no signs of decomposition. Her hair hadn't yet lost its luster. She must have died that day, the night before at the earliest. How had she been living this whole time? Months had passed since the world ended. While Jacob was hiding in his basement, dicking around with crazies, and drowning his Darkness in alcohol, this girl had somehow been surviving among all the death and chaos. She made it this far only to end up gutted on the floor of a run-down auto shop, a monster feeding on her body.

The Ghoul pressed an especially sharp claw to the unbroken skin of the girl's chest. Blood blossomed along a line just underneath where a breast had only recently started to develop. He plucked out a bit of flesh and brought it to his mouth. Eyes closed, he savored the tender morsel. "She'll be ready soon."

He pulled another lump from the girl's gut and held it out to his guest. "Want to taste?"

Jacob's stomach turned. Unable to speak, he violently shook his head.

"Suit yourself." The Ghoul flicked the meat into his mouth, swallowed it whole, and licked his lips. The dark beads of his eyes glittering in the candlelight, he regarded Jacob with the amiable curiosity of a chatty bartender on a slow night. "I bet you see this as a waste."

"What do you mean?"

The Ghoul looked at him in an uncomfortably conspiratorial way, as if he meant to tell a dirty joke and trusted Jacob not to take offense. "Oh, I don't know," he said, his voice a notch lower. "Maybe you're the kind of guy who would have preferred this little one's company when she was warm and fresh, with all her pretty parts intact. There are all sorts of things a person could have done with her then, hmm?"

A dark scowl emerged from the stony expression Jacob had been trying to maintain. Pressure built where his powers lived.

"Whoa... Relax, friend." The Ghoul raised his arms in mock alarm. "To each his own, right? I don't judge."

Jacob let the topic drop, despite feeling he had been made complicit in something vile. Wanting to quickly change the subject, he asked, "How did she end up here? Did you kill her?"

"Killing's not my thing." The Ghoul's lips pulled back into a horrifyingly toothy grin. "I am but a humble scavenger. After the rest of the world has had its fun, I clean up what's left."

"So, you found her like this," Jacob said.

"Not dead, no. I met her in the library's basement, where the old newspapers are. She was all alone, the poor thing." A wistful expression passed over the Ghoul's grotesque face. He ran one of the clawed horrors he had for hands over the girl's cheek and gazed into her lifeless eyes. "At first, she just curled up in her hidey-hole, shaking like a leaf." He brushed a stray strand of hair from her face, losing his train of thought for a few seconds. "But after a while, we got to be buddies."

Jacob didn't know if he could believe a word this man said. The idea of a thing like him taking care of a child was unimaginable. "That doesn't explain how she ended up here," he said.

"How do you think? She died."

"Yes, but how?"

"Quietly," the Ghoul said and sighed. "She didn't want to live anymore, so she ate some pills."

"She killed herself?"

"That's right. She asked me to stay with her until the end if it wouldn't be too scary for me. Imagine that, a little thing like her worried I might get scared."

Part of Jacob wanted to thank his host for a lovely afternoon and get the hell out of there. Another part of him needed to know more. What was this thing with the voice of a man? Could Jacob really be the same kind of thing?

"But this..." he began.

"It's what she wanted. I'd have burned her or whatever she asked, but she wanted this. Even after she took the pills, she made me promise not to wander off so she'd be the freshest thing I ever ate. Just between you and me, friend, I like to let my meals mellow a bit, but I didn't tell her that. It's the thought that counts, right?"

Sounding more defeated than upset, Jacob said, "You manipulated her. You drove her to suicide so this could happen."

The Ghoul's eyes flashed with anger. "What do you know? You weren't there when she woke up screaming for her mom. You didn't see how she scurried away from the smallest sound. She didn't deserve to suffer like that; it wasn't right."

Taken aback by the sudden display of emotion, Jacob failed to respond.

The Ghoul placed his hand on the girl's shoulder. "She'd had enough. This is what she wanted."

"I don't believe you," Jacob said, regaining his taste for argument. "Even if I did, I'd still hold you responsible. You didn't stop her."

The Ghoul laughed to himself. "Responsible? Who says things like that these days? The little one was a leftover from the dead world. What else was she supposed to do?"

"Live," Jacob snapped.

"Oh? Let her suffer for suffering's sake until someone with a taste for living girls had their way with her then dumped her in the street like garbage? That would have been better?"

"It didn't have to be that way. She might have found somewhere safe, somewhere to learn how to be happy again. But now..." Jacob turned to the girl's butchered body and lifted her hand from the pool of blood. It was cold and stiff. "Now she's gone. There's no hope."

The Ghoul frowned. When he next spoke, a hint of uncertainty darkened his aged voice. "The world is what it is. Pain, fear, and a messy ending—that's all there is for her kind."

"You genuinely believe she's better off dead?"

"Doesn't matter what I think. It was her life, not mine. She wanted to go out quietly, feeling good about it. How many of those people scurrying around out there like rats on a sinking ship would do the same if they thought it over?"

"But she was a child!" Jacob shouted. "You should have—"

"What? Kept her? Don't let my innocent face and friendly ways fool you. Babysitting isn't in my nature."

"No, you're more into eating kids than protecting them," Jacob said, incensed.

"Ahh...now we're getting somewhere. Yes, hunger is what I am. *That's* my nature. Oh, I watched over the little one, kept her safe and sound. And I was nice to her, a perfect gentleman. Just like I'm being right now." The Ghoul flashed a gory grin to demonstrate how nice he was. "But after dark...well, things change after dark. You know a little something about that, don't you, friend? My hunger grew and grew until I wasn't anything but hunger. I wasn't so nice then. The little one's smells, the thumping of her heart, the air whistling in and out of her lungs—she made me sick."

The Ghoul's black eyes shimmered. He paused to stroke the girl's hair. "She saw all that. She was always watching, my clever little one. Always watching. And she understood. There's no place in this world for sweet, gentle things like her, not anymore."

"So make one!" Jacob yelled. "The world isn't some monolithic lump of misery. It's a place where things happen. It can change."

The Ghoul regarded him with an expression both amused and pitying. "You're an odd one, all right. Why would someone like you want to change the world? You belong here." He paused to dip a claw into the blood spilling across the girl's chest from the incision he had made earlier. "I did what I could for her, which is more than she'd have gotten from most of our kind."

Our kind. The words cut like a razor. Creatures of Darkness, monsters. Was there truly no place left in the world for that poor girl? Or for Micah and Rebecca?

The Ghoul's voice startled Jacob from his thoughts. "Maybe you wish you'd found the little one first, hmm?" His laid-back good humor had returned. "What would have become of her then, I wonder. Don't be shy, friend. Tell me about *your* nature."

A wave of anger rose in Jacob but failed to crest. His emotions dissipated in the garage's heavy stillness. "You don't know anything about me. I would have..."

He faltered. Had this girl been a crazy? Did it matter? He had met crazy children and left them alone, which almost certainly doomed them to a death worse than this girl's. But what else was he supposed to do? He couldn't bring them home. Did the universe expect him to run some kind of orphanage for deranged, often violent children? A queasy feeling rose in his gut as he realized his power would allow him to do precisely that if he cared enough to make the effort.

Flustered, he let a string of words sputter from his lips. "Well, at least I wouldn't have carved her up and ate her!"

"I don't imagine you would have," the Ghoul said and laughed, a sound like stirring broken glass. "But what's done is done. She's dead. Might as well make the most of what she left behind." With that, he stuck his entire hand into the girl's stomach and pulled out a sloppy mess of entrails.

Jacob turned his head. He didn't want to see what happened next. Unsure how much more of this he could take, he decided to redirect the conversation to topics he had intended to ask about from the beginning. "Do you know how all of this happened? Why is the world like this?"

Talking with his mouth full, the Ghoul replied, "The how and why of it don't much matter. We're here now."

"Humor me," Jacob said. "What happened?"

The Ghoul shrugged, his gaunt frame barely visible under the bulk of his black hoodie. "I woke up hungry, ate my fill for a while, then met this little one. That just about sums it up."

"You don't remember anything from before?"

"Bits and pieces. I used to stand in front of a room full of little ones and tell them about math. They were about the same age as this one here. Maybe that's why I took a liking to her."

"Anything else?"

"Nothing that will satisfy the hunger you're working up. Take my advice: let the dead world lie in peace. This is your world now. Live in it."

"But how—"

The Ghoul cut him off. "Listen, friend. It'll be dark soon, and my meal's almost ready. It's been nice chatting with you while I have a snack or two, but when it comes time to dig in, I'd like some privacy. No offense. But before you go, I've got a story that might help you. Want to hear it?"

With a frustrated sigh, Jacob nodded and leaned back on his stool.

"Good. This came to me while I was flipping through the old newspapers at the library. It's a fable.

"Once there was an artist who made wooden statues; figurines, he called them, since they were small. He made all kinds: animals, people, buildings, weird shapes that didn't look like anything at all. He was good at it too, really good. And the only tools he needed were his trusty carving knife and a file.

"This artist, he loved what he did and he didn't want to do anything else. Every day was the same: he picked up his tools in the morning and didn't put them down until dinnertime. He was happy.

"One morning the artist woke up with a different hand than he had gone to bed with. Instead of fingers and a palm, his right hand had changed into a knife and a file. A perfect carving tool! He didn't even notice—that's how excited he was to get to work. All morning and through the day he carved and carved. Never in his life had he made such fine figurines.

"When dinnertime came around, he went to put his tools away but realized he didn't have any tools. For the first time, he saw what had happened to his hand. Scared half to death, he ran off to the hospital.

"His doctor didn't know what to do, so other fancier doctors came from out of town. None of them had ever seen anything like that before. They argued about the cause of it all, but they agreed on one thing: metal tools didn't belong where hands were supposed to be. So, they cut the poor guy's arm off.

"He never carved again. The end."

Looking satisfied with himself, the Ghoul asked, "What do you think?"

"Interesting."

"That's it? Hmph. And I used my storyteller voice and everything. Did you at least get the moral?"

Jacob thought for a moment, then answered somewhat flippantly. "Don't trust strangers who like to cut people up?"

The Ghoul let loose with a dry cackle. "I guess it's like any other story; it means what you want it to mean. Or nothing at all. I'll tell you one thing though: that artist would have been happier if he had never remembered a time when he *didn't* have tools for a hand."

Leaning low over the dead girl, he extended his long tongue and licked the thickening blood that oozed from her chest.

The air changed. Or had it been changing for a while? Warm and heavy, it beckoned Jacob into its embrace. The candlelight grew softer and blurred. So hard to think...this place. Waves of drowsiness lapped at his senses. More questions...tools for hands...glassy green eyes...such a waste...

The Ghoul's voice came to him as if from a great distance. "One more thing, friend, before I let you go. A warning: we're at the center of the world. Things scarier than me come out at night. It's not safe to talk to strangers."

Jacob tumbled off his stool and fell into the girl's blood. The last thing he saw was the Ghoul's hideous grin.

Learning the Ropes

Jacob awoke on the steps of city hall, groggy and disoriented. The sky was a dingy gray with only a trace of light. A single thought rang through his head like the tolling of a bell: *Go home.*

Muscles stiff from having slept on stone stairs, he made his way through downtown. A belligerent crazy yelled incoherently from the fifth floor of an office building then hurled a bottle at him. Another shuffled across the street a block in front of him. *Coming out early tonight*, he thought. Considering sending a telekinetic wave to bust a few windows around the jerk who had tossed the bottle, Jacob looked up. His attention moved past the office building to the sky. Yellow? It was supposed to be getting darker, not brighter. It took a few more seconds for the puzzle pieces to fall into place. Dawn! He had been unconscious all night.

A panic-induced explosion of adrenaline propelled his aching body into a full sprint. Thirty-two minutes and six miles later, he burst into his house. "Rebecca!" he yelled.

Silence.

His insides a knot of dread, he raced to the basement door and shoved it open. The deadbolt on the other side tore away from the doorjamb with a snap. Taking the stairs two at a time, he raced into the shadowy space below. And there they were, huddled together in their nest under the stairs, afraid but unharmed. He fell to his knees before them—an act of contrition, a prayer of thanks, and sheer exhaustion wound into a single gesture.

Two days later, Jacob convinced Rebecca to let him go out again for a few hours. Arguing with her about it was more a courtesy than anything else. She couldn't have stopped him.

He returned to the auto shop. It was a supremely reckless thing to do, but he had to know if the Ghoul was still there, if he'd always be there. Ducking under the still halfway open door, Jacob stepped into a completely ordinary garage. No air of hypnotic serenity. No Ghoul. An empty feeling, some variation on loneliness that only monsters know, fell over him.

Dried blood covered much of the floor, but there was no sign of the dead girl at first glance. Then Jacob saw her. On the shelf, next to her clothes, reduced to a neat pile of bones. Her skull sat on top, as if in a place of honor. Its crown was crushed, revealing a cavity as dry and clean as the rest of her remains.

There was nothing more to see. He went home.

Life had been so much easier when Jacob imagined himself the only freak with superpowers in the world. Like a cozy blanket snatched away on a cold night, that delusion had vanished. He wasn't even the only one in town.

The next scheduled exploration day found him sitting on the living room couch, pretending he had never heard of exploration days. After his encounter with the Ghoul, he was lucky to be alive. What would have happened if he had died? How long would Rebecca and Micah have lasted?

Although Jacob didn't want to go out anymore, his Darkness had other ideas. By the time seven days had passed moping around the house, it *needed* to go out. If he didn't give it a release, it would drive him crazy. So, one day he packed some weapons and a "lunch" that consisted solely of whiskey into a backpack and walked out the front door.

It felt like starting over, only this time he knew the world held secrets more frightening than he had imagined. For the first few excursions, he only went a few blocks from home, but before long, he worked up the courage to walk to Hyde Park Square. (Some crazy had put a hat on the statue on top of the fountain. It suited her, so Jacob left it there.) Bit by bit, his confidence returned.

He had thought he could handle the Ghoul and been put in his place. No point in denying it; he had been bested. If he ever saw the old man again, he'd have to thank him for the lesson about overconfidence and for leaving him alive to learn it. But the end hadn't come for Jacob Freeman yet. Until it did, he owed it to himself not to give up. He pictured himself as a gladiator in ancient Rome. There was more to surviving the games than brawn. The ones who got lucky enough for long enough learned the tricks and became the most successful of all. Jacob had always been lucky.

The Lady of the Waters

What if Cincinnati had been uniquely unprepared for the end of the world? Other places could have reacted quicker or had better emergency-response infrastructure. There might be fully functional cities, or even entire states out there. It didn't seem likely, but maybe.

Cincinnati sat at the intersection of three states, so it wouldn't be difficult for Jacob to take a quick peek over a couple borders. He could even take a day trip to Louisville, Indianapolis, or one of the other larger cities in the region if he found a motorcycle to navigate the dead traffic clogging all the roads. Opting to start with the low-hanging fruit, he made plans to visit northern Kentucky. It was a short walk across the Ohio River from downtown, not much farther than he went on his regular excursions.

Rebecca loved the idea. One of the largest army bases in the country was in Kentucky. For all they knew, the military had secured the borders and turned the entire state into a giant refugee center. Although Jacob doubted that was the case, he chose not to burst her bubble.

A light, jaunty feeling drove him on as he set off for the river. He had embarked on a voyage of discovery, a post-apocalyptic Lewis and Clark charting civilization's ruins. An hour and a half later, he stood at the mouth of the Roebling Suspension Bridge. There were other bridges he could have crossed, but they lacked a sense of adventure. This one's stone arches topped with golden ornaments promised great things. A slight breeze played with his hair. Comfortable and confident, he finally understood what the Ghoul had meant when he said this new world belonged to people like them.

Halfway across the river, everything changed, radically shifting as though he had stepped over some invisible line that marked the edge of reality. Time stopped, suspended between one moment and the next. There was no sound, no motion. Jacob's heart froze midbeat, clenched tight. He couldn't move or use his powers.

It might have lasted hours or days or only an instant. Without change, time didn't exist. Panic eventually ran its course, leaving Jacob wondering if the world he knew had been a dream, the lifeless images of buildings and bridges around him nothing but its fading echoes. Soon those would be gone too. He'd be alone, a universe of himself.

Somewhere far below, water sloshed. Another of the dream's dying whispers, perhaps. Then the river moved. Past the edge of the bridge, at the exact point where his eyes were fixed, a circle of water bubbled and rippled. Everything else remained in stasis.

A woman's figure rose from below the river's murky surface. Beyond a distinct sense of femininity, she was indescribable. Nothing covered her, but she couldn't be seen. She was a shadowy blur, an abstract watercolor done in lunar white and swirling black.

The sky darkened.

Finally, the last muddy drops of water dripped from the woman's feet as she hovered a few inches above the river. She looked up at Jacob. Her eyes were dark and infinite. His head spun. Surely he'd lose himself forever in those eyes.

Rising higher, she glided toward the bridge. Jacob wanted to run, hide, die, anything to get away. She was too much. Such intensity. Such power. Floating in the air on the other side of the bridge's railings, close enough for her to reach out and touch him. She was everything, all that is and ever could be.

Too much...

The woman made a small gesture, and she inexplicably changed. Jacob could now be near her without feeling on the verge of losing his mind.

She had withdrawn part of herself, tucked it away where it wouldn't hurt anyone. She was still overwhelming, but her presence no longer warped perception and made a joke of sanity. Human features emerged from the field of dark distortion around her. An impossible amount of black hair cloaked her body as though part of the river had clung to her. Milky skin, softly glowing. A half-smile, as wicked as it was beautiful. Eyes like voids, black beyond black.

Looking into him, through him, she spoke. Her voice was a strange kind of music. It conjured feelings or symbols in Jacob's mind, occasionally coalescing into something like words.

"♥∞♡? stubborn child. □✦ Ω □ ❣"

Her voice filled him. He couldn't do anything but listen.

"Strayed so far. *(pain and laughter)* ☙ ♄ Can I see? ✪ ⊛ ∞□...★ □★...✧□✦✧□."

She reached a slender arm toward him. *No!* his mind screamed. *Don't! I'll split. I'll explode. I'll—*

Her icy hand settled lightly on his left cheek. Something vital in him rushed to her touch. She was a magnet, his soul a pile of iron shavings. Toying with his Darkness, she sampled its flavor, adding a little power and taking a bit for herself. Jacob felt like an overripe grape held between her two fingers. Any second, with no effort at all, she could end him.

Her smile took a fiendish turn as she leaned over the railing that separated them. Jacob saw nothing but her face—such terrifying beauty. Then she came closer still, close enough for him to feel the chill of her body.

Stop, please stop.

Soft lips brushed his, lingering for a moment. And that moment was all time. A black ocean rose around the two of them. Images, memories, and emotions flashed like lightning. Jacob saw his own cruelty, every heartless thing he had done, every time he had existed for self and self alone.

He's in his dorm room at the university. A young woman sits beside him, sobbing into her hands. She blubbers on and on about some drama with her boyfriend, ex-boyfriend now by the sound of it. Jacob has had a few drinks and is having a hard time keeping all the tedious details straight, which is fine. It only needs to appear as though he cares. Her eyes red from crying, she looks to him for comfort. She trusts him. Good. He can work with that.

Soothing words. Hollow compassion. With feigned tenderness, he puts his arm around her.

A party. He has just graduated law school. People are swarming around him, offering congratulations, best wishes, phone numbers, job tips. In a corner, his cousin Steve sits alone, drunk, high, and miserable. Fucking loser. *Jacob swells with pride. Two years later he'll have the same thought when he learns Steve has blown his brains out with a shotgun:* Fucking loser.

He's a child standing on third base, watching a boy bleed. A pitch hit Danny right in the face and his nose burst like a blood balloon. Danny the popular. Danny with the perfect smile. Danny who Joy said she likes. Look at him now, bawling like a baby. Jacob hopes Joy is watching this. He wants that with all his heart.

Nicole lies under him, flushed from wine and pleasure. With a subtle shift of his weight, he eases into her flawless body.

At home, which is an entirely different world, Rebecca and Micah would be getting ready for bed. They aren't expecting him anytime soon. In that universe, he's having dinner and drinks with an important client.

Although he did have dinner and drinks with Nicole, she isn't a client. She's a free-spirited paralegal with a taste for things she can't afford. Having a benefactor—someone handsome and charming who has the resources to treat her how she deserves to be treated—makes her feel like a fairy-tale princess. She feels that way now, enjoying being enjoyed, relishing the passion she enkindles. Fairy tales might not include this part, but it's implied.

Jacob is happy too, though for reasons far simpler and more immediate.

The visions went on and on, growing worse, showing Jacob things he had wanted to forget. So many people he had hurt, so much suffering orbiting his life.

His family, everyone he knew, Darkness was in them too. It always had been. The way his sister used to dig her nails into the back of his neck, clawing him until blood or allowance money flowed. How Grandpa used to touch her, whisper in her ear, while Grandma sat watching game shows, indifferent.

Spiraling out of his own existence, Jacob saw Darkness stretch through time and across the earth, pulsing through history like blood through a body.

The killer is removing a head, working slowly and meticulously. It'll look marvelous when he's done, much better than the last one. Look at how clean the cuts are! He likes to keep mementos like this. After all the violence and heated emotions, it's nice to step into the walk-in freezer and reflect on how far he has come.

It's a time of war. Far from home, soldiers rake through a decimated village. They're supposed to be verifying the area is secure. Instead, they're looking for souvenirs, alcohol, anything they want.

Piles of rubble smolder where houses once stood. Nothing is left standing.

"Shithole town. These dirt farmers ain't got nothin' worth taking," one says.

Warily, another soldier uses the end of his rifle to lift the door to a root cellar. Peeking inside, he sees a woman holding a baby, her face a tear-streaked mask of dust. He lights up like a Christmas tree. "Looky here, boys," he calls, then flings the door open with a bang.

The baby cries.

Rough hands drag the woman from her hiding place. She struggles, screaming in a language the men don't understand. "Bitte! Bitte nicht!"

A soldier rips the baby from her arms and tosses it onto a pile of crumbled stone. His friends wrestle the woman to the ground.

They take what they want.

The landowner's wife has broken another rod. Curse that boy's thick hide! And with it so hot today, she's positively dripping sweat. She shouldn't have exerted herself so.

Joseph will surely scold her for going into the fields again. When he does, she'll tell him he has only himself to blame. If he had hired a proper overseer in place of that loafer Mr. Hodges recommended, she wouldn't need to handle things herself.

"Maude? Maude, dear, I believe I'll retire to my sitting room. Bring me tea at half past four."

She beats them because she can. She beats them because it thrills her. There are other things she'll do, but those are yet to come.

The fat old king, wine sloshing in his gut, lies naked on perfumed pillows. All around, scattered across the marble, draped over the gold, are broken children he calls nymphs.

The Lady of the Waters' beautiful smile wove through everything like a diseased soul. Jacob collapsed. As he fell from her touch, the visions dissipated, leaving nothing but the deepest black. Blinded, his mind boiling, he writhed, beating his head on the ground. "Out! Get out!"

The music of her voice came to him from a distance. "♫ ♪ ♄ ♫ *(amusement and curiosity)* ∞♥ ♫"

The Disciple

He lay on the bridge, the sunless sky pressing down on him. Hot. How had it gotten so hot? He had no name, no memory—a mindless speck of life withering in the merciless heat. Time moved in a dizzying blur from nowhere to nowhere. It sped up then slowed down, occasionally disappearing into pits of oblivion.

Yet he was alive. The idea emerged from a haze of heat and light like a shimmering mirage: Alive. He had life and he wanted to keep it. Weak fingers scratched the concrete under his body. Solid, real. He pulled himself into a fetal position then stretched out again. Moving hurt. The pain was real too; it helped him focus. There was a sky above and water below. Somewhere between, he lay on a bridge. A trickle of memories returned.

Home. He needed to go home.

Focused on the pavement in front of him, Jacob forced himself forward on hands and knees, each inch a battle. Eons later, he finally lifted his eyes to check his progress and came to a dead stop, stunned.

Dozens of people had gathered at the end of the bridge, blocking his path. They were armed with assault rifles and dressed in black combat fatigues complete with tactical helmets, like a Special Forces unit preparing for a midnight raid. It didn't make sense. Crazies never gathered like that.

The crowd split, and a man in a black shirt—buttoned all the way to his throat—and dark jeans stepped forward. A white porcelain mask hid his face, its expression severe with a mouth set in a grim half-frown under censorious eyes. In his left hand, he held what looked like a metal baton with a sharp end. Some kind of spike? Even from a distance, it was clear he wasn't human. Darkness pulsed around him; Jacob could *see* it.

As the man got closer, Jacob realized he didn't have a spike in his hand; the spike *was* his hand. About a foot long and the dull gray of lead, it surfaced from a puckered ring of skin at the cuff of his shirt. The thing didn't reflect light in a normal way; it drained the space around it of color and vitality.

The masked man spoke—no, there was no sound. His voice formed inside Jacob's head, as pure and soulless as the pealing of a bell. *Imposter. Fraud. Filth.* Each syllable was a dagger of hatred, delivered in a flat, steely tone. *She appeared for* him? *A mongrel cheat?*

An angry murmur rose from the crowd. The man must have been in their heads too. They all surged forward, bearing down on Jacob. He tried to summon a telekinetic wall to hold them back but didn't have the strength. Dust stirred around their feet, nothing more.

The masked man's voice sounded where only Jacob's thoughts had a right to be: *A blight upon her lands. Unworthy.*

Growing more agitated by the second, the crowd continued to advance. Again, Jacob tried to call his powers. His head whirled and he worried he might pass out. Whatever that woman in the river had done had left him completely drained. The man stood over him now, his mask glaring like a pitiless sun. His Darkness, as unyielding as a wall of steel, crushed Jacob.

Once again, he spoke. *I have awaited Mother's blessing, watching over this place each night. Why would she rise for an insect creeping about in the light? Why?* He lashed out with a heavy boot, delivering a vicious kick to Jacob's stomach. *There must be a reason.*

Writhing in pain, Jacob made a futile effort to crawl away, but the man swooped down on him in a black blur. A gloved hand grabbed the back of Jacob's neck and drove his face into the concrete. Something sharp poked into his back. The spike. It was impossibly cold, as if it had been dipped in liquid nitrogen.

Jacob braced himself. There was no escape.

A test, the masked man intoned. *It's a test of faith. I have traveled far and given much, but the Mother of All demands more.* He paused as if weighing his options. *It's fitting that the gifts wasted on this usurper be returned to Mother at night when she is most ready to receive them. Let him scurry off to his hole. I'll meet him where he is strong to prove my worth beyond question.*

The masked man turned his back to Jacob and walked away.

Home

Pushing his battered body to its limits, Jacob stumbled down a bike path that led from the riverfront parks to his neighborhood. Nowhere was safe. He needed to warn Micah and Rebecca. Every scrap of energy he could muster fueled motion. Faster, he needed to move faster.

An hour later, he collapsed into the entryway of his house. The sky had darkened to charcoal gray. "Help," he gasped.

Rebecca ran into the room, chef's knife in hand. "Jacob! What happened?"

"We have to leave," he said, trying to get to his feet. His eyes darted wildly. "Get Micah. Where's my car?"

"Calm down," Rebecca said. "You're hurt. Let me see if there's anything I can do."

She turned to close the front door and paused, staring at something outside. Her mouth opened as if to speak but she thought better of it. With a resolute grunt, she dismissed whatever had distracted her and got to work. After locking the door, she helped Jacob to his feet. Supporting much of his weight, she guided him to the kitchen where she eased him into a seated position against the dishwasher. Once he was stable, she busied herself collecting towels and bottles of water to clean his injuries.

The basement door opened a crack, and Micah peeked out. When she saw her father like that—pale and shivering, his face bruised, blood on his clothes—she screamed and ran to him.

Rebecca held out an arm to block her. "Not too close," she warned. "You know what happens if you touch."

"Is he okay?" Micah asked.

"I don't know. He's exhausted. I think he ran here from somewhere far away."

Tugging at her clothes, Micah shifted anxiously from foot to foot. "What do we do, Mom? Can you make him better?"

"I'll try. His body isn't the kind I know how to fix, but I'll try. Can you do something for me?"

"Y-yeah."

"Talk to him while I clean his face. See if he wants anything. He might know what'll help."

"Okay."

The Freemans' kitchen became a surreal emergency room. Wheezing one syllable at a time, Jacob asked his daughter to bring him whiskey, a pillow to hold to his chest, a beer, a pencil and paper (which he used to draw a mess of black swirls and a feminine smile), more whiskey, and so on. All the while, Rebecca examined his body, pelting him with questions he didn't answer. There was only one thing he asked her to do: wash his lips. He wanted her to do that over and over.

The moon rose, huge and heavy, and the light in the kitchen shifted from muted gray to cold silver. As night set in, Jacob's condition improved. The bruises vanished from his face, his strength returned, and the feverish whirlwind in his head became something closer to rational thought.

The family moved into the basement, where he paced anxiously while lifting random objects with his mind. He still wouldn't tell Rebecca what had happened, but insisted they needed to pack up and find another place to live.

"I don't understand," she said for the third time.

"It's simple. We're leaving town. Tonight."

"But it's dark out," Micah protested, her eyelids drooping.

"I know, M," Jacob said. "I'll keep you safe. The bad guys always run from me."

"But, Dad—"

He held up a hand to cut her off. "There's no time to argue. Go find your backpack and pack up some books and toys."

"Hold on," Rebecca said. "We can't just leave. Where will we go?"

"I don't know. Somewhere far from here."

"Does this have anything to do with those people who were outside?"

Jacob stopped pacing. The pile of clothes he had been levitating dropped to the floor. "What people?"

"Two men were standing across the street when you came in. I meant to tell you earlier, but with everything—"

"That was hours ago!"

"I know! I'm sorry, okay? I was kind of busy."

Sick with dread, Jacob crossed the basement and peered into the darkened stairway that led to the kitchen above. The door at the top was closed. Motioning for the others to stay put, he crept up the stairs. Each groan of the old wood beneath his feet made his heart leap and sent a sick jolt through his stomach. At the top, he took a deep breath then cracked open the door.

Beams of light danced across the moonlit kitchen. Two people dressed in black stood on the patio, shining flashlights through the sliding glass door. *Damn it!* Crazies didn't work together like that. They had to be those people from the bridge.

Jacob retreated into the basement. There might still be a way out of this. There must be. He pulled a ladder to one of the windows that looked onto a strip of grass between his house and the neighbors'. All he could see from his ground-level vantage point was a wall of weeds. "Shit," he muttered. Something had to be done, and brilliant ideas weren't presenting themselves.

He undid the latch and swung the window into the basement, straining his ears for any clues as to what might be outside. The faint rustle of a breeze. Crickets chirping. With a silent expression of gratitude to whatever mysterious force had given him such an agile new body, he pulled himself up and snaked through the window.

Lying in the weeds outside, ready for anything, he waited. Nothing happened. No one had noticed him sneak out.

He followed the contour of a shadow to the corner of the house to peek at the back yard. The strangers were still on the patio, and they weren't alone. Barely visible in the dark, another pair stood by Micah's swing set at the edge of the yard. They carried what appeared to be long rifles with scopes.

The house was most likely surrounded, which meant there would be a fight. Beyond subduing the occasional crazy, Jacob had no experience using his powers as weapons. The prospect of taking on an organized, heavily armed group sent bolts of panic shooting up his spine. Desperate for reassurance, he reached out to his Darkness and found it eager for action. *They're nothing to us,* it whispered.

But even his Darkness feared one thing: the man in the mask. Flashes from earlier that day flickered through Jacob's mind: the bridge, a voice in his head, that spike digging into his back. He needed to act quickly.

Crawling through knee-high grass on his belly, he made his way to a spot where both the people by the swing set and the ones on the patio were within range of his power. Then, after taking a deep breath to steady his nerves, he attacked. A wave of telekinetic energy shot toward the snipers, whooshing through the grass like an invisible train. It hit like a train too, sending a tangled mass of swing set and bodies flying off into the night.

Jacob spun around and charged at the patio. The two people who had been peering into his kitchen reached for pistols holstered at their hips, but they weren't nearly fast enough. He seized them in an invisible bubble, which he immediately constricted into something the size of a large beach-ball. After tossing the intruders' crushed remains in the same direction he had sent their friends, he scanned the yard. Was that all of them?

Pop!

Something whistled past Jacob's ear. "What the—"

Pop!

He spun as if someone had punched him. A mist of blood clouded his vision. It took a second for the stabbing pain in his shoulder to register.

Pop!

The third bullet hit the side of the house with a loud thud. A glimmer of light flashed in the window on the side of their detached garage. A riflescope had caught the moonlight. Jacob whipped his arm, and most of the garage's wall blew apart. With a clatter and crack of breaking wood, the structure's roof caved in.

He ran to the patio door and shattered its glass with a punch rather than mess with the board Rebecca had used to lock it. Before entering, he peeked through the open kitchen into the dining room and the living room beyond that. Quiet and dark. But the instant he stepped inside, a loud bang sounded from the direction of the front yard and the living room window shattered. Blinding light flooded the house. An ambush! Cabinets exploded around him, spraying shards of broken plates and glasses; bullets ricocheted everywhere. Jacob dove across the room, tore the basement door off its hinges, and scrambled halfway down the stairs.

After a moment, the shooting subsided, giving way to nerve-wracking silence. Too scared to breathe, he stared into the harshly lit wreckage of his kitchen. Had they given up? Four of them already lay dead in the back yard, maybe they would cut their losses and—

A dark figure stepped through the patio door. Heavy boots, black shirt, and a white mask that gleamed like polished bone—the man from the bridge. Turning toward the basement, he held the spike he had for a hand before him.

Jacob focused. This was his chance. He'd crush that creepy fuck into paste.

Just then, three people in black fatigues burst into the kitchen, disrupting his view of the masked man. Each held what appeared to be a plastic toy pistol. Two pops in rapid succession. Jacob hopped farther down the stairs, narrowly dodging the taser wires, which fell uselessly where he had just stood. Before he could recover his balance, the enemies rushed forward, their weapons replaced by handheld stun guns with fizzing arcs of electricity at the tips.

The stairwell became a jumble of flailing limbs as Jacob knocked the weapons away before they could touch him. Everything was moving too fast; he couldn't fix his eyes on anything long enough to use his power. He punched someone hard enough to collapse their face, snapped an arm like dry kindling, grabbed a man by the throat and—

A gray blur shot through the tangle of bodies. The masked man's spike pierced Jacob's shoulder, cutting through muscle and bone as if they were nothing at all. He went numb. His vision dimmed. The strangest kind of pain he had ever felt radiated from the wound. It was like an enervating poison, spreading weakness and a deathly chill. He fell to his knees.

The masked man's voice filled his head, as cold and hollow as before: *The time has come.*

Pain tore through Jacob's entire body as the spike's tip ground against the inside of his shoulder blade. He was burning from the inside out. No, not burning—freezing.

The Mother of All has marked a path. I, alone, will follow. Where her gifts have fallen on barren soil, I will root them out. These malformed children, unworthy of her sight, must be purged. The masked man drove him backward into the basement. With an excruciating downward thrust of the spike, he forced him to his knees. *The purification begins.*

Jacob's Darkness writhed. The spike was somehow attacking it directly. As icy roots spread through him, a fissure opened, dividing man from Darkness. But those weren't separate things anymore; they couldn't be split. The fissure became a yawning chasm, sucking life and warmth from the world.

A metallic drone filled his head: *May the Mother see my work; may she—*

From out of nowhere, a whirlwind of blonde hair and skinny limbs flew at the masked man. Micah jumped on his back, wrapping her arms around his neck. He doubled over and fell to his knees as though she weighed much more than she did. His chest heaved with quick, shallow breaths.

The sickness! That strange thing that happened whenever Micah touched Jacob worked on the masked man too, and she had weaponized it. Clinging to him with all her strength, her face set in a grimace of tortured determination, Micah fought through her own sickness.

The masked man reached over his shoulder, feebly pawing at her. He looked frail, as though he were a hundred years old.

Rebecca burst from the shadows, a crowbar raised over her head. She swung at the man's ribs, narrowly missing the arms and legs Micah had entangled him in. He collapsed in on himself. Grasping at Micah, he lost his balance and crashed headfirst to the floor. His porcelain mask shattered, revealing a smooth stretch of ghostly white skin as featureless as a hard-boiled egg. The man had no face, not even bone structures that hinted at one.

Rebecca stared in open-mouthed horror, her crowbar poised for another strike. Trembling, she dropped her weapon and laid a hand on Micah's back. "Let go, honey. We need to get out of here."

Still clinging to the apparently unconscious monster, the girl didn't respond.

While Rebecca unwound Micah's arms and legs, Jacob sat on the stairs to recover. The stab wound in his shoulder felt like someone had shoved a hot coal into it. He sensed his Darkness healing, but he was too weak to fight. Luckily, the human soldiers had left their master to execute Jacob in privacy.

Rebecca lifted Micah's limp body from the faceless man and carried her to the nest under the stairs, where she laid her down.

"We don't have time to look her over," Jacob said. "We need to—"

She flew across the room, snatched the crowbar from the floor, and swung it at the faceless man's head. It connected with a solid thud, as if she had hit a tree trunk. Her face speckled red, Rebecca stood frozen, staring at a bloody gash of torn skin and exposed bone where the man should have had an ear.

Jacob went to her and gently removed the crowbar from her hand. "That's enough. We need to leave before the others come back."

While Rebecca retrieved Micah, he cleared the abandoned bodies from the stairs and piled them in a corner. After completing that grim task, he crept upstairs to assess the situation. Spotlights still shone through the house, casting the kitchen in stark light and deep shadow. Two men and a woman, all with stun guns in hand, huddled near the sink, looking out the back window. They seemed worried about something outside.

Before they could notice him, Jacob swept them up in an invisible fist as though they were a bouquet of flowers. He lifted them to the ceiling, flipped them over, then slammed them headfirst into the granite countertop. An explosion of gore splattered the room. His powers had recovered.

A cluster of enemies crouched on the patio, guns aimed away from the house. One, a boy who couldn't have been more than fifteen, stood in the broken back door, about to come inside. He gaped at Jacob, his eyes and mouth three perfect *Os* of shock.

Jacob blocked the doorway with a telekinetic barrier. That should keep them from shooting at Rebecca as she carried Micah up from the basement. Now there was only one way out. He dashed into the living room. A wall of light blasted through the front window, making it impossible to see outside. There wasn't time to worry about that. Moving as quickly as he could, he destroyed the front door with an energy bolt and blindly charged through the space where it had been, ready to bulldoze a path through anyone outside.

The expected storm of gunfire failed to materialize. Instead of a hostile army, he found dozens of semi-conscious people sprawled across the lawn like sunbathers on a beach, forgotten weapons beside them. Not one of them reacted to, or even seemed to notice, his sudden arrival.

Something was very wrong. The air felt heavy and warm. High above, the moon shimmered. Crickets chirped beyond the harsh glare of an array of spotlights in the road. *What a beautiful night...* Jacob thought. His mind drifted to campouts in his parents' back yard as a kid. All those people lying on the grass looked so relaxed, so comfortable. Wouldn't it be nice to—

He bit down hard on his tongue. The jolt of pain was real; the rest of this wasn't. Putting everything he had into resisting a powerful urge to lie down, he raised his eyes. On top of the graffiti-covered ambulance still parked out front, the Ghoul sat cross-legged like a nightmare yogi. Partially obscured by a gray curtain of scraggly hair, his cavernous mouth lined with shards of teeth widened into an unspeakable grin. He regarded Jacob with an expression of cheerful surprise.

The creature began to speak but was interrupted by Rebecca as she carried Micah out the front door. She must have misinterpreted the lack of violence as a sign that it was safe to go outside. The Ghoul flinched. A wave of tension shot through his hypnotic field, causing the crowd of dreamers to stir. He stared in stunned disbelief, his beady eyes fixed on Micah.

Before the soldiers awoke, the Ghoul's spell stabilized. It only took a moment for his shocked expression to morph into something resembling delight. "Oh, friend," he called. "What have you gotten yourself into?" He waved his hand, and the fog cleared from Jacob's mind. "Relax, I won't hurt you or these fine folks with you."

Jacob shook his head, forcing out the last of the Ghoul's influence. "What are you doing here?"

"I followed these guys. They're new in town, but they've made quite a splash. Bodies drop like flies wherever they go. I'm a big fan of their work."

"That's disgusting."

The Ghoul tilted back his head and laughed, putting his jagged row of teeth on full display. "To each his own. They spotted me this time though, so all this had to happen. I was about to skedaddle when you showed up."

While the Ghoul talked, Jacob checked on Rebecca, who lay on the front porch, covering Micah's body with her own. The hypnosis or whatever it was must have affected her as well. She rubbed her eyes and looked around, confused. Noticing the creature on the ambulance for the first time, she grabbed Jacob's arm and gasped.

The Ghoul, who appeared to be enjoying himself, turned his gaze on Rebecca. "Evening, ma'am! Have a nice nap?"

Jacob scowled at him. "Don't talk to her."

"Apologies. I didn't mean to offend." He smiled broadly, which was a traumatic sight to behold. "Let me make it up to you. How about I keep things nice and mellow here for a little while? You can hang out if you want, but if I were you, I'd get out of here while the getting's good."

"Why should I trust you? How do I know you won't follow us?"

"Beggars can't be choosers, friend," the Ghoul replied with a congenial chuckle. "There's no guarantees in life. Do whatever you want. I know I will."

Jacob didn't have a choice. He needed help, even if it came from a repulsive monster who ate people. "Fine," he said. "But I know your trick. If I feel you anywhere near us—"

"Yeah, yeah," the Ghoul interrupted. "You'll smash me into gooey bits. Just like this poor guy." He held up a severed hand that had been sitting on his lap. "I found this behind the house. Your handiwork, I assume?" A thick rope of saliva dropped from his lower lip as he eyed the hand.

Rebecca picked up Micah and allowed Jacob to usher her down the driveway and onto the road. They'd have to walk, since he had collapsed the garage on his and Rebecca's cars earlier.

"One more thing, friend," the Ghoul said as the family warily passed the ambulance he sat on. "Don't go near any rivers. There's no telling what *she* would think of that freaky little one you've got there."

Jacob nodded and set off down the road. Neither he nor Rebecca looked back. There were too many horrors prowling Cincinnati's darkened streets to spare a thought for the ones they had left behind. Finally, he saw some of the others. A child with bat wings, a woman who had six arms, a centaur—so many of his kind. Something the Ghoul had said the first time they met came back to him: *We're at the center of the world.*

The strange creatures watched his family from a distance. Some were curious, others threatening, a few frightened. But none approached. It didn't take long for Jacob to realize it wasn't him they were afraid of. Their gazes invariably fell on Micah.

Micah's Rules for a Better World

Protect the people you love. Even if you're small and weak, even if you know it'll hurt, do what you can to keep them safe. Without them, you aren't anything.

A Dream

This cannot be. In full sight of Mother—no, impossible.

I will make amends. I will prove my worth.

The usurper's stench lingers in me, mocking me. If he can hear these words, he will know this to be true: Oblivion awaits.

As unworthy as he is, I give him my name so that he might fear it. I am Caleb.

Interlude

"Oww!"

The Ghoul hopped around on one leg in absolute darkness. He'd just banged his shin on one of the little stepping stools that were scattered around the library. How'd one get all the way down to the basement? It hadn't been there when he left a couple nights ago. Fumbling in the dark, he searched for the flashlight he kept on a table next to the door. Gone.

"Blasted thing! Where'd you run off to?"

That's when he noticed the smell. Sour and sharp, with a little funk—food before it's food, something alive. A wacko, had to be. People like him, changed people, didn't smell that way, and leftover humans never came to this part of town.

"Hello?" the Ghoul called into the wall of darkness. "Don't be scared, little wacko. I won't hurt you. Unless you messed up my newspapers. Then I might." He chuckled, a raspy rattle he knew sounded like death itself to wackos.

Nothing happened.

Fishing around in his hoodie's pockets, the Ghoul found a small candle and his trusty lighter. (It wasn't really trusty, but he hoped someday it might be if he thought nice things about it. The power of positive thinking.) With a click and a fizz, the lighter flared to life. He lit his candle so he could get his bearings.

Back in the dead world, the library's basement must have been used for storage. A sign on the door upstairs read *EMPLOYEES ONLY*, and that sign meant business. Whoever "employees" were, they must have had special training to make sense of the maze of shelves and cabinets down there overstuffed with dusty books, huge volumes of bound newspapers, boxes of forgotten magazines, and binders full of who knew what. Lots of places for a spooked wacko to hide.

"Come out, come out, wherever you are," the Ghoul called. He set off on a leisurely search, sure he'd hear the clatter of falling books any second as the wacko made a break for it—probably with his missing flashlight. He smiled; a good scare would serve the thief right.

As the Ghoul came to a stop near the center of the basement, a pungent scent scalded the inside of his nose. There was a living thing nearby. *Bleh!* Death smelled so much better. Following his nose, he came to a suspiciously body-shaped object wrapped in a blanket, lying on a mostly empty bottom shelf. "What's this?" he asked. "A visitor?"

He hooked a corner of the blanket with his claw and peeled it back to reveal a small face. Green eyes, huge with fright, stared up at him. "A little one!" he shouted, holding his candle closer to get a better look. (To the Ghoul's constant annoyance, he didn't have very good eyesight.) "Tell me, little wacko, what brings you to my humble abode? For your sake, I hope you weren't planning to eat me. I'd taste terrible!" He let out a hearty laugh, his long tongue sliding all over the place, as it tended to do.

Tears trickled down the little one's cheeks.

She didn't try to eat him. (The Ghoul decided his visitor smelled like a she, although it was hard to tell with little ones.) She just stared at him with her mouth partway open, as though a scream had gotten stuck there. *What a weird wacko*, the Ghoul thought. He didn't say that out loud though. It would have been rude.

After a few minutes of the silent treatment, she asked, "Are you going to kill me?"

"Do I look like the kind of guy who'd do a thing like that?"

Gravely, as though it were the most serious thing she'd ever done, the little one nodded her head.

Tickled, the Ghoul doubled over in a fit of cackling giggles. It had been ages since he'd had such a good laugh. He liked this wacko, even if she smelled bad.

It took a while, but the girl eventually got brave enough to come out of her hidey-hole and be sociable. She turned out to be more of a medium-sized one than a little one, but the Ghoul decided to keep thinking of her as little. And she wasn't a wacko! She was a leftover named Lily. She didn't like him to call her Lily the Leftover though, so he didn't.

As luck would have it, the Ghoul happened to have a stash of food cans he thought she might like. He used to trade with a group of leftovers who lived in a different library: food for their dead. Those guys loved the slop in those cans. Then one day they all disappeared, and he got stuck with a bunch of extra cans. The Ghoul hated waste, so he was happy to find a use for them. He brought one that said *tomato soup* to Lily and ripped it open for her. She eagerly slurped up the red goop inside, licking the can's insides with her ridiculously small tongue. The poor thing was hungry. The Ghoul understood that all too well. He told her she could have as many cans as she wanted.

After she'd eaten, Lily curled up in a corner with her blanket. The Ghoul promised not to bother her if she needed a rest. Her body very much wanted to take him up on his offer, but the scary things spinning around in her head wouldn't let her relax. She squeezed her blanket tightly and cried for people who were gone.

The Ghoul felt bad for her. Gradually, so it wouldn't startle her, he used his special gift to make the basement feel cozy and safe. Happier thoughts filled Lily's head, and she drifted into a peaceful sleep.

Days and days passed, maybe months; the Ghoul wasn't good at keeping track of time. Once Lily convinced herself she wasn't about to die, she warmed up to him. He loved listening to her stories about the dead world and looking at the strange pictures she drew—groups of people all together, a yellow ball in the sky, a four-legged thing she called Chester the Puppy. Her company added a welcome dash of flavor to the times between eating and getting hungry again.

Life in the library basement was mostly good. Although, sometimes after drawing one of her pictures, she cried for reasons the Ghoul couldn't understand. And things got rough at night. After dark, he thought with his stomach, which didn't like Lily. Her smells made him sick. The sounds of life within her body drove him out of his mind. Being hated by the Ghoul's stomach was a very scary thing, so the little one hid, her heart beating so hard it nearly burst out of her chest.

She knew what he ate. He washed up after meals and put on a fresh hoodie, but she figured it out. She was clever, the little one. Each night, after he satisfied his hunger, she made him promise he wouldn't eat her. And each night he traced a cross over his heart like she showed him how to do and promised, each night except the last. Different promises were made that night.

The Ghoul thought Lily might be happier with other leftovers, so he offered to find some for her. That meant going out during the day, which made him nervous. Bright light hurt his eyes, and the others whispered about some guy with horns skulking around while everyone else was resting, but he'd have gone out if she asked him to. She didn't want to leave the library though. Bad things had happened to her out there.

Not long after Lily settled into her new normal, a shadow fell over her. She might have been safe, but safe wasn't enough. She ate her cans with less gusto. Her stories about the dead world more often ended in tears instead of smiles. She didn't even hide anymore when he got scary at night. She was dying without dying.

The Ghoul did everything he could think of to cheer her up, all his favorite jokes and tricks: dancing skeleton legs, talking skulls, knuckle-bone showers. He even brought home a fresh heart to show her the trick where he threaded his tongue through the tubes inside, so it went in one hole and came out another. That last one made her run for her old hidey-hole.

For over a week before the end, Lily only wanted one thing: the Ghoul's aura of peaceful feelings. He gave it to her, even though he worried too much might not be good for her. Who was he to judge?

One day she handed him a big book she had found upstairs. It didn't have any stories in it, not at all the kind of thing she usually read. The front cover read *Pharmacology*. She wanted him to bring her some pills that were mentioned in the book.

Her dad had taken those same pills after he had been forced to kill her big brother, who went wacko and tried to stab everybody. Lily's dad had asked her to take the pills with him. She said she would, but at the last second, she got scared and spat them out. He'd already swallowed his, so there wasn't much he could do about it. He died chasing after her, begging her to keep her promise. More and more, her dad's ghost visited her to tell her he had been right all along.

The Ghoul could read. He knew what those pills did to leftovers if they took too many. Scared, he put the book on a shelf too high for her to reach and said he'd never bring her anything like that, not in a million years. He didn't want Lily to be gone.

But she cried and begged. She told him the world didn't want leftovers anymore. It hunted them down and made life so miserable, they'd be better off not living at all. People like her ran, hid, ran some more, then died in a nasty way. He tried his best, but he couldn't convince her she didn't need to feel that way, not with him there to protect her.

Once the Ghoul resigned himself to the fact that Lily had made up her mind, he agreed to help. It crushed his heart, but her life was her own. It wasn't fair to make her keep living on his account. He went to a place with a sign that read *Pharmacy* and got the pills. Later that day, she took them. As her heart slowed and her eyes grew drowsy, the Ghoul put his peace aura on her one last time. When the end came, only happy thoughts filled her head.

Chapter 4

Prelude

Life exists for its own sake, requiring neither purpose nor pleasure. Even after civilization fell, life persisted. There was a lot less of it, but it persisted. Plagued by madness and hunted by monsters, survivors plodded on with nothing but fear to drive them from one day to the next.

On the Run

Night Zero

Rebecca rode in the backseat of a stolen car. Darkened houses crawled by the window, looming shadows under a monstrously huge moon. There were no signs of life anywhere. She hadn't been outside the house for months, now all she wanted to do was go home and never leave again. The things she had seen as they made their way through the city...horrible, unspeakable things. How could the world be like this?

Micah hadn't regained consciousness since they pulled her off the thing with no face. She lay sprawled across the backseat of the car, shivering and groaning. More than ever, Rebecca needed to know what to do, but she didn't. As far as she could tell, Micah's only injury was a two-inch cut on her lower left leg. The monster must have gotten her with that weapon he had instead of a hand. The wound wasn't deep, not much more than a scratch, but it looked awful. Pus oozed from it, and the surrounding skin had turned red. How could an infection take hold so quickly? A toxin maybe?

"Where are you going?" Rebecca asked Jacob, who was in the driver's seat, navigating a mess of wrecked cars clogging the road ahead.

"North."

"Why aren't we at a hospital? I need medicine for Micah."

"Which is why—" He hit the brakes as a young boy wearing the remains of several dogs dashed across the street then disappeared into the darkness beyond the car's headlights. "I *am* taking you to a hospital."

"There are hospitals close to home. I don't even know where we are."

He sighed, a sound that carried more menace than irritation. "When the fanatics who attacked our house come after us—which they will—where do you think they'll look first? The closest hospital, or one of the many not-so-close ones?"

"Jacob! Can you stop being a jerk for two seconds and tell me where we're going?"

"The finest healthcare facility in all of suburbia. They'll have everything you need and more. Sit back and enjoy the ride, we'll be there soon."

"Goddamn it," Rebecca muttered. Talking to him late at night was pointless.

Day One

They got to the hospital a little after dawn—Memorial North, one of the largest medical facilities in the Greater Cincinnati region and the most well-equipped trauma center outside the city proper. It would have been an excellent choice if there were anyone to staff it, which there wasn't. Nor was there electricity to power the diagnostic equipment Rebecca needed to use. The hospital's emergency generators must have failed long ago.

Those issues might have been manageable, but post-apocalyptic Memorial North had another problem: it was full of dead bodies. In the chaos of the outbreak, the hospital's staff must have abandoned the patients.

Rebecca could smell the rot from the parking lot. Under no circumstance would she take Micah in there. Besides the stench, the place was undoubtedly festering with disease. It would have been safer to treat her in a dumpster.

As Jacob brooded over the many ways his plan had been ill-conceived, Rebecca formulated a plan of her own. She needed to find a powerful, broad-spectrum antibiotic in case an infection was the underlying cause of Micah's symptoms. That could still happen. The drugs in the hospital pharmacy should be usable, at least the ones that didn't require refrigeration. Someone just had to go in there to get them.

After the antibiotics were secured, she would need a clean bed and wound-care supplies. The two ambulances parked outside the emergency room should have all of that and more. If Jacob got one of them moving, they could transport Micah to an outpatient clinic that would have been closed when the outbreak took place.

Jacob eagerly agreed to get the medicine. Rebecca gave him a list of what she needed and did her best to explain how pharmacies were typically organized. She didn't know where this hospital's pharmacy was, so he'd need to figure that out on his own. After watching him disappear into the emergency room, she locked herself in the car with Micah and waited. Although she knew it wouldn't do any good to worry, she worried anyway.

An hour and a half passed before Jacob returned. To Rebecca's immense irritation, he walked out of the hospital wearing scrubs and looking freshly showered. Had he stopped to wash up? How long did *that* take? At least he wasn't empty-handed. Two very full duffel bags swung from his shoulders.

"What took you so long?" Rebecca called as she stepped out of the car. "I was about to—"

Behind him, the emergency room doors swung open. A filthy, naked man waving fistfuls of hypodermic needles over his head ran out and charged at Jacob.

"Watch out!" Rebecca screamed.

Jacob spun around, and the man instantly flew backward, as if an impossibly strong gust of wind had blown him away. He slammed into the side of the building with a thud and stuck there, pinned to the wall a dozen feet above the ground.

The man stared at Jacob in utter incomprehension. Whatever insane impulse had compelled him to attack an indestructible horned monster had vanished. Lost and confused, he could only stare. Then his rib cage imploded. Blood shot out his nose and mouth. His chest crumpled into a shapeless mass.

Too shocked to think, Rebecca gaped at the crushed thing that seconds before had been a living body. Jacob dismissed his invisible weapons and the man flopped to the ground. A large splatter of blood on the wall marked where he had been killed.

Killed. Jacob had killed him.

"Come on," Jacob said gruffly, approaching her.

Rebecca sat back down in the car's back seat beside Micah, not knowing what else to do. Numb, her mind a blank, she failed to accept what she had just witnessed. A trick, an illusion...

One of the ambulances still had its keys in the ignition. After loading Micah into the back, Rebecca got busy setting everything up. She removed the patient's dirty clothes, dressed her wound, and started an IV to infuse antibiotics and keep her hydrated. Meanwhile, Jacob busied himself raiding the other ambulance for supplies. Rebecca worked furiously, doing everything she could think of, probably more than she needed to. Fussing over her daughter kept her mind off everything else.

Eventually, Jacob climbed into the ambulance. He shoved a load of spare sheets, first-aid supplies, and batteries into a cabinet and took a seat next to Rebecca. She looked up and was surprised to see it was growing dark.

"How's it going?" he asked.

"Not good. The acetaminophen isn't doing anything for her fever. She hasn't shown any signs of waking up."

Jacob put a hand on Rebecca's shoulder. It was an intimate gesture, something he might have done before—before he was a monster, before he was a killer. She didn't know how to feel.

"What's the plan?" she asked.

"We should move on. If they're searching the hospitals, it's only a matter of time before they make it up here."

"Do you think they'll take it that far? What do they want?"

"I don't know," Jacob said. He sounded tired. "I made their leader angry. I... It's hard to explain." He rubbed his eyes with the heels of his hands.

"But you beat them, you and that thing with gross hair."

"They didn't strike me as people who gave up easily."

Rebecca took Jacob's hand and sat with him in silence. She needed moments like this, when he spoke to her as a partner like the man he used to be. She wished she could tell him that, but knew anything she said to this Jacob would be distorted and thrown back in her face by the Jacob who came out at night.

"Come on," he said. "We should find somewhere to lay low until tomorrow. It's too dangerous to drive around at night."

Night One

They parked the ambulance in a garage attached to the most nondescript house they could find in the middle of a generic subdivision. Hopefully all that sameness would serve as effective cover. Rebecca wasn't comfortable with the idea of spending the night in such close quarters with Jacob, especially not in almost total darkness. After finding an electrical outlet in the front of the ambulance, she plugged in a hot-air balloon-shaped nightlight she had found in the garage. It was intended to ward off imaginary monsters, not keep real ones at bay, but it would have to do.

Micah lay on a gurney inside the ambulance, so pale and still that she appeared to be dead. Rebecca tried to keep busy, checking her patient's temperature and doing other tasks that didn't need to be done for hours. It got harder and harder to work as the night dragged on. Her eyes dried out, and she kept nodding off. Some minutes felt like hours; others disappeared into a hazy mist.

Eventually Jacob broke the silence, the poison silk of his nighttime voice uncoiling in the semi-dark. "A brutal day. Misery, bloodshed, and decay. Rest, weary one. Let this wretched world slip away."

Was that supposed to be a poem? Rebecca *really* hoped he hadn't decided to speak in verse from now on. Nothing good could come of responding, so she didn't. But as much as she hated to admit it, Jacob had a point. Micah would need her in the morning, if not sooner. She should sleep while she had the chance. But how could she with him there watching? She sat quietly, her hand resting on the chef's knife she still kept close.

Time passed.

"Jacob?"

The sound of her own voice surprised her. Rebecca had told herself she wouldn't let Jacob goad her into conversation, and now she found herself starting one. Stress, loneliness, and the delirium of fatigue must have taken their toll. She needed to talk, even if it was with the monster.

"Hmm?" he responded from his dark corner of the ambulance, his voice dripping venom.

"Can I ask you something?"

"Questions? And here I was resigning myself to another evening with the wall of sullen hostility. What's come over you, Becky?"

"Call me that again and I'll remove your tongue." Rebecca couldn't believe she had said that. She was so tired she felt drunk.

The many shadows cast by the little nightlight obscured Jacob's face, making it impossible to read his expression. After a moment, he laughed. It was a deep, complex, and decidedly sinister sound.

"I can do it, you know," Rebecca continued. "You'd be surprised how easy it is—snip, no tongue."

"You should," he said, still laughing. "I'd like to know if it grows back."

Rebecca nodded off again. It was inevitable. She wasn't a monster; she needed rest. But not like this, not with Jacob's sneering laughter echoing through her head. "Why did you kill the man at the hospital?" she asked.

He didn't answer for a few seconds. When he did, a trace of humanity had crept into his voice. "I didn't want you to see things like that. Micah wasn't awake, was she?"

"No."

"Good."

Rebecca paused, unsure what to say. "Did you have to kill him?"

"Crazies are dangerous."

"I know, but couldn't you have locked him inside? Or...I don't know, done something else?"

"Sure. I could have shoved him through a fifth-floor window and hoped he didn't find his way back down before we left. Or maybe I should have tossed him over the building and let gravity take care of him in the back parking lot. Less traumatic that way. Not for him, of course, but for everyone else. But when some psychopath with a handful of needles is charging at your family, you tend to go with the first thing that pops into your head."

"He was suspended in the air, twenty feet away," Rebecca said pointedly. "You had options and time to think them through."

"I don't need to justify myself to you," he said, his voice midnight black. "Some filthy vermin reeking of corpses attacks *me?* It's absurd." His eyes flashed in the dark. His horns glowed a ghostly white, catching the meager light in a way nothing else did.

"I figured it was something like that," Rebecca said, refusing to let him intimidate her. "You didn't do it to protect us. You're just some narcissistic jerk who can't stand to have his pride dinged."

"Ungrateful bitch," Jacob said in a seething hiss. "If it weren't for me, you'd be some crazy's plaything. You both would—"

He choked on his words, doubling over in his seat clutching the sides of his head. After a few seconds, he spoke again, "I shouldn't have said that. I'm sorry."

"Why apologize now?" Rebecca asked. "You say things like that every night. It's who you are."

"You don't mean that. I..." Jacob's voice trailed off. He sounded utterly spent. "Never mind. Let's get some rest."

As Rebecca lay down on the bench, her thoughts returned to the maniac at the hospital. She wanted to hate Jacob for what he had done. He deserved to be hated. Maybe she deserved to be as well, because despite everything she had said, she couldn't muster any genuine outrage. She only felt relief that nothing had happened to Micah. A realization as darkly comforting as it was unsettling ushered her into sleep: every crazy in the world could come for her child and Jacob would slaughter them all; she didn't have to stop him.

Day Two

Jacob drove the ambulance to Dayton's southern suburbs, which blended seamlessly into Cincinnati's northern ones. Wanting to avoid obvious search patterns, he stuck to smaller roads. A wreck or a couple of abandoned cars could—and frequently did—bring their progress to a halt. Through a combination of physical and telekinetic labor, he cleared the road and kept them moving, but it was slow going.

All day, Micah tossed and turned, groaning and whimpering. Sweat matted her hair. Her skin went pallid as her fever raged. While rolling her over to prevent bedsores, Rebecca noticed Micah had lost weight, which made sense, as she hadn't eaten for days. She didn't look malnourished though. Weird.

With a frustrated sigh, Rebecca lay down to rest. There wasn't anything for her to do but monitor Micah's condition and try to make her comfortable.

Night Two

Jacob sat in the back of the ambulance, fidgeting with a hunting knife he had found in the garage where they had parked for the night. He scratched the floor, cut his fingers to watch them heal, tossed it from hand to hand, and did whatever other tricks kept him entertained. Rebecca could tell her questions about the crazy man at the hospital had gotten to him. Rarely did she feel she had an advantage in this relationship, so it gave her no small measure of satisfaction to push things a little further.

"Jacob?"

He missed a toss and the knife clattered to the floor. "What?" he snapped, not disguising his irritation.

"Stop calling me Becky."

"You don't like it? I think it's cute."

"You know I don't like it. That's why you're doing it. I'd sleep better if you cut it out."

"Spoilsport," he said, then thought it over for a few seconds. "Fine. I'll try."

Too much emphasis had landed on the word *try*. Jacob was always like this when he felt wounded; he'd say anything to avoid meaningful conversation, so he could run off to sulk somewhere.

"Promise?"

"Rebecca, I solemnly swear I will, from this moment forward, never again address you as *Becky*. Satisfied?"

Now he was being facetious. Rebecca got up, felt her way around Micah's bed, and stood directly in front of him. "I'm serious. You want Micah to get better; I know you do. Creeping me out so I stay up all night isn't helping. You've got no reason to do it other than being a jerk, so cut it out."

Jacob's expression told her he hadn't expected her to be quite so persistent about this. He fumbled for a clever response but came up blank.

"Now promise, and seal it with a kiss."

They used to finalize agreements that way. It had even found its way into their wedding ceremony: "I now pronounce you man and wife. Seal it with a kiss."

Jacob's expression morphed into a wolfish grin. "You want me to kiss you?"

"Just a peck. If there's anything left of the real you, that'll help you honor the deal."

"Fine, if it'll make you stop pestering me." He stood up and looked into Rebecca's eyes. "I, Jacob, promise to never again call you Becky." He bowed his head and kissed her on the nose.

Something changed. No, *everything* changed. A solemn, almost sacramental air fell over the ambulance. Jacob's words echoed through Rebecca's head. Her heart skipped a beat. She couldn't breathe. This must be some new trick he had learned.

Expecting to see him grinning in that smug way he did when his power scared her, she instead found his face frozen in an expression of raw terror. Waves radiated from his body like heat rising from asphalt. She wanted to call it energy or light, but it was the opposite—nothingness. With absolute certainty, she knew this was the thing that had taken him from her. She could see it!

A link materialized between the two of them, pulsing with strange power. It tightened, pulling at her in some indescribable way. Then there was a *click* like the turning of a lock. She heard it. She felt it.

The bond vanished, leaving only quiet and a sense that something profound had taken place. A status indicator on one of the medical devices turned from red to green.

"What the..." Jacob said, his voice quivering.

Rebecca didn't know what to say. He was the magical monster with horns; shouldn't he understand this stuff?

Tentatively, as if uttering a witch's hex he was afraid just might work, Jacob said, "Becky." A retching sound erupted from his gut and he collapsed into a miserable heap, clawing at his stomach.

Rebecca crouched beside him and put her hand on his back. "What's wrong?" She had no idea what to do. This wasn't a human sickness.

"Get away! Don't touch me."

A minute passed, and then another. Jacob's condition gradually improved. His muscles relaxed, and his breathing slowed. He leaned back against the ambulance wall as someone recovering from a vomiting fit might, except there was no mess.

Rebecca went back to her seat. Despite everything that had just happened, or maybe because of it, she fell asleep.

Day Three

Determined to move farther north, Jacob pulled the ambulance out of the garage at first light. In a foul mood, sullen and testy, he didn't want to talk about whatever had happened the night before.

Rebecca checked Micah's vitals and changed her bandages. The cocktail of medications she had administered hadn't done a damn thing. Micah's temperature fluctuated between 100 and 102, as it had all day the day before. The redness around her cut had spread across most of her lower leg. Thick, black fluid leaked from the cut itself. An odor more like something burning than the putrid smell of gangrene rose from her leg.

For the third time that morning, Rebecca set the bags of drugs on a bench and went through them. There had to be something that would help.

Night Three

Jacob climbed in the back of the ambulance and closed the doors. He had heard something outside and went to investigate, otherwise he wouldn't have left Rebecca and Micah alone after dark.

"See anything?" Rebecca asked.

"Just a cat."

"Did you smash it against a wall? Rip it in half?" She knew better than to antagonize him, but couldn't resist the urge.

"Oh, Beck—"

Jacob cut the word off so violently it was like someone had punched him in the throat. He sat down hard on a bench, clutching his stomach, and glared at Rebecca as though his monster problems were her fault. Without another word, he retreated to his corner and closed his eyes to rest.

Much later that night, as Rebecca lay half-asleep beside Micah's gurney, Jacob whispered her name. Instinctively, she slid a hand under her pillow to grip her knife. It was an ineffectual weapon, designed for slicing vegetables, not people, but it comforted her.

"Rebecca? Are you awake?"

"Leave me alone."

"Tell me why you keep that weapon."

"My knife?"

"You always have it, even when you're safe and sound here with me. Why?"

He sounded closer, although Rebecca hadn't heard him move. She sat up stiffly. "You woke me up to ask about that?"

"Clinging to a thing like that is indicative of an unhealthy frame of mind. How about you swap it for a teddy bear?"

"Funny," Rebecca said in a dry tone. "It's for protection."

"It puts me on edge. Would you mind getting rid of it?"

Annoyed beyond belief, Rebecca glared into the shadows around him. "You know damn well this knife can't hurt you."

"It hurts my feelings," Jacob said in a sugar-coated parody of sincerity. He moved to the bench on the opposite side of Micah's gurney. Although he was only a few feet away, Rebecca still couldn't see his face. The nightlight had somehow been unplugged, leaving the status indicators on the medical equipment as the last remaining source of light.

"The only feelings you have are the kind that deserve to be hurt," Rebecca said.

"I blame myself." He let out an overly dramatic sigh. "It's partially my fault you've become such a spiteful shrew. I haven't always been as kind as I could. How about we declare a truce and start fresh? If not for our own sake, then for that of our poor lambkin here."

Lambkin? Did he mean Micah? Rebecca massaged her aching head. He could go on like this all night. "Fine, a truce. Whatever you want. Can I go back to sleep now?"

"After we clear up one final sticking point. As a sign of goodwill, I'd like you to get rid of the knife."

Rebecca laughed, but there was no humor in it. "Of course there's a catch! Forget it, Jacob. You wouldn't keep a truce anyway."

"And what have I ever done to warrant such suspicion?" he asked in a devil-politician voice. His face was lost in shadows, but she knew what expression he wore: wounded justice, a card he would play in court whenever someone accused some scumbag he was representing of wrongdoing. He had no intention of letting this knife business drop.

"Fine," Rebecca said, not wanting to spend the entire night caught up in his spiraling arguments. In the morning, he'd apologize, give her knife back, and lie to her about how he'd never badger her like that again. "I'll get rid of my knife if you promise to leave me alone for the rest of the night."

"Agreed. Let's make it official. Seal it with a kiss?" With little more than a slight movement of air, Jacob was standing over Rebecca. He grabbed her arm and forcefully pulled her up to face him. Her left hand grabbed the knife, but she couldn't raise her arm to stab him. His goddamned telekinesis!

"A deal is a deal," he said. "Do you promise never to touch that knife again?"

"You're insane!" she yelled, futilely struggling to free herself.

"Repeat after me. I, Rebecca, promise to never touch that knife again."

"You're hurting me," she said through gritted teeth.

Jacob's grip tightened. "Say the words."

"Okay! I, Rebecca, promise not to touch my knife ever again. Now let me go!"

Jacob looked around as though he expected something to happen. "It's not done yet! Seal it."

She clenched her jaw, struggling not to scream, her face a grimace of pain and frustration. She had never seen him like this. He wasn't playing. "I promise, you sick son of a bitch, not to touch my knife again." She leaned forward and touched her mouth to his jaw.

Everything changed. The evil in Jacob rose from his body, heavy and fluid. It touched something in her, then a link formed between them with an audible click—a lock that bound the soul. It was the same as the night before.

Held uselessly in her hand, the knife suddenly became repellent to her. A cramp like none she had ever experienced seized her midsection as a wave of nausea turned her stomach in on itself. She dropped the knife and fell backward, away from Jacob.

"It worked," he said to himself, unconcerned with her suffering. "How though?"

Rebecca curled up on the bench along the side of the ambulance. "Ugh… What did you do?"

Chuckling to himself, he withdrew to his corner. "I didn't do anything. You're the one who broke your promise." He opened the ambulance's back doors and stood silhouetted by moonlight, his horns gleaming.

Enraged, she grabbed a pair of scissors she had set on a shelf and lunged at him. Jacob caught her in a forced embrace. She swung the scissors side-armed and sunk them two inches into his liver. He didn't even flinch.

Gently guiding her back to the bench with invisible hands, Jacob's smile became a smirk. "As promised, I'll leave you alone for the night." With that, he jumped out of the ambulance and slammed the doors.

Day Four

First thing in the morning, Rebecca used a tire iron to knock her now-toxic knife out the back door. Being near it made her sick. Like a sorcerer from a fairy tale, Jacob had put a curse on her. No, a contract with magical teeth. A promise and a kiss, the kiss had sealed the deal. She'd have to be careful not to promise him anything else, and she sure as hell wouldn't kiss him again. Rebecca shook her head to scatter the distractions. Dwelling on Jacob's ever-expanding arsenal of horrifying abilities wouldn't accomplish anything. There was work to do.

The swelling and redness around Micah's wound appeared to have diminished; not much, but noticeable. After sliding her hands under the unconscious child's shoulder and hip, she rolled her onto her side. The sheets under her were soaked with sweat. Those needed to be changed. Hopefully the moisture hadn't irritated Micah's skin. Her weight loss had continued. Before her illness, Micah had weighed sixty-seven pounds. She couldn't be more than sixty now. Oddly, she didn't look any thinner. Unless she woke up soon, a feeding tube would be necessary. They should be able to find—

Rebecca's blood turned to ice. Her stomach knotted up, and her vision swam.

Micah's back was wrong, fundamentally wrong. The bones had moved—no, they *were moving*. Nodules, ridges, and bulges formed and unformed under the skin of her upper back. With a trembling hand, Rebecca touched something that looked like a rib bone repositioned to run vertically between Micah's shoulder blades.

"Stop!" she screamed and pounded on the wall between the back of the ambulance and the cab. Before she could take three breaths, they came to a shuddering halt and the back doors flew open.

"What happened? Wha—" Jacob's face locked up mid-word. He saw it too.

The ambulance erupted into a flurry of confused activity. Micah was washed, repositioned, and checked in every conceivable way. Through it all, she showed no signs of discomfort or distress. She slept peacefully as the flesh of her back rolled like the sea.

Afraid he would make everything worse by inadvertently touching Micah, Jacob went back to driving. They needed to get somewhere safer than the open road. That morning, they had settled on a destination, so he knew where to go. One of Rebecca's friends from medical school had joined a group practice near Dayton called the Maple Valley Family Medical Center. The facility had an on-site lab, basic imaging equipment, and an urgent care center. Most importantly, it should have been locked up when the outbreak took place.

Thinking of the diagnostic tests that needed to be done—most of which required specialists, technicians, and sophisticated equipment—made Rebecca's head spin. And almost all of it required electricity. For some reason,

Jacob thought he could restore power to the building if it had emergency generators. Other than baseless machismo, she didn't have a clue what gave him that idea. He had never done any electrical work more advanced than plugging something in. There wasn't time to worry about it though, not with all the preparations she needed to do.

One step at a time. Focus on the next thing. Work kept terror at bay. There was a conclusion Rebecca desperately wanted to avoid coming to. If she had allowed it to take shape, it would have looked like this: *My daughter is turning into one of them, a monster.* No. Rebecca expelled the idea before it snowballed into something she couldn't handle. If she thought like a mother, she'd fall apart and be no use to anyone. She was a doctor caring for a patient. No names. No identities.

The dressing on the patient's wound needed changing. She'd take care of that on the way to the medical center. As the bandage peeled back, a chill climbed Rebecca's spine. Her hands trembled. Micah's cut emitted a pink glow as if a small light had been embedded in her leg. Tiny wisps of smoke drifted up from the wound's edges, carrying a distinct odor of burned meat. Rebecca palpated the surrounding tissue and found it hot to the touch. She noted that the dark-colored drainage had stopped, and a scab appeared to be forming...or that might have been charring. She decided against redressing the wound, as the heat might damage the bandages.

After an eternity of stops and starts, the ambulance's engine shut off. Jacob opened the back doors. While he broke into the medical center to make sure it was safe inside, Rebecca busied herself preparing the patient for transfer. He returned a short time later to tell her the building hadn't been looted or vandalized. Other than a layer of dust, it appeared to be a normal doctor's office. Finally, a bit of luck.

Night Four

By the time they had moved Micah into an examining room, done what they could to secure the building, and gathered supplies from the urgent care clinic, dark had fallen. Exhausted, Rebecca pulled an extra bed into

Micah's room and lay down to rest. She had meant to get back to work later that night but fell into a deep sleep. Her dreams weren't good.

Day Five

The patient's fever broke at dawn. By midday, her cut had healed, leaving an inch-long scar. The bones in her back had stopped shifting in a way that could be seen by the naked eye but hadn't yet stabilized. Both shoulder blades protruded and appeared misshapen. The patient's collarbones had thickened and grown more pronounced, presumably to support the unnamed muscles growing there. New bone tissue covered her upper thoracic vertebrae. The symmetrical nature of these abnormalities suggested controlled development.

We've been down this path before, a voice in Rebecca's head suggested. She uprooted the thought and pushed its remains into the dark place where she kept things that couldn't be acknowledged.

Surprisingly, Jacob figured out how to change the emergency generator's fuel tank without blowing himself up. He fixed the electricity after all. Still paranoid about the people who had attacked them, he tried to convince Rebecca to let him turn it off again at dusk to avoid lighting anything up that might attract attention. She insisted on having power in at least a few rooms well into the night though. There were a lot of machines she needed to learn how to use.

Night Five

Late at night, as Rebecca lay awake, beating herself up over how little she had gotten done, Jacob crept into the room she and Micah shared. Her first impulse was to demand he leave, but she didn't have the energy for an argument.

Tears glistened on Jacob's cheeks in the moonlight. Rebecca couldn't remember the last time she had seen him cry. Had she ever? "Micah," he whispered. "Can you hear me?" He spoke tenderly, without any trace of his nighttime persona. "I'm so sorry, M. You have to fight it though."

Minutes passed as he stood with his head bowed.

"Dad?"

Rebecca sat up, sure she must be dreaming. The voice had been so small, little more than a breath.

"Dad? Is that you?"

A weight fell from Rebecca's heart. She leaped from her bed and ran to her daughter. "Thank God! Are you all right?"

Micah's eyes fluttered open. "Mom? I...I can't see."

"We're both here," Rebecca answered. "Dad and I, we're right here next to you."

"Why can't I see you?"

"I don't know, honey."

"Micah," Jacob said. "Listen carefully. Don't trust the Darkness. Fight it. Think about us or your friends or your favorite toys, whatever you love more than anything in the world. Use that as a weapon. Don't let it take you."

The room fell silent. Micah's eyes darted left and right without settling on anything. "Darkness? It's not dark. All I see is light. Bright, bright light. It hurts. It hurts really bad."

Her eyes closed, and she lost consciousness. Rebecca and Jacob sat with her through the night, helplessly watching as seizures wracked her small body followed by periods of limp exhaustion. She cried out and moaned, but didn't speak.

The thought that her daughter might die was a knife twisting into Rebecca's heart. At any moment, Micah could slip away, and no one could stop it. All of Rebecca's training and hard work, Jacob's terrifying powers, the love they both felt for this child—none of it would mean a thing. For the first time since Jacob had changed, she wanted to be near him. Monster or not, he was the only person in the world who cared about that little girl the way she did.

Day Six

Rebecca proceeded with the diagnostic tests she had planned to do. None of the results were encouraging. Micah weighed forty-six pounds, a third of her body inexplicably gone. Yet she still didn't look like she had lost much weight. Rebecca didn't question the data though. She only needed to roll Micah over or shift her in her bed to verify the measurements. It was as though parts of her body that used to be muscle and bone had been replaced with balloons.

X-rays revealed an underlying order to the gnarled mass of tissue on Micah's back. As Rebecca had suspected, the scapulae had changed shape. They were larger and arched over a cavity that had formed on each one's medial edge. Thick knots of unclassifiable tissue filled in all the new gaps.

Micah's clavicles and sternum were affected as well, although not nearly as radically as the bones of her back. Both collarbones appeared thicker and more pronounced, and her sternum arched up slightly from her chest. Like the other changes, these were perfectly symmetrical and appeared to follow a nonhuman anatomical design.

The lab results were as alarming as the imaging tests. Although Rebecca only knew the basics of pathology, she immediately saw that Micah's blood wasn't normal. It didn't look anything like the pictures in the lab manuals or the sample she had taken from herself. With a little research, she learned why—Micah's red blood cells had nuclei. Human blood didn't work that way. It shouldn't be possible. No disorder could change blood in such a fundamental way.

Humans weren't unique in having red blood cells with no nuclei; it was a trait shared by all mammals. Other animals, however, had blood similar to Micah's. One group stuck out in Rebecca's mind: birds.

Night Six

The evening passed quietly. Jacob looked at the X-rays and other test results. Despite his pleas for explanation, Rebecca didn't interpret them for him. She didn't understand most of them herself.

Day Seven

Sometime between Micah's morning and midday assessments, two hard lumps grew on the inside edges of her shoulder blades. Rebecca forced a fresh wave of horror and revulsion into the same pit she had put the others and got back to work. She had a job to do.

Throughout the day, the growths continued to develop. There was no bleeding, just some skin irritation. Rebecca kept everything sterile. It was all she could think to do.

Micah slept peacefully.

Night Seven

"Dad? Mom? I'm scared!"

Micah sat up in bed, frantically looking around the darkened room.

Rebecca rushed to her. "Micah!"

"Mom? Where are we? I want to go home."

Tears flowing down her cheeks, Rebecca wrapped her arms around Micah and held her close. "So do I, honey. So do I."

Over the next few days, Micah rested and regained her strength. She said she felt fine. There were no more bouts of unconsciousness, only the usual sleepiness that set in once night fell. Nothing remained of the cut on her leg except a rapidly fading discoloration.

Rebecca clung to a desperate hope that the nodules on her daughter's back would disappear. They didn't. Two days after Micah woke up, finger-like protrusions sprouted from the growths, which for some reason didn't concern her at all. Jacob normalized the situation without much effort. Rebecca found herself alone in despair.

Thankfully, Micah showed no signs of cognitive or behavioral issues. She laughed, goofed around, and expressed a keen interest in being reunited with her friends—blessedly normal reactions for someone her age.

The only non-physical change was a newfound fixation on rules. Whenever a problem arose, Micah would respond by making a new rule. A coping mechanism, Rebecca figured, her way of reasserting control over her life. Nothing to worry about.

Micah's Account

"Can you tell me one more time?" Jacob asked.

Micah slumped down in her bed. "Do I have to?"

"Just once more. I'll record you this time, so I don't have to ask again."

"Okay. I still don't remember much though."

"That's all right. Tell me what you can."

She blew a stray strand of hair out of her face. "The last thing I remember is running up to that creepy guy in the black shirt. When I got close, I felt sick, just like when I get too close to you. That gave me an idea: if he made me sick, maybe I made him sick too."

"That was smart," Jacob said.

Rebecca rose from her chair by the window and began her midday assessment of Micah's condition. "I wouldn't call blindly charging at a monster *smart*. I told you to stay put while I found something to use as a weapon."

Micah rolled her eyes. "Anyway, my leg started to hurt really bad all of a sudden, like when salt gets into a cut. I don't remember anything after that. At least not anything that makes sense, only weird stuff."

"Tell me about that too," Jacob said.

"I...I don't like that part."

"I'm sorry, M. One more time. Okay?"

Micah sighed in resignation. "The main thing I remember is a bright light. There wasn't anything else, just light. It talked to me. Not like we're talking now though. Different. I knew what it meant without words. Crazy, huh?"

"No, honey," Rebecca said. "Dreams are like that sometimes."

Jacob and Micah exchanged a glance that made it clear neither of them thought they were talking about a dream. In the margins of the notebook she used to chart Micah's medical information, Rebecca made a note to confront Jacob about blurring the lines between fantasy and reality.

"Tell me about the Light," he said.

"It saved me from whatever the man in black did to me. It didn't want me to die."

"So, it's good?" Jacob asked.

Micah shook her head in an emphatic *no*. "It just wanted to save itself. It needs me. I think it's trying to make us into the same thing."

"Don't let it," Jacob said.

"I know, Dad."

"And did the Light want anything else?"

"Yeah. It kept showing me a place far away, a shiny city with mountains all around. I call it the Golden City. The Light wants to go there."

"Why?" Jacob asked.

"It said this is a bad place full of bad people. The Golden City is safe."

"Do you want to go there?"

Rebecca, who was now inspecting the spot on Micah's leg where the cut had once been, glared at Jacob. "Don't give her any ideas. That isn't a real place, and you know it."

"I don't want to go anyway," Micah said. "Dad isn't allowed into the Golden City. I'm not sure about you, Mom, but I know Dad can't go. That's a rule."

"Says who?" Jacob asked. "I'll file a complaint for discrimination against people with horns."

Micah giggled. "I don't think there's anybody to complain to."

"Oh well. The paperwork would have been a nightmare anyway. So, I take it this Light of yours told you I wasn't invited to its special city. Did it say why?"

Micah shrugged. "Something about poles and opposites. I didn't get it."

"I see. And what did you think of the Golden City?"

"I told the Light I wanted to go home and be with my mom and dad. It got mad when I said that." The color drained from Micah's face. She shuddered. "It was scary when it got mad."

"I'm sorry, M," Jacob said. "Did it hurt you?"

"No. It tried all kinds of things to make me change my mind, but I kept telling it I wanted to go home."

Jacob leaned in closer. "How'd you make it let you go?"

"It was worried some bad guy would eat us up while we were asleep. I knew you and Mom would keep me safe, but the Light didn't think so. It ended up scaring itself with all that talk about being eaten and wanted to wake up. I made it promise to do things my way before I'd let us."

"Leverage," Jacob said. "Good negotiating."

Micah grinned widely. "Thanks!"

"So, it let you go?"

"Sort of..."

"It's all right," Jacob said. "Tell me the rest."

"I couldn't come back unless I brought the Light with me. It's part of me now. Maybe it always was, even before I got sick. It just mixed in with the other parts instead of trying to take over."

"Is it in you now?"

"Yeah. It's sleeping though," she said.

"What do you mean?"

"Being so far from the Golden City makes it tired. It can't do much. Plus, there are rules."

Jacob raised an eyebrow. "What kind of rules?"

Micah beamed, glowing with pride. "I knew the Light was getting nervous about being asleep, so I told it we weren't waking up unless it agreed to my rules."

"See," Jacob said to Rebecca. "Sometimes it pays to be stubborn."

She scowled at him.

Micah's expression darkened. "I just hope my rules are good enough. You can't trust the Light."

Micah's Rules for a Better World

When you're turned around and confused, when you don't know what's true and what's a lie, be stubborn. Dig your feet into the ground and don't do anything at all until you figure out what *you* want to do.

A Dream

The usurper's fruit ripens, and he attends to its every need. Sickening. Mother, take these visions from me.

Chapter 5

Prelude

One of the first lessons parents teach their children is "don't talk to strangers." There are good reasons for that.

An Intruder

Almost a week had passed since Micah had woken up. For the third day in a row, Jacob made the case for moving on. Rebecca, who argued their enemy couldn't possibly search all of southwestern Ohio, refused to consider leaving until she had subjected Micah to every diagnostic procedure available at the medical center. She needed to be certain she hadn't missed a clue that might lead to a breakthrough. There had to be a way to slow down Micah's changes—hormone therapy, chemotherapy, surgery, *something*.

As darkness fell, Jacob entered the examining room Micah slept in to say goodnight. Rebecca sat at a table near her own bed, reading by candlelight. He levitated a stuffed rabbit his daughter had adopted to her waiting arms from where she had left it on a counter. Rebecca rebuffed his offer to bring her a bottle of water or a snack.

Jacob didn't need sleep, so he spent each night in an examining room across the hall, reading novels and worrying. He made a point of checking on the others at least once an hour. When the time came for his first visit that night, he found Micah asleep and Rebecca writing a list of some sort. Just for fun, he blew her a kiss. She set her pen down and put her hand on a large hunting knife sitting on her desk, the same knife Jacob used to play with in the ambulance. She could touch *that* one. He chuckled and turned to go.

Then he froze. Blood rushed to his head in a thundering deluge. A young woman, early twenties maybe, stood in the doorway. Large yellow eyes shrouded in dark makeup glimmered in the candlelight. Her mouth was a scrawl of black lipstick across a bone-white face. A dark tangle of hair spilled over her shoulders. Behind her, a feline tail swished in the shadows.

No. Oh, fuck no, Jacob thought.

The woman's look was hard-edged, dirty, and mean—black leather jacket, frayed jeans, combat boots. Wiry and poised, she held herself like an animal stalking its prey. An air of savage mischief emanated from her.

Jacob's eyes flicked at the floor, and a barrier rose behind him to cordon off Micah and Rebecca's half of the room. More than anything, he wanted to join them in relative safety. Telekinetic walls were soundproof though, and someone needed to talk to the stranger.

"Who are you?" he asked.

As if that were an invitation, the woman stepped into the examining room. She moved tentatively, testing the floor with each step. Keeping an eye on Jacob, she pawed at a book Rebecca had left on a counter, examined cabinets, and turned a faucet handle on the sink. She came to a stop where Jacob's barrier met a wall and stared at the apparently empty space in front of her nose. Her tail twitched nervously as an inner debate played across her face. Curiosity won out over caution, and she extended a finger to poke the barrier.

"Is this what you do?" she asked, her voice as bright and melodious as a pixie's. "Force fields? Cool."

Jacob glanced at Rebecca, who hadn't moved an inch. Still seated at her desk, pen in hand, she watched the intruder with laser focus. Thankfully, Micah slept under a small mountain of blankets. Other than a lump here and there, she could barely be seen.

"I can make shields, among other things," Jacob replied. He assumed a calm demeanor, not entirely welcoming but not hostile either. His first bet was placed: dialogue would prove more effective than a show of force.

The woman made a semi-musical humming sound as she inspected the telekinetic barrier. She gave it a little shove. "So why's there a force field right here? Scared I'll mess with your stuff?"

She flashed a predatory grin, which Jacob countered with a stony gaze. Hopefully, his display of indifference to her attempts at intimidation was more convincing than it felt. The stranger glowered at him, clearly upset. Failing to make an impression bothered her? Interesting.

Upping the friendliness in his manner, he said, "The barrier gives my friends here a sense of security. They make a terrible racket when something spooks them." He gave his visitor a knowing look, as though they were the only adults in a room full of toddlers. "You know how their kind can be."

"Yeah, a real pain in the ass." The woman walked along the barrier, tracing its curved surface with her finger.

"Is there something I can do for you?" Jacob asked. Too much irritation had slipped into his voice. He really wished she would stop touching his barrier.

"This won't work, you know," she said.

"What won't?"

"The force field." She gave it another poke, contemptuously this time. "Watch." With that, she disappeared. One second, she was there; the next she wasn't.

Dumbfounded, Jacob stared at the space where she had been. A long shadow glided across the floor at his feet. He spun around to find her standing by the window behind Rebecca's bed. She had crossed the barrier! Seized by panic, he thrust an arm at her, and his telekinetic shield became a wrecking ball. The bed crumpled like paper. The widow exploded. Rebecca screamed and ducked under her desk. Micah sat up with a gasp.

The intruder was gone.

"Boo!"

Jacob spun around again. The woman stood in the doorway on the opposite side of the room, brandishing a pair of knives. Primed for a fight, she swayed slightly on bent knees. Her weapons, a dagger and a curved combat knife, winked silver in the candlelight.

Barriers couldn't contain her. She was too fast to grab. And where the hell had those knives come from? Jacob's mind plunged into chaos. There had to be an answer! A wide-area telekinetic bludgeon—no, not with Micah and Rebecca in the room. He could...he could...

With a Herculean effort, he suppressed his panic and forced a smile. "So that's what *you* can do," he said to the woman.

"Among other things," she replied flippantly.

"Sorry for trying to push you out the window. You startled me."

"Push me? Seriously? You tried to squash me!" Her voice rang with impish glee. "I guess that's another thing you can do, huh? Smash stuff."

Bold. Aggressive. Jacob made several mental notes. "I think we've scared my friends here enough. I'd hate for one of them to die of a heart attack. Why don't we go across the hall and have a little chat? You know, just us demons."

At the word *demons*, the woman's composure fractured. He had a name for what they were, and she evidently didn't. That bothered her. Interesting. Of course, Jacob had just then started calling himself a demon. The crazy woman he had found tied to a fountain back in Cincinnati deserved credit for coining the phrase. He'd be happy to borrow it, though, if it got under this woman's skin.

"Okay," the intruder said after thinking it over for a moment. "Not across the hall though. I choose the room."

"Fair enough. After you." Jacob gestured toward the hallway.

As they walked, she moved around him, not maintaining her position for more than a second or two. In front, then behind, then beside him, slipping through the dark like a fish through water. Her black leather jacket and mass of dark hair camouflaged half her body. Jacob only caught flashes of her blades in the light of the candle he carried and glimpses of her tail swishing across her jeans.

They entered a room identical to Micah's except without the extra bed Rebecca had brought in for herself. He set his candle on a countertop. Its orange glow created an island of warmth in the cool moonlight that streamed through the window.

"Introductions are in order," Jacob said, and reached out to shake hands. "I'm Jacob Freeman."

After a moment of hesitation, she took his hand. Darkness flowed under her skin, throbbing with her pulse. Touching her like that, feeling the ebb and flow of her power... It was an unexpectedly intimate gesture. He didn't want to let her go; he couldn't. Yes, he'd pull her closer and—

A sharp, sudden pain caught his attention. Some remnant of sanity had caused him to bite his tongue before he did anything stupid. This wasn't the time for his Darkness to fly off the rails. For fuck's sake, was he *trying* to get himself killed?

As soon as the intruder took Jacob's hand, her face tightened into a grimace of self-reproach. She had acted without thinking it through, something her expression suggested she often reminded herself not to do. Jacob read her body language as easily as he'd scan billboards along the side of a road. The woman either couldn't hide a thing or wasn't bothering to.

"I'm Judith," she said. "I...uh...don't have a second name."

Reluctantly, Jacob released her hand. "Nice to meet you. I hope you won't think I'm rude if we dispense with the pleasantries. I'm quite busy. What exactly do you want?"

The directness of his question seemed to throw Judith off balance. Her swagger slipped as she struggled to frame a response. "I was just curious, you know?" Embarrassment cut across her face. Her tail flicked. She had obviously wanted to say something more befitting a demon punk, or whatever she saw herself as.

Jacob smiled inwardly. Despite his uninvited guest's discomfort with conversation, she allowed herself to be coaxed into it. If she had kept her mouth shut and her knives up, he'd have been fucked, but in a verbal exchange he had an advantage.

"Anyway," Judith said. "I saw you had a couple of Muggles. I was going to take them. Or maybe trade."

"Muggles?"

"You know, people who aren't special but aren't psychos either."

"I like it. Why do you call them that?"

She shrugged. "That's just what they are."

This woman didn't remember the Harry Potter stories, but she had carried the concept of Muggles to the other side of the apocalypse. Darkness worked in mysterious ways.

"They call themselves normal," Jacob said. "I take offense at that, so I shorten it to norms. Your word's better though, very creative."

"Normal?" Judith's asked, affronted. "Boring's more like it."

Jacob flashed an easy smile. "Can't argue with you there. So, what do you want them for?"

"To model my fashions."

"Model?"

"You know, I dress them up and make them move around. They're better than mannequins, because you can see how the clothes move."

Jacob didn't know what he had expected her to say, but that most definitely wasn't it. "You keep people as...fashion slaves?"

Her sharp, feline features pinched in a bit around her yellow eyes, expressing confusion. "They're just a different kind of mannequin. I like that they move, but it sucks that they die for no reason. That's why I need new ones. Mine died."

"Norms don't drop dead for no reason. Did you take care of them?"

Judith shrugged under the thick, armor-like leather of her jacket. "I don't know. When they cried too much, I locked them in a garage. Maybe they didn't like that?"

The conversation had taken an odd turn, but it seemed to have veered away from the brink of violence. Judith's knives were nowhere to be seen. Where they had gone remained a mystery, as she didn't appear to have anywhere to put them, but they weren't in her hands.

"Owning norms isn't easy," Jacob said. "It takes a lot of work. You need to find food and clean water for them. They get upset if there isn't a private place to relieve themselves. And, of course, keeping them safe from crazies is—"

"Okay! I get it," Judith said. "Norms are a pain in the ass."

"You have no idea. Do yourself a favor: stick with non-living mannequins." This might be easier than Jacob had thought. If he could convince Judith his "Muggles" were more trouble than they were worth, she might give up on the idea of taking them and leave peacefully. "Believe me, I'd be happy to let you take those two in the other room off my hands, but, as it happens, I need them for a while longer. So if that's all you wanted, I believe we're done here."

A sly smile spread across her face. Her eyes sparkled gold in the flickering light. "But not everybody in that room *was* a norm. There's something weird about that girl on the bed. Why do you have a thing like her?"

Jacob underlined a mental note he had made earlier about curiosity. "The child? Yes, she's unique. Unfortunately, I'm not at liberty to discuss her case."

"Okay. I guess I'll pop over there and check her out myself then." Judith feinted toward the door.

"Stop!" Jacob yelled. "She's weak. A sudden fright could kill her." He paused, slumping his shoulders and gazing at the floor. "She doesn't know anything about her condition anyway."

Relieved he still had an audience for this part of his performance, he paced the room, massaging the point where his right horn met his skull and muttering curses. "Look, I'll tell you what's going on, okay? Just leave her alone."

"I'm waiting." Judith radiated confidence. In her mind, any missteps she might have made up to that point were redeemed. She had reclaimed the position of dominant demon.

"Not that it's any of your business, but I'm doing an experiment," Jacob said, as if the words were being pulled from his mouth with pliers.

"I decide what's my business."

Her excitement was palpable. For no reason other than an inability to pass up a good secret, Judith seemed to want this very badly. Jacob wondered if loneliness didn't also play a role in all this. He might very well be the first person she had had anything resembling a conversation with since the world ended.

"Fine, let's talk then," he said. "Remember the experiment I mentioned? Well, that girl is what happens when it fails." He took a seat on a chair in the corner, buried his face in his hands, and groaned. "If anyone finds out about this..."

Judith was practically drooling. Her tail curled up, peeking over her shoulder as though it were listening too. "She's a mutant freak like on the story discs?"

"I'll tell you," he said, and hopped up from his seat, "but first we need to make a pact."

Judith's mouth opened and closed again without producing any sound. Her tail dropped to the floor. She stared at him blankly. A social ritual had come her way and she had no idea what to make of it. That wouldn't have mattered if her demonic transformation had completely erased the human need to belong, but that didn't appear to be the case.

"What's the matter?" Jacob asked. "We can't sit down for a friendly chat if we're at each other's throats." He let a little impatience creep into his voice. Not enough to make her angry, just a touch. "So let's make a trust pact."

"Trust pact..." Judith repeated as though the words had come from a language totally alien to her.

"I'm in a hurry, so let's get this over with." Jacob pulled the only chair in the room toward Judith and sat in it. "Oh, and we can also discuss the trade you mentioned if you're still interested. The girl is off the table, but I could part with the woman after I'm done with my experiment. One pact can cover both your questions and any trade negotiations. Agreed?"

"I...uh... Okay."

"Then get on with it. You're the one making the request."

The silence between them grew heavier by the second. Utterly lost, Judith scanned the room as though the secret to getting out of her predicament lay hidden somewhere. Tension lines twitched around her eyes.

Displaying a decorous smile tinged with condescension, Jacob said, "Oh, I see. You haven't done this before, have you?" He paused for a moment to let her wonder if she should dig herself a deeper hole by lying, but not long enough for her to question the tower of bullshit he was building. "Sometimes I forget I'm not in the city anymore. Not much need for social graces out here, huh?"

Judith's eyes narrowed. Her face twisted into a vicious snarl. Perhaps the air of casual snobbery he had sought to project had come off too well. He wanted to hint at a demon society she had been left out of but might want to join, not make her feel like a bunch of assholes she didn't know saw her as a backwoods yokel. This was groundwork; Jacob didn't want her to get violent, not yet.

"Don't worry about it," he added hastily. "Let me explain. As I'm sure you know, demons are dangerous. We're liars, thieves, killers, and cheats. But we still need to deal with each other, right? So, we've worked out a ritual to facilitate communication. It's totally symbolic, of course, but it helps set people's minds at ease. Demons who get a reputation as pact breakers find themselves isolated. Particularly egregious offenders are hunted down for sport. It's not worth it."

Judith looked both relieved to be off the hook and humiliated to have been on it in the first place. She'd have liked to come off as savvy, but the opposite had happened. And although she hadn't realized it yet, she had also shown herself to be dangerously gullible. Darkness hadn't intended for this one to engage in conversation with con artists or attorneys.

"It might come in handy to know how trust pacts work," Jacob continued. "You're bound to run into situations like this again, especially if you come into the city. You should visit us, by the way. Wouldn't it be nice to show off your fashions to an audience more sophisticated than a bunch of crazies? I'll show you how pacts work so you'll be ready."

"Yeah, sure. Whatever," she said in a poor imitation of nonchalance.

"It's simple. First you say, 'I, Judith, promise not to hurt (fill in name here),' then you kiss the other demon to seal the deal."

"Kiss?"

"Don't worry. Some guys will say you have to kiss them in rather exotic ways, but that's a bunch of bull. Don't let them fool you. It only takes a quick peck on the cheek like they used to do in France."

"What's France?"

Apparently, the Ghoul wasn't the only demon to suffer near total memory loss. "It's not important," Jacob said. "Do you understand the ritual? Easy, right?"

"I guess..." Judith seemed worried, but not about the right things. "Okay, let's try it. I, Judith, promise not to hurt you, Jacob Freeman." In the blink of an eye, she dashed forward, touched her lips to his cheek, and withdrew. It happened so fast, he barely saw her move.

The air grew heavy and still. Strange energy buzzed and crackled between the two demons. Jacob's promise magic drew Judith's Darkness out of her like a fox pulled from its den. Frantic, it snapped and bit as it fought to free itself. He didn't understand how he held a thing like that, but he did. His own Darkness, a black ocean of power, emerged. He forced Judith's into his, deeper and deeper, drowning it. *Click.* The promise sealed. Everything was quiet again, a normal room lit by a candle and the moon.

"What...what the fuck?" Judith stammered.

"Hmm? Is something wrong?"

"What did you do to me?"

"I don't know what you're talking about," Jacob said dismissively.

"Bullshit!"

This was a critical point in the plan. If she blinked past him and went to Micah's room, everything would be ruined. "Whoa... Calm down," he said, backing away from her with his hands up to indicate he had nothing but the purest of intentions.

"Where do you think you're going?" She lunged forward and grabbed his shirt. Panic streaked through him. Judith's eyes were red slits of bestial rage. Her breath burned his skin. "Did you curse me?" She shook him violently. "What did you do?"

He shoved her back with a burst of telekinetic energy. It took every ounce of courage he had not to run away the instant he was free of her. "Get your filthy hands off me! I never should have left the city. There's nothing out here but crazies and feral—"

She vanished. If Jacob hadn't been waiting for that exact thing to happen, he'd have been dead. He spun around to catch a glimpse of silver slashing at his neck from behind. A wave of energy shot out from his body and sent Judith flying across the room. She crashed into a wall of cabinets, then hit the floor in a clatter of medical supplies and broken wood.

Blood gushed from Jacob's neck. He had worried about executing his counterattack prematurely, but he had very nearly been too slow. The candle was gone, leaving moonlight from the window as the only source of light.

Judith hunched over, clutching her stomach and choking. It had worked; the promise's magical enforcement had triggered. Even on something like her, his new trick worked.

Jacob rushed at her as quickly as he could, which felt sluggish compared to how she moved. He grabbed a fistful of her hair and slammed her face into the floor. From there, his Darkness took over. Its voice, as slick as oil, seeped into her ear. "Poor kitten, pawed at things she shouldn't have. Cats aren't the only things with claws, you know."

Judith made a feeble attempt to fight, but in the grip of sickness with him pressing her face into the ground, she could barely move. Pathetic, muffled whimpering rose from the pool of blood fanning out around her head.

"I should end you," Jacob said. "I'd be doing the world a favor."

If he had any confidence in his ability to do so, he might have tried it. Trying and failing would have been disastrous though. He wanted to keep her fearing for her life, not force her to fight for it. Or at least that's what he told himself. There was also the matter of how much he was enjoying this creature squirming under him, helpless. With a malicious scoff, he gave her head one more smack against the floor for good measure, then released her.

Judith sat up. Blood poured from her nose and mouth, flowing onto her leather jacket. Her eyes were infernos of rage. She lunged at him again. Such incredible speed! Jacob didn't stand a chance. If she had done that a hundred times, he wouldn't have dodged her once. Fortunately, he didn't need to. She fell to the floor at his feet, sickness tearing her apart from the inside.

"Disgusting," Jacob said. Towering over Judith, he spat on her. That wasn't part of the plan, but his Darkness couldn't be restrained. "I don't have time for trash like you." He paced the room a few times, staging a performance of supreme irritation. "There's a way for you to feel better again, a trick you can use. If you promise not to leave this room until I finish my work, I'll tell you."

"You lying sack of shit," Judith coughed. "I'll get you for this. I'll fucking—"

"It's a simple question. Do you promise?"

"Argh!" She crawled at him then collapsed again, hit by a fresh wave of sickness. After a moment, she whispered, "Make it stop."

"First things first. Repeat after me: I, Judith, promise not to leave this room. Don't forget to seal it with a kiss."

"I, Judith, promise not to leave this room."

"And..." Jacob waved his hand in front of her face.

She pressed her lips to a knuckle and the ceremony repeated.

"Good kitty," Jacob said once the new promise had sealed. Then he turned away and walked out the door.

"Wait!" Judith yelled. "What's the trick? How do I feel better?" Black rivers of makeup ran down her cheeks.

Jacob paused, his back to her. "It's simple. Don't break your promises."

Fiendish laughter rang through the halls.

The Captive

"Can we keep her?" Jacob asked his wife. It had been two days since he captured Judith, and he hadn't yet decided what to do with her.

"What are you talking about?"

"The person we have locked up down the hall. Judith. I was thinking of drawing up a contract that would let her come with us. She's been surprisingly cooperative."

Speechless, Rebecca stared at him in utter disbelief.

"She could help with nighttime guard duty," Jacob added. "And who knows, maybe she's seen a refugee center or two. It would also be good to have another person like me to talk to. We might be able to figure some things out if we compare notes."

"Have you lost your goddamned mind?"

"Hear me out."

Rebecca held up a hand to cut him off. "No! We are *not* taking a monster with us."

"But I can—"

"You've got to be kidding me." She let out a long groan of disgust. "You were so eager to leave before. Now it's nothing but excuses to stay. It's because of her, isn't it?"

Jacob shrugged. "Partially."

"What are you thinking? She's dangerous! How do you not see that?"

"She was at first, but—"

"Don't give me that 'surprisingly cooperative' crap. I hear her in there. She's a rabid animal."

"That's not true," Jacob said unconvincingly. Somehow it hadn't occurred to him that other people could hear Judith's...episodes.

"Wait." Rebecca shot him a look of pure, hot loathing. "You want to sleep with her."

"Don't be ridiculous. It's not like that."

"Really? Then tell me, Jacob, what is it like? Because I'm having a hard time seeing where you're going with this."

"I'd feel bad leaving her. And we could use some help."

"Feel bad? You'd feel bad for *her?* The psychopath who almost killed us? *She's* the one you're worried about?"

"She's sick, just like me. I want to help her."

Rebecca took an exasperated breath in a failed attempt to regain her composure. "Two things. First: she's not sick, she's a monster. Second: you're full of crap. You know goddamn well you aren't trying to help anyone but yourself."

"If you'd just listen for a minute, I can tell you my plan."

"I'm not talking about this. The medicine is packed and ready to go. Micah and I are leaving."

They didn't leave though. How could they go anywhere if Jacob didn't want to?

On the fifth day of Judith's captivity, Jacob ran into Micah in the medical center's lobby. She wore only shorts and sandals. Rebecca had ruined all the kid-sized shirts she had collected from nearby houses, trying to alter them to accommodate the rapidly growing protrusions on Micah's back. (Micah had taken to calling them wings, but to Rebecca they were protrusions.) Almost nine inches long now, the new appendages had baby versions of all the bones and joints bird wings should have. Although they were currently covered in pale, goosebump-prone skin, Jacob knew they would be beautiful someday.

"Good morning, M."

"Morning, Dad."

"How're you feeling? Does your back hurt?"

"No. It's fine."

"Glad to hear it."

"Dad?"

"Yeah?"

"You're going to let the lady with a tail go before we leave, right?"

"Don't worry," Jacob said. "I'll figure something out."

"I think Mom wants to leave her here forever. That would be wrong."

"Well, I can't speak for your mother, but I want to let Judith out of that room."

"Promise?"

"Don't worry, M. I promise I'll—"

Jacob cut himself off. Best not to phrase things that way. "She's dangerous, but I'll find a way to get her out of there."

Micah slumped her shoulders, dejected. "You didn't promise. New rule: We don't trap people in rooms forever."

She closed her eyes. An expression of intense concentration creased her brow. For not the first time, Jacob got the unsettling impression Micah was keeping track of all these rules.

"Dad?"

"Yeah?"

"It would be better to be dead than trapped like that. If you aren't really going to let her go, kill her."

That night, when Jacob went to check on his prisoner, she greeted him with a barrage of verbal abuse. No violence though. Progress. After giving her a few minutes to vent, he asked, "Do you want to get out of here?"

"What do you think, asshole?"

"Well, today's your lucky day!" There was a long pause for dramatic effect. "But nothing comes without a price. Before I cancel your promise, we'll need to make a new agreement, a contract of sorts. Loosen up those mouth muscles, you've got a lot of kissing to do."

Micah's Rules for a Better World

Show mercy. That means being kind when you don't have to, when nobody expects you to. You don't need to forgive. You don't need to love. Those are harder. All you need to do is show mercy.

A Dream

The usurper has become a slaveholder, shackling Mother's children to himself. No purification can remove the taint of such bonds.

This girl he defiles will have a quick end. The usurper will not.

Interlude

"Fuck!"

Judith slammed her fists down on the bathroom sink, almost knocking it off the wall. Her reflection in the medicine-cabinet mirror was a mask of rage done in smeared makeup and wild hair. Behind her, a pile of soggy clothes lay in the bathtub. They were the only things she cared about in that piece of shit house—no, in the whole piece of shit world.

An hour earlier, she'd come home from her latest attempt to hold down a waitressing job feeling she'd be less of a whore if she made her money selling blowjobs at a truck stop. She didn't get out of the diner until after midnight, and she was dead tired.

Pulling up to her dad's house, she found the junker her sister, Liz, called a "sports car" blocking the driveway. That skanky bitch would be passed out by now, snoring like a pig. Her car wasn't going anywhere anytime soon.

Judith thought about laying on the horn, but knew it would bring out the redneck neighbors with their guns and their dogs. Then her dad would stumble out of the house, drunk as shit and ready to beat somebody's ass—and she had a pretty good idea whose ass that would be.

She put her hand on the horn and applied a little pressure. It might be worth it. A bunch of pissed-off morons running around in their pajamas (dirty underwear, more likely), screaming their heads off; dogs going ape shit; her sister's fat face pressed to the window, hoping the chaos didn't get too close to her car—it would be fun. And who knows, maybe her dad wouldn't see her and would go after one of the rednecks instead. Maybe somebody would get shot. Judith took her hand off the horn. Someday...

She parked her car half on the road and half in the front yard. Where had Liz taken the junker anyway? Most days she wouldn't haul her ass off the couch if the house was on fire. Happy images filled Judith's head as she walked across the weed patch her family thought of as a lawn: her sister on a burning couch—TV clicker still in hand—bitching about nobody saving her while her cheap, synthetic-fiber clothes melted into her skin.

Then Judith saw what lay in front of her sister's car. The world spun. She felt like she was going to throw up.

Clothes spilled out from under the junker: *her* clothes. More were scattered across the driveway. Ripped, crushed, and stained—they'd been run over. Repeatedly. The car's front tire sat on a dress Judith had made a few months before, grinding its white linen into oil-soaked concrete. The jeans she wore when she wanted to feel like a badass hung from the bumper, one leg nearly torn off. Her sexy shorts lay wadded up in the weeds, caked with mud and car grime.

Her brain locked up like a seized engine, unable to process what she saw. Those clothes weren't just things that made her look good—they were her voice, the only way she knew how to say anything worth saying. And that fucking bitch ran them over!

Judith's breath came in violent bursts. Her mind was a white-hot haze, incinerating all thoughts, leaving only hatred and rage. In an explosion of movement, her paralysis broke. She scooped up as many clothes as she could carry and ran for the house. It didn't even matter which ones she held in her arms. If she saved the sexy shorts, she'd be sexy. If it was something else, she'd be that. She just needed to save *something*. If they were all gone...

For over an hour, Judith knelt beside the bathtub, scrubbing, rinsing, soaking, doing anything she could to repair the damage. It was no use. Most of her clothes were ruined. Sobbing, she slumped into a miserable heap on the floor. Tears burned her cheeks. She'd put everything into those clothes—time, money, energy, passion. Now they were rags sunk in dirty water.

A badly scuffed leather boot caught her attention. She turned toward the sink to find a towel to polish it and saw herself in the mirror—the wreckage of her makeup, her hideous work uniform, her defeated expression. It all came crashing down on her. Not just what had happened that night, but her whole life.

"Fuck!" Judith screamed. She spun around and viciously kicked the side of the bathtub. Pain shot through her foot. It helped clear the other shit from her head.

She crouched down and pulled the heating register out of the floor. Reaching into the vent, she fished out a plastic case designed to hold eyeglasses. Inside were needles, razor blades, and a couple scalpels she'd stolen from the biology lab at her old high school years ago—everything she needed.

It had been almost a year since Judith stopped cutting. She'd thought she was over it. But what was she supposed to do? The anger and frustration needed somewhere to go. Cutting helped. Pain became an external thing, something that happened to bodies, not souls. The court-appointed therapist she had to see after her last run-in with the law said there were healthier ways to process life's challenges. What the fuck did he know? Cutting worked.

Judith took one of the razor blades out of the case and held it to her upper arm. Just a little; too much and somebody might notice. That would mean more therapy. As skilled as a surgeon, she put pressure on the blade. A familiar push of resistance, then the skin broke. Blood swelled like a flower blooming. Blood and the blade's sting—that was all there was. This stinking pile of shit she called a life disappeared.

She stopped, the razor blade still biting into her arm. An idea came into focus, as clear as a fire burning in the darkest of caves, the kind of idea that changed the world: a revelation. With more certainty than she'd ever had about anything, Judith knew this: she wasn't the one who needed to be cut.

A scalpel in each hand, she stepped into the dark outside the bathroom and turned toward Liz's room. This was going to be fun.

Chapter 6

Prelude

Relationships grow like a blackberry thicket—a tangled, thorny mess. There's fruit, and the fruit is sweet, but getting it will cost you.

Introductions

How does one rebrand yesterday's deadly menace as today's reluctant ally? It wouldn't be easy. Jacob had a crazy impulse to wrap his former captive in shiny paper and bring her home like a holiday surprise. He doubted she'd go along with that though.

Judith had shown remarkable restraint since winning her freedom by agreeing to Jacob's terms. She hadn't tried to kill him, not even once. Although there had been a regrettable escape attempt, the clause in her contract intended to deter such behavior proved effective. She was, if not cooperative, at least sullenly compliant. Of course, Jacob understood she was biding her time while she planned her next steps. That didn't worry him. Scheming and plotting he could handle. What he didn't want to deal with was an enraged madwoman. She needed to make a good impression on his family, the perfectly reformed demon.

Hours ago, Judith had gone off somewhere to clean up. Apparently, that was going to take all day. Jacob began to regret not including language around promptly following instructions in her contract. Too late now. He had lost his leverage the second she walked out of that room. The only bargaining chip left to him was true freedom, which he had no intention of surrendering.

While he didn't expect gratitude, Jacob hoped his new assistant realized how lucky she was. The new world was brutal. All manner of atrocities and obscenities could await someone who found themselves trapped as she had been. Judith had her health, a reasonable amount of autonomy, and no obligation to do anything excessively degrading. In exchange, all she had to do was not hurt him or his family, stay within two miles of them, and do anything in her power to protect them from bodily harm. It was an almost unimaginably good outcome for her. Jacob felt downright benevolent.

As generous as the terms of Judith's contract were, it must not have been easy for her to accept. Darkness didn't serve anyone or anything but itself. Bending to another person's will went against its nature, as the Ghoul might have said. On top of the humiliation of defeat, she was most likely dealing with a Darkness in full revolt. Taking her along on this road trip through hell presented all sorts of risks, but Jacob had confidence in his contract and the strange power behind it, which he admittedly didn't understand at all.

Where the hell was she anyway? It would be dark soon. He waited on a dusty couch in the medical center's lobby, dousing his irritation with vodka.

About an hour before twilight, Judith stepped through the double glass doors of the main entrance and turned Jacob's world upside down. His heart beating double time, he watched her move through deepening pools of shadow. The clever, self-assured things he had planned to say when she arrived vanished like soap bubbles popping. This couldn't be the same woman he had let out of the examining room, no way.

Her hair, now clean and lustrous, was a deep, smoldering crimson streaked with black. She had swept it up into an artfully messy bun, delicate tendrils dangling off the sides to kiss her neck. Smoky shades of plum had replaced the black makeup, lending her elfin features an air of mystery. Her eyes caught and amplified the waning light, shifting between gold and red, neither color yet both.

A black cocktail dress embellished with lace brought the curves out of her slender figure. Moonlight slipping through dark clouds, her skin flowed in and out of the elegant garment. Silky black fur coated her tail, which swished behind her. An ingenious sleeve-like modification freed it without disrupting her dress's lines.

Her appearance carried a message: the girl with a fierce smile and flashing blades was gone. This was Judith the shrewd, fully prepared for subtler forms of combat. She had assessed his vulnerabilities and knew precisely what she needed to do to throw him off balance. The realization that he might be in deep trouble struck Jacob like a fist. His faith in his ability to control this creature nosedived. A panicked urge to release her then and there nearly overcame him.

Then she spoke. "So, where are these people I'm not allowed to kill?"

"Hurt. You promised not to hurt them."

She shrugged. "Whatever you say, boss."

Her voice struck him as overtly flippant with too much edgy attitude, not very sophisticated at all. Jacob didn't respect that voice, much less fear it. Judith's mystique wavered. It didn't disappear, but it slipped enough for him to see through the mirage. He could handle her. Probably.

They walked together to Micah's room. After knocking, Jacob opened the door and stepped inside. "Micah, Rebecca, I'd like to re-introduce you to Judith. She'll be traveling with us for a while."

Micah sat on the examining table, clutching a pillow to her chest as if it could shield her. Rebecca stood next to her as rigid as stone. Neither said a word.

"Come on, guys. Don't be rude."

He turned to see Judith in the hallway behind him, backing away. Her impeccably made-up face contorted into an expression she hadn't planned on wearing with that outfit: raw, visceral panic.

"I'm not going anywhere with that girl!" Judith had changed into a snug, knee-length pencil skirt and a white blouse. It was the sort of outfit Jacob's female colleagues would have worn to court. The cocktail dress must have been deemed inappropriate for this conversation.

"Correct me if I'm wrong," he replied. "But didn't you promise to stay within two miles of us? Sealed with a kiss, as I recall." He made a kissy-face that would have gotten his lips cut off if Judith weren't contractually obliged not to do that sort of thing. He continued in an affected, regal tone. "However, I'm feeling magnanimous. So, by all means, share your objections to my family."

Judith paced the lobby, her tail lashing. "Shut up! Just shut the fuck up! That girl isn't like us. I mean, she is, but she's all wrong. What did you do to her?"

"You've seen her before. Remember? You wanted to trade me for her. Didn't you notice her peculiarities then?"

"She's different now!"

"What do you mean?" Jacob asked.

"When I saw her that night, she had a weird vibe and a fucked-up back. But now she's different. She glows!"

Jacob laughed, and it wasn't a friendly kind of laugh. "Glows? That's ridiculous. Your eyes just aren't used to daylight."

She scowled at him incredulously. "You're bullshitting me again, right? That room was brighter than the others. And it wasn't normal light; it wanted to burn me." Judith's eyes, red now, bore into him. Her tail hung low and rigid, its fine hairs standing on end. A pair of knives that hadn't been there before gleamed in her hands. Everything about her screamed of triggered survival instincts. Up to this point, she hadn't shown any indication of being capable of performing a lie this convincing.

"Wait here," Jacob said.

Making his way back through the medical center, he paid attention to the empty rooms he passed. Weak, green-tinted light filtered through their windows, casting them in murky gloom. Then he came to Micah's room and stepped into golden sunshine. Light from the window coalesced around her like a shimmering veil, giving her hair and skin a barely perceptible glow. Rebecca, who sat at her desk with her head down, didn't glow at all. If anything, she appeared shaded. The room's two occupants were experiencing different weather; Micah's world enjoyed a sunny day, whereas Rebecca Land was overcast.

Deeply troubled, Jacob returned to the lobby. "You're right," he mumbled to Judith.

"No shit."

Lost in thought, he stared off into space. "She's unusual, I'll give you that, but she won't hurt you. As long as you don't touch her, you'll be fine."

"What happens if I touch her?"

"You'll get sick. Probably. We should test that."

Judith glared at him, murder in her eyes. "Are you fucking serious? I'm not going anywhere near her." She sat on a couch and crossed her arms in a childlike show of defiance.

"Fine," Jacob said firmly. "We're leaving at dawn. You can come with us or stay here to experience all the unpleasantness that broken promises bring. If you're smart, you'll join me in the ambulance. Or find your own car if you want. I don't care."

"I have a car, asshole."

Team Building Exercises

Judith's "car" turned out to be a large truck of the sort moving companies use. Although Jacob questioned the wisdom of taking such a bulky, gas-hungry vehicle, he didn't say anything. It was best to avoid conflict on the first full day of his and Judith's highly charged relationship.

Giving Jacob a look that said she wanted to crush him under her truck's wheels, Judith pulled it behind the ambulance. The Freemans weren't ready to go yet, so she listened to extraordinarily angry music on the stereo while they packed.

An hour after dawn, the little caravan pulled onto the desolate streets of Dayton. They planned to investigate Wright Patterson Air Force Base, located just east of the city. Rebecca hoped to find some surviving remnant of the military. Although Jacob doubted they'd find anything but crazies and corpses, he kept his opinions to himself. This morning was all about conflict avoidance.

Problems circled like hungry vultures, but they could wait. Simple thoughts occupied him as he drove. For a little while, he'd enjoy being a random guy on a lonely stretch of highway, letting his mind wander. There was something very few people knew about Jacob, a bit of his internal life he preferred not to share. Jacob Freeman—respected attorney, devoted father, and loving husband—harbored an appreciation for beautiful women that bordered on mysticism. For him, beauty possessed an intrinsic value apart from any other qualities a person might have or lack. He found nothing unusual about being enchanted by a woman he knew to be abhorrent in every way other than a magical mix of characteristics he interpreted as beautiful. This wasn't objectification, but rather prioritization. How many other people could one realistically appreciate in all their complexity? For him, that number could be counted on one hand with a finger or two to spare. He didn't have the time, patience, or energy for more. While he recognized each of his acquaintances' uniqueness, he chose to focus only on the aspects of them that interested him, which tended to be aesthetic.

Jacob understood this way of thinking would make him a bad person in the eyes of many, which didn't bother him. If he had anything resembling a core belief, it was this: Everyone is a bad person, some are just better at hiding it than others.

The ambulance rocked gently as he steered around a jackknifed tractor trailer. A skilled, almost certainly insane street artist had painted a picture of a nude (and evidently excited) Abraham Lincoln on its side. Jacob's mind returned to Judith in her black lacy dress. For all he knew, she was the most beautiful woman left in the world. He needed to be careful not to let that distract him from her proclivity for violence, the variety of lethal abilities at her command, and her raging hatred for him.

Pondering the dangers Judith had introduced into his life brought Jacob's thoughts around to Rebecca and the vastly different threats she presented. Rebecca...

Curiously, she had never sparked the same kind of desire in him those other women had. He had fallen for her in a different but no less powerful way. Her lack of pretense, her rock-solid stability, her honesty—as he entered a certain stage of life, she had captivated him in ways no one else ever had or ever would. Why had someone like her given him a second glance? Had she seen something in him she thought she could trust?

All his life, Jacob had been alone. Surrounded by friends and lovers, to be sure, but alone nonetheless. He hadn't realized that until he met Rebecca; he was so steeped in loneliness he didn't know anything else. She brushed all that aside like a curtain of smoke. "Are you done playing games? Do you want a real relationship or not? I won't wait long, so make up your mind." She had never said that, but it was the message he received. And he welcomed it. If only he could have proven equal to his ambition and become the man she deserved.

Planning dinner parties, devising an equitable system for changing diapers, supporting each other—he and Rebecca did such things remarkably well. They made a great team. And while physical attraction may have lost its edge over the years, the sex had always been good. No complaints there. Yet a need had gone unmet, and now that need had manifested as Darkness, leaving him a monster.

He had never fallen out of love with Rebecca, but love was a day-to-day thing built to endure. His feelings for Judith came from a different place, a world of fire. There was no day-to-day there; everything burned.

The air force base's main gate stood wide open, but its guard post was empty. Dangerous-looking equipment littered the roads and parking lots. The closest building to the entrance had been burned to the ground. Wreckage from at least two plane crashes spread across the airfield. With grim stoicism, Rebecca surveyed the scene, refusing to allow her disappointment to crush her.

After an exhausting and dispiriting day of searching for survivors, the Freeman family settled down in the base's infirmary. Or rather, Micah and Rebecca did. Before Jacob could enter, Rebecca slammed the door in his face and locked it. With a heavy sigh, he sat on the ground next to the ambulance and produced a flask of gin he had been saving for such an occasion.

Hours later, still sitting by the ambulance, he spun the now-empty flask in a telekinetic bubble over his head, catching the moonlight. He was about to crush it when he saw movement in the knee-high grass surrounding the infirmary. Jumping to his feet, he raised a shield around himself.

Judith stepped out of the shadows, wearing a camouflage miniskirt with black fishnets and a t-shirt that featured a grinning skull. Her considerable amount of hair was pulled back into a high ponytail. Tough Judith had returned, with sexy Judith in a supporting role.

"How's it going, boss?" she asked as his invisible shield disappeared.

"You look perky. Find a crazy to murder?"

"Just enjoying my two miles of freedom." She sat across from him with her legs folded under her. "Let's stay here a while. I want to check this place out. There's lots of cool stuff lying around."

She had a point. The base had been ransacked, but it looked like the work of crazies rather than looters. If crazies couldn't eat something, fuck it, or use it to fuel their obsession, they had no use for it. There might be all kinds of useful supplies looking for a good home. Rebecca wouldn't want to stay, but he could persuade her with the prospect of finding food and medicine. Rebecca was nothing if not practical. And Jacob had to admit, he could use a break from clearing roads of broken-down cars.

"I'll think about it," he said in the most noncommittal voice at his disposal.

"Oh, shut up. Decide already. I need to put an outfit together before it gets light out. Should I dress for driving or exploring?"

"Fine. We'll stay, but only for a day or two."

"You're the boss." She served the words up with a thick glaze of contempt.

"Hey, Judith."

"Yeah?"

"Do you know how to fly an airplane?"

"What?"

"I want to steal a fighter jet. Wouldn't it be fun to fly one of those things around?"

She stared at him as though he were the most disgusting creature to ever disgrace the earth with its presence and he had just pissed on her shoe.

"Or maybe a bomber?" Jacob mused. "There's a guy back in Cincinnati I'd like to bomb."

"Hey, Jacob."

"Yeah?"

"You're a fucking moron."

He laughed; it was a full, heartfelt laugh. It had been a long time since he'd had one of those.

The base turned out to be a goldmine. There were weapons, spare parts for the trucks, food, clothes, medical supplies, and much more. There were even vehicles (with keys!) if anyone wanted to upgrade. Jacob toyed with the idea of setting up a permanent home there, but he worried the group was still too close to the fanatics in Cincinnati. Besides, Rebecca would never agree to stay long-term. She still believed there was a civilization to find out there.

The two demons took turns guarding Micah and Rebecca while the other went out to scavenge. Before long, an impressive pile of loot formed next to the ambulance. Jacob had assumed most of it would go in Judith's truck because the thing was huge; but when the time came to pack everything up, she said she'd only take the "good clothes" and a few curiosities she had found. No food, medicine, guns, or anything else.

Exasperated, Jacob insisted on knowing what she kept in her truck that was so much more important than the supplies they'd spent all day gathering. After several minutes of threats and abuse, Judith begrudgingly opened the back of her truck. Racks of clothes and piles of fabric lined its interior walls. A large table with a grid-patterned cutting mat dominated the center. Clear plastic bins stuffed with thread, needles, scissors, and other sewing supplies were stowed underneath.

"You can't be serious," Jacob said.

"Fuck you! I won't ditch my fashion stuff." Her words crackled with hysteria. The knives reappeared in her hands. "You can't make me! I'll chain myself to the truck. I'll—"

"Settle down. Your contract doesn't oblige you to follow orders, an oversight on my part. I'm not going to fight you over this. Keep your dress-up collection."

He knew he shouldn't have reminded Judith of that flaw in the contract, but it was easier than telling the truth. They'd haul around a truckload of useless crap because Jacob couldn't bring himself to take it from her. He had already taken too much.

"You'll find room for some guns though," he said. "Two for each person, children included. Put them in the cab if there's no room in back. You aren't using the passenger seat, are you?"

For a fleeting moment, a half-second if that, he glimpsed something in Judith he hadn't thought her capable of: gratitude.

That night, Jacob once again found himself alone outside the infirmary. There was a real possibility every day from then on would end with Rebecca slamming a door in his face. Nursing a beer, he leaned against the ambulance and tossed around the idea of smoking cigarettes for the first time in his life. Why not? It would give him something to do while everyone was avoiding him.

"We need to talk," Judith said from somewhere off to his left, then she abruptly materialized six inches in front of him.

Jacob took a startled step away from her, almost tripping over his own feet. In a minor miracle of telekinesis-eye coordination, he caught his beer bottle midair as it dropped from his hand. Fortunately, none spilled on the clean khakis and black t-shirt he had found earlier that day, an outfit he was rather pleased with.

"Careful," he said. "What if I had fallen? Hurting me violates your contract."

"Sorry," Judith replied in a bright chirp that told him she was anything but.

"What do you want? I'm busy."

"Getting drunk?"

"And what if I am, kitten?" he asked, his nighttime voice's derisive tone coloring his words.

Judith's eyes ignited, their fire brighter than the moonlight. From out of nowhere, a knife appeared in her right hand. "Don't call me kitten."

"Whoa... Calm down. No more nicknames, got it. You're so cute and cuddly though, just like a kitten."

He kept his eyes on Judith's knife. She relaxed her grip and it vanished. So, she could summon her weapons at will. Interesting. It would be difficult, if not impossible, to disarm her. He made a mental note and filed it away.

"We need to talk," Judith said again, growing impatient.

"Okay, what's on your mind?" Jacob drained his beer and pulled a half-bottle of Irish whiskey from underneath the ambulance.

"Why am I here?"

"The meaning of it all? I didn't peg you for the philosophical type, but I'm game. Where to begin? The ancient Greeks thought—"

Both knives appeared in her hands. "One more word and I'll stab you in the fucking mouth. I don't care if I get sick. It would be worth it."

"Suit yourself," Jacob said. "But don't blame me when you come down with a serious case of existential angst."

"Why are you making me follow you around? It can't be that horseshit you fed me back at the doctor's office. Where are we going?"

Jacob didn't respond. Would knowing he didn't have a plan make his captive more dangerous or less?

"Tell me!" Judith yelled after waiting a few seconds, her voice hot and shrill. "You already got what you wanted. You don't need to lie anymore, right?"

"Your contract speaks for itself. Stay close. Don't hurt us. Do what you can to keep us safe."

"Why? Who are you people?" Judith's eyes flared red. She lunged forward and shoved Jacob hard, knocking him into the side of the ambulance. They both froze. Would that break her promise? It didn't.

She turned away and started pacing, her tail thrashing. "This would make sense if you made me clean your truck or give you blowjobs every night, but I'm just here. Why? What are you going to do to me?"

Jacob took a long swig of whiskey; he didn't have enough energy for this conversation. "Listen, Judith, we don't treat you like a slave because we aren't the kind of people who'd do that."

"I'm not stupid," she spat. "Nice people don't grow horns."

She was right. What he had done to Judith, the places his thoughts drifted when he let his mind wander, the visions he had experienced on the bridge—none of it was nice. He put on a good show of decency, but at his core, where others had a soul, lie a hungry void. Jacob wasn't nice. He never had been.

"You don't trust me," he said. "That's smart. People used to pay good money for me to weave webs of lies so intricate you wouldn't know where to start looking for truth. Like some kind of wizard of words, I worked my magic and truth didn't exist anymore, only words. After that, it was easy to bring people around to whatever I wanted to pass off as truth."

He fell silent for a moment, gazing off into space. Had there really been a world like that, a place of laws and regulations? And all of it so easily corrupted by interpretation, the whole system a sham. Had people really filed into the courtroom to have their lives ruined or redeemed? Then filed back out again, accepting the proceedings as though the judge's black robes imparted some sort of mystical authority?

"Anyway," he said, "lying is second nature for me. Hell, it might be my only nature. You'd be a fool to trust me. But I'm not lying to you now. Like you said, I have no reason to. There's no secret plan. All I expect of you is what's in your contract."

"Bullshit."

Jacob downed a swig of whiskey and stood leaning against the ambulance, relaxed despite everything. Overhead, the moon neared its zenith, a pale disc against solid black, casting just enough light to generate shadows. He had spent a lot of time studying the moon these last few months and knew its path like the pattern of his own breathing. How long had it been since he had talked freely to anyone without worrying about judgement and consequences?

"I should have made you promise to go away and never bother us again," he said. "That would have made sense and been an easier contract to draw up. I didn't though. I wish I had a simple explanation for why, but I don't."

"How about a complicated one then?"

"Fine, I'll take a stab at it. You have to promise to listen though. No interrupting. No violence."

"I'm not promising shit," Judith said, "but I'll listen."

Jacob told her everything. His transformation and the deal he had struck with Darkness, meeting the Ghoul, the woman in the river, the faceless fanatic—all of it. He told her he remembered the old world as vividly as the new. Its ways of thinking, its fears, its morality clung to him as the smell of smoke lingers in clothes. He told her of his fears and weaknesses, although letting her of all people in on such secrets couldn't be smart. He even showed her the corruption at his core, the place where Darkness and humanity mixed. Someone had to see it. Someone had to understand.

Silence, crackling with tension, filled the space between them when he finished.

"That's messed up," Judith said at last, still digesting the story. "You got lonely, so you kidnapped me to listen to your crying and bitching?"

"Well, there's more to it than—"

"And I'm supposed to play bodyguard, because you pissed off some über demon?"

The questions kept coming, but she wasn't interested in his explanations. Before long, he gave up on fielding them and settled in for a verbal flogging, which was what he got. At least Judith had paid attention to his story. Once the words stopped, leaving only her fiery glare, he said, "It's all so pathetic, I know. I never claimed to be a hero."

The anger faded from her eyes. She sat on the ground and slumped against the ambulance. Jacob joined her. Side by side, they gazed up at the sky. The night was quiet and still.

Minutes passed.

Judith spoke first, her voice small, her eyes fixed on her hands fidgeting in her lap. "What you did to me, doesn't it feel wrong even to you?"

A tired smile added years to Jacob's face. "There aren't any rules here. You know that."

"Yeah, I get it. I fucked up. But this is...unnatural. Know what I mean?"

He shrugged. "Everything's like that for me."

With a look of mournful resignation, Judith stood and walked away.

The next morning, the Freemans found Judith waiting for them outside the infirmary. She wore a white, knee-length sundress embroidered with tiny red flowers. Braided pigtails draped over her narrow shoulders. She almost certainly intended the look to be ironic; breezy, rustic charm didn't suit her. Any objective observer would have noted her features were too hard and sharp to pull it off, her body too wiry, her complexion too bloodless.

Far from an objective observer, Jacob stared at her in dumbstruck wonder. Judith as a wolf in the clothing of a doe-eyed innocent—the image affected him like magic. He couldn't say whether his fascination was in spite of or because of the ironic purity of her outfit, and he didn't care.

Realizing he was gawking in a way that violated the bounds of propriety, he averted his eyes, hoping no one had noticed. Everyone had. Always observant, Rebecca scowled at him, no doubt making all sorts of unfortunate connections and assumptions. Micah cast confused looks from one adult to the next. Judith beamed a roguish grin.

Surprisingly, Jacob found he didn't much care what any of them thought. A light, carefree happiness lifted him above the mire of their judgments. For the first time in a long time, he didn't feel like he was performing a role. He was what he was.

Judith had heard his story with nothing edited or omitted, and she understood. She might not have been entirely sympathetic—she had directed a fair amount of scorn his way—but she understood. When she looked at him, she didn't see a freak or a monster, just some asshole who had tricked her. This horrifying new universe made sense to her; it was the natural way of things. Someday, he'd like to feel as comfortable with the world and his place in it. He belonged here too, after all.

And here Judith was, despite everything, greeting the new day with a razorblade smile and sarcastic sunshine. She knew how to have fun, and Jacob wanted to learn. He boldly reaffixed his eyes on her. Why shouldn't he? He was a horned demon in a world gone to hell. He'd look at whatever he pleased.

Jacob decided to spend the day with Micah. She seemed the safest choice if he wanted to delay the consequences of his behavior that morning, which he most certainly did. They were in the officers' lounge, ostensibly searching for food. Jacob, however, harbored hopes of finding some decent liquor.

Micah folded her wings against her bare back and crawled into a floor-level cabinet. A few days before, her new limbs had sprouted thin needles of a fingernail-like material. Just that morning, white fuzz had blossomed from the spikes. Feathers.

She would be beautiful. Jacob didn't care to delve any deeper into what might be happening to his daughter. Micah plus wings and that was all. She wouldn't become a demon. How could she? She didn't have Darkness—something else maybe, but not Darkness. Judith had sensed that. And the Ghoul had seen it right away. She was different.

"Dad?" Micah called from inside the cabinet.

"Yeah?"

"Why does Judith change her clothes all the time?"

"Maybe she likes to dress how she feels, and her feelings change a lot."

"I think she's pretty."

"I bet she'd be happy to know that. You should tell her." A secret jolt of joy shot through Jacob as he imagined Micah trying to tell Judith anything. The poor demon still acted as though Micah suffered from a deadly, highly contagious disease.

"She doesn't like me," Micah said.

"She's just nervous. Give her some time."

"Is it because I could hurt her?"

"Hurt her?" Jacob asked.

"Yeah. My skin tingles a little when she gets close. She's like you. We can't touch."

That answered one question. Judith was off the hook for Micah-reaction testing. More evidence that Darkness hurt Micah and she hurt it, which meant she couldn't be a demon. But what had caused her to grow wings?

She scrambled out of the cabinet. "Hey, Dad, do you think Judith would make me a shirt? Like her tail clothes, but for wings. I mean, I don't really need one. It's just you guys here and it never gets cold. Mom keeps trying to make shirts for me and messing them up though. It's stressing her out. I even tried to make a no-more-shirts rule one time."

"How'd that go?"

"She yelled at me before I finished saying the rule."

Jacob laughed. "I'm not surprised. Your mom doesn't like to be told what to do."

Micah giggled. Her messy blonde hair, which hung down in her face, caught the daylight and turned to gold.

An eruption of heated shouting outside where they had left the ambulance disrupted the conversation. Jacob and Micah ran out of the officers' lounge to find Rebecca and Judith standing toe to toe in the parking lot, both bristling with anger. Judith snarled, her eyes blazing. The color in Rebecca's face had drained, leaving it a stony white.

Micah ran to her mother, wings spread as though she'd fly there if she could. "Mom! Stop it!" Judith hopped back a step, recoiling from the girl.

"She was sneaking up on you," Rebecca said. "I caught her climbing into a window."

"Rebecca," Jacob began in his most calming voice.

"Shut up." Her words slashed at him like a knife. "Why is she even here?"

"I've got everything under control," he said. "She won't hurt us. It's like I told you—"

"You told me a bunch of crap! Every word that comes out of your mouth is crap. Nothing you say means anything. What you've *done* is put us in danger so you can ogle a monster wearing the skin of a slutty girl."

A curtain of cool fell over Judith, wiping her anger away. The focus of the drama had shifted, giving her a chance to disengage. And seeing Jacob ripped into by his wife had done wonders for her temperament. She enjoyed that immensely. "Jacob," she said, trying to emulate the measured tones he used during the daylight hours. "Your pet norm pulled my tail. That's *not* okay. I'll let it go this time, but you need to keep her under control."

Everything played out in slow motion. Rebecca, her face a mask of rage, shoved Micah aside and lunged at Judith. The hunting knife shot out before her. Jacob's mind locked up like a set of misaligned gears. Not happening, none of this was happening. Then, at the critical moment, when Rebecca's blade should have met flesh, she stumbled through empty space.

From behind the group, Judith's voice rang out. "Hey!" Everyone spun around to find her standing on top of the ambulance with her hands on her hips. The weird light washed over her bare shoulders and lit her blood-red braids as though they were sprinkled with ruby dust. "Somebody tell that bitch to leave me alone. This isn't fun."

"What the hell, Rebecca?" Jacob yelled. Judith was his responsibility. If she hurt anyone, he had no one to blame but himself. Still, what had Rebecca been thinking? She never lost control like that.

Sitting at a table in the officers' lounge, Rebecca poured herself another shot of bourbon. She rarely drank liquor, but she was now. "I had to know if it worked," she said.

"If what worked?"

"Your deal with her."

"Are you telling me you planned that?" Jacob asked. "It was a test?"

She shrugged. "More or less."

"For fuck's sake..." He sat down hard on a chair across from Rebecca. Her whiskey bottle rose into the air and floated to his waiting hand. He took a long swig.

"Don't look at me like that," Rebecca said and snatched her bottle back. "What kind of idiot would trust a magical promise to keep her child safe? I needed to make sure it worked."

"And are you satisfied?" Jacob asked. "Can we never do that again?"

"No, I'm not satisfied! Your contract worked this time. Congratulations, Mr. Lawyer Man. I saw fear in her eyes when I touched her. But what happens when she finds a loophole? You think you're so goddamn clever. This isn't a game, Jacob. The second she gets a chance, she'll kill us all."

"Which is why you shouldn't provoke her. You're lucky she didn't slit your throat, consequences be damned. She's not exactly a champion of impulse control."

Rebecca took another drink, her eyes blurry and unfocused. "And what about you? How's your impulse control holding up?"

"What's that supposed to mean?"

"You know exactly what I mean, you bastard."

"Rebecca—"

"I see how you look at her. And if you think she doesn't see it too, you're crazier than I thought. What'll happen when she figures out how to use that against you?"

"You're drunk."

"What do you care?" Rebecca took a defiant gulp from her glass. "Why'd you bring us this far if you were just going to throw us away as soon as some shiny object caught your attention? You should have left us to the crazies back home."

Heat rose in Jacob, burning the words from his mind. His face flushed.

"Micah's growing wings!" Rebecca shouted. "And what are we doing about it? Finding help? Looking for a cure? No! We're screwing around in Dayton while you try to get that thing into bed."

"Enough!" Jacob's eyes were as hard as steel.

Rebecca slammed her glass on the table. "It's her or us! If we aren't on the road tomorrow without her, Micah and I are setting off on our own."

Later that night, well after dark, Jacob slipped into a large storage room in the officers' lounge. His horns glowed in the moonlight trickling through the room's only window. Without a sound, he crept to Rebecca's cot across the room from where Micah slept. He kneeled beside his wife, his face inches from hers.

She lay rigid, glaring up at him, her eyes a blizzard of hostility.

"Rebecca, I don't know how this will end. It's dark and there's no path. You and Micah deserve better."

"Send her away. Rework your deal and let her go."

"I can't."

"Then I don't have anything more to say to you."

"Rebecca," Jacob whispered. Her name hung between them like an unfinished prayer. "I promise not to hurt you." He leaned down and pressed his lips to her forehead. Magic filled the room.

A Table for Two

Jacob sat alone in the officers' lounge, simmering in a toxic brew of misery, loneliness, and tequila. A single candle tenuously lit the area around his table. Light and dark played a game as the flame shifted and swayed, driven by imperceptible forces.

Somewhere a door opened. The candlelight fluttered madly, almost going out. Judith stepped from the shadows and sauntered to his table. "Rough day, boss?" she asked, a Cheshire-cat grin smeared across her face.

"You could say that."

She moved the candle aside and, with a nimble hop, took its place on the table. Her long legs stretched out before Jacob, coyly crossed at the ankles. She still wore the sundress from that morning. Twin braids of sleek hair flowed over her shoulders like blood swirled with ink, one resting on each breast. In the indistinct, otherworldly candlelight, she made a different impression than earlier. That morning's playful charm had ripened into the relaxed allure of a steamy summer night. Under the thin cotton of her dress, she was alive with a slow, languid sensuality.

Darkness flowed between them, humming, purring. Jacob looked into Judith's eyes. He had been thinking about her, there was no point in hiding it.

"So..." she began. "You look like a man who's got something to say. Don't be shy. Let's hear it."

"Okay. How about you tell me why you were threatening my wife?"

Her eyes flashed red with a surge of anger. "*She* pulled *my* tail! If it weren't for your stupid curse, she'd be bite-sized Becky bits right now."

"How about you keep your tail away from her? And don't call her that."

"Call her what? Bite-sized?"

"No," he said. "The other part."

"Becky? Why not?"

"Just don't." Jacob took another swig of tequila. He wished the B-word hadn't come up. His accidental promise still bothered him. "Speaking of this morning's drama," he continued. "Your account of what happened is missing a few key details, like *why* Rebecca pulled your tail. Were you spying on me?"

"Maybe," Judith replied indignantly.

"Anything specific you hoped to learn?"

"I wanted to find out if what you told me was true. It's kind of hard to believe. Somebody like us wandering around with a real family, protecting them just because." She scanned his face, searching for additional clues. "You guys act like one of those families on the story discs though. That weird girl is your kid. You're all dopey for her. And the bitchy norm is your wife. Why else would you let her talk to you like she does?"

"Very perceptive."

Jacob found it increasingly difficult to focus on what had happened that morning. So many things about the here and now were clamoring for his attention: the elegant lines of Judith's neck, the taut cords of muscle in her arms, her lips, the smell of fresh linen. A shade of Darkness he had been trying to ignore stirred in him. Shadows danced across her svelte form. Her skin glowed in the warm light. So close, she was so close.

Words failed him, and words were what he needed most. In conversation, he had a chance. But sitting here like this, with nothing but Darkness between them, he was lost. If anything happened—no, he couldn't give Judith that kind of leverage.

Thankfully, Judith seemed more interested in chatting than seduction. Clearly, the woman didn't know how to press an advantage. "Tell me about the old world," she said. "Did it look like it does on story discs?"

"You really don't remember?"

"Quick flashes, but they're all messed up and scrambled. I see myself, but I don't know what I'm doing or why."

"Tell me something you remember. Maybe I can fill in the context."

"Hey! You're supposed to be telling *me* stories." Judith shot him a look of mock anger.

"Later," Jacob said. "I want to know about you." He took another drink from his bottle and offered it to her, but she ignored the gesture.

"Sure, I can talk a while. I get to ask a quick question first though. How old is that wing-girl thing? I mean, how old was she when she was a regular girl?"

Jacob hesitated. Talking about Micah with a demon made him uncomfortable. "Ten. Why?"

"In one of my memories, I look kind of like her. Not blonde and glowing, but the same size. I think I was a little older than ten though. Somewhere between there and whenever you get boobs. I don't have many kid memories, so it's special."

"Tell me," Jacob said, easing into his chair, enjoying the soft, warm sensation of alcohol seeping into each cell in his body.

"It was the first time somebody kissed me."

"Let me guess," Jacob interrupted. "You saw an especially succulent boy walking down the street. Unable to resist, you dragged him to your lair and—"

"Do you want to hear the story or not?" she snapped. Her anger was less playful this time.

"Sorry. That was my Darkness talking. And most of a bottle of tequila."

"It sounded like an asshole talking to me. Anyway, there's not much to tell. It was just a kiss. I can't remember the boy's name or anything."

"How'd it go?" Jacob asked. "Embarrassing? Exciting?"

Judith's eyes briefly lit up. "Exciting. We were alone in a dark place—a closet, I think—giggling. Then everything changed...like time slowed down. Know what I mean? The rest of the world wasn't real anymore. We could do anything we wanted, anything at all." She paused, a wistful, faraway expression replacing her usually intense focus. "My heart was pumping so hard, I thought it would explode. It was fun."

"Cute," Jacob said. The word came out as a question. He had assumed Judith's human memories would consist of nothing but trauma inflicted and trauma received. How else do you explain what she became? "Just curious, why did you share that memory? There's not much context for me to add."

Judith shrugged. "I think about that girl in the closet sometimes. I know she's me, but how? I can't figure it out."

"I know exactly what you mean."

Silence settled between them. That wasn't good, not if Jacob wanted to avoid doing anything stupid. Perhaps a little too hastily, he asked, "So, you don't remember having a boyfriend or anything like that?"

"There were other kisses with other boys, but I don't remember details. One time, some lady who was as old as my dad kissed me. Not like a mom though. More like the boys kissed me. She flicked out her tongue and licked my lip afterward. That freaked me out. Weird stuff like that didn't happen often though, maybe just that one time. I feel like most of the romance stuff I did was pretty fun, nothing special."

Jacob sighed, half in relief and half in disappointment. As intriguing as it would have been to get Judith talking about her more advanced sexual exploits, it wouldn't have been conducive to keeping things platonic. He could revisit the topic with her some other night, after he had more firmly established the power dynamics between them.

"Oh! I've got another one," Judith said. "There's none of that mushy stuff you're perving over, but it's a good story."

Apparently, she was more perceptive than he had given her credit for. Under normal circumstances, an accusation of "perving" would have been mortifying; but these circumstances were far from normal. What did he have to be ashamed of relative to a violent, possibly evil, psychopath whose only moral grounding was fashion?

"I'm a man of varied interests," Jacob said.

"Okay," Judith began. "I like this one, because I remember who some of the people are. It happened at my cousin's house. I'm pretty sure his name was Dickhead. No, wait... It was Barry. Anyway, he was an asshole, like you but stupider and fat. In this memory, we were both teenagers.

"Barry's family lived in a huge house with a pool in the back. Not the shitty above-ground kind, either; this was a real pool, like the one in the park. Some kind of party was going on, which is the only reason me and my dad were there. Barry's family didn't like us being around all their fancy shit, so we only went to their house when some big family thing happened.

"I was in the pool, lying on one of those blow-up raft things. The sky was super bright and really hot, like a huge light bulb. I was having a good time until my cousin's girlfriend started giving me shit. She looked like a… What are those things that look like giant pigs but float around in gross water and get eaten by crocodiles?"

"Hippopotamuses?"

"Yeah! A hippopotamus stuffed into a skanky bikini, that was her. She walked up to the edge of the pool and yelled, 'Oh my God! There's a skeleton in the water! Somebody call the police!' That pissed me off, but I ignored her.

"Then my cousin started yelling at me. He was all like, 'Get your scrawny ass off my raft. We want it.' When stuff like that happened, I used to sing a song to get people to fuck off."

In a bright and surprisingly melodious voice, Judith sang the tune to "Mary Had a Little Lamb," but with lyrics very much her own.

Fuck off, asshole. Fuck fuck off.

Fuck fuck off.

Fuck fuck off.

Fuck off, asshole. Fuck fuck off.

Fuck off and die, asshole.

"I sang that really loud. Barry didn't like it, so he splashed me from the side of the pool. I was just about to take things to the next level, but I saw my dad watching. He'd have gotten pissed if I got in a fight at his brother's prissy party, so I went to get some food instead. But before I left, I pulled the little plug out of the raft."

A sputtering laugh jumped up from Jacob's belly, nearly making him spit tequila all over Judith. "That dick cousin of yours deserved it."

Judith's smile relaxed, her devilish air softened by humor. "Oh, it gets better. Later, I was coming out of the bathroom upstairs when I ran into Barry. He blocked the hallway and went off on me about popping his raft. I told him to pretend he had a brain and check the plug. That really got him going. He said I was a crazy bitch and called me white trash. What's that mean? I forget."

"It isn't nice," Jacob replied.

"No shit? Anyway, Barry's face got all pink and splotchy from yelling. I didn't mean to laugh, but it was so funny. Then he pushed me. Big mistake. I busted out a karate move my dad had taught me so I wouldn't get raped or some shit. You're supposed to sweep the other person's feet out from under them with your leg, but I did it higher, right to the side of the knee. Barry dropped to the floor, bawling like a baby. Found out later I'd torn one of his tendons or something."

Jacob took a long swig of tequila. That story lined up better with his expectations. "What happened next? Did your dad get mad?"

"I can't remember. It would have been worth it though, to see that asshole lying there crying for his mommy."

"If you say so." Jacob put another dent in his bottle.

He wondered how he'd have reacted if a teenaged Micah had done that. Naturally, he'd worry about a lawsuit, but how do you handle something like that as a dad? Micah wouldn't do anything like that though, not ever. Was that thanks to her personality, his parenting skills, or the fact that no one would think to call someone from a family like hers white trash. Her background didn't matter now though. What kind of person would she become in a world like this? No social norms or expectations to mold her, nothing secure or safe, violence all around. Her elite education and refined manners wouldn't do her much good anymore.

Lost in thoughts of her own, Judith issued a wistful sigh. "You don't see things like that on the story discs."

"Do you mean movies?" Jacob asked. "I bet there was a market for swimsuit-clad, teenage girl violence, but it would have been more of a YouTube thing."

Judith cocked her head. "YouTube?"

"Not important. Movies were entertainment. Most people wanted stories where the good guys won, and all the nasty parts ended up meaning something in the end."

"What a bunch of horseshit," Judith said. "That reminds me of the Oz disc with all the singing and that annoying dog. I loved the parts where the girl and her friends were running through spooky forests, finding magic flowers, and fighting monkeys. But then it got stupid after the witch melted. Nothing but a bunch of crying, giving out prizes, and watching the dog fuck things up. And why'd they have to make the giant head be some old guy behind a curtain? That pissed me off."

"Then it all turned out to be a dream," Jacob said. "That's the part I hated."

He sat back in his chair, sipped at his bottle, and watched Judith. She bit the corner of her lower lip, her brow knitted. Her tail had swung up to rest on the table beside her. It looked so silky and smooth; maybe she wouldn't mind if he...

Jacob dug his fingernails into the palms of his hands. Not a safe place for his mind to wander. "You wanted to ask me about the old world," he said, hoping he sounded more relaxed than he felt. "Go for it."

"Huh?" It took Judith a second to reengage. "Oh, right. I've got a bunch of questions." She absent-mindedly stroked her tail. "I forget what eating was like. What happened to people who didn't do that?"

"They got hungry."

"Yeah, I saw that on the discs. But what if they *still* didn't eat?"

"Their bodies got thinner and thinner until they were nothing but skin and bones. Then they died. Starving to death, we called it."

"They didn't show that on any of the discs," Judith said.

"It was one of those things we preferred not to think about."

"Hey, Jacob?" Her tone grew dark. "Let's say I locked Becky up in a little room and sat there watching her starve to death. Would that count as hurting her?"

He didn't know the answer, which alarmed him. "Yes," he said unequivocally. "And even if it didn't, I'd stop you."

Judith pouted. "You're no fun."

"Any other questions? Preferably ones that don't involve murdering my family?"

"Yeah. One of my favorite discs is about this lady who goes somewhere called New York and becomes a famous fashion designer. Do you think I ever did that?"

"Do you remember putting on fashion shows or anything like that?"

"No," she replied glumly.

"You're a bit young to be a well-known designer. What are you? Twenty-two? Twenty-three?"

She shrugged, as if he had asked her the circumference of the moon.

"You don't know. Sorry." Jacob sighed and sunk into his chair. "It's more likely you were studying fashion in college or just interested in it. I guess you could have been a model."

"It doesn't matter now, huh?" Judith asked. "Everything I remember, all the stuff on the story discs, it's all gone. My dad, my asshole cousin, that boy I kissed in the closet."

"I suppose so."

A relaxed silence settled between the two demons. Judith was lovely, bathed in a soft blur of candlelight and drunken haze. Despite the panic-inducing directions in which her thoughts sometimes flowed and Jacob's suspicions as to why she was talking to him at all that night, he was enjoying her company. Would every night be like this from now on? That wouldn't be so bad.

Minutes slipped by as he reassured himself the things he had done were the right things to do. Everything would work out.

He glanced at his companion, hoping to find her in a state of comfortable resignation, all thoughts of murder by starvation set aside. Instead, he met the hot, hungry glare of a wolf that had cornered its prey. Her eyes were flames. Her mouth twisted into a dark grin.

"Do you want to hear a more interesting story?" Judith asked, her voice a purr. "This one's from the new world, so I remember every detail."

Jacob guzzled about four shots of tequila. "Why not? It's just us demons." He listened to himself respond with the helpless horror of watching a car skid off the road and over a cliff. If Judith had set a trap, he had just blundered into it.

"Cool," she said. "I think you'll like this one." Faster than his eyes could track, she snatched the tequila bottle from him and returned to her lounging position on top of the table. After taking a long drink, she began.

"A while back, this crazy guy started coming around my house after dark. He was super scared of me, but he kept coming every night anyway. And guess what he did, like non-stop?"

Jacob shrugged.

"Jerk off!" She let loose a peel of ringing laughter. "Fucking crazies. He'd get as close to me as he could without freaking out, take off this gross parka he always wore, and go to town. Each night he got a little bit closer. It took him a while, but the crazy motherfucker finally made it all the way up onto my porch with me sitting close enough to smell him.

"One night he took off his parka like usual but didn't start wanking. Instead, he grabbed his cock and waved it at me like I'd be happy to see it. Then he spouted off a bunch of crazy shit. I thought about scaring him away, but decided it would be more fun to mess with him."

Judith leaned back on the table, propping herself up with her hands. She regarded Jacob with a fiendishly cute look of expectation. If he wanted more, he'd need to ask for it.

"What did you do?"

"I asked him if he wanted to play a game. The rules were easy. I'd take off one piece of my clothes for each time he let me cut him. Just little cuts, I promised. He could quit anytime he wanted, but we'd have to start over the next time."

"Did he understand?" Jacob asked, borrowing the tequila bottle she had stolen.

"Enough to nod and plop his ugly ass down on my porch. Didn't even think about it for a second. You know how they are—there's no stopping them from doing their thing, and this guy's thing was me.

"I had a lot of clothes on, so the game lasted a while. That crazy guy didn't complain once, not even when I only took off an earring or one stocking. And when the cuts came, he barely flinched. He was totally into it.

"The price for my petticoat—like I said, I was wearing a *lot* of clothes—was a shallow cut all the way around his cock. Not much more than a scratch, but enough to bleed. I wanted to see if he'd stop rubbing it. He didn't.

"By the time I took off my bra, he was covered in blood and his face was white as a bone. He still had a goofy grin though, like he was having the time of his life. I leaned over and squeezed my boobs together." Judith paused to demonstrate this maneuver over her dress. "That was free; I didn't take a cut for that. Then he passed out. A few minutes later he died, that stupid smile still on his face."

Jacob's breath came rough and erratic. He couldn't speak.

"I guess I won," Judith said. "I still had my special tail-girl undies on and a choker I'd been saving for the grand finale. The choker was supposed to be the last tease before letting him see all the goodies. Too bad he ran out of blood."

"Holy shit," Jacob murmured.

"What's the matter, boss? You don't look too good." Judith's golden eyes sparkled.

As if emerging from a dream, Jacob realized he had scooted his chair so close the edge of the table dug into his chest. His hand was resting not two inches from Judith's thigh. Under the table, an insistent erection argued the case for closing that gap.

"You know," Judith said in a hushed, intimate way. "We could play games too. On nights like this, when there's nothing to do…" She rolled a lithe shoulder, allowing the strap of her sundress to slip off.

Jacob's heart quickened, pounding out a rhythm that made a lie of all things civil and tame. His body ached with desire, Darkness churning through him. He took the bottle from Judith's hands and drank deeply.

"Just kidding," she chirped. "That's not in my contract."

She hopped off the table and trotted away. Lost in the swish of her tail and the sway of her hips, Jacob watched her disappear into the night.

A Diversion

The Freemans spent another day in Dayton, arguing about where to go next. Rebecca, who still refused to call the old world *old*, wanted to search for outposts of civilization. Preferring to avoid big cities and the demons who likely lived in them, Jacob thought they should find an isolated farmhouse in Iowa or maybe Kansas and settle down.

After wasting most of the daylight hours locked in indecision, the group put the matter to a vote. Micah abstained, so Judith was unexpectedly asked to decide. Horrified by how boring Jacob's plan sounded, she voted against him. Although Rebecca normally wouldn't have stood for giving Judith a vote, she begrudgingly accepted the demon's support. It was decided. The next morning, they'd leave for a city of Rebecca's choosing.

Jacob and Judith spent their final night at the air force base watching "story discs" on a portable DVD player she had in her truck. There was a little flirting on his part and some malicious teasing on hers, but mostly they watched movies. As she had mentioned, one of her favorites was a rags-to-riches story about a young woman from the Midwest who makes it big as a fashion designer. Other movies Judith liked included a sentimental story about a girl who adopts a stray cat that turns out to have magic powers, a series of slasher movies about successive groups of teenagers getting slaughtered at the same campground, and a period drama about a wealthy family in Victorian London which she watched solely for the costumes.

Early the next morning, everyone gathered by the ambulance so Rebecca could go over her plan. Jacob, who was struggling to rein in certain

Darkness-charged impulses, had a hard time staying focused. Rebecca wore faded jeans with a tight tank top, and her hair was pulled back in a tight ponytail—a look he recognized as her "cleaning clothes." It had always attracted his attention, often leading to sweet rewards should he help with the chores. Not that Rebecca had ever made the connection between her attire, his contributions to housework, and sex. It had been a while since he'd felt stirrings of longing for his wife, several days at least. She looked good now though.

Judith sat next to him, cleaning her fingernails with one of her disappearing blades and pretending to yawn. She wore an air force flight suit modified to accommodate her tail. Her great mass of deep red hair, streaked with black, was set in side-buns that stuck out from her head like stubby horns. Jacob couldn't help but notice the zipper on the front of her flight suit was a bit lower than regulation.

"Jacob!" Rebecca snapped. "I asked you a question."

"Sorry. I was—"

She cut him off with a glare sharper than any knife. "I know what you were doing. I swear to God, it's like talking to a bunch of teenagers."

"Hey!" Micah protested. "I was paying attention. You said we're going to Columbus because it's a state capital and there's a big college there with lots of scientists and stuff. Then you asked Dad if he put gas in the ambulance."

"Exactly," Rebecca said. "We're leaving in ten minutes. And so help me God, if the ambulance doesn't have a full tank, someone is going to wish they were never born."

***

Corpses in various states of decay littered the streets of Columbus, some arranged into installation pieces by artistically inclined crazies. Burned buildings peppered every neighborhood, and a few scenes of mass destruction made quite the impression on the band of explorers, but as was the case in Cincinnati and Dayton, the agents of chaos had preferred human casualties over attacking the city itself.

Oddly, dozens of crazies were wandering around Ohio State University in broad daylight. Although not exactly hanging out, they seemed to tolerate one another's presence. It was a more relaxed, easygoing bunch of psychopaths than either Jacob or Judith had yet encountered. Unfortunately, these crazies didn't appreciate moving vehicles disturbing their peace. They had a habit of rushing the trucks on sight. Once they saw a demon at the wheel, they fled. Still, a bunch of screaming lunatics charging the group made for a slow and nerve-wracking tour of the ruins.

Jacob devised a plan. After much cajoling, a few threats, and a considerable amount of bribery, he convinced Judith to lock her truck in a garage and ride on top of the ambulance. She'd be a living scarecrow, except not for birds. It didn't take long for her to get over her grumbling and find a way to have some fun. The ambulance became a mobile horror show, with her dancing around, making spooky noises, teleporting from one side to the other, and lunging at any crazies who ventured too close.

In high spirits, she called, "Come up here!"

Jacob stuck his head out the driver's side window. "Me?"

"No, the bitchy norm. Yeah, you, dipshit."

"Why does she call me a norm?" Rebecca asked from the passenger seat.

"It was something I made up when I was negotiating with her," Jacob said quietly enough that Judith couldn't hear. "She's latched onto it. Do you want to know what you were before that?"

"I'll bite. What?"

"A Muggle. I guess she was a Harry Potter fan."

"That makes me a half-blood!" Micah chimed in through the small window that connected the back of the ambulance to the cab.

"I don't think it works that way," Jacob said. "You're more like a Crumple-Horned Snorkack."

"Those aren't even real!"

"Sure they are. I've got one in the back of my ambulance."

Micah fell away from the window, seized by a fit of laughter. A smile cracked Rebecca's dour expression.

With a deafening boom, Judith stomped on the ambulance's roof. "Come on! I want to try something!"

Rebecca shot Jacob a disapproving scowl. "I'll drive. She'll punch a hole in the roof if you don't go."

What Judith wanted to see was how crazies would react to two demons, and it was a sight to behold. Any crazy unfortunate enough to cross their path flew to previously unimagined heights of hysteria. Many went into a stunned paralysis, frozen mid-cower like Medusa's victims. More than a few pissed themselves. One ran around in a circle, squawking. Another stood in the middle of the road pulling at her hair, her mouth an *O* of shock. (To Rebecca's great annoyance, she had to drive around that one.) A girl around Micah's age tried to dig a hole to hide in with her bare hands. An old man, who must have been the craziest of the crazies, cackled then threw a rock at Judith.

Both Judith and Jacob found the double-demon effect hilarious. Giving up all pretense of looking for refugee centers or whatever else Rebecca imagined might be out there, the demons dreamed up new ways to torment the local crazy population, bouncing increasingly elaborate ideas off each other. Judith even let Jacob levitate her for a few of their pranks. For an hour, maybe more, they set aside the thorny knot of their young relationship and let their demonic natures play. They were children—demented children with the power of gods.

The scaled-down caravan came to rest for the night in a fenced-in parking lot behind a suburban police station. It wasn't the most defensible position in the world, although the fence would keep crazies from wandering in. Judith said she'd patrol the fence, which set Jacob's mind at ease, but first she wanted to search the station. She hoped to find a police officer's uniform reasonably close to her size.

Rebecca and Jacob sat on the ground next to the ambulance, trying to figure out how to load the guns they had collected at the air force base. Working with the guns was one of the few activities they did together. Rebecca wanted to learn how to shoot but didn't know the first thing about firearms. Jacob didn't either, but he was willing to risk taking a bullet or two if a gun accidentally went off while he fooled around with it. For that one task, they made a good team.

Moody and sour-faced, Micah emerged from the ambulance and squatted next to her parents. She poked at a pistol with a stick she had found somewhere.

"Micah, please don't do that," Rebecca said in her Mom voice.

Micah didn't stop. She had a bad habit of provoking conflict when she was in a foul mood. Usually guns weren't involved, but these were strange times.

"Micah! I said stop."

Feigning a sudden interest in pistols, Jacob snatched Micah's plaything off the ground and inspected it.

"Hey!" she yelled.

He pawed at the gun, hoping it wasn't loaded. "Aren't you supposed to be in the ambulance?"

Micah traced designs on the ground with her stick, refusing to make eye contact. "I want to go back to Dayton."

Jacob set the pistol aside, taking care not to leave it pointed at anyone. "Why, M?"

"Is traveling scary, honey?" Rebecca asked. "Did the base feel safer?"

"No. I want to travel, but in the other direction. We're going the wrong way."

Her parents exchanged looks of low-grade concern. "What do you mean?" asked Jacob.

"I saw the Golden City again. I was resting while you guys drove, and it popped into my head. It's the other way."

Another exchange of looks—this time suppressed parental panic.

"Micah," Rebecca said. "That's not a real place."

"It is! There are people there right now, lots of them."

Rebecca's face tensed. Jacob saw the mechanisms of her brain whirling into high gear as they did when Rebecca the doctor and Rebecca the parent merged. Micah was about to be whisked away for some frantic and thoroughly unproductive diagnostics.

Taking custody of the parental voice, he spoke before his wife could shut the conversation down. "But isn't that a bad place?"

"Yeah. I don't want to go *to* the Golden City, just *toward* it."

"I don't understand."

"The Light showed me another city too, the Dark City. That's the worst place in the world for me. It showed me *home*, Dad. There's something in Cincinnati that's poisonous to me."

A feminine smile appeared in Jacob's mind. Cold breath prickled his skin. The woman in the river. What had the Ghoul said that night? *We're at the center of the world.*

Micah went on. "I didn't believe it at first. The Light lies. But since we're farther from home now, I know it's true. I can feel the Dark City reaching for me. I can feel the Golden City too. It's that way." She pointed west.

Rebecca was about to smack someone, and Jacob had a good idea who that might be. Preempting any attempts to derail his line of questioning, he asked, "If both cities are dangerous, shouldn't we go away from them? North maybe?"

"No! Something else is up there. We need to find a place between the Dark City and the Golden City. We'll all be safe there. At least I think we will."

Rebecca wasn't happy, not at all. Her expression carried an indictment. Jacob stood accused of pandering to the delusions of a mentally ill child. Only the habit of not fighting in front of Micah kept her from passing sentence then and there.

"Well," Jacob said. "Indianapolis is west of here and it's a state capital like Columbus. How about we search for refugee centers there? Hoosiers are tough; maybe they're better at this whole apocalypse thing than we are."

The fig leaf of rationality he had placed over Micah's unapologetically irrational request wouldn't satisfy Rebecca, but it might buy him time to think of a way to discuss this in a less confrontational way. Rational or not, the strains of fear in his daughter's voice were real. If going west made her feel better, they'd go west. There was no reason not to.

Micah's face blossomed into a smile that shone like the sun used to. "Do you mean it?"

"Of course. We'll leave first thing in the morning."

She jumped to her feet. For a moment, it seemed as though she might fling herself into Jacob's arms. Instead, she hugged herself, beaming light and warmth to the whole world.

Judith was late for the next morning's logistics meeting.

Eager to get moving, Micah extended and contracted her wings in an anxious, fidgety way. Their fuzz-tipped spikes had grown into a fluffy coating of white pre-feathers. She had crossed that line in avian development when a chick transforms from an ugly, fetal-alien thing into an adorable puffball.

Rebecca sat cross-legged on the ground next to Micah, aggressively flipping through the pages of a thick book. At daybreak, she had ambushed Jacob to beat him over the head with the fact that their daughter weighed forty-five pounds. Naturally, this was his fault. Everything was. He didn't try hard enough to find help; he didn't worry enough; he didn't care. What did she expect him to do? As far as he could tell, Micah was strong and healthy. She certainly didn't look like she weighted forty-five pounds. No one understood the changes she was going through. In his mind, interfering might do more harm than good.

The addition of Judith to the group had thrown fuel onto the flames of Rebecca's suspicions around his motivations. She couldn't see the benefits of having another demon around, even after Judith had helped them get the ambulance through the horde of crazies at Ohio State. Of course,

Judith had also distracted him into spending half the day playing super villain instead of searching for a refugee center.

Where the hell was Judith anyway? They should have been wrapping the meeting up by now.

Just then, she arrived, looking harried and dressed in a swimsuit. It was a no-frills, black one-piece outfitted with a snug tail sleeve, as it would be impossible for her to wear such a thing without one. In a huff, Judith plopped down on folded legs, her tail mercilessly flogging the ground beside her.

Jacob gave her a moment to address her tardiness, bad mood, or wardrobe choice, but she just sat there scowling at everyone. "Judith," he prodded. "If you don't mind my asking, why are you wearing a swimsuit?"

"I *do* mind," she said, and returned to her sulking.

To everyone's surprise, Micah broke the uncomfortable silence. "Um... Do you mind if I ask?"

Judith recoiled. For a second, it seemed she might run away. Instead, something wholly unexpected happened. Her stunned expression curved into a mischievous grin. "I don't mind at all, Ms. Micah," she said brightly. "*You* can ask me anything you want."

Micah smiled, doubly pleased that Judith had spoken to her *and* she had found a way to interject herself into a logistics meeting.

"Okay! Why are you wearing a swimsuit?"

"I'm glad you asked! I actually wear this pretty often. You just don't see it unless you're a huge perv." She shot Jacob a pointed glance. "It's an undersuit. I wear it under short dresses or skirts, so I don't flash my ass whenever my tail moves."

Micah giggled. It was good to see she still had a ten-year-old's appreciation for butt-related humor, although Jacob would have preferred Judith use more age-appropriate language than "ass."

"But why's it a swimsuit?" Micah asked. "Don't you have underwear?"

"Nope, and I'll tell you why. It's the same reason you're running around with no shirt on all the time. A lot of clothes don't work with my body. I can't find many undies that fit over this thing." Judith made her tail do an undulating dance like a serpent emerging from a snake charmer's basket.

Micah's laughter quickened, threatening to grow into a full-blown giggling fit.

Judith continued, clearly enjoying the opportunity to discuss the fine points of tailoring for people with tails. "Swimsuits are stretchy and strong. The top part helps hold up the bottom part. If you're careful, you can cut a tail hole into it without messing up how it fits. There's other stuff I can use, but swimsuits are easy to find."

"But wait, why are you wearing your swimsuit-underwear-suit thing now?" Micah asked. "Where's your other clothes?"

After putting on a show of exaggerated unease, Judith replied, "That's a *scary* story. Are you sure you want to hear it?"

Fading giggles found new life. "Yeah!"

"Okay," Judith said in a ghost-stories-around-the-campfire voice. She gulped dramatically. "I was walking past the ambulance, wearing one of those cute tennis dresses with a pleated skirt, when I came face-to-face with..."

"What?" Micah begged.

"*A pigeon!*"

Judith's audience of one went wild. It had been a long time since Micah had had so much fun.

"The ugly shit was on top of the ambulance," she continued. "Sitting there staring at me with its creepy, red eyes. Then it opened its beak and in this whispery voice said, '*Coo...coo.*'"

Micah squealed, thrusting her arms forward and her wings out in an impressive display of alarm.

"I wanted to run, but my legs wouldn't move. And then it...it..." Judith buried her face in her hands and pretended to sob. "I can't go on. It's *too* horrible."

"Tell me!"

"It dove right at me! I thought for sure it would peck out my eyeballs, but it did something worse. *Much* worse."

Micah leaned forward, eyes wide. "What?"

"It *pooped* on me!"

Micah surrendered a fit of laughter that nearly knocked her over.

"Stupid bird got me right on the chest," continued Judith over the noisy reaction to her story. "I was so mad I ripped the dress off and threw it at the pigeon. Then I looked like a dumbass standing there in a swimsuit with socks and shoes on, which pissed me off all over again.

"That, Micah, is why I'm at your parents' boring-ass meeting barefoot and wearing a swimsuit."

"You're good with kids," Jacob said after Micah and Rebecca had gotten into the ambulance.

"I can be nice if I like somebody."

"Oh? Since when do you like my daughter?"

"Since a little while ago. She laughed at my story, and I liked that. I think it'll be more fun to talk to her than cut her. With most people you meet, it's the other way around."

"That simple, is it?" Jacob asked, a steely edge to his voice.

"Yep."

"But you *can't* cut Micah; your contract doesn't allow it. Wouldn't you have killed her before you found out you liked her if it weren't for that?"

Judith shrugged again, already bored with the conversation. "Maybe. You win some, you lose some. Stabbing is always fun though, so it wouldn't have been a total loss either way."

"You know," Jacob said, heating the metal in his voice. "If for one second I thought you were endearing yourself to Micah as part of some half-assed plan to use her against me, your life would suddenly become very unpleasant."

"Not my style, boss. That kind of bullshit is your game."

"Just remember, nothing in our agreement precludes *me* from hurting *you*. Don't test me."

Judith laughed, her eyes flashing contempt. "Good luck with that! I could run around my two miles of freedom forever and you'd never catch me. You can't lay a finger on me unless I let you, which I won't."

A sliver of a smile cracked the shield of Jacob's expression. Despite everything that had happened to her, Judith still hadn't learned the perils of overconfidence.

Home Away from Home

Having gotten such a late start, the group decided to only go as far west as Dayton. They had just left the air force base the day before, so it seemed a safe place to spend the night. As the light faded from the sky, the trucks backed into an empty hangar and parked side by side. Jacob slid the airplane-size doors shut behind them.

After his family had settled into the ambulance and Judith had run off to sort through a pile of shoes she had looted from a store in Columbus, Jacob found a spot near the ambulance to work on his telekinetic tricks. It was impossible to know if practice would help him grow stronger, but it couldn't hurt to try. One day he might be able to crush crazies by the dozen while sipping a dry martini safe and sound inside an impregnable fortress of mind magic.

As things were, however, he felt somewhat restricted. He could only have two telekinetic objects active at a time with a finite amount of energy to distribute between them. Managing it all was a balancing act; too much strain on one of his objects or not enough energy allotted and things fell apart. Barriers broke; projectiles failed to do any damage; force waves hit like a gust of wind instead of a speeding train.

Quiet and still, the hangar was a world apart from the madness that consumed the city streets after dark. Judith had put her shoes away and was on guard duty, an activity that mostly involved flipping through fashion magazines by flashlight in the cab of her truck. Jacob, who had snuck to the officers' lounge for a bottle of vermouth and a jar of olives, sat in front of the trucks, working on the martini part of his invisible fortress fantasy. He debated asking Judith if she wanted one.

In an instant, everything changed. A thunderous boom, like the world itself being violently knocked from its foundation, shattered the peace. White light ripped the hangar doors away like the claws of a great beast. Hell had unleashed its fury.

Jacob jumped to his feet, martini glass still in hand. A bullet whizzed over his head and demolished the ambulance's siren. Gunfire poured through the blown-out hangar doors. After quickly placing a telekinetic shield in front of the ambulance to protect those inside, he dashed through the gap between the group's vehicles and ducked behind Judith's truck. His barrier should hold if he stayed within thirty-six feet.

The screech of metal tearing into metal reverberated through the hangar as the exposed front of Judith's truck took a beating. Was she still in the cab? No, she could teleport out. Cautiously, Jacob peeked between the trucks. His heart lurched then seemed to stop. He couldn't breathe. An enormous, lumbering silhouette took shape in the field of light at the hangar entrance. Then another. And another.

"Shit," he muttered. Where was Judith? He had never clearly defined how the "Protect the Freemans" clause of her contract worked, but this would be a great time for it to kick in.

The figures entering the hangar grew more distinct as they got closer. Four monstrous blobs, about ten feet high and five feet wide, lurched toward the trucks. Their top halves resembled human-shaped balloon art—pinched at the joints and grotesquely inflated everywhere else. Tiny heads perched on top of their massive, puffed-out chests. At first glance, the creatures' bottom halves appeared to be unbroken masses of creeping flesh, like a snail's body, but there were legs, three extra-wide limbs set in a triangular configuration. Loose skin hung between them, squishing together in overlapping folds as the things moved. Backlit by floodlights blasting in from outside, it was hard to make out any more details.

With a thrust of his arm, Jacob projected a narrow force wave through the space between the trucks, then fanned it out to about ten feet wide once it had passed the ambulance's shield. If he was lucky, he'd hit at least two of the things.

The wave broke on the first creature like the ocean meeting a cliff. The monster's wide profile, extra leg, and sheer size made it incredibly stable. All four of the things responded to Jacob's attack by retracting their heads into their bodies. Although they probably couldn't see anymore, they moved forward.

He launched a more focused attack. An invisible cannonball struck the lead monster in the chest with a fleshy slap and a pitiful groan. It sounded more like an old man struggling to get out of bed than something hit by magical artillery. A nasty bruise, two feet across at least, bloomed on the creature's body. It paused, wobbling a bit, then resumed its plodding advance.

Time for Plan B. Jacob had been working on a defensive countermeasure in case of an attack on their camp. It was a crude weapon designed to be effective against humans, not three-legged giants. Still, it would have to do. He reached out with his mind for a cardboard box full of smashed liquor bottles stashed under the ambulance, and it slid across the floor to him. After scooping a watermelon-size ball of shrapnel from the box in a telekinetic bubble, he looked around the corner of the truck and fired.

Each shard of glass became a tiny missile, propelled with devastating force and accuracy. They tore into the nearest creature, transforming its torso into a Pollock painting done in blood and skin.

That got a reaction. The wounded monster's ridiculous head popped out to release a shrill scream. Jacob must have hit on a glitch in the thing's human-turtle hybrid wiring. It could take a hit, but a flurry of cuts sent it into a panic. Before its turtle brain could reassert itself, he launched a follow-up attack. A well-placed telekinetic punch knocked off the creature's head as neatly as a golfer driving a ball from its tee.

The thing's hulking body shambled forward, then stood still, as if it couldn't believe it had just lost its central nervous system. Blood sputtered from where the head had been in a thin stream more like a squirt gun than the gush of gore generally associated with decapitation. Finally, the monster collapsed into a pile of pasty flesh.

One down, three to go. Jacob reached for his shrapnel box to prepare another attack, but it wasn't there. The box lay on its side a few feet from where it had been, its contents strewn across the floor. He must have been in too much of a hurry last time and knocked it over as he swung his ammunition into position.

Thoughts whirling, his heart went into a frenzy. What now? Why hadn't he made more boxes? Those creatures were getting closer by the second. Gunfire from outside converged on the gap between the ambulance and Judith's truck. Bullets ricocheted wildly, ripping holes in the vulnerable metal along the side of the ambulance.

Escape. That was the only option. He had to get his family out of the hangar. There was an emergency exit in the back, behind the trucks. But someone must be watching it, snipers probably. Maybe if he went out first and—

A piercing scream rang through the hangar. At the risk of getting shot in the face, Jacob looked around the corner of the truck. One of the monsters was slapping at itself with clumsy, overstuffed hands. A second later, its head popped out. Much closer now, Jacob could see it had a face. Warped, stretched, and disfigured, yet undeniably human. That thing used to be a person.

From behind the monster, a black-and-white blur dashed around its towering form and scampered up its front as easily as a squirrel runs up a tree. The terrified creature was leaking blood everywhere. Coming to a stop behind its shrieking head, the blur became Judith. Her face a study in bloodlust, she straddled the thing's neck like a little girl on her dad's shoulders, a blade gleaming in each hand. With a move too fast to register, she plunged her weapons into its eye sockets.

As it fell, a tsunami of gunfire pounded its corpse, targeting Judith, but she had disappeared.

Jacob raised a barrier behind the next monster to shield it from snipers. He was on defense now. It would be up to Judith to do the killing. With two telekinetic objects, including the barrier in front of the ambulance, his power had reached its limit.

"Next one!" he cried into the bright bedlam of the hangar.

Another monster screamed, flailed, and fell. As quickly as he could, Jacob redeployed the shield.

"Last one!"

Once again, the grisly sequence replayed, only this time, Judith added a touch of demonic flair by ripping the creature's head off with her bare hands.

Jacob's partner in slaughter materialized beside him. "Thanks for the assist," she said, panting. "Getting shot would have messed up my flow."

A crooked smile peeked out from her blood-splattered face. Covered in monster muck, eyes ablaze, she was their guardian angel of Darkness. Jacob wanted to kiss her. He very well might have if something else hadn't demanded his attention.

Unsure how to proceed without their tank-like front line, the snipers stopped shooting. In the relative quiet, a new sound asserted itself from the hanger's rear. Scratching and chittering, it sounded like a horde of angry raccoons trying to get through the emergency exit behind the trucks. As Jacob turned around, the exit door flew off its hinges with a loud pop and a heavy clatter.

The noise exploded into a cacophony of clicking, scraping, chirping, and hooting. A moment later, a wave of bouncing, leaping, rolling balls of muscle and grey-white skin poured into the hangar through the emergency exit. Each one was the size of a toddler except reshaped into something like a hairless chimpanzee. Their round, infant-like heads served as platforms for freakishly large mouths lined with jagged teeth. The rest of their faces were a hodgepodge of mismatched eyes, malformed noses, and asymmetrical ears. Only their mouths were consistently well-designed. Mouths were the entire point of those things.

Monkey-baby monsters, a swarm of them, raced toward Jacob and Judith. Most moved on all fours, propelled by muscular legs, but a few ran on two legs with a swaying, simian gait, screeching and waving their clawed hands over their heads. Within seconds, they closed the distance between the door and the trucks. A wave of them leaped at the stunned demons.

Jacob's paralysis broke just in time. A telekinetic blast sent dozens of the things flying backward, flinging them into the hangar's back wall. Before those hit the ground, more were airborne on his right. He wasn't fast enough to fight that way, with them coming from every direction. Backing up against the rear of Judith's truck, he raised an invisible wall around himself. Within seconds, countless bundles of claws and teeth crowded around his barrier, clamoring to get in.

Fresh gunfire erupted. The snipers were trying to hit Judith, who had left cover and was madly dashing around the hangar with one of the monkey-babies attached to her shoulder. A dozen more of the things trailed her as others leaped around her. She spun, twirled, and slashed at them, but there were too many.

Inside Jacob's telekinetic barrier, the chaos around him played out in silence. With the helpless passion of a sports fan screaming at their TV, he urged Judith on. "Teleport! Why don't you teleport?" He wanted to use his power to grab her, but it didn't work through any kind of obstruction, even one of his own creation. Dropping the barrier low enough to act would let the monsters jump over it. Could he levitate himself? No. He had tried that before; telekinesis didn't work on his own body.

An idea struck him. Platforms, like he had used in the magic shows he had staged for Micah back home. Just one, about six feet in the air, and he'd be able to climb onto the roof of Judith's truck. Scrambling up a six-foot ledge would have been difficult, if not impossible, for old-world Jacob, but now it would be easy.

His shield in front of the ambulance would have to come down while he climbed; a barrier to protect him plus a platform equaled two telekinetic objects in play. There was no other way. He'd need to work fast.

The ambulance's barrier dissolved, and a platform took shape over his head. He pulled himself up. For a second, he appeared to be floating—a poor man's levitation—before he scrambled onto the truck's roof. The platform and barrier behind the truck disappeared, and a fresh shield popped up at his new position on top.

Before shielding the ambulance, he needed to do one more thing. Across a roiling sea of monsters, Judith fought a losing battle to keep the little fuckers off her. Two had affixed themselves to her back and another was chewing on her thigh. Thankfully, she was still on her feet and within range of his power. He swept her up into an invisible bubble.

A demon floating through the air in full view of the hangar doors made a compelling target for the snipers, which kept them from shooting at the unshielded ambulance. Bullets soundlessly bounced off Judith's protective bubble, raining down on the frenzy of monsters below. Jacob set her down behind his barrier on top of the truck. Two dead monkey-babies flopped to the ground as he removed her bubble. A third still clung to her upper back.

"Get it off me!" she screamed, flailing at the thing. "Get it off!"

Jacob threw a new barrier in front of the ambulance, then grabbed the monkey-baby on her back and squeezed. Its spine broke with a crack. After a final spastic movement, the monster went limp in his hand. For a second, as its life slipped away, he felt something other than writhing muscle and rubbery skin: Darkness. It was weak, not much more than a spark, but unmistakable. The dead thing in his hand had possessed a Darkness of its own.

Judith sat in front of him, dazed and exhausted. Blood flowed freely from her mangled back and leg. She wore the blank expression of severe shock.

"Are you all right?" Jacob asked, crouching beside her.

No response.

"Judith?"

Just as he reached the edge of panic, her eyes snapped back into focus. Her face ignited into a blazing inferno of rage. "Does it look like I'm all right?"

Gunfire pummeled the shield, while yapping monsters swarmed around the truck. Something had to be done, and Jacob couldn't do it alone.

"We can get out of this," he said. "But not while I'm getting shot at. It's taking everything I've got to keep these shields up. We need to find cover or make it safe enough up here for me to work."

Judith's back was a mess of blood, shredded skin, and exposed bone as though the business end of a food processor had attacked her. She wouldn't be able to walk, much less fight.

"You can take those little shits out?" she asked.

"Yes. But not while I'm blocking bullets."

"I'll see what's outside. Maybe I can do something about the guns."

"But you—" Jacob began.

Judith waved him off. "Shut up and give me a minute."

With a flick of her wrist, she produced a long, thin spike made of the same metal as her blades. Fine, impossibly intricate etchings wrapped around the shaft. It looked like a sacred artifact from some forgotten culture that was also a knitting needle. Judith reached behind her back and ran the needle's tip over her wounds. Then she jabbed it three inches into her own body.

Jacob gasped. "What the—"

"Quiet," she hissed. "You're going to make me mess up."

A second needle appeared in her other hand. Craning her neck to see behind her, she executed a series of complex maneuvers, part sewing and part surgery. The needles danced across her back, weaving in and out of the gore. Ravaged skin regenerated. Torn muscles mended. By the time she flicked her wrists again to dismiss the needles, the tattered remains of her t-shirt revealed a painfully raw but serviceable back.

"Ready," she said. "Things are still kind of fucked up inside, but I'll fix that later."

"Wh-what did you do?"

"The world's full of mysteries, old man." Judith stretched to test her handiwork. "Now you just sit here sucking up bullets. I'll handle the fun stuff." She got to her feet, dashed to the edge of the truck's roof, and disappeared.

Suck up bullets was exactly what Jacob did, not that he could do much else pinned down with his powers maxed out. A minute or two later, all hell broke loose outside the hangar. The gunfire became frantic and confused. People screamed. A truck engine roared to life then sped off into the distance. Everything went quiet.

Judith reappeared at Jacob's side. "Took care of the gun guys, boss. There were ten of them. Six are dead. The others got away. Oh, and one of those giant freaks is wandering around in the road by the big lights."

Jacob took down his bullet shield and moved to the side of the truck. With a downward thrust of his hands, he squashed a group of monkey-babies like foul grapes. The others didn't run. The revolting things had only one thought in their heads: *Kill.* In a frenzied rush to get at the truck, the survivors filled the spaces where the dead had fallen. They were meat pouring into a grinder.

When Jacob knocked on the back of the ambulance, Micah flew out the door, her wings spread. She rushed to her father, barely restraining herself from leaping into his arms. Still inside, Rebecca slumped onto a bench, buried her face in her hands, and wept.

Doing his best to clear a path through hundreds of monkey-baby corpses, he led his family out of the hangar. Rebecca carried Micah to allow the girl to close her eyes as they made their way through the carnage. They found a quiet place along the side of the building where Rebecca and Micah could... Do what? There would be no recovery from this. Trapped, gunfire all around, no idea what was happening, all that death outside—there wasn't a way to leave that behind.

Judith stayed with them, her needles stitching up a few wounds she hadn't had time to attend to before, while Jacob went back into the hangar to assess the situation.

The ambulance had suffered heavy damage. Two of its tires were destroyed and a pool of fluid seeped out from under it, gasoline by the smell of it. They were lucky the damned thing hadn't caught fire yet. Judith's truck, which hadn't been partially shielded like the ambulance, looked even worse. None of its tires had survived the onslaught, and countless bullet holes peppered its cab, guaranteeing the engine had taken a beating. A stream of oil flowed from under the truck to mingle with the gas leaking from the ambulance. Even if they had a mechanic in the group, which they didn't, there wasn't time to make repairs. The people who had attacked them might return any minute with reinforcements.

Driving away didn't seem wise anyway. Only a few roads led out of the air force base, all of which were excellent spots for an ambush. The group would have to set off on foot. Jacob handed out hiking packs he had stashed in the ambulance in case it ever broke down and gave the group fifteen minutes to grab whatever they could carry.

Despondent about leaving her clothes and tailoring supplies behind, Judith refused to cooperate. Jacob tried to talk sense into her, but it only made matters worse. Surprisingly, it was Micah who managed to calm her down. A dash of heartfelt empathy and a promise to help find even better clothes once they got to Indianapolis did the trick.

While the others got ready, Jacob walked around the hangar to make sure no one was sneaking up on them. Everything he saw led him to believe the enemy had bungled the attack. An explosive device that had been rigged to the back door, presumably to let the monkey-babies in, hadn't gone off. From the state of the door, it appeared someone had waded through the knee-high monsters clamoring to get in and manually knocked it down. In all likelihood, the plan had been to send the small monsters rushing in while he and Judith were still engaged with the big ones. The two demons wouldn't have stood a chance.

Jacob circled back to the front of the hangar. As Judith had said, a fifth giant was wandering around the enemy's abandoned spotlights. It didn't attack or even retract its head as he approached. Looking scared and confused, its disfigured face peeked at him from atop a mountain of flesh.

With a wave of his hand, the giant's head popped off. It felt like an act of mercy.

Micah's Rules for a Better World

When people fight to kill, they change. They aren't people anymore. No more wars, no killing.

A Dream

The usurper slips away. No matter. He has felt only the tip of one finger on the hand that will crush the life from him.

Interlude

I was all there was and all that could be, a universe complete, no beginning and no end.

In the waters of the Allegheny, the Mother of All touched me. It was but an echo of her glory, a shadow, but it changed everything. For the first time, I truly saw her creation, this world I had walked but never known. So many things I couldn't have imagined.

She touched me. *Me.* The concept was new. In a universe of "I," there is no "me." A sanctum formed to keep me from dissolving into everything else, to define me as Caleb.

Yet I exist. I take. I give. I destroy. Why? How does it all fit together?

This I know: all things flow from Mother, even the power I command. She is the source. She has revealed her truth to me. I alone am worthy.

Together, we will rid this world of her misbegotten children, purify it. We will form an unbroken, undiluted river of power flowing from her to me. She is the beginning and I am the end.

Chapter 7

Prelude

Life runs deeper than these bursts of consciousness we experience as lives. It's a primal thing—a great serpent racing through time. If you're lucky enough to grab it, you're in for quite a ride. For a while, you can dress it up and call it your own. You're a star, the center of your own universe.

But when your grip loosens, clarity cuts illusion away. In those desperate moments of grasping and clawing, you understand. The fluff and frill of identity falls away and the charging beast is all there is. Any life, even its most miserable manifestations, is precious beyond measure. Unless you've been there, hanging on by your fingernails, you don't know what you would do to keep from slipping into oblivion.

Exodus

"This isn't what I signed up for!" Judith screamed.

"The only thing you signed up for was getting out of that room. Anything else that happens is well within the scope of our contract."

"Fuck the contract!" She stepped forward, blades out. "Let me go. Do it now or—"

Sickness hit her like a punch to the gut. She doubled over and took a step back, her face a smear of pain and fury. Just a taste of the promise's full, debilitating potential.

Everyone's nerves were strung so tightly they were on the verge of losing their minds. Memories of the day before felt like visions from a different life in a different world. Monsters had attacked them, driven them from their camp, stripped them of most of their supplies. And it wasn't over: they were being hunted.

Shouts and the roar of engines had filled the night as the group escaped through a hole in the air force base's perimeter fence. Spears of light perforated the sky to the south as helicopters bore down on the base. (Helicopters? Who were these people?) For hours, the group had run, dodging between buildings and clusters of trees. Trucks rumbled past their hiding spots, scanning the roadside with spotlights. The ominous *whump-whump* of helicopter blades shook the night.

When Rebecca and Micah couldn't go any farther, the group took refuge in a diner several miles from the base. The place must have been run-down long before the world ended. It blended seamlessly into a ramshackle road, which in turn blended into a dilapidated neighborhood. The perfect place to hide, or so they hoped.

Outside, the sky shifted from inky black to a dull gray-green. It was hard to call such a tepid thing "dawn," but it signaled a new day, nonetheless. Decisions needed to be made.

Judith paced the length of the diner's counter, her eyes gleaming red in the meager light. With a spin too fast to see, she lashed out at a table. Condiment bottles and salt packets flew everywhere. "Fuck!" she shouted. "At least tell me who's trying to kill us. That über demon you pissed off?"

Jacob shrugged. "Probably."

"What do you mean, 'probably'? Does he have an army of norms and mutant freaks or doesn't he?"

"It's a definite yes on the norms. The mutants...maybe?"

Judith heaved a sigh. "You don't have a fucking clue what's going on, do you?"

"No, not really."

Not long after Judith had retreated to a back room to fume, Jacob settled on a plan. Hiding wasn't a great idea. This enemy didn't seem inclined to give up anytime soon, and they might very well have the manpower to search whole neighborhoods building by building. He needed to put as much distance between his family and their enemies as possible. With any luck, they'd be able to disappear into the industrial wasteland outside Dayton, then make their way out of town. Those bastards couldn't search the entire Midwest.

He'd let everyone rest during the day, then leave the diner as soon as it got dark. No one was in any shape for traveling and wouldn't be anytime soon. Besides, the helicopters might have a harder time spotting them at night. Crazies would be out, but two demons should suffice to keep them at bay.

When the time came, the four fugitives emerged from their hiding spot. They hesitated, standing on the edge of a vast and terrifying unknown. The thumping of helicopters echoed all around. Insane things howled and shrieked in the distance.

With a step forward, the night swallowed them.

The new world was a carnival of horror, and the streets of Dayton were no exception. A lunatic dressed in a tuxedo sat in a booth at a fast-food restaurant, dining on raw cat by candlelight. Outside a jewelry store, Jacob nearly tripped over a handbag full of severed hands. A burned-out police car with a charred corpse at the wheel blocked an intersection; the body's head had been replaced with that of a pig. Something resembling a six-foot-long cockroach scuttled into a house as the group walked through an otherwise quiet subdivision. Maybe it had been a demon, maybe something else.

Until then, Jacob had shielded his family from the worst of what the world had become. The basement, the ambulance, the medical center, the base—those places might not have been truly safe, but they offered shelter. The scary things had always been on the other side of a wall. Not anymore.

Stoic as ever, Rebecca took it all in stride. She had caught glimpses of the new world and must have guessed at the rest. But Micah—eyes wide with terror, she clung to her mother's arm and crept along as though the earth might swallow her at any moment. Jacob wanted to sweep her into his arms and let her hide her face in his chest, but if he so much as held her hand sickness would swoop down on them both like a hawk. Walking beside her, he opened his mouth to offer some small reassurance, but no words came. What could he say? The world was what it was.

The group made its way north, then west. Traveling under the cover of darkness proved more difficult than Jacob had anticipated. The further Micah's condition advanced, the quicker her energy drained at night. They hadn't gotten two miles before she slowed down. Another mile after that, and Rebecca needed to carry her like sleeping baby. Although Micah didn't weigh much, it didn't take long for the extra effort to exhaust Rebecca to the point that she needed to rest. Having only gone five miles, the group stopped in a small, ranch-style house surrounded by dozens of nearly identical houses.

While his family slept and Judith seethed like a caged tiger, Jacob formulated on a new plan. They'd set off at dawn, sticking to residential roads so they could duck into a house or under a tree if a helicopter got too close. When dark came, they'd find somewhere to hide. Repeat until the enemy gave up or spread themselves so thin the group could slip past them and leave town.

"What do you think?" he asked Judith after running the plan by her.

"I think you're a fucking moron."

"Not helpful."

"Okay, how about this? We find a car and get the fuck out of here."

Jacob shook his head. "Too risky. Do you hear those helicopters patrolling the streets? We'd be the only moving vehicle for miles around; they'd spot us for sure. We're more flexible on foot."

Judith scowled. "Why'd you ask what I think if you're just going to throw the stupid idea you already decided on back in my face?"

"Because you're a respected and valued member of this team," he said in the hollow tone of a corporate vice president addressing his underlings.

Failing to suppress an unprofessional smirk, he added, "I'd like to come across as open to new ideas. Is it working? Do you feel empowered?"

Before he knew what had happened, Judith lay at his feet, choking with sickness, blades in hand.

Day after day, the group snaked through Dayton's ruins, hoping to lose their pursuers in the labyrinth of abandoned streets. It was slow going, punctuated by frequent stops to rest and bouts of scurrying for cover when a helicopter came too close. No matter how far they went, what direction they headed, or how clever of a route Jacob chose, their enemy was always right behind them. The hunters floundered during the day, but every night, they converged on the group's location like a pack of wolves picking up a scent.

At first, Jacob suspected Judith had found a loophole in the section of her contract that dealt with indirect damage to him or his family and was tipping the enemy off. But she seemed as surprised about their mysterious tracking ability as anyone else. Besides, nothing indicated she was capable of scheming even if she stumbled upon an opportunity to do so. Deceit simply wasn't her style.

Thankfully, whatever the hunters did to zero in on their prey lacked precision. They seemed to have a general idea of where to search each night, but they still needed to search.

Jacob sat in an office at the center of a warehouse, a candle flickering on the desk in front of him. Once upon a time, the office had served as the nerve center of a bustling hive of activity—forklifts rushing through a maze of pallets and shelves, trucks rumbling at the loading docks, workers shouting to each other over the din. Now it was nothing, a darker-than-average spot in a very dark world.

"Dad?" Micah called from the corner where she lay in her sleeping bag.

"Yeah?"

"I'm scared."

A tired smile softened Jacob's expression. "Don't worry. I'm on guard duty. Get some rest."

"Can Judith sit by me?"

That was unexpected. The two of them had grown more comfortable around each other, but Jacob thought their relationship could best be described as mutually apprehensive.

"I don't know," he said. "Mom might not like that if she wakes up."

"Please?"

Judith, who was sewing by candlelight, put her project away and moved next to Micah.

"Is this okay, kid?" the demon asked.

"Better."

A dusty road stretched to the horizon, slicing through an endless expanse of cornfields. The sky was a sheet of steel, generating an oppressive heat but little light. Judith had pestered Jacob all morning about going on the offensive. Surely, two demons could take out a bunch of armed norms, helicopters or no helicopters. He refused. That must have been what the enemy wanted, to flush them out into the open. If that happened, things more dangerous than human soldiers were bound to show up. And somewhere out there, the faceless man waited to strike.

Although Jacob hated to admit it, Judith had been right all those days ago when she suggested they find a car and make a run for it. Back then, the dragnet around them had been less organized and plenty of cars had been available. Not anymore. Every motorized vehicle the group came across on these rural roads had been disabled as though a car-destroying storm had raged through the area. Evidently, the hunters went to great lengths to search the sparsely populated area for garages, parking lots, stretches of roads, anywhere they might find vehicles. They ripped out fuel lines, stole tires, punctured radiators, and did whatever else they could think of to limit their prey's mobility. So, the group walked, traveling by day when the enemy seemed less active.

The countryside west of Dayton proved more difficult to navigate than Jacob had imagined. Roads were scarce and enemy jeeps constantly patrolled the larger ones. That left a handful of rural routes without any buildings or even a grove of trees for miles at a stretch. If a helicopter flew by, the only thing to do was lie still under a blanket of weeds in one of the many overgrown soybean fields or duck into a cornfield.

Despite the calendar claiming it was January, the fields were still green. Someday, science might figure out if environmental changes had confused the plants or if whatever had given Jacob horns and Judith a tail had changed corn into evergreen, demon corn. And for that, the group was grateful. Living plants provided better cover than dried-up dead ones.

Finding places to rest for the night was a constant worry. Other than a smattering of towns, most little more than a handful of buildings clustered around a stop sign, there were few places to seek shelter without venturing perilously close to the heavily patrolled freeways. Isolated farmhouses presented the best options, but with nothing but hundreds of acres of fields around them, they made inviting targets for scrutiny from above.

Whump-whump-whump. An approaching helicopter ripped Jacob from his thoughts. Everyone dove into a cornfield alongside the road. Like a god-size hawk, the thing passed overhead, booming thunder. Micah clung to her mother, biting her lip to keep from crying. Judith crouched beside Jacob like a coiled spring.

The same scene played out three more times before the group came across a derelict barn where they could rest. Huddled around their packs, which were running alarmingly short on food for Rebecca and Micah, they watched daylight bleed from the sky. Soon, night would fall like an ax.

With so few roads to survey and barely any buildings to search, the hunters could cover huge swaths of land with relentless efficiency. Another brutal day passed, then another after that.

Just as Jacob reached the point of utter hopelessness, opportunity presented itself at last. Judith spotted a pickup truck rolled onto its side in the brush along a dirt road. Creeping vines had grown over it, concealing it somewhat. It hadn't been tampered with.

Using a combination of telekinetic and physical strength, the demons managed to get it on its wheels and pull it back onto the road. The keys were in the ignition, and it started on the first try.

Jacob had paid careful attention to the enemy's movements. Although it made sense to move while the hunters were spread out and mostly stationary during the day, one could argue for a bolder strategy. When the hunters received their mysterious update on their prey's location each night, there must be a period of logistical confusion as they redeployed. If the group fled at that exact time, taking advantage of the enemy being unaccustomed to a moving target, it might be possible to slip past them and make a run for it. As long as the group's vehicle held up, they could make it to Indianapolis before anyone figured out what had happened.

Jacob drove the pickup down a quarter-mile-long driveway to a farmhouse in the middle of a cornfield. After parking under a carport, he and the others went inside to wait. As soon as night fell, they'd pack into the truck and head west. He and Judith possessed excellent night vision; they should be able to make good time on the rural roads even without using headlights. They could gas up or switch cars in Indianapolis, then head farther west. If everything went their way, they'd be hundreds of miles away by dawn.

Into the Fields

Everything didn't go their way.

As soon as Jacob stepped out the front door of the farmhouse that night, he noticed movement near the pickup. A figure, barely visible in the moonlight, hopped and twirled in a free-form dance. It appeared to be a child or a young teen—a girl, Jacob thought, although he couldn't tell for sure. She wore the black combat fatigues of the enemy with a snug cap pulled over her head and dark camouflage paint on her face.

Micah gasped.

The stranger froze mid-arabesque, her eyes locked on the group staring at her in amazement. After righting her body, she came closer with a jaunty bounce to her step. No one knew what to do, so no one did anything. Not twenty feet away, the girl stopped, and her camouflaged face stretched into a broad grin. She bowed deeply with a theatrical flourish of her arm.

There was something in her hand, a remote control.

Click.

Jacob swept his arms over his head to raise a telekinetic dome over his group. Light flashed under the pickup, and then a fiery explosion lit up the night sky. Under the dome, it happened in silence, but the blast must have been heard for miles around. Flames engulfed the pickup, black towers of smoke billowing up from it.

The strange young saboteur darted to the edge of the cornfield with the effortless speed of a gazelle. Before disappearing into the black of night, she spun around and blew a kiss.

Jacob dropped his barrier. Beyond the roar of the fire, the sound of multiple helicopters approaching beat like mad drums. "Move!" he ordered.

The group plunged into the field. Long leaves of corn whipped their faces as they ran in single file along a rut between two rows. The plants were more than six feet high, making it impossible to see anything but dark sky above and leaves all around.

From the rear, one of the helicopters thundered past, its spotlight compressing the field's pools of darkness into razor-thin slits of shadow against searing white. Another helicopter approached from their left, while a third hovered somewhere in front of them. The cornstalks swayed as the group ran, marking their path to anyone observing from above. They might as well have been waving flags over their heads.

Jacob needed to see where they were going, so he fell back and signaled Judith to lead the others ahead. He climbed onto a telekinetic platform three feet in the air to peek over the top of the stalks. A helicopter hovered to their right, well beyond the range of his power. As he weighed the pros and cons of moving close enough to attack, something that looked like a dog but wasn't jumped out of the helicopter. Then another. And another.

He hopped off the platform and ran after Judith, who trailed behind Rebecca. "Wait!" he called. "There's—"

As she turned toward him, a hairless wolf-like creature burst through the swaying wall of cornstalks and knocked her to the ground. There was no sound, no warning. It was just there. The monster sank its teeth into Judith's shoulder and dragged her off into the dark sea of foliage.

Following a trail of broken stalks, Jacob tore through row after row of corn after her. A sick feeling rose in his gut, growing more intense each time he burst through a wall of leaves to find only more leaves. Judith couldn't be gone! He needed her.

Just as he realized he had left his family behind, he stumbled onto a dirt road that cut across the field. There, not twenty feet away, Judith fought a losing battle against two monstrous canine creatures. Relief washed over him—a strange reaction to finding a woman being mauled by hairless, oversized wolves, but relief nonetheless. Rebecca and Micah stepped out of the field and into an invisible dome of protective energy. Jacob rushed forward to help his partner.

One of the monsters had Judith pinned flat on her back with its paw on her shoulder. Her forearm pressed into its throat, shielding her face from its snapping jaws, but she couldn't get her hand in position to summon a blade. The second wolf jerked her other arm around like a chew toy. The things must have possessed incredible strength to keep her down. Built for speed, Judith wasn't as strong as Jacob, but she was more than strong enough to cast aside a couple ordinary dogs.

As he sprinted to her, he brought down a telekinetic hammer on the one yanking her arm. Its hindquarters crumpled into a useless mass of disconnected muscle and splintered bone. The creature released Judith and whipped its head toward him. It didn't cry out in pain or make any sound at all; the expression on its face was one of curiosity rather than fear or rage. Jacob grabbed the beast's head in invisible hands and squeezed, crushing it like a juicy melon. Judith summoned a dagger into her now-free hand and thrust it into the other monster's skull. A split second later, the wolf went limp and flopped down on top of her.

"Motherfucker!" she howled, flinging the dead thing away and springing to her feet.

The creature was roughly the size of a Great Dane, only heavier and more muscular. Its hairless skin had a faint yellow-white glow in the moonlight—a putrid color, like spoiled milk. There was something disturbingly human about it, as if a person had been melted down and poured into a dog-shaped mold. It resembled a werewolf, the kind that moved on four legs not two, but bald.

Jacob didn't have time to gawk. The fight had pulled him away from Rebecca and Micah; any farther and they might fall out of the thirty-six-foot range of his power, causing their shield to disappear. He grabbed Judith's arm and dragged her back to where he had left his family.

A half-dozen wolves circled Rebecca and Micah. Eerily calm, they observed their targets with clear, intelligent eyes. On the edge of the dirt road, a man spoke into a walkie-talkie. As Jacob approached, the enemy drew a pistol from a holster on his leg, but he never got a chance to fire. Judith appeared behind him and slit his throat.

The wolves around the barrier dome divided into teams. Three charged Judith. She leaped and dodged, moving more like a dancer than a fighter, blinking in and out of existence as she carved them up one by one. The remaining three came at Jacob in a tight V formation. That was a mistake. He swept them all up into an invisible bubble and hoisted them into the air. The bubble collapsed, compressing its squirming captives into a mess of mangled monster parts.

Jacob tossed the dead beasts into the field then dismissed his family's shield. "Follow me," he called to them. "Judith, stay behind us. Watch out for—"

Three more wolves shot out from the curtain of leaves behind Rebecca and Micah. Judith teleported into the path of the swiftest one and grabbed it by the hind leg as it raced past her. Jacob jerked his arm to raise an invisible wall in front of the other two. It was the quickest thing to do other than blindly cast a telekinetic wave, which might have hit his family. One of the wolves hit the barrier headfirst and collapsed in a concussed daze. The other jumped. Not expecting that, Jacob had made his wall wide but only as tall as his eye level.

The creature's paws hooked over the top edge of the barrier; the rest of its body swung down and smacked against what appeared to be empty space. For a second it hung. Then, pumping its hind legs, it scampered over. A bolt of telekinetic fury struck the ground with an impotent *whomp* where the wolf had landed, but it had bounded toward Rebecca, who stood in front of Micah as a last line of defense. It lowered its head and rammed her, sending her flailing into the cornfield.

Wings pinned back, arms raised to shield herself, Micah took a step back. The wolf barreled into her, slamming her small body to the ground. It put a heavy paw on her chest to pin her. Powerful jaws seized the arm she still held before her and wrenched it aside. Micah's scream cut through the night. The beast towered over her, fresh blood dripping from its teeth. Prey secured, it raised its head to deliver a killing blow.

Just as Jacob shot an invisible hand toward his daughter, a mass of muscle slammed into him from behind. The wolf that had run into his wall seconds ago had recovered. It drove him face-first into the ground and dug its teeth into the back of his neck. His line of sight broken, he cast a desperate glance to Judith, who was tangled up with the wolf she had caught. Although it was slicked with blood and missing a leg, it had her by the shoulder and wouldn't let go. She couldn't teleport.

A tortured scream came from where Rebecca had fallen. Drowning in despair, Jacob gave himself up to the monster on his back. If the Darkness that had taken him possessed a shred of pity, it would return his human body so the beast could kill him then and there.

Nothing happened. The sounds of Micah's life being ripped away didn't come. Instead, an inexplicably still-living child let out a miserable groan. Jacob pressed his hands to the ground and lifted both himself and the thing on his back to get a better view. The wolf crouching over Micah was looking around as though it had forgotten what it was supposed to do. Its fierce alertness had given way to confusion. Head cocked, it looked down at Micah like it wanted to ask her a question. Wisps of smoke wafted from its nose. As it turned an inquisitive gaze to its belly, the skin there shriveled and crisped. The wolf was burning from the inside out.

Finally untangling herself, Judith teleported to Micah's side. With a vicious swipe, she slashed the monster's throat. Greasy smoke poured from the wound.

There wasn't time to think about what had just happened. Helicopters beat the air nearby. Hidden enemies rustled the corn on both sides of the dirt road. Judith dispatched the wolf on Jacob's back while Rebecca gathered Micah into her arms, folding her crumpled wings. Blood flowing freely from the wolf bites on his neck, Jacob shepherded his group back into the field.

They ran through a blur of whipping leaves. Shouts all around punctuated by gunshots. Helicopters droned in the distance. A minute later, Rebecca grabbed Jacob's arm, begging him to stop. She couldn't take another step. Judith materialized in front of him, anxiously shifting her weight from foot to foot. They needed a plan, and he didn't have one.

Red streaks shot into the sky from nearby, bloody gashes in the black. Flares. Engines popped to life only a few rows of corn away. Something else, something that rumbled and roared in deeper tones, entered the sonic landscape. A trap! They had run directly into an ambush. Unsure which direction—if any—was safe, the group froze.

Boom!

A sound like thunder but channeled sounded in the distance. Something shrieked through the air overhead and struck the ground behind the group with an earth-shaking thud. A patch of field exploded, knocking everyone to the ground, soil and shredded cornstalks raining down on them.

Boom!

Jacob raised a telekinetic barrier a split second before the second shot hit. It was a near miss, striking the ground not ten feet away. The force of it popped his shield like a soap bubble. Rebecca crouched on the ground, her body over Micah. Another invisible dome replaced the one that had been destroyed, but would it be enough?

Judith appeared next to Jacob, her eyes glowing red as though a fire burned inside her skull. "Whatever did that is dead, fucking dead."

"Wait, what are you—"

"Keep the girl safe," she said, then vanished.

Jacob scooped the others up in a bubble. Touching his telekinetic objects made Micah sick, but it couldn't be helped. With his family in tow, he chose a direction at random and ran as fast as his demon body would go.

Boom!

The place they had stood five seconds before became a crater.

Something sped through the field to Jacob's left, behind a ribbed veil of cornstalks, rattling as it bounced over the rough terrain. After pulling ahead of him, it turned sharply and cut into his path. An ATV. The driver came to a skidding stop, raised a pistol, and fired.

A bullet tore into Jacob's chest, sending him staggering backward. His hands instinctively flew to his heart. Instead of a life-ending wound, they found a torn t-shirt, a splash of blood, and a bruise that hurt like hell. A flood of disjointed profanity gushed from his mouth.

Wolves charged past the ATV, ghostly in the moonlight, loping toward him. With a sweep of his arm, the corn flattened in a thirty-six-foot arc. The ATV blocking his path tumbled away through the field. A wolf with at least one broken leg struggled to get to its feet on the edge of the arc. Another lay crushed near where the ATV had been.

Something moved to Jacob's left. Another telekinetic wave smashed into more wolves preparing to flank him. Footsteps behind him. One hand still pressed to his wounded chest, he spun around just in time to shield himself as two men opened fire with assault rifles. The bubble he carried his family in whipped out like the business end of a giant flail and struck the enemy soldiers with the force of a truck.

Too many noises to track, Jacob backed up until he felt Rebecca and Micah's bubble behind him, then opened a gap so he could join them inside. After resealing it, he put everything he had into making it the strongest telekinetic structure he had ever created.

Wolves, at least ten of them, emerged from the field. An ATV pulled up and shone its lights on Jacob and his family. Seconds later, two more arrived. Someone threw a flare that bounced off the telekinetic dome and fell to the ground, casting a pink-orange glow. Seeing that their targets had taken a defensive position, the ATV drivers traded their guns for walkie-talkies and reported to still more enemies. The wolves circled, their hairless bodies absorbing the flare's unnatural light. Jacob guessed the soldiers were radioing in targeting information. Another bomb, artillery shell, or whatever had caused those explosions would strike soon, almost certainly shattering his shield. That would be the end. He took Rebecca's hand.

Startled, the wolves all jerked their heads in the same direction. The ATV drivers fumbled for their weapons, muted curses on their lips. What the—

A steel goliath burst through the corn like a whale breaching the ocean's surface. Wolves scattered, soldiers jumped on their vehicles and fled. It was a tank, a fucking tank. Jacob's mind sputtered, failing to process the scene unfolding before him. After almost ramming his dome, the tank came to a jerky stop. A moment later, the hatch where the crew would enter flew open and Judith's head popped out.

Time moved like snapshots flashing across a screen. Judith gestured wildly for the rest of the group to get into the massive weapon she somehow controlled. Dazed, Jacob lifted his family up and deposited them into the hatch before climbing in himself. It wasn't until he took a seat behind Judith in the cramped cockpit that words returned to him.

"What...what is this?" he asked.

"A tank," she shouted over the engine noise.

"Yeah, I can see that. But why are you driving it? *How* are you driving it?"

"Those assholes were using this to shoot at us. Scared the shit out of the guys who were in here when I popped through the wall." Her shoulders shook with a self-satisfied chuckle. "It's actually pretty easy to drive if you ignore most of the switches and lights and shit. Look here to see where you're going." She pointed to a monitor displaying a black and white video feed of the field ahead of them. "Then hit the gas and turn this steering thing."

"Right," Jacob said, fairly certain he had died and gone to some bizarre version of hell. Only then did he notice the blood splattered across the tank's interior. Hopefully there weren't dead bodies crammed into storage compartments. "How do they have a tank?" he asked nobody in particular.

Judith shrugged. "Don't know. This isn't the only one though. I found the big road by accident while I was figuring out these controls. There's a fuck ton of trucks and army shit heading for the house. More tanks too."

"Damn it! Get us out of here!"

"Sure thing, boss," Judith said. Her tone was light, playful even. Nearly being ripped to pieces by naked werewolf things evidently hadn't put a damper on the thrill of driving a tank. "But we have to go get the backpacks first."

"What? No we don't."

"My sewing stuff's in there, all my projects."

There wasn't time to argue. Jacob stood up and began opening the hatch.

"What're you doing?" Judith asked.

"Being the gun. Anything that gets in our way won't stay there for long. And if one of those helicopters gets too close, I'll pull the fucker out of the sky."

Judith flashed an impish grin. "I like it."

To his surprise, Jacob found himself smiling too.

They rumbled back to the farmhouse as quickly as a novice tank driver navigating a cornfield could get them there. All the while, helicopters monitored their progress from above. Occasionally, an airborne sniper took a shot at Jacob's head sticking out of the hatch, but mostly the enemy just watched.

Lights were already bobbing down the road when Judith pulled up to the house. Jacob climbed out of the hatch and, one at a time, levitated the abandoned packs into the tank. Engines roared on the long driveway that led to the road. Any second, gunfire would break out around them.

A deafening boom sounded from the driveway. With a terrific crack and clatter, half the farmhouse collapsed. The tank lurched forward, throwing Jacob off balance and tossing him into the hatch. Behind them, a vicious *rat-tat-tat* of machine-gun fire erupted. High-caliber bullets pinged off the tank's armor in furious bursts. Jacob picked himself up from the floor, cursing Judith for nearly throwing him into the enemy's path, and scrambled back to the hatch to look outside.

Helicopters converged on the farmhouse's ruins, their spotlights searching for the stolen tank. Jeeps with machine guns mounted on their backs sped across the lawn. A dozen ATVs fell into formation at the jeeps' flanks. In the rear, larger trucks—armored personnel carriers—could be seen along with at least one more tank.

Bullets whizzed and whistled past Jacob as he peeked over the rim of the hatch. The jeeps were gaining fast. Judith sped toward another cornfield. Good idea. The tank would do much better on the furrowed terrain than anything moving on four wheels.

"Slow down!" Jacob called.

"Are you out of your fucking mind?" Judith called back.

"Trust me. Don't go into the field until I say so."

Although Judith didn't reply, the tank slowed. Jeeps and ATVs closed in. Helicopters maneuvered to surround them. This would be tricky. Everything was moving at different speeds, and the cornstalks would interfere with his vision if Judith went into the field.

Closer...

Bullets ricocheted around Jacob. One grazed his cheek. Ignoring the fresh blood flowing down his neck and the throbbing of his still-healing chest, he focused on the enemy vehicles.

A little closer…

The faces of the enemy drivers and gunners came into view. People who, just a few months ago, had had jobs and kids, normal lives. People like he used to be. In this impossible world, hell made real, they found themselves hunting a horned demon who destroyed things with his mind, and they were scared.

Now.

Jacob raised a barrier, the widest one he had ever attempted. It didn't need to be tall or strong, just cover a lot of space. Jeeps slammed into it, flipping forward then skidding upside down across the grass. ATVs tumbled into the chaos. In an instant, the enemy's formation degenerated into a pileup.

A helicopter swiveled toward the carnage, swinging its tail toward the tank. Jacob stretched his invisible hands as far as they would go. Close, but not close enough.

"Back up!" he yelled.

A storm of profanity so dense that individual words blurred and lost meaning rose from the cockpit below, but Judith did as Jacob had asked. Sweat beaded on his forehead as he strained the imaginary muscle that controlled his powers. If he could just get an extra foot—

There! Telekinetic fingers met metal. He grabbed the preoccupied helicopter's tail and pulled. Its body tilted, shifting the position of the rotor blades. The machine lost lift, swung wildly, then plunged from the sky, crushing a group of soldiers trying to rescue their comrades from the wreck.

"Go!"

Judith sped off into the cornfield. Flames painted the sky behind them.

Rebecca did her best to attend to Micah as the tank rumbled down county roads. It wasn't easy though. The ride was bumpy, and she didn't have much room to work. Worst of all, she didn't know what to do. Micah's physiology wasn't human anymore. The wound where the wolf had bitten her leaked black pus and glowed faintly, just like the cut she had received from the faceless fanatic's spike. To everyone's relief, it healed much faster though. Within an hour, the bite had begun to scab over.

Micah would recover physically. How she was holding up mentally, however, wasn't at all clear. She sat on her mom's lap as still as death, staring into empty space.

The thing that had attacked her... What happened to it? Jacob replayed the scene over and over in his mind: The wolf crouching over Micah, exhaling smoke. Did she do that to it? He had felt a weak Darkness in the wolves as he fought them, just like the monkey-baby thing he had pulled off Judith in the hangar. Was what happened a reaction between the wolf's Darkness and whatever had given Micah wings?

Jacob closed his eyes and rubbed his throbbing temples. Next time they'd need to capture one of those creatures and do some experiments. Next time. There would be a next time, wouldn't there? This wasn't over.

The corpses of mega stores and car dealerships rose like zombies from the countryside. At long last, the group had reached Indianapolis's sprawl. There was no celebration, not even a sigh of relief. They weren't safe, and everyone knew it. An army of monsters and men, complete with armored vehicles, stood against them. Maybe they had put enough distance between themselves and those who would harm them, and maybe they hadn't. So far, nothing had stopped the hunters from tracking their prey.

Ten miles from downtown Indianapolis, the tank's fuel gauge hovered a hair's width over empty. Judith pulled into a fire station beside a fire engine that miraculously hadn't been called out on some doomed mission the night the world ended. Its gas tank remained full and ripe for siphoning. Rebecca wanted to stop for a while to let Micah recuperate in a proper bed. No one argued. If the hunters caught up to them on the road, neither Jacob nor Judith was in any shape to fight. Even demons needed rest. In a few hours, dawn would come. They'd continue west then.

Rebecca found some folding cots and set a couple up between the tank and the fire engine for herself and Micah. Meanwhile, Judith got to work on her injuries with her healing needles. Jacob pulled a cot into a corner and sat down to attend to his own wounds. His ribs had deflected the bullet that hit his chest, but a wound above his right hip felt like it might have one lodged in it. Figuring that was as good a place as any to start, he picked at the gory hole in his jeans with a butter knife from the kitchen. His body would expel the bullet eventually, but it didn't hurt to help the process along. (Strictly speaking, digging around in there hurt quite a lot, but he'd be fine. Probably.)

A little while later, Judith walked up to his cot, stretching her arms and twisting her torso to test the repairs she had made. She looked down at Jacob with an expression that was both contempt and pity. "Lie down," she ordered.

"I'm kind of busy. Do you need something?"

"Just take off your shirt and lie down." Her needles reappeared. "I don't know if this'll work. I've only done it to myself."

"Are you serious?"

"I don't want you to be all fucked up like this if we get attacked again."

Jacob stared at her in disbelief.

Her gaze hardened. "If you don't want my help—"

"No. Don't go. I'll take whatever help I can get." He peeled off his blood-soaked t-shirt, reopening half-healed wounds in the process, and lay on his back.

Judith leaned over him, inspecting the damage. "Holy shit... This'll take a while."

"That bad?"

"Yep. I'll see what I can do, but if your stupid curse thinks I'm hurting you, I quit."

"Got it."

Jacob didn't feel the needles go in—two drops in an ocean of pain. Judith's nimble hands moved over him with the skill and precision of a surgeon. Bullets dropped to the floor. Bites healed. As the pain diminished, the sensation of the needles moving in his body became more pronounced. It hurt, but in a warm, pleasant way, like stiff joints getting a good stretch—only much better.

Judith worked on him for over a half-hour, flipping him onto his belly, rolling him onto his side, attending to every cut and bruise. When she finished, she put her needles away and inspected her work. "Looks okay. How's it feel?"

Lost in a fog of bliss, all Jacob could manage for a reply was a contented groan.

She laughed—a light, musical laugh, almost girlish in its honest simplicity. Not in a million years would he have expected to hear such a sound from her. An echo of who she had once been, perhaps. His eyes slid shut, and he entered a state not unlike sleep.

The Pale Gentleman

Crack. Crack. Crack.

Jacob jumped to his feet. Judith appeared at his side in a combat stance. Someone was at the fire station's side door. Knocking. That didn't happen anymore, not in the new world. People hid, fled, or attacked. Knocking didn't make sense.

Crack. Crack. Crack.

Again. It sounded more like a machine than anything made of flesh and bone. Micah and Rebecca woke in unison, sitting bolt upright in their cots.

Jacob threw a barrier over his family and placed a second in front of the doorway. Judith disappeared.

Crack. Crack. Crack.

Seconds after Judith had gone, she returned. "Some weird guy is out there, a big motherfucker. Definitely a demon. I think he's alone."

"Does he look dangerous?"

"How the fuck should I know? He's not carrying any weapons or anything, but he's a demon."

"Damn it."

Crack. Crack. Crack.

Jacob approached the door and moved its barrier to a position behind him. Only a couple inches of wood stood between him and the visitor.

Judith teleported into a dark corner, preparing an ambush. Behind them, Micah scampered to her mother's side.

"Who is it?" Jacob called. It sounded ridiculous, like he was back home in the old world, getting ready to talk to kids selling cookies door to door. Particles of dust drifted through the stale air, catching the waning moonlight. Nothing else moved. Jacob held his breath.

"I mean you no harm," a man said from the other side of the door, his voice monotone. "I've come to make a proposal."

"What kind of proposal?"

"It's a matter best discussed face-to-face. Suffice it to say, I'm aware of your situation and I would like to offer some assistance, if it be in my power to do so."

Jacob looked to Judith, who shrugged. No help there. He wanted to jump into the tank, crash through the fire station door, and get out of there. But what if this stranger was telling the truth? What if he *could* help? After dismissing the shield he had placed over Rebecca and Micah, he motioned for them to hide inside the tank. "I'm opening the door," he said to the demon outside. "Do anything suspicious and you're as good as dead. Understand?"

"Of course."

With a trembling hand, Jacob grasped the doorknob. "I must be out of my goddamned mind," he muttered, then opened the door.

A gaunt, freakishly tall man dressed in a black trench coat and a fedora stood on the other side. Deathly pale, his long face carried no expression whatsoever. His nearly lipless mouth pulled into a straight line. His eyes were sunken so deeply into his skull they appeared to be pools of shadow.

"Allow me to introduce myself," the man said. "My clients refer to me as the Pale Gentleman."

He extended an enormous, bony hand. Jacob took it and found the stranger's grip firm but accommodating. A powerful current of Darkness moved through him. It had a magnetic quality that pulled in unsettling ways.

"Jacob Freeman," he said, then withdrew his hand more urgently than good manners would dictate.

"Pleased to make your acquaintance, Mr. Freeman."

The tall demon stood in silence, patiently looking down at Jacob. It seemed he'd be happy to stand there all day. That kind of thing might attract unwanted attention should an enemy helicopter fly by.

"Would you like to come in and explain this proposal of yours?" Jacob asked.

The man nodded. "I would. Thank you."

Micah and Rebecca hid within the tank's thick steel armor, while Judith lay in ambush. If trouble had found them, they were as prepared as they could be. Jacob stepped aside to admit his guest. The Pale Gentleman entered, ducking so as not to bump his head on the top of the doorframe. He turned to face Judith's hiding spot and tipped his hat. (So much for the element of surprise.) Jacob scanned the small parking lot outside and the road beyond for signs this strange demon hadn't come alone, then shut the door.

With no urgency whatsoever, the Pale Gentleman said, "Congratulations on escaping your adversary's snare. Until this evening, the presence of hostile forces has thwarted my efforts to meet with you. I hope you are recovering well from the ordeal."

"If it's all the same to you, can we dispense with the pleasantries? I don't mean to be rude, but I have other matters to attend to."

"Indeed, you do," the stranger said with grave certainty. "I've monitored your progress with great interest. If I may speak plainly, I did not expect you to make it as far as you have. Your adversary is formidable."

"Yeah, no shit," Judith said, evidently giving up on the idea of hiding. She twirled and tossed her blades as she sashayed toward the two men standing near the door. Jacob hoped her cocky display of confidence wasn't just for show.

"Your...associate?" their guest asked. For the first time, he didn't seem to have the precise words he wanted to use lined up ahead of time.

"You could say that. Judith, meet the Pale Gentleman."

She replied with a contemptuous snort.

"Now that we're all acquainted," Jacob continued, "can we discuss your proposal?"

"Of course. As I'm sure you have noticed, those in the service of your adversary possess an uncanny ability to approximate your location. I've developed a theory as to how they are accomplishing this, based on a thorough review of their communications. There might be a way to prevent them from continuing to do so."

"You have my attention," Jacob said.

"I suspected that would be the case." The Pale Gentleman nodded, an ambiguous gesture that might have been intended to compensate for his apparent inability to smile. "Before we proceed, I must determine if it's within my power to assist you. If it isn't, I will take my leave so as not to waste any more of your valuable time."

"You want to make sure you can negotiate in good faith?"

"That's correct."

"Commendable," Jacob remarked, only partially concealing his skepticism. "What do you need to do?"

"Conduct a test, of sorts, with the aid of this." The Pale Gentleman pulled a human ear out of his pocket. Other than not being attached to a head, it looked like a perfectly healthy ear.

Judith yelped and jumped back a few feet. "What the fuck?"

"Please don't be alarmed," the man said. "With Mr. Freeman's permission, I will use this artifact to verify my suspicions as to the nature of his problem."

"How does that work exactly?" Jacob asked, eyeing the ear.

"I will simply touch it to your head."

"It's a trick," Judith said. "And it's fucking gross."

"What does it do?" Jacob asked, ignoring the commentary.

"It hears."

"Somehow that doesn't surprise me. Can you be more specific?"

The Pale Gentleman slowly shook his head. "I'm afraid I cannot. I will, however, offer you my assurance that you will come to no harm."

Assurance. Jacob wasn't comfortable with that. Not at all. He knew he had to do what the Pale Gentleman asked anyway though. He didn't have much choice. Sooner or later, the hunters would catch up to them. If there was any chance of losing them for good, he had to take it.

"Judith, anything weird happens and you take this guy's head off. Got it?"

She shot him a look that blended shock and disgust. For a second, he worried she would revolt, but she nodded and took a position behind the strange demon.

"Do it," Jacob said in a whisper.

The Pale Gentleman stepped forward, extended his hand, and pressed the ear to Jacob's forehead. Warm and alive with Darkness, it released an eager energy that romped through his brain like a boisterous puppy. While not painful, the sensation was profoundly disconcerting. He looked up into the other demon's eyes and found he had no eyes. What had earlier appeared to be sunken sockets were dark, empty pits.

"Yes," the Pale Gentleman said after less than a minute. "It is as I suspected." He put the ear back in his pocket. "Thank you for your cooperation, Mr. Freeman. Please reassure your associate as to your well-being. It would be unfortunate if there were any misunderstandings."

"It's okay, Judith," Jacob said. His head spun, and he felt nauseous, but the effects were dissipating. He turned back to the Pale Gentleman. "What just happened?"

"I'm afraid I can't discuss my methods."

"Okay. Then will you at least tell me what you learned?"

"I will. A connection has formed between you and your adversary, a link he can exploit to sense your physical location within a certain range. By moving about and sensing where you are not, he can deduce where you might be. It's an imprecise means of finding someone; however, it can be effective given sufficient resources to undertake a search. Your adversary possesses such resources."

"Link? What does that mean?" Jacob asked.

"In a general sense, you could think of it as a distortion in the energy that sustains us, one that grows more acute the closer your adversary is to you."

"Energy? Do you mean Darkness?"

"An apt description," the Pale Gentleman said. "Yes, that's the energy to which I refer."

"He's connected to my Darkness? How the hell did that happen?"

"I'm afraid I don't fully understand the process. All I can offer is speculation."

"Then speculate," Jacob said, growing animated. But even as he said it, he already knew. That night in the basement, the faceless fanatic had stabbed him with his spike, something about a ritual. It felt like death itself—no, worse than death. Then Micah broke the connection before it was meant to be broken. Something must have remained.

"As you wish," the Pale gentleman said. "Your adversary can directly interact with the sustaining energy of other Transcendent—their Darkness, to use terminology you're familiar with. Although rare, such abilities aren't unheard of. Typically, they allow one Transcendent to weaken or manipulate another. Your adversary's abilities, however, are atypical. He destroys, or perhaps absorbs another's Darkness."

The Pale Gentleman waited for a response. Not getting one, he changed the subject. "In the interest of fostering goodwill, I'm prepared to offer you a summary of the information I've gathered on your adversary as well as additional information from the listening test. Are you interested?"

"Extremely. Tell me everything you know."

"My pleasure. A Transcendent named Caleb pursues you. He..." Again, that pause as though there weren't words for what needed to be said. "Suffice it to say, he exists in a world of himself. He's physically present in this shared experience we think of as reality; however, his mind operates in a world of its own creation. You were drawn into this private universe, and part of you remains there still."

"Why?" Jacob asked. "Why would he do that?"

"Caleb's intentions aren't known to me, but I'm certain he meant to do you great harm."

"Who doesn't?"

This elicited a bitter laugh from Judith. "What did you do to him anyway?" she interjected. "Trick him into some bullshit promise? Is he supposed to be washing your undies or something?"

"Funny," Jacob said. "If you don't mind, can we get back to the part where this guy helps us? Or is there more sensitive information you'd like to share with the room first?"

Judith let her stormy expression respond for her.

"If I may," the Pale Gentleman continued. "Prior to your encounter with Caleb, his inner world experienced a breach of sorts. Overwhelmed by stimuli which he had no way to process, he developed a rather interesting system of beliefs to make sense of his situation. The nature of these beliefs has made him hostile to his fellow Transcendent.

"He's consumed by hatred, much of which has been focused on you, Mr. Freeman. Frustration stemming from your success at eluding his forces is partially to blame. A strong desire to rid his inner world of the echo of your presence plays a role as well. However, his animosity runs deeper than any of this. He believes you are an abomination, a thing that has no right to live."

Dawn would break soon, and Jacob hadn't learned anything useful. As fascinating as all of this about destroying Darkness and magical links was, none of it would save his family's lives. The time had come to see exactly what this demon wanted. "You did your test," he said. "Can you help us or not?"

"I'm pleased to say I can."

"I imagine you'll expect compensation for this service," Jacob said, shifting into negotiation mode.

"Naturally. My price is a specimen from each of the Transcendent in your party. Demons, I believe you call us."

"A specimen?"

"You might say I'm a collector. In exchange for my assistance, I ask for a small part of each of you, something physical."

"You...you want pieces of our bodies?" Jacob stammered.

"Precisely."

Judith backed away. "Fuck that!"

"Calm down," Jacob said in the most soothing voice he could muster. Nothing good could come of walking away from the table at this point.

"No!" Judith yelled. "I've already been cursed once. I'm not giving this creepy motherfucker a finger or whatever so he can do something even worse."

"Your concerns are understandable," the Pale Gentleman said in his lifeless drone. "However, there is no cause for alarm. The harvesting process seldom results in permanent damage. As for being 'cursed,' rest assured that any artifact derived from your specimen will do you no harm. Others, perhaps, but not you."

Jacob took a moment to mull over everything the Pale Gentleman had said. Darkness as energy filling each demon, flowing between them, manipulated by this man to make tools of body parts or by Caleb to breathe life into his monstrosities. "Darkness is in our bodies," he said to Judith. "And it never forgets us. Let's say he turned your finger into a death ray. While it might kill me, it wouldn't hurt you—or something like that. The artifact's power is still somehow you."

"Very astute, Mr. Freeman," the Pale Gentleman said. "While an oversimplification, that is essentially correct."

"What about indirect harm?" Jacob asked, ignoring Judith's bewildered agitation. "Could an artifact be used to initiate a sequence of events that would foreseeably harm its originator?"

"Artifacts have a way of knowing. None derived from your flesh would intentionally bring you harm. However, not every contingency can be accounted for. As I'm sure you're aware, it's impossible to eliminate risk from any undertaking."

"Shut up!" Judith screamed. Her tail lashed, and her blades were in hand. A cornered animal, desperate and dangerous, she radiated violence. "What the fuck does that even mean?"

Unfazed, the Pale Gentleman went on in the monotone voice he had maintained throughout their conversation. "It means you will be uniquely protected from the specimens I harvest from you."

"Excuse me," Jacob said before Judith could respond. "May I confer with my partner?"

"Of course. Take your time."

Jacob took Judith's arm and led her to a remote corner of the firehouse. "Listen," he began. "We can't go on like this. You must see that. At some point we're going to screw up or just get unlucky. Whatever this guy has in mind can't be worse than what Caleb will do to us. We should at least hear him out."

"You're the one that Caleb asshole is after. He's tracking *you*. Let me go!"

"I can't do that."

"Fuck you!" Judith shouted, and stormed off to fume by the tank.

With a deep sigh, Jacob walked back to the Pale Gentleman, who patiently awaited his return. Thankfully, Judith had terrible instincts for negotiation. Despite the considerable leverage she held at the moment, she didn't think to ask for any concessions. If she had asked for a longer leash, Jacob would have given it to her. She might have even forced him to free her, depending on how all of this played out.

"I hope all is well with your associate," the Pale Gentleman said.

"Don't worry about her," Jacob said dismissively. "About this deal of yours, I'm intrigued. But how do we know you aren't withholding information? All of this about magical artifacts and connections through Darkness... You claim to know a lot and we have no way to verify any of it." He paused a moment to cast an appraising glare over the Pale Gentleman. "Will you at least let me draw up a contract so we have all this in writing? It's an empty gesture, I know, but my partner puts a lot of stock in that sort of thing. It would set her mind at ease. You see, there's this promise ritual—"

The Pale Gentleman held up a massive hand to silence Jacob. "You disappoint me, Mr. Freeman. I'm well aware that promises made to you are anything but empty gestures. I'm negotiating in good faith and I expect you to do the same. You have my word that everything I have told you is true and I have omitted nothing pertinent to this discussion. My word is all I offer, nothing more and nothing less."

"Fine," Jacob said, annoyed. "Hypothetically, if we agree, what happens next? Do you start cutting off ears?"

"In most cases, specimens are less structurally significant than an ear. Should you consent, I will evaluate all three of you to determine the nature of the specimen required."

A knot formed in Jacob's gut. "Three?"

"Yes. There are three Transcendent in your party." The Pale Gentleman turned the black pits of his eyes toward the tank. "I suspect the third is inside the armored vehicle you commandeered last night."

Jacob clenched his fists, trying to suppress his panic. There was no point in lying. The Pale Gentleman knew everything else, of course he knew about Micah too. "She has no part in this."

Judith appeared in front of the Pale Gentleman, her weapons raised. "Not happening, asshole."

"I hope we haven't arrived at an impasse," the Pale Gentleman said. "My terms were clear: a specimen from each Transcendent in your group."

Jacob made a conscious effort to shift from father mode to lawyer mode. Micah's Dad wouldn't get them anything but a fight, but Jacob Freeman, the sought-after attorney, might find a way out of this. In his most reasonable voice, he said, "I wouldn't call it an impasse, but we need to clarify a few key concepts. I had assumed you meant people like us when you said 'Transcendent.' The girl isn't like us."

"An interesting assertion. Would you care to elaborate?"

"No, I wouldn't," Jacob replied, bringing as much menace to bear as he could. "She doesn't use Darkness. She's not one of us."

"Do you claim she's human?" the Pale Gentleman asked.

Jacob shot him a hard look. "I'm not claiming anything other than what I said. She's not like us."

"Mr. Freeman, I'm sure I don't need to remind you that the child is in grave danger, a situation that grows more dire by the minute. I've given my word that I won't harm her. Your adversary will offer no such assurances."

Jacob didn't know what to do. It would be unthinkable to offer Micah up as a bargaining chip. But did he have an alternative? There was no telling what Caleb would do to her when he caught them, and if this connection existed between them, he would catch them eventually.

"Dad."

Everyone's eyes leaped to the tank. Like a white carnation absurdly misplaced, Micah's head stuck out of the hatch, strangely lit by a lantern left there to help people get in and out. Struggling to restrain her, Rebecca pleaded with her in frantic whispers.

"Let go!" Micah yelled. "I can help."

Jacob glared at the Pale Gentleman, who stood in front of him as impassive as ever. "Watch him," he told Judith.

He rushed to the tank and climbed onto its body. "What are you doing? Get back in there," he said to Micah in a strangled hiss.

Rebecca's desperate voice rose from the hatch. "Jacob! She's too strong. I can't hold her back."

"I have to tell you something," Micah repeated, refusing to be talked around.

Jacob peeked over his shoulder. The Pale Gentleman still stood in the same spot with Judith hovering around him. A telekinetic barrier went up over the tank, more to mute the conversation with Micah than for protection.

"What do you think you're doing?" he asked. "Get back in there and do exactly what your mother tells you to do."

"Dad! Listen to me!"

Jacob cast another anxious glance at their visitor, then took a seat in front of the hatch. Micah's jaw was set, and her voice held a steely edge. There was no talking her down when she got like this. The girl would say what she meant to say and nothing would stop her. "Fine. You have one minute."

Tension shot through the muscles around her eyes, letting him know she'd take as long as she damn well pleased. "I can help," she repeated. "The Light can help. It... Sometimes, it tells me things."

"What kinds of things?"

"If a person is good or bad, if they're telling the truth. I've only ever tried it on Mom, but it would work on anybody, even him." She pointed to the Pale Gentleman, only a trace of fear in her voice.

"And I suppose that's how you know about him in the first place: it told you."

"Yeah..."

"Do you think it's a good idea to listen when it speaks?"

Micah scowled at him. "I'm not stupid, Dad. I know it's not my friend, but it wants to keep me alive. We're in trouble, the kind of trouble that might get me killed, and it knows it."

Jacob wanted to protest but didn't have any arguments to use against Micah, only emotion and authority. What she had said made sense. It worked the same way with his Darkness. He didn't trust it, but when it came to survival, its interests aligned with his own. If this other thing, this force that had infected his daughter, could save her life, wouldn't he be failing as a father if he didn't let it?

"Let me talk to him," she said as though reading his thoughts. "I need to get close for it to work. I'll tell you if we can trust him."

Jacob thought about it.

"No!" Rebecca cried from below.

Jacob leaned toward the hatch to see his wife. Only her eyes caught the light from the lantern outside, furious eyes. "We need to do something, Rebecca. There's a man out here, a...changed person. If what he says is true, we can escape and leave all this fighting behind. I don't trust him, but what if Micah can tell us if I should?"

"She's just a kid!"

"She'll be a dead kid if we don't get help!" Jacob snapped. He closed his eyes and massaged the base of one of his horns. He hadn't meant to be so blunt, not in front of Micah. "What am I supposed to do? This might be our only chance."

Seconds ticked by like nails driven into a coffin. Rebecca didn't have a solution. None of them did.

"Don't worry, Mom," Micah said. "Dad and Judith will keep me safe. Even though you're mad at them, you know they won't let anything bad happen to me. Let me help."

"I'm going with her," Rebecca said after a moment. Her horror and fury had transformed into grim resolve.

Together, the family climbed down from the tank and walked to the Pale Gentleman. Judith shot them a damning glare as they passed her. To the towering nightmare looking over them, Jacob said, "My daughter wants to speak to you. Stay where you are, keep your hands where I can see them, and answer her questions."

"Of course," he replied.

Jacob stepped aside so Rebecca and Micah could move forward. Gripping her hunting knife, Rebecca said, "I'll kill you if you hurt her. I don't know how, but I swear to God I'll do it."

The demon nodded politely.

Micah let go of Rebecca's arm and took another step closer. The Pale Gentleman stood motionless—the gallows on a moonless night, patiently waiting. She stood close enough for him to feel her strangeness, the alien energy that struck a sickening discord with Darkness. He didn't react.

"Are you going to hurt me?" Micah asked, her voice trembling.

He lowered himself into a stooped crouch, bringing his face level with hers. When he spoke, a hint of warmth softened his dry monotone. "With you, child, I can make a promise: I mean you no harm."

"What about Mom, Dad, and Judith? You won't hurt them either?"

"No. I have no malicious intent toward your father or his associate. As for your mother, I require nothing of her."

Micah gazed into the emptiness of his eyes. For a moment, silence, then she gasped—a raw, bloody sound torn from her chest. Fear darkened her face like an eclipse. She tried to fight it, calm herself, but failed. Panic.

Terror. She turned away from the Pale Gentleman and flung herself into Rebecca's arms.

Jacob raised a barrier around the Pale Gentleman. Judith appeared, knives poised.

"Wait," Micah called in a broken voice. She pulled away from her mother, tears streaming down her cheeks. "Don't hurt him. I saw... I..." She wiped her eyes and took a deep breath. "That man is *not* a good guy. He's evil. Cold, mean, and *evil*. But he's not a liar."

The Pale Gentleman's slit of a mouth bent into something akin to a smile.

That settled it. Without further discussion, the group put their faith in Micah's proclamation. Even Rebecca went along with all that followed, questioning none of it. It didn't make sense, relying on the psychic impressions of a girl who only a few months ago had been a perfectly ordinary fifth grader, but nothing made sense anymore. They needed a path, and one had opened before them.

The Pale Gentleman performed some sort of demonic evaluation on those he demanded payment from. This involved laying his hands on Jacob and Judith. He simply looked Micah over. The price was set: one of Micah's feathers, a vial of Judith's blood, and a shaving from Jacob's horn. No need for anyone to sacrifice anything so gruesome as an ear. The last item, however, proved difficult to collect. Nothing could damage the horn. After ruining two saw blades and a drill bit, Judith finally chipped off a sliver by using one of her own blades as a chisel.

Once everything was in order, the Pale Gentleman produced something that looked like a sharp canine tooth from his overcoat. "This, Mr. Freeman, is an artifact that severs bonds of servitude. Strictly speaking, your situation is not the sort of problem it was intended to resolve. I believe, however, it will prove effective. Should it fail, I will of course return the specimens I have collected from you and your companions. Please bear in mind that this procedure is not a guarantee of safety. Caleb will most likely continue his pursuit, but he'll do so at a great disadvantage."

"I understand."

"Very well. You must focus your thoughts on your adversary," the Pale Gentleman said. "If there are bonds you would prefer to remain unbroken, purge them from your mind. This artifact is one of destruction."

Jacob cast a quick glance at Judith, happy to find she hadn't caught any of that about this thing breaking bonds. "I don't suppose I could keep that tooth when you're done with it," he asked. "You know, for safekeeping."

"You may not."

The Pale Gentleman took Jacob's hand and spoke words that didn't come from any human language. He pressed the business end of the tooth into Jacob's palm. The initial spike of pain gave way to an intense feeling of relief, as though the strange demon had performed acupuncture. A light, buoyant sensation rinsed his mind and body clean. How had he not realized how sluggish he had felt?

All of it, everything the Pale Gentleman had said, was true. Caleb had taken part of Jacob, something he didn't have a name for. Life force? Soul? And now the missing piece was destroyed. At long last, healing could begin.

"It's done," the Pale Gentleman announced. "The bond is no more."

After letting Jacob's hand drop, he pulled a handkerchief from yet another of his endless pockets to wipe the blood from his hands and the tooth. Without further comment, he walked to a nearby table to collect his payment, producing three small boxes to hold the items.

"That concludes our dealings," he said. "As I'm sure you're eager to move on, I'll take my leave."

"Wait," Jacob said. "Can you tell us anything about what's out there? Is there somewhere safe we can go?"

"Information has value, and I'm afraid you no longer possess anything to trade." He paused for a moment, considering. "I will, however, offer a bit of advice at no cost."

"I'd appreciate it."

"What is lost can never be restored. What is done can never be undone. For better or worse, every step we take changes the world. Tread carefully, Mr. Freeman."

A somber mood settled over the fire station. No one ventured a reply.

"It has been a pleasure," their visitor said. "I look forward to doing business with you again, should the opportunity arise."

With a tip of his hat, the Pale Gentleman left.

Micah's Rules for a Better World

Survive. Keep going no matter what. When there's no hope, keep going anyway. Make surviving the reason to survive. As long as you don't give up, hope might come back someday.

Interlude

His clients called him the Pale Gentleman. A craftsman and a trader, he wandered the land in search of specimens. Specimens became artifacts. That was his work.

Although he had seen many things during his travels, his encounter with Mr. Freeman's party would be unique. The Pale Gentleman had never had occasion to interact with more than one Transcendent at a time. The prospect of doing so gave him pause. To further complicate matters, there was an uncomfortable level of uncertainty around the resources these Transcendent might have at their disposal.

In preparation, the Pale Gentleman deployed an unprecedented assortment of defensive measures. He held a severed finger in his right hand. Were its bone to break, the finger would transport itself along with anyone touching it to the hand from which it had been cut. That hand currently sat on a table in the basement of a hardware store several miles away. He had applied a transparent gel derived from the crushed eyeball of an arachnid Transcendent to his forehead to prevent mental interference. Additionally, a strip of dried intestine lined the Pale Gentleman's coat to disrupt Mr. Freeman's telekinesis should it be applied to his person. Half a tongue, cut lengthwise, squirmed in one of the interior pockets of his coat. This artifact emitted a deafening noise if squeezed with sufficient force, stunning those caught unawares. This should temporarily impede the tailed Transcendent's mobility.

After satisfying himself that everything was in order, he straightened his hat and knocked on the firehouse door.

Days later, the Pale gentleman sat at his workbench, his mind blank. Once again, his attempts to attune himself to the specimens he had harvested from Mr. Freeman's group had failed. Casting his gaze on each in turn, he opened himself to them. Blood. Bone. Feather. As was the case with every previous attempt, no connections formed.

The horn fragment's energy and that of the vial of blood had inexplicably become entangled. Anything done to one affected the other, which in turn triggered wholly unpredictable reactions in the first. Although such a conglomeration couldn't be transmuted into an artifact, the phenomenon merited further study. This strange pairing might, in time, yield new insights into transcendence itself.

The feather lay on a clean black handkerchief folded and placed inside a wooden box with a hinged lid, which lay open before him on the workbench. He ran his fingertip along the specimen's pearlescent shaft, and a bone-deep chill came over him. The sensation could not be accurately described: weakness, disorientation, and a profound sense of dread.

While undoubtedly a product of transcendence, the feather differed in fundamental ways from anything he had yet encountered. Rather than reacting to his experiments, or having no reaction, it actively negated everything he did. Applying his own power to it was not unlike dropping an ice cube into a cup of hot water: the feather's energy canceled his.

An idea took root in the Pale Gentleman's mind, then blossomed into a question so radical it made him dizzy: What if there was more than one way to transcend? Mr. Freeman had been correct when he said the child wasn't like them. And yet she was. An entirely new avenue of research opened before the Pale Gentleman. He experienced a level of satisfaction that could almost be described as happiness.

Once again, he touched the feather.

Chapter 8

Prelude

With nothing to apply itself to, the mind grows wild—lurid blooms of desire and fear's strangling vines, nothing more.

Respite

After seeding the fire station with false clues hinting that the group had fled toward Chicago, they drove into the countryside west of Indianapolis. It needed to be west. Micah would tolerate a little north or a bit of south, but west had to be the main ingredient in their route.

Rebecca chose Springfield, Illinois, as an initial destination. Not only did it meet Micah's geographic requirements, but it was yet another state capital, making it as plausible of a place as any to continue the search for civilization. Rebecca hoped the city's small size relative to Columbus or Indianapolis meant it had a higher concentration of government officials. Perhaps that had increased the odds of some agency or other surviving to organize a recovery effort. For his part, Jacob thought the lunch-shift crew at a random fast-food restaurant would have had a better chance of rebuilding society than a bunch of bureaucrats, but he kept that to himself.

By the time the meeting with the Pale Gentleman had wrapped up, dawn had long since passed. There wasn't much daylight to work with, so the group didn't get as far as they would have liked. A couple hours before dark, Judith drove the tank into a state park near the Indiana-Illinois border.

Several square miles of densely forested terrain made for better cover than a cornfield. Better safe than sorry. There was no way to know if the Pale Gentleman's ritual had worked; their enemy might converge on them that night as they had every other night.

The park's nature center had a clean, secure basement without any windows—a perfect shelter. Provided they didn't make too much noise, the group could do pretty much anything they wanted without giving away their location. Lanterns cast weird shadows on the walls as everyone prepared for the long night ahead. Excited chatter and muffled laughter filled the basement, bringing to mind memories of the bedtime bustle of a slumber party or a family camping trip.

Judith rummaged through her pack on the floor near one of the lanterns. She wore a bit of reclaimed fashion she had worked on during the anxious nights spent hiding from Caleb's army. It had started off as a frilly, old-fashioned dress she had found somewhere. The thing had screamed "Grandma's church clothes." Judith took in the waist and bust until its faded fabric squeezed her small frame. The hemline soared, and the neckline plunged. Scraps became a loose-fitting tail sleeve. Now a sexy take on farm-girl cute, she had christened the reborn dress "Slutty Susie's Sunday Best." Classy, as always.

"Judith," Micah called from the corner where she had laid out her sleeping bag. "Can you tell me a story?"

This would be the third story she had gotten out of Judith that day. Although Jacob wasn't entirely comfortable relinquishing bedtime story responsibilities to a bloodthirsty demon, he didn't have the heart to intervene. Micah had been through hell; if Judith's stories took her away from it all, she could have them.

"Okay," Judith said. "What kind of story?"

"A scary one!"

Micah didn't like scary stories, and she knew she wouldn't get one. As usual, Judith's idea of "scary" would be an amusing anecdote about an ill-fated item of clothing. Her stories were crude, silly, and irreverent—exactly the kind of entertainment a ten-year-old might enjoy.

Judith took a seat next to Micah, carefully placing her tail where the unruly appendage couldn't accidentally touch her. "When I was little," she began, "I got to be in a wedding. I was the... What's the kid with the basket of flowers called? Flower child?"

Micah giggled. "Flower girl."

"Yeah, that's it. I didn't care about the wedding, or my flower-throwing job, or any of that. I was in it for the clothes. My dad wasn't some rich asshole like yours, so I didn't get to dress up very often. The people getting married bought me this lacy, cream-colored dress with a coral sash. I was cute as fuck!"

"Language," Jacob called.

A duet of giggles rose from Micah's corner. "Sorry, Dad!" Judith responded in a sarcastic singsong. It was a good thing Rebecca had gone outside to answer nature's call. She wouldn't have been happy about anything going on at the moment.

Jacob grabbed a flask of whiskey and headed for the stairs. He had first watch. As he climbed into the darkened nature center upstairs, he wondered what tragedy would befall little Judith's fancy dress.

The night passed peacefully.

The next morning, Rebecca and Judith got into an argument about how much of the tank's storage space should be reserved for clothes as opposed to food, medical supplies, and guns. Evidently, the planned morning departure would be delayed. While the two women worked things out (hopefully without Judith losing her temper and falling prey to promise sickness), Jacob took Micah for a hike in the park.

Cool, lush forest wrapped around them like an embrace. It was a world apart from the dusty expanses of farmland they had traveled through for so long. The two of them walked on and on, walking for the sheer pleasure of walking. They didn't need to run or hide; they were safe.

Micah entered a narrow gorge, moss-covered walls of limestone towering over her on both sides. If she stretched her arms out as far as they'd go, she could run the fingertips of both hands along the walls. She tried it. Looking back over her shoulder, she smiled at her father.

The gorge widened into a basin. On the far side, a waterfall made its way down terraced stone, feeding a crystalline pool. Micah stepped to the water's edge and took a deep breath of clean, moist air. Weak, post-apocalyptic light soaked into her skin as rain might into thirsty soil. She accepted it gladly, refining the sickly stuff into golden warmth—what sunlight used to be. Stretching her bare back, she unfurled her wings. Long white feathers glittered like fresh snow. She had the wings of a swan.

Jacob's breath caught in his chest. She was beautiful beyond words.

Layover

Welcome to Springfield, the sign read.

Despite everything, they had made it. They had defeated an army, stolen an undoubtedly valuable piece of military hardware, entered into fruitful negotiations with a man who might have been the devil himself for all they knew, and escaped into the American heartland. They ought to be dead. No one would say it, but they all knew it.

Jacob thought about everything his family had been through, the incalculable trauma they might never recover from. Anger, as thick and hot as lava, seeped into places that had known only fear until recently. Never again would he allow the people he cared for to be reduced to helpless prey. When danger found them again—and it would—he'd be ready.

"Judith," he called over the growl of the tank's engine.

"Hmm?" she answered from the driver's seat in front of him.

"Let's spend some time training together. There's a lot we could do if we coordinated our abilities."

After mulling it over for a few seconds, she said, "Okay. Sounds fun, and you need the practice."

That went more smoothly than he had expected. "Don't get cocky," he said through a confident smile. "I've got a trick or two you might find instructive."

Musical laughter filled the tank's cockpit, clearing the storm clouds from Jacob's thoughts. "Whatever you say, old man," Judith said.

"Nothing wrong with some spirited competition, but this isn't a game. The better I understand what you can do, the better I can support you. I'll make you look good."

"I already look good." Judith flipped her hair dramatically, flashing a view of her exquisite neck. Yes, she looked good all right, very good indeed. "And what's there to understand about how I fight? I blink around and stab stuff."

"But how does that work?" Jacob asked. "Can you blink as many times as you want?"

"I wish! If I do it real fast, I can only blink three times before I run out of juice. I try not to do that though. If I pace myself and rest a little between blinks, I can keep it up for a while."

Rebecca, who had been sitting stiffly in the gunner's seat, said, "Can you two talk about this some other time? I've had more than enough of monster powers for one lifetime."

"I think it's interesting," Micah chimed in.

Ignoring his wife, Jacob asked Judith, "How far does one blink go?"

"I don't know. Ten feet maybe?"

"Unless something is holding you," Jacob said. "Then you can't go anywhere."

"How do you know that?" She turned her head from the tank's periscope to shoot him a suspicious glance.

"I pay attention."

"Yeah, I bet you do." She mumbled something to herself then went on. "You're right though. I can't blink if something's got me. Can't carry anything either. Except my blades; they're part of me."

"But—"

"Before you get all pervy, no, I don't need to be naked to do it. My clothes are part of me too. I put my heart into them."

"I wasn't going there," Jacob said, which was a lie. He didn't understand why clothes would be different from anything else, but he chalked it up to Darkness working in mysterious ways and let the matter drop.

"Done grilling me?" Judith asked. "I've got a tank to drive."

"Last question. How did you steal this thing?"

"Blinked through its wall."

"You can teleport *through* things?" he asked.

"I guess you don't pay that good of attention, huh? I go through your force fields all the time, don't I?"

"Yeah...good point." Jacob took a moment to chastise himself for asking a stupid question. "Hold on a second—you can see through telekinetic objects, but you'd be teleporting into this thing blind. What if you reappeared where someone was sitting?"

"I'd have ended up inside them, and they'd have exploded."

"Gross!" Micah yelled, more delighted than disgusted.

Judith turned around to flash her a grin. "Just kidding. It doesn't work if there's nowhere to land."

Jacob leaned back in his aggressively uncomfortable tank-commander seat. This was going to be interesting. Working together wouldn't be easy; it didn't seem like the kind of thing demons were naturally inclined to do. Natural or not, he would make it work.

"Missed me!"

Judith darted behind a storage shed. Jacob raised an invisible wall on the other side, hoping she'd run into it. A dark swoosh, she circled back the way she had come. Tricky.

"No fair laying traps," she called from behind an overturned sedan that had ended up in the back yard of this house, their third Springfield home.

(Jacob insisted on moving every few days to confuse anyone who might be conducting surveillance on them.)

"All's fair in love and demon tag," he yelled, preparing to scoop her up as soon as she went for the shed again. Instead, Judith dashed off in the opposite direction. "Crap!"

He scanned the yard. She couldn't have gone far. It was against the rules for her to teleport or leave the yard. Jacob's rules stipulated that he couldn't move objects or destroy anything, which turned out to be a major pain in the ass. If it weren't for rules, the wrecked car would have been tossed out of the field of play and the shed Judith kept hiding behind would be a pile of splinters.

Something rustled behind Jacob. He spun around and threw a dome over a row of bushes along the back of the house. Trapped! Now she'd have to forfeit and live with the ignominy of being "it" until next time. "Got you!" he yelled triumphantly, although Judith wouldn't be able to hear him in her telekinetic cage.

Another rustling noise, from above this time. He looked up just in time to receive a foot to the face. He hit the ground hard.

"You're it," Judith jeered, doing a little dance over him.

With a heavy groan, Jacob got to his feet. "How did you do that? Teleporting is cheating."

"I climbed that tree. You were right under a branch, so all I had to do was drop. *Bam*! Judith wins again."

"Climbed it?" The tree must have been thirty feet tall, with the lowest branch a dozen feet off the ground.

"I used my blades as spikes and went right up. Easy."

Easy. Of course it was. Judith had the strength of a gorilla and the body mass of a ballerina. With climbing spikes, she could scamper up a tree like a squirrel. Jacob spat out a mouthful of blood. He probably couldn't have gotten a shield up in time to block her, so he should have lowered his face and let her hit his horns. He was both heavier and stronger than Judith. If he had planted his feet and used his horns as a shield, he might have deflected the blow; then she'd have been the one sprawled out on the ground. Lesson learned.

"Damn it," he muttered and spat again. "I could have sworn you were in those bushes."

"That was a squirrel I found in the tree. I threw it at the bush to mess with you."

"You threw a squirrel at me?"

"At the bush."

Jacob gave her a look of playful disapproval. "Poor little guy, just minding his own business."

"He's fine," Judith protested. "Squirrels fall out of trees all the time, right? They probably bounce or something."

"Micah!" Rebecca shouted from inside the house. "Get away from there!"

A puff of blonde hair disappeared from a second-floor window. Micah had been spying again. Jacob didn't mind. Demon tag must be fun to watch. Rebecca, however, hated her seeing demons being demons.

"Busted," Judith said, a slash of a grin across her face.

"Come on," Jacob said. "Let's go inside. It's getting dark."

After cleaning up and changing his dirty clothes, he went upstairs to say goodnight to Micah. She was sitting at the foot of her bed, her wings hanging over the back edge. She looked troubled.

"Dad?"

"Yeah?"

"I saw Judith in the tree. Would it have been against the rules to warn you?"

"We didn't make any rules about spectator interference," Jacob replied. "Unless Mom's rules have changed, there shouldn't be any spectators."

"Mom just yells at me. She never made an official rule. Don't tell her, okay?"

"My lips are sealed."

"I'm making a new rule for myself," Micah said. "No helping when you and Judith are playing your games. It wouldn't be fair. Will you tell Judith for me?"

"Sure thing. Goodnight."

Jacob found Judith in the living room, working on a sheet of black leather draped over her lap. He took a seat on the couch and cracked open a warm beer. (He really needed to outfit the tank with a mini fridge.) "Micah says she won't warn me the next time she sees you cheating," he announced.

Judith's sharp features melted into an uncharacteristically warm expression. "Good girl."

Jacob had assumed they'd stay in Springfield two or three days, but Rebecca had other plans. She wasn't going anywhere until she had scoured every government building, police station, hospital, and anywhere else she could think of for information. She even wanted to search veterinary hospitals for some reason.

On the first full day of her investigation, Rebecca made him drag a portable generator to the state capital's data center so she could power up some computers. Her hacking skills being about what one would expect of a physician, she didn't have any luck bypassing the state of Illinois's security measures. That's didn't stop her from trying though. Rebecca was nothing if not persistent.

After two weeks, Jacob resolved to talk to his wife. Springfield wasn't their last chance to unravel the mysteries of the apocalypse. Plenty of other state capitals, military bases, and universities awaited them farther west. At that very moment, civilization might have been thriving in Topeka. The conversation didn't go well. Rebecca threatened to lace his whiskey with Quaaludes then surgically remove several vital body parts after he had slipped into a coma. Jacob resigned himself to staying in Springfield indefinitely.

He and Judith settled into a routine: guard Rebecca as she conducted her investigation, train in the evening, then come up with novel ways to stave off boredom at night. The days began to bleed into each other. Time became a blur.

Slow-Motion Montage

"What do you want to do tonight?" Judith asked. She was sitting on a coffee table in front of the sofa Jacob had just settled into. Her tail hung over the table's edge, lazily sweeping the dingy carpet below.

Judith did one of three things after dark: disappear until the next morning, sulk in a corner with one of her sewing projects, or torment Jacob. Since she was talking to him, he assumed this was a night for option three.

When the mood struck her, Judith could mix a potent cocktail of flirtation, cutting mockery, and a twist of teasing. Despite constantly telling himself he'd turn her away for the sake of his own mental health, he never failed to drink deeply of her poisoned charms. When she came to him—eyes flashing gold, lips set in a crooked smile—he was powerless.

Jacob had wanted things to work out differently. As delusional as it sounded in hindsight, he had hoped to make friends with his unwilling partner. And maybe, on lonely nights like this—

"Anybody home?" Judith asked. "I'm talking to you."

"Sorry. I'm drunk."

"I asked what you want to do tonight."

Jacob shrugged. "I don't know. Want me to teach you how to play chess?"

She rolled her eyes. "Ugh. Let's go out."

"Why? We've already driven all the crazies out of town. There aren't any left for you to torment."

"Or for you to fuck," Judith quipped. A malicious grin threatened to engulf her entire face.

Jacob had never had sex with a crazy. Since transforming into a demon, he hadn't had sex with anyone, which sent his Darkness into fits of despair.

Nevertheless, the idea of him raping every vagina-enabled crazy he came across had become a recurring theme in Judith's needling. Perhaps he had divulged too much information about the urges he had experienced during the heady days of his demonic awakening.

"Go out then," he said. "Nobody's stopping you. Maybe you'll find some cool clothes."

"I can only go two miles."

"In any direction you please." Jacob closed his eyes and slumped down in his seat. He wished she'd go away.

Judith scowled at him. "I can't go anywhere new unless you come with me. So get off your ass and come with me."

"I doubt you're missing much. Springfield wasn't much for nightlife even before it became a ghost town."

"Come on! Rebecca has like ten guns under her bed. She'll be fine."

"No."

Her eyes ignited into fiery gems and she flew off the table she had been sitting on. "You're a fucking embarrassment. You know that, right?" She leaned forward and flicked one of Jacob's horns. "How'd you get this shit? You're not a demon. You're a dog. An ass-sniffing, face-licking dog."

With that, she stormed out of the room.

***

Later that night, Jacob went outside to relieve himself. He still needed to do that when he drank. Anything that went into his body needed to come out. Happily, those processes worked the same as they always had, a fun fact of demon life which gave him some small measure of comfort. As he stood there, musing on the miracles of nature, something popped into his peripheral vision.

"Boo!"

"Shit!" Jacob yelled, spinning away from Judith.

She giggled impishly. "That's what you get for hanging around with your dick swinging in the breeze."

Jacob finished his business and zipped up his jeans. "I was taking a piss."

"I can see that." With slow, lazy movements, she wandered to a rose bush gone wild near the house's back door and stroked one of its blooms. "You know, if you laid off the booze, you wouldn't have to do gross stuff like that."

"Yeah, well, drinking helps me deal with what a pain in the ass you are."

Judith grinned. If there was a point to this harassment, she wasn't in a hurry to get to it.

"What do you want?" Jacob asked.

"Actually, I was going to ask you the same thing." She stepped out of the shadows, her eyes sparkling in the moonlight. "What do *you* want?"

"To take a piss in peace."

"Is that all? How sad." She stepped closer, seeming to glide through the overgrown grass. "But it isn't, is it? I think you want more. Much, much more." Her voice was low and silken.

"Don't you have better things to do than making a pest of yourself?" Jacob asked.

"I was thinking about you," Judith said. "What do you do with your life? Protect people, right? You're the best guard dog in the whole, wide world. Good boy. But you must want something for yourself too. So, what is it? What's the treat that'll get this doggy's tail wagging?" She wagged her own tail in a canine way.

"Call me a dog again, and I'll toss you in the air and let you drop. I'm not in the mood for this, Judith. Leave me alone."

"You're the one keeping me here. What's the matter? Don't like me anymore?"

Judith had been drifting closer. As lightly as a butterfly landing, she placed a hand on Jacob's shoulder. Her Darkness soaked into him. Anytime they stood close to each other, he could feel it, that electric hum. But touching... This was so much more.

"You might not act like it," she said. "But you're a demon. And demons always want something. *Always.*" She moved closer still. They might have been coming together for an intimate dance. Her tail stroked the back of his leg.

"You shouldn't do that," Jacob said, his voice unsteady.

"I don't see you stopping me." Judith ran a finger down his chest. "Do you know how demons get what they want?"

He found himself unable to respond. His throat was tight. His entire body throbbed with the rhythm of his pulse.

Judith's lips brushed against his cheek. In a breathy whisper, she said, "They take it."

Slender arms wrapped around his waist like serpents. She eased into him, pressing her deliciously soft chest to the unyielding bone of his. Golden eyes. Cool breath on his neck. The cedar and musk smell of her hair.

Darkness flooded Jacob's mind, obliterating thought and reason, charging his senses. A need more urgent than any he had ever known overwhelmed him. He grabbed Judith by the hips—a drowning man grasping for a raft. She was as close as she could be, but he wanted her closer. He would have consumed her if he could. For one shining second, she was his. Her body, supple yet strong. Skin as soft as velvet.

With a spin and a shove, Judith slipped out of his arms and vanished. His embrace collapsed, leaving him holding nothing but himself. She stood a dozen feet away, bathed in silver moonlight, her smile sharper than a blade.

Jacob's Darkness raged.

Playful, patient, and merciless, Judith was a cat that had cornered its prey. She started visiting Jacob almost every night, eager to wind him up and watch him unravel. In her captivity, she lived for these bursts of fun. She only had one toy, and she intended to squeeze as much enjoyment out of it as possible. Or perhaps she simply meant to break him, torment him until he let her go.

Lost in spectacularly dangerous territory, Jacob floundered. When he hit his lowest point, mad with desire, everything but Darkness stripped away, what would he do? It killed him to admit it, but Rebecca had warned him of this exact situation.

Judith had forced him into an uncomfortable admission. His nature, the thing that had gone wild and become Darkness, had always been there. Throughout his life, a deeper impulse had lain at the root of so many of his impulses. He didn't want to see it—such an ugly, desperate thing—but she had laid it bare. Every demon wanted something, they were creatures of desire. And for Jacob, it was the most basic desire of all: lust.

Despite Judith's cocksure certainty that he couldn't do anything to her unless she let him, he knew he could. The training they did together had proven it. Grab her under her clothes or by the hair—anything to entangle yourself with her body—and her teleportation trick failed. Hit her hard enough, and she'd run off to lick her wounds. But none of that was his style. He'd bide his time. And as degrading as Judith's games were, they thrilled him. When she brushed against him or leaned in close to whisper poison into his ear, he burned.

<hr>

"Break it down," Rebecca ordered. She stood in front of an unassuming door in the Illinois State Capitol.

"Do you even know what's in there?" Jacob asked.

"I said break it down."

"Fine."

With one quick shove, he knocked the door off its hinges. It fell into a broom closet, toppling a tower of toilet paper rolls, which spilled out into the hallway at their feet.

Jacob smirked. "Happy?"

Rebecca wasn't happy, not at all.

<hr>

One morning, Rebecca sat at a picnic table, staring blankly at a stack of papers she had found in a police station. They were handwritten, so she figured they might have been generated after the computers went down. Eager for clues, she took them outside to read in the daylight. A florid, looping script covered the pages, offering detailed instructions for making *Beauty Balm*, a skin cream that used human tallow as a base. Rebecca shut her eyes and drew an unsteady breath. "Damned crazies..."

"Hey, Mom," Micah called from the road. She stretched the appendages on her back as she approached. Rebecca's skin crawled.

"For God's sake, Micah, how many times do I have to tell you? You can't go outside half-naked."

"I'm dressed. See?" She held up a fistful of skirt for inspection.

"You know what I mean. Until we figure out how to make shirts that fit, wear your robe."

"I don't like it. It's too hot and I can't move my wings."

"It doesn't matter if you like it." Rebecca said. "You need to wear *something*."

"But there's nobody here to see me!"

"That's not the point. Besides—"

"New rule," Micah said, cutting her off. "People can wear whatever they want." Her voice was steel, her eyes ice.

Rebecca's hands clenched into trembling fists. She opened her mouth, but words failed.

***

Other than her research, the only thing Rebecca showed the slightest interest in was her ever-expanding arsenal of firearms. Not a day went by that she didn't demand Jacob escort her to one of the firing ranges in town for target practice. Although he worried about her mental state, he didn't know what to do. She wouldn't talk to him. If only she'd accept that the state of Illinois hadn't solved any great mysteries before it closed up shop, the group could at least move on.

One day, Rebecca burst into his room, carrying a laptop computer. She slapped a piece of paper on his desk, followed by a memory card, the small kind that digital cameras used. The paper was blank, except for a few lines of handwritten text across the top. It read:

Joint session of the Illinois State Legislature and the Springfield City Council. Representatives of the Illinois National Guard, the Department of Public Health, the National Security Agency, and other federal and state agencies in attendance.

"I found this in the capitol building," Rebecca said, beaming. "It was just sitting on a desk. Can you believe it?"

"What is it?" Jacob asked.

"You'll see."

She plugged the memory card into her laptop and opened a video file that showed about a dozen people huddled around a podium in the state legislature's chambers. Lanterns lit the proceedings, casting ghostly shadows over haggard faces. A crowd murmured in the seats behind the camera. Periodically someone went to the podium to speak, but mostly they argued, their voices a garbled din. A fat man wearing a sweat-stained suit kept holding up what looked like a map and pointing to various spots. The camera had been placed too far away, making it impossible to hear most of what was said.

"I told you!" Rebecca crowed after the video had finished. "Did you see?"

"See what?" Jacob asked, annoyed he had wasted his time watching doomed norms pretend they had a chance.

"The meeting! Those were survivors."

"We already knew people survived. Notes taped to doors, abandoned camps, there have been all kinds of clues. Most of them are dead by now or hiding in some basement somewhere."

"Those people were organized. And look how many there were!" Rebecca shouted, growing increasingly animated. "Didn't you see that guy with the map? They found somewhere to go. That's why there aren't that many dead people here."

Jacob sighed. "Or we just witnessed bureaucracy's last hurrah. If they agreed on a plan, which I very much doubt they did, it probably fell apart. Crazies got them, they starved to death, or maybe some demon ate them. One way or another, whatever they tried to do failed."

Rebecca glared at him. "You don't know that. They might have gone somewhere safe. And if they did, I'm going to find out where." She snatched the paper and the laptop and left.

"Great," Jacob muttered. "Now we're never leaving."

Judith glided into the living room, wearing what appeared to be a fairy costume complete with sparkly wings, and executed a flawless pirouette. "The Fashion Fairy has arrived to make all your dreams come true." She tossed a bundle of white cloth to Micah, who perched on the arm of a sofa.

Surprised, Micah bobbled it before pulling it to her chest. "What's this?"

"You have to unfold it, dummy."

The word "grin" failed to capture Judith's expression. She looked like a cross between a kid on Christmas morning and the evil witch ushering Hansel and Gretel into her candy house.

Micah unfolded the bundle, ready for there to be something inside. There wasn't. She looked it over for a few seconds, puzzled. Then a smile bloomed across her face, as big and bright as a sunflower. The gift was the cloth itself. She held up a short Grecian tunic supported by a strap around the neck, so it didn't require a back or anything draped over the shoulders.

"What do you think?" Judith asked. "There's room for your wings. You don't have to wear it if you don't want to. The topless thing's cool. I just thought you might want to mix up your look now and then."

"I love it!" Micah squealed. "This is *way* better than a robe!"

Judith's smile widened. "That's really nice fabric, isn't it? Light and it moves really well."

Micah hugged the tunic because she couldn't hug Judith. "It's so soft," she breathed.

"Try it on," Judith said. "I want to see if it fits. I eyeballed the measurements."

It fit perfectly. The neck strap fit snugly enough to do its job but not too tightly. A sash around the waist embroidered with a subtle geometric pattern in blue gave the garment shape and helped hold the bottom in place. Judith had clearly put a lot of thought into the design. The tunic's simple elegant lines gave it an airy quality that suited Micah, and its vibrant white fabric accentuated her subtle glow. She was a winged goddess straight out of ancient mythology.

Across the room, Rebecca's reaction shifted from surprised to incensed. She stood up in a huff and left the room. Jacob excused himself and went after her. Fortunately, Micah was too busy admiring the embroidery on her tunic's sash to notice her mother's disapproval. Good things happened so rarely; it would be a shame to ruin this.

He found his wife fuming in the garage. "Who does she think she is?" she shrieked at him. "That...bitch!" She lunged at him as if she were going to slap him. "You told her to do that, didn't you?"

"No. Micah wanted me to ask Judith to make her a shirt, but I forgot. Judith must have come up with the idea on her own."

"You're trying to bring the two of them together, aren't you? You want to take Micah from me!"

"What are you talking about?" Jacob asked. "Micah is reaching for Judith all on her own. She's lonely."

"So you let her play with that monster? That's your solution?"

"A monster who saved our lives!" Jacob shouted, frustrated and hot with a rush of anger. "A monster who thought to give our daughter new clothes when I'd forgotten she wanted them. A monster who keeps Micah safe while you spend all day playing detective. For fuck's sake, she's watching her right now so you can have this little episode."

Rebecca flinched. Tears welled in her eyes.

Jacob immediately regretted what he had said. "Rebecca..."

As she turned away, her body quaked with suppressed sobs. "Did you see how Micah smiled? She's never smiled at me like that, not once."

After four weeks of fruitless effort, Rebecca made the unilateral decision to search the areas around Springfield for signs of a mass exodus. Thus began the group's descent into a hell of endless wandering. They scoured freeway exits and picked through small towns, driven on by Rebecca's obsession. A dog leashed to a pole, they never ventured far from Springfield for fear of straying too far from the only solid evidence she had found.

When the group finally ran out of places to search within fifty miles of their home base, a heated argument broke out over which direction to expand the investigation. Predictably, Micah insisted on west. There were a few issues with that though. First, both Jacob and Judith felt a vague, inexplicable apprehension about going any farther that way than they already had. That couldn't be good. Second, it would prove difficult to convince Rebecca not to investigate the bridges over the Mississippi River. The Ghoul's warning about not bringing Micah's strange energies near major rivers lest the Lady of the Waters take notice haunted him.

Fenced in by the Mississippi, Ohio, and Illinois rivers, the group couldn't go much of anywhere. As much as Jacob didn't want to admit it, Springfield might have been their best option for a permanent home.

After several days of furious debate, they set off again to explore what towns they could while avoiding rivers whenever possible. At the University of Illinois Urbana-Champaign, they fended off an unprecedented mass assault by crazies on the frat house they had claimed. Judith hadn't had so much fun in ages.

Outside of Normal, they fled from a Minotaur.

On a stretch of I-55 suspiciously free of wrecked and abandoned cars, they encountered a werewolf-like demon dressed in a leather biker outfit. He drove up alongside the tank on a flame-painted chopper with a human skull mounted between the handlebars and let out a blood-curdling howl.

Jacob popped his head out the hatch to see what their visitor wanted. The other demon yelled, "Nice ride!" and sped off.

There were other adventures, but mostly the group drove around chasing phantoms.

Exhausted and disheartened, they returned to Springfield after five weeks on the road. Five long weeks...and that only accounted for the second part of Rebecca's study of post-apocalyptic Illinois. All together, it had been almost nine weeks since they first left Springfield. Four months had passed since they escaped Caleb. It seemed more like four years. How long had it been since the world changed?

Without anywhere to go that didn't involve crossing rivers, everyone began to think of Springfield as home. Everyone, that is, except Rebecca. Her zeal for finding other humans knew no bounds. There were constant arguments about risking a dash across this or that river, but nothing came of it.

The flow of time slowed to a barely perceptible crawl punctuated by islands of activity when anything disrupted the monotony.

Jacob wandered the house early one morning, lonely and restless. For no reason in particular, he opened the door to an unclaimed bedroom and his heart stopped. The world flew from its axis and spun into the unknown.

Judith stood with her bare back to him, examining herself in a full-length mirror. Naked from the waist up, a flowing white skirt hung from her hips. She watched him over a bony shoulder but made no effort to cover herself. Instead of surprise or anger, her expression was one of curiosity. She wondered what he'd do next.

A sinister Venus de Milo in the semi-nude, her beauty was devastating. The long, graceful lines of her back. Skin like liquid moonlight. Lush hair flowing freely—the deepest shade of red, streaked with black. Dark, silky fur ascended from the hidden root of her tail, crossing the threshold of her skirt to coat the base of her spine.

The night before, when the moon hung heavily in the sky and Jacob's Darkness burned, he would have embarked on yet another pathetic pursuit of her. But now, with daylight filtering through the windows, he stood conflicted—torn between desire and pride, acutely aware of the danger he had put himself in. He did nothing.

Judith's demeanor shifted. Disappointment. Boredom. She flicked her wrist and a dagger appeared. With a lazy toss, it took flight. Jacob could have dodged it or shielded himself, but he didn't. He watched it spin toward him. Blade...hilt...blade...hilt...blade.

Her aim was true. The dagger's tip met his forehead like a viper's kiss. Blood beaded up from the wound and dripped into his eyes, a black river to drown his gaze.

Every minute of every day, Jacob and Judith felt the weight of their contract. It was a chain wrapped around each of their hearts, binding her Darkness to his. As days dragged into weeks, the bond changed in subtle but alarming ways. They began to sense each other's feelings and intentions. At first, they attributed this to all the joint training they had done and celebrated it as progress. The two demons had gotten preternaturally good at anticipating each other's actions. Neither could catch the other off guard anymore. Their sparring matches looked more like choreographed performances than brawls. Demon tag became a chess match. They stopped playing their violence-enhanced variation on hide-and-seek because the seeker immediately knew where to look every time.

Before long, the changes crept into their lives off the field of combat. The demons could sense each other's state of mind from a block away. If one needed rest or was upset, the other knew it. Darkness was acting on them in ways neither could understood or control.

"What are you doing to me?" Judith asked late one night, her voice sunk in despair.

"I'm not doing anything."

On the verge of tears, she grabbed his arm. "The contract is *your* magic. You expect me to believe you aren't the one messing with it?" She did believe it though; the hopeless look in her eyes said as much.

"The promises are a mystery," Jacob replied. "Even to me."

"And you're okay with that? It's changing you too!"

"I know."

The space between them grew heavy and still.

After what felt like hours, Judith spoke. "You can fuck me if that's what you want. You can do anything to me; just let me go afterward. No more promises. I won't hurt anybody. I'll just leave."

"Is that really what you want?"

Her anger flared. "I want to choose!"

That made sense. Who wouldn't? Jacob still didn't let her go.

"Aren't you ashamed of yourself?"

Jacob looked up with a start. He was sitting at the kitchen table, flipping through the pictures on a phone he had found earlier that day. (It never ceased to amaze him how many people had set their phone's passcode to 123456.) Rebecca stood in the doorway glowering at him.

"Excuse me?" he said.

She took a seat across the table. "I asked if you were ashamed of yourself."

"For any specific reason, or are we talking about a generalized sort of shame?"

"If you can't keep from drooling over that girl you've kidnapped, at least save it for when Micah's not around."

"Ah...more drive-by parenting." Jacob leaned back in his chair. This would take a while, might as well get comfortable. "Did you pull yourself away from your research long enough to be displeased by something you saw?"

Rebecca struck the tabletop with her fist. "Don't talk to me like that! If I could make Micah stay with me, I would. Since she refuses, I expect you to show some decency when you're responsible for her."

Jacob turned his attention back to the phone he held. Its screen displayed a picture of a handsome couple and two smiling children on a boardwalk, a blazing sunset behind them. The picture looked fake. "I'll take it under advisement," he said without looking up from the phone.

Rebecca lunged across the table and slapped it out of his hand. "Listen to me!"

Anger surged through Jacob's body but was immediately snuffed out by a wave of sickness. The promise he had made that night in Dayton—he couldn't even want to hurt her. "You have my attention," he said, seething. "What exactly do you want me to do?"

"Stop acting like a creep! For God's sake, Jacob, that girl is half your age!"

"I don't know about half. More like sixty to seventy percent." He cast a forlorn glance over the empty table before him, wishing he'd had the good sense to pour himself a drink before he sat down. "Although, you could say she was reborn the day she transformed into a demon, which might very well make us exactly the same age."

"Shut up!" Rebecca shouted. "Stop talking for a minute and listen to me." She stared him down. "This isn't about her. This is about *you*. Do you want to be the kind of man who chases around girls barely out of high school, a pathetic pervert who can't help but make a fool of himself?"

"For the record," Jacob said, "is this conversation supposed to make me a better person, or do you just enjoy calling me a pathetic pervert?"

"You shouldn't need me to tell you to be embarrassed."

"Do you want to know a secret?" Jacob asked, leaning toward her over the table.

"You're about to tell me some bullcrap about none of this being your fault, aren't you?"

"Not at all. I'd like to share an insight I had recently. It was something of an epiphany."

Rebecca sighed wearily. "I don't want to hear—"

"Bear with me. This'll only take a minute. Not long ago, I'd have told you all this stuff with Judith was in your head, a veritable tsunami of denials and rationalizations."

"You aren't about to do that right now?" Rebecca asked.

"No. And do you know why?"

"Because you don't care enough to bother."

"Exactly!" Jacob paused to flash a suitably demonic grin. "Why should I care? The old world is gone. Its facile moralizing, thirst for punishment, and rank hypocrisy—all gone. There's no one left to judge me but myself."

Rebecca gave him a blank stare. She didn't know how to respond to something so casually horrible, but felt she needed to. "What about basic human decency? Right and wrong don't change depending on who's watching."

"I disagree," Jacob said. "I'd argue the entire concept of 'wrong' depends on people watching. Let's say you drag me out for a public flogging, maybe parade me around so a bunch of sheep can work themselves into a self-righteous frenzy as they spit in my face. Who benefits? The sheep themselves, because it's fun to spit on people you feel superior to. And, of course, whoever gets to derive moral authority by condemning me in the first place."

"Everyone benefits," Rebecca said. "Society benefits. It's not about the crowd or the judge; it's about you and whatever shitty thing you did. Didn't they mention accountability in law school? Maybe the idea of justice rings a bell?"

"Oh, sure, we learned all about justice. It's a nonsense word the powers that be throw around to help ordinary people sleep better at night. As lawyers, it was our job to make it mean whatever they wanted it to mean."

Rebecca looked away, disgusted. "Listen to yourself. You're a comic book villain twisting everything around to fit some cynical worldview. In the end, it amounts to one thing: run-of-the-mill selfishness."

Jacob shrugged. "The world is what it is. I just adapt to it."

"What a load of bullcrap." Rebecca cast him a vicious glare burning with contempt. "You're the one making the world the way it is!"

Bored with the conversation, Jacob pulled a comb from his pocket and made sure his hair hadn't crept over his horns. He hated when that happened. "I'm not hurting you or Micah," he said. "I am, as always, your humble shepherd. If only you'd let me guide you."

"Ha!" Rebecca scoffed with a bitterness she had rarely allowed herself to express. "What does that look like? Should I find some psychopath to waste my time lusting over?"

"Think what you want about me...or Judith, for that matter. There isn't a goddamned thing you can do about it. Without an angry mob, authority doesn't exist." Now Jacob *really* needed a drink, and that half-bottle of wine he had left in the kitchen wasn't going to cut it. Eager to end this tedious conversation, he said, "Look, Rebecca, we'd all be better off if you took some time for yourself, stop worrying about what everyone else is doing and get your own house in order. We're doing okay, all things considered. Why not relax a bit?"

Rebecca didn't have the energy to argue anymore and Jacob knew it. Talking was his thing. He didn't want to, but he could do this all night. Tired, frustrated, and more miserable than when she had sat down with him, she stood up and walked away.

Jacob didn't stop her.

In the doorway, she paused to look back. "Are you sleeping with her?"

"No."

"Liar."

Jacob released a deep, multi-faceted sigh. "Would it matter if I was?"

"I don't know. Would it?"

He didn't have an answer.

A couple nights later, just before dawn, Jacob spotted Judith walking down the road in front of their latest house, a modest ranch on the outskirts of town. She was something out of a nightmare—black spirals smeared on her face and arms, most of her white tank top deeply stained, her hair slicked back with viscous fluid, glistening in the moonlight.

He leaned on a car in the middle of the road, waiting for her. Tail bobbing behind her, she sauntered up to him, a carefree smile adorning her painted face. Up close, it became apparent she had decorated her body with blood. After so much exposure to the stuff, Jacob was good at identifying it, even if the dark had rendered it black.

"Keeping yourself busy?" he asked.

"I caught a crazy snooping around the house."

"I assume you took care of the threat?"

"You assume right, boss."

"What did you do with the body?"

"Relax," Judith said. "Becky won't find it. I don't want her bitching at me. I played with him for a while, then stuck what was left of him in a refrigerator in some random apartment building."

"Played?"

She nodded, a twinkle in her eye. "Yeah, we tried out this card game I saw on one of the story discs. I don't think I got the rules right, but it was fun anyway. He lost."

"I gathered as much. And did this crazy participate of his own volition?"

"You mean did he want to play? No, but I talked him into it. He was way into this doll he had and only wanted to play with it. Kept licking it in weird places. It was gross."

"So, how did you get his attention?" Jacob asked.

"First, I told him he'd better play with me or I'd skin him alive, but he just kept talking to that stupid doll."

"An obsessive. I've run into my fair share of those."

"He was pissing me off," Judith said. "So I took his doll. I said he could have it back if he beat me at the game."

"And he didn't."

A grin spread across her gore-painted face. "Nope. After a few rounds, he kind of...popped."

"Hence the blood-based body art."

"Yeah. Do you like it? I was going for scary."

"Nailed it," Jacob said. "You'll wash that off before morning, right?"

"On it. There's a stream about a mile away. I'll rinse off. You can't come though. No peeking."

"Darn."

Judith turned to leave, tickling Jacob's chin with her tail as she did.

"Hey," he called after her. "Just out of curiosity, what does the word 'shame' mean to you?"

She thought about it.

In that moment, there was nothing human about Judith. A primal flame—bold, pure. Slick with blood, she didn't need a reason to kill. The hot thrill of it was enough. Jacob shuddered. If only he could have seen her in action, helped decorate her body, run a bloody finger along the ridges of her muscles. He would have—

"Nothing," Judith answered. "It doesn't mean a fucking thing."

Jacob poured himself another glass of wine. He sat at a fold-up card table in the basement of a Victorian mansion. It wasn't the best ambience for a glass of wine, but it would have to do. The parlor upstairs would have been nice, but he might run into Rebecca or Judith there and he didn't have the energy to deal with either of them.

Something had been bothering him all day. What had happened to the population of central Illinois? He and Judith had dispatched the occasional crazy in Springfield, but they hadn't encountered anything like the horde that emerged each night in the cities to the east. Where had everyone gone?

Micah called Cincinnati the Dark City. It was the opposite of the Golden City. How exactly the places were in opposition, she couldn't explain. Although her visions didn't make sense, something about them rang true. As Jacob traveled farther west, the world seemed to fade in some indescribable way. The air in Springfield didn't hum like it did back home.

Perhaps crazies had sensed that too. They migrated east for a more stimulating, Darkness-infused atmosphere. It wasn't like they had jobs, families, or anything of the sort to root them to any particular place. Didn't some mysterious calling along those lines draw Micah in the opposite direction?

He lit another candle on the table in hopes of driving the shadows back a bit. This basement was creepy, even for a demon. As it turned out, more flickering candlelight only made it creepier.

Maybe the local crazies had simply starved to death in their basements, attics, and other hiding places. How long could a bunch of psychopaths obsessed with some dark desire or another survive on their own?

Jacob's thoughts returned to his daughter and her strange visions. If Cincinnati truly was a focal point for Darkness, what kind of place was this Golden City? A shiver ran down his spine. For no reason he could articulate, he didn't want to go one inch farther west.

"Dad?" a small voice called from the basement stairs.

"I'm down here."

Micah shuffled up to the card table wearing a flannel nightgown with long slits down the back to slip her wings through. "Can't sleep," she said.

"That's a first. Want to hang out with me? I'm exploring a wine rack I found down here."

"Yuck." Rubbing her eyes like a sleepy toddler, she took a seat on the other side of the table.

Jacob drained his glass of cabernet then poured another after toying with the idea of switching to malbec. How could this perfect little person, his sweet girl, be possessed of anything like the Darkness he had in him? Impossible. He swirled his wine, such a deep red it appeared black in the dim lighting. Maybe he'd had too much to drink; a shimmering mist of sentimentality had settled over his mind. *That's fine*, he thought. *I might look like the devil made flesh, but I can still enjoy the occasional tender moment.*

"Dad?"

"Yeah, M?"

"What would've happened if those helicopter guys caught us?"

That wasn't what he wanted to think about just then. A reassuring answer failed to materialize, so Jacob said nothing.

"It would have been bad, right?"

"Yeah, it would have been bad."

"Mom says all the stuff she's doing will help us find a safe place to live. Is that true?"

"I don't know. She thinks so."

There was a long silence as Micah mulled things over. "She doesn't believe me about the Golden City and us going west. She thinks I'm crazy."

"Oh, no, honey. She doesn't think that. She just… She wants to do things her way."

A couple minutes later, Micah fell asleep in her chair and Rebecca came to carry her back to bed.

The next day, Jacob sat in the living room, ostensibly reading a novel but mostly eying Judith. She lay on her belly on the floor flipping through a fashion magazine. Her white blazer, unbuttoned with nothing but a bra underneath, held his gaze at the moment, but her skintight jeans demanded a lingering glance every now and again. Her tail swayed over the rest of her body like a lone palm tree on a picturesque beach.

Micah waddled into the room wrapped so thickly in blankets she resembled a laundry pile. "Daddy! Pick me up!" she said, giggling.

He did. It was ridiculous. It was amazing. He felt her weight, the outline of her body. She was there, wiggling inside her cocoon, laughing with joyous abandon.

Micah sat on a barstool in a sunny kitchen. Well, not sunny exactly, but close. Each time they changed houses, she found the room with the most windows and polished them until they sparkled. It focused the light. This kitchen had lots of windows.

She decided to ask her dad if they could stay a while the next time she saw him. Maybe he'd even agree to make this their only Springfield home. He said moving around confused anybody trying to spy on them, but Micah thought all that spying stuff was in his head. Who would be dumb enough to mess with him and Judith?

The second Micah thought of her, Judith walked into the room. Maybe summoning people by thinking about them was a new superpower! She thought about her mom to try to make her appear too, but it didn't work.

"Morning, kid," Judith said as she rummaged through a drawer.

"What're you looking for?"

"A rubber band. I want to do pigtails, but I only have one hair tie."

"Here," Micah said. "You can have mine." She pulled out her ponytail, hopped off her stool, and put her hair tie on the counter near Judith.

"Thanks. This'll feel better than a rubber band." With a flick of Judith's wrists, the scary needles she used to fix herself and Micah's dad when they got hurt appeared. Muttering bad words, she used the needles to pick knots out of her hair.

"I wish I could help," Micah said. "Your hair's so pretty."

"Not as pretty as yours. I mean, look at that stuff! It's lit up like a light bulb. I'm jealous. I don't glow at all."

Micah giggled, which happened a lot when she hung out with Judith. "Hey," she said. "Bend down. Let me see something."

Judith brought her face level with Micah's. Being so close, they felt each other's magic. It made Micah a little sick to her stomach, but not too bad; she was used to it. Judith's magic was quick, like lightning bolts shooting off in every direction—not at all like her dad's heavy, liquid magic. Micah looked deeply into Judith's eyes.

"What? Is there something gross on my face?" Judith asked.

Micah looked deeper, past the golden mirrors of her friend's eyes, past muscles and bones, into the place where—

Judith's eyes flashed red. Then she was gone, leaving Micah staring at empty space.

"You're not supposed to do that," Judith said from behind her.

Micah turned to face her. "It's not fair. Dad can smash walls and pick up cars just by looking at them. You do all kinds of cool stuff. All I have is that soul-peek thing, which takes so long to do that people always escape before I can finish. Light magic sucks."

The kitchen filled with Judith's laughter. "Demons are the scariest things around, but when one catches a glimpse of you, they piss themselves and run crying for their mommy. That's got to count for something."

Micah sulked. "I guess."

"You shouldn't do that to your friends though," Judith added. "You might not like what you see."

Micah remembered peering into the black pits the Pale Gentleman had for eyes. The things she had seen...bones pulled from screaming people's bodies, tongues and ears cut off, skin peeled away. She had seen it all through his cold, clinical mind. The people he did those things to were nothing to him, just bodies.

But it couldn't be that bad to look into Judith's eyes, not a chance.

***

Micah saw more than anyone wanted her to. She knew the tension between the adults in her life was a screw being driven deeper and deeper into brittle wood, splitting it with each turn. Something needed to be done, and she had an idea: a camping trip.

Setting aside his concerns about easily spotted campfires and roving crazies after dark, Jacob agreed to make it happen. He didn't want to be the one to disappoint Micah. As it turned out, no one else did either. Supplies were gathered; tents were procured; and with only a minimal amount of bickering, the Freemans (plus one) piled into the tank and set off for a nearby lake.

Fresh air smelling of trees and earth; clean, cool water; green everywhere—nature had a miraculous calming effect on everyone. Even Rebecca lightened up. They explored overgrown trails, swam in the lake, skipped stones, and did all the other things families do on camping trips.

As the sky faded to gray, the group settled in for the night under a dense canopy of trees. Firelight lazily flickered over the campsite. Although darkness pressed in all around, the world was safe and warm under their dome of light. Crickets chirped. Micah toasted some marshmallows she had found somewhere. Rebecca did nothing at all, which was unprecedented in recent memory.

A log shifted in the fire. Jacob leaned forward to poke at it, which proved to be a bad idea. His back spasmed and cramped up. Earlier that evening, Judith had gotten carried away during an impromptu game of King of the Rock they had played in lieu of training. She pushed him off a ten-foot-high boulder into a shale creek bed, where he landed flat on his face. Not satisfied she had sufficiently won, she then launched herself from the top of the boulder and delivered a flying kick to Jacob's spine as he lay prone. Things weren't quite right back there.

"Still hurt?" Judith asked.

"Yeah. I think I'll lie down. That might help."

"Do that. On your stomach. And take off your shirt." Her healing needles in hand, she got up from where she had been crouching by the fire.

Jacob eagerly followed her instructions. He had come to love the needles. Straddling his body, Judith took a seat on his backside. Her healing instruments pierced the skin on either side of his spine, and she got to work.

Pleasure and pain struck a perfect harmony. He melted into the soft, fragrant earth. As his eyes closed, he noted that no one was especially alarmed by the display of demonic surgery. Micah watched with interest. Rebecca paid them no mind.

For the first time, the group truly felt like a group. Maybe everyone was getting used to each other. Maybe things would work out.

Cat Sandwich

The camping trip had been such a success, Jacob decided to arrange another outing a few days later. How had he not thought of this earlier? After the nonstop barrage of horror this group had endured, what they needed was some semblance of normalcy; only then would healthy relationships have the space they needed to grow. And what better way to bring all of this about than wholesome, fun family activities?

Several lifetimes ago, Jacob's childhood had been a prison. His father didn't know any way to live other than working himself to death. Far from emotionally dead but bound by fear and pathological restraint as surely as a ship trapped in a frozen sea, his eyes betrayed a desperate longing that would never find words. Jacob's mother had surrendered to depression and alcoholism before he started middle school. On her worst days, she was nearly catatonic. His sister, four years his senior, was a waspish girl prone to erratic bursts of violence, but only against him and only when no one could see.

Each night, the family gathered around a meticulously set table—complete with lit candles for a centerpiece—and ate under an oppressive cloud of silence. Jacob had always suspected this daily display of dysfunction was his mother's cry for help, a cry no one knew how to process, much less respond to.

When Jacob started a family of his own, he was determined to do it right. He'd establish a warm, welcoming home full of life. The results had been mixed, but he had certainly done better than his parents. Saturday afternoons in the park, dinners where people actually spoke to each other, family vacations—endless opportunities for his family to experience life together. Sure, there was his drinking problem and the occasional extramarital adventure. And it didn't help that he wasn't inclined toward the openness and honesty close relationships need to thrive. Still, he had done okay, hadn't he? All that engagement had definitely helped.

Yes, that was precisely what this new iteration of his family needed: more ways to have fun together.

Sightseeing seemed absurd, given the circumstances, but Jacob wanted to visit Lincoln's Tomb. It was Springfield's main tourist attraction, and they hadn't properly explored it yet. Micah loved the idea. (She had always found Lincoln's top hat funny, so Jacob said she could have it if they found it. Why not?) Judith was excited as well, although she didn't remember anything about Lincoln. While less enthusiastic than the others, Rebecca agreed to go along if she could bring some guns to get in a little target practice.

So here they were, on another outing. Jacob leaned against the tank, gazing up at the soaring obelisk that marked Lincoln's grave. It used to mean something, that spike of stone thrust into the sky like a middle finger held up to the universe. Strength, resilience, dignity—supposedly timeless truths from a world whose time had passed. What did it mean now?

A sharp pop echoed from the other side of the monument. That would be Rebecca and her guns. At least her slavish work ethic had paid off there; she was a better shot than any of the snipers Jacob had had the displeasure of being targeted by. Who would have guessed she had harbored a latent talent for marksmanship?

Micah and Judith were using a phone they had found somewhere to take pictures of each other in front of a large bust of Lincoln. Its bronze nose was shiny from being rubbed by generations of tourists, which both girls found hilarious. Judith teleported to the top of Lincoln's head and struck a queen-of-the-mountain pose. Adoring giggles rose from below. She dismounted with a double flip and landed neatly at Micah's side.

Micah wanted to try too. She jumped as high as she could, spreading her wings for a couple unsynchronized flaps. The results weren't spectacular, but she got a few extra inches of lift for her effort.

Seeing his daughter happy filled Jacob with a warmth positively unbecoming of a demon. It felt like thumbing his nose at the Darkness inside him. Despite his misgivings about leaving her in the care of a volatile demon whose pastimes included blood-based body art, murder by striptease, and collecting fashion slaves, Jacob could see why Micah enjoyed spending time with Judith. She was young, free-spirited, and not Mom or Dad.

Who had Judith been before all this? She must have had hopes and dreams, relationships, and all the other things that make up a human life. If by some freak occurrence Jacob had met her then, what would they have thought of each other? No doubt she'd have hated him. He'd probably have hated her too—still been attracted to her, naturally, but hated her. You never know though. Maybe—

A burst of panic knotted Jacob's stomach; something was wrong. He surveyed the area. Judith and Micah were still playing. The pop and crash of Rebecca shooting bottles hadn't changed. Everything seemed okay. There! Footsteps on the other side of the tank. He leaped onto the turret and took a position behind a telekinetic barrier. If anything dangerous was back there, he wanted to draw its attention to himself.

A well-dressed, well-groomed woman in her mid-thirties tiptoed toward the tank. She held a piece of black construction paper in front of her face as though she were hiding behind it. Jacob expected her to run away when he made his presence known, but she didn't. Maybe she hadn't noticed him? He shuffled his feet to make some noise, but she continued her advance. When she finally came to a stop, not ten feet from the tank, she slid her paper shield aside enough to reveal half of a pretty if not beautiful face framed by a blonde bob. "Don't be afraid," she whispered loudly. "I won't hurt you."

Jacob stared, dumbfounded.

"I'm here to help. Yes, I am." She lowered the paper and looked off to the side, as though addressing an invisible audience. *"And to get the prize. Yes...yes...the prize."* For that last bit, her voice had taken on a mustache-twirling, cartoon villain quality.

Jacob raised a hand to do something—contain her, push her back, crush her like a bug, some sort of demon business. He hadn't decided on the particulars yet.

Just then, Judith materialized between him and the stranger. The woman fell to her knees, grasping the paper in front of her face with both hands. Shockingly, she still didn't run.

"Mistress!" the woman yelled, her voice quivering with fear and awe. "You're here!"

"I am," Judith said brightly, although she obviously had no idea what was going on.

Jacob removed the barrier he had placed in front of himself and climbed down from the tank. "What are you doing?" he asked Judith.

"Being polite. What are *you* doing?"

"Protecting us. Where's Micah?"

"Locked up under Lincoln's tower, in the room where they buried him. I told her not to come out, no matter what."

"And you're not with her because..."

"Because we have a guest. This lady came here alone and unarmed to..." Judith turned her attention to the woman. "Why are you here again?"

"To save you!" she answered from behind her paper.

"Got it," Judith said. "See? She's here to help us. Don't you want to hear what she has to say? Maybe pull the stick out of your ass and have some fun?"

"No, I don't. I want to get out of here before anyone else shows up. Do you think we can do that?"

Judith glared at him, disgusted with his lack of demonic spirit. She turned to her new friend and said, "Don't mind him. He's an asshole."

Jacob glared back at her.

"What should we call you?" Judith asked their guest.

The woman shrank from the question, her paper rustling in trembling hands. "Me? I... You want to know about me?"

"Of course!" Judith said with a friendly smile.

"Sue. I'm Sue."

"Nice to meet you, Sue." Judith walked over and stuck out her hand for a shake. Violent tremors spread through Sue's entire body. She released one side of the paper, but couldn't bring herself to reach out to the grinning demon.

Judith grabbed her hand and shook heartily.

Peeking around Sue's ridiculous mask or shield or whatever it was supposed to be, Jacob saw a crazy who looked like she might drop dead from shock right then and there. He gave her a second, but no such luck. She just stood there, paralyzed by Judith's attention.

As if the situation weren't difficult enough, Rebecca stepped around the corner of the tank, a pistol pointed at Sue's head. Something in Jacob deflated. He could forget about finding an easy way out of this now.

"Who is that?" Rebecca demanded.

Jacob spoke before Judith said anything stupid. "Her name's Sue. She showed up a few minutes ago. We've got everything under control. If you want to check on Micah, she's—"

"Shut up. Is she with those people who were trying to kill us?"

"Of course not," Judith said. "You're not trying to kill us, are you, Sue?"

Sue looked mortified. "Me? That...how...I..." She fell into a fit of babbling.

"It's okay," Judith assured her. "We know you don't want to hurt us." As she spoke, she casually touched Sue's shoulder. The woman reacted as though Judith's hand were a live wire.

"She's crazy, isn't she?" Rebecca asked. "Why is there a crazy here?"

"Hey! That's not nice," Judith scolded. "Sue might not have her shit all the way together, but that's no reason to call her names. She's here to help us, isn't that right?"

Sue stood silently next to Judith in a state of bewildered terror, desperately clinging to the paper that covered her face.

"Don't worry," Judith continued. "I won't let the mean old norm get you." She put her arm around Sue's shoulders.

If this act of maternal concern didn't give the crazy a heart attack, nothing would. Unfortunately, it sent her into a state of manic ecstasy instead. She lowered her paper, revealing her whole face for the first time. "Don't be afraid! I'll save you. The White Witch's magic won't work on me. *And collect my prize. Yes, the prize.*"

"White Witch?" Jacob asked.

"The angel, the one who glows, the White Witch. She's got you under a spell. Where is she? I'll go find her." Sue set off toward Lincoln's tomb.

Judith grabbed her by the shoulders and pulled her back. "Hold on. Not so fast."

"But I can stop her," Sue said, her expression the sad confusion of a dog that had been yelled at for something it couldn't possibly comprehend. "The White Witch won't see me with this." She rattled her paper. "It's black."

"Of course she won't." Judith patted Sue's head. "But I need you to stay here with me for a little while, okay?"

Jacob's patience had reached its limit. "Are you finished?" he asked Judith. "We need to leave. Now."

"You've got to be kidding," she replied in disgust. "You really don't want to have fun with her? Not even a little?"

Sue pressed her nose into the paper and tried to sneak off. Judith retrieved her again, not offering any reassurance this time.

"I don't want to do anything with her," Jacob said.

Judith stamped her foot. Her tail jerked and twitched behind her. "Come on! You can even go first. You won't make as big of a mess as I will."

"Forget it."

"What's the matter? Not your type? Get over it. She's not ugly or anything. And she's hot for demons. I can tell. Give her a few minutes to calm down, and she'll be all over you."

"Fuck off, Judith. We're leaving."

"Because *she's* here?" Judith pointed at Rebecca. "Grow a pair. You're a fucking demon!"

"You make me sick," Rebecca interjected. "Is that all you think about? Violence and murder?"

"I don't have to listen to this bullshit!" Judith shrieked, her face flushed. She clenched her fists and gritted her teeth. "You can't make me feel bad about being what I am."

Seeing everyone was distracted, Sue made another attempt to excuse herself, but Judith forced her into a seated position on the ground.

Ignoring Judith, Rebecca cast Jacob a withering scowl. "This is who you let take care of our daughter? Little Miss Monster Pride?"

"I would never hurt Micah!" Judith protested.

"Why not? People are nothing but toys to you. What would stop you?"

"People," Judith said, spitting the word out as though it were a piece of rotten fruit. "What does that even mean? There's you, me, the fucking tank over there...we're all separate things. I like Micah, so I won't hurt her. That doesn't mean I have to be nice to the rest of you assholes." A dark cloud of frustration formed over Judith. For a second, it seemed she might give up on the argument and go sulk somewhere.

Perhaps thinking everyone had forgotten about her, Sue started to stand up again. Judith shot her a murderous look. "Try that again and I'll break your fucking neck." Sue cowered behind her paper.

An idea struck Judith; her face positively lit up with it as she turned her attention back to Rebecca and Jacob. "You guys used to keep animals as pets back in the old world, right?"

"Yeah," Jacob replied, unsure where she was going with this and positive he didn't want to find out.

"But other animals got eaten. You killed them, sliced them up, and ate them."

"Yeah, but—"

"I saw this on the story discs, so don't try to bullshit me. If you liked an animal, a cat or whatever, you kept it as a pet. You fed it, brushed its fur, and called it some cute name like Professor Poopy Pants or whatever. And no matter what, you didn't hurt it, even if it scratched you.

"As soon as you got hungry, though, you went to the kitchen and made yourself a nice meat sandwich. Oh, and what's meat again? Sliced-up animals! Guess you didn't care too much about those animals, huh? That's cool. Take care of the cats you like and fuck all the rest." Judith beamed a triumphant grin.

Rebecca's anger morphed into overt scorn. "We didn't eat cats, you idiot."

"What?" Judith looked to Jacob for confirmation, which he reluctantly gave with a nod. "Why not? Do they taste bad or something?"

Desperate to put this conversation out of its misery, Jacob spoke up. "We didn't eat the same kinds of animals we kept as pets. We mostly ate cows, chickens, and pigs."

"Seriously?" Judith asked, baffled. "Wouldn't it have been easier to eat what was around?"

"No," Rebecca said. "We loved our pets but also loved cats and dogs in a general way. It's called compassion, something you'd know nothing about."

"What about pigs and chickens?" Judith asked, genuinely curious.

"Forget about them!" Rebecca shouted. "The point is love is bigger than an individual person. If you can't feel at least a little compassion for everyone, you aren't a good enough person to truly care about anyone."

Judith thought it over for a moment. "That's dumb," she decided, and sat down beside Sue. "Just because one cat is cool, it doesn't mean some other cat isn't an asshole who needs to get turned into sandwich meat. Same with pigs, I guess. How did you know you weren't eating some really cool pigs, ones it would have been more fun to make friends with? All of this putting things in groups is bullshit. Each thing is its own thing. Right, Sue?"

Sue pulled as much of herself as possible behind her paper.

"Anyway," Judith continued. "Micah is Micah. I like her, so I'm not going to hurt her. Not even if she scratches me or pees on my clothes or whatever."

"I've had enough of this," Rebecca said, disgusted. "Let's go."

"Well then, Queen Norm," Judith said, putting on a show haughty airs. "What do *you* think we should do with Sue? Bitch at her until she runs away?"

"No," Rebecca replied coolly. "She's crazy. That makes her dangerous. We have to get rid of her."

Shock slapped Jacob across the face. He took a step back, as though Rebecca had just burst into flames. "You mean kill her?"

"You heard her, she wants to hurt Micah. If we let her go, she'll follow us and try again. And what if those soldiers find her? She knows we're here."

"Rebecca," Jacob said. "Judith and I can handle this. "You don't have to—"

"We'll do it quickly and humanely," Rebecca said. "Nobody is going to 'have fun' with her. I'll make sure of that."

Jacob didn't know what to say. How had she gotten like this? She was a doctor, for fuck's sake! Doctors didn't think in terms of getting rid of people.

Judith sprang to her feet. In a blur of motion, she stuck a dagger into Sue's forehead. It happened so fast, the crazy didn't even flinch. Not bothering to pull out the blade, Judith simply made it disappear. Sue's body flopped to the ground, a dead hand still gripping her paper shield. Thick, dark blood oozed from the wound.

"Was that humane enough for you?" Judith asked.

Catalyst

Nothing was the same after Lincoln's Tomb. At the heart of the group lay a molten core of hostility, resentment, and suspicion which had now been breached. Conflict erupted everywhere. Suddenly, questions everyone had avoided for months needed answers. Had they given up on the idea of finding civilization? Why were they still in Springfield? Did Micah's condition need treatment? Was Judith family or a prisoner? Resentment settled thickly over the group. They could scarcely stand to be in the same room, much less come together to discuss a path forward. Their descent into dysfunction became a free fall.

One day, while on patrol, Judith picked up a bottle off the sidewalk and flung it at Jacob. He caught it in an invisible bubble then crushed it into sparkling dust, which he let fall like snow. She picked up another bottle but lost interest in the game before throwing it.

"One time I saw this story disc where a guy said he was dying of boredom," she said. "Can you really die from that? Because I think I'm about to."

A long sigh unfurled from Jacob's chest like a white flag of surrender. He leaned against the brick façade of a post office and gazed up at the sky. The same weird, fake sunlight halfheartedly shining on the same streets they had been walking for ages. Just another eighty-four-degree, February day in Illinois. "A change of scenery would be nice," he said.

"Then why, in the name of all-mighty fuck, don't we go somewhere?"

"Rivers," Jacob said vaguely. It was what he always said when the issue of travel came up.

"There's got to be *somewhere* we can go that we haven't already been. I mean, it's just Micah who can't do bridges, right? Why don't you and me—"

Judith stopped short. A male voice crept around the next corner, which was where they had left the tank. The demons sprinted ahead. Two armed men in green combat fatigues stood in front of the tank. Rebecca was with them. The bottom dropped out of the world. Time seemed to simultaneously speed up and slow down.

Judith vanished then seconds later appeared behind one of the men, holding a blade to his throat. The other didn't have time to raise his gun before a telekinetic dome rose around him. Jacob placed another over Rebecca as he ran toward her.

"Wait," he called to Judith. They needed to know if these men were alone, information they wouldn't get from a couple corpses.

Rebecca frantically beat the inside of her barrier, desperate to get Jacob's attention. He opened a gap in the shield and stepped inside. "Are you okay?" he asked, scanning her for injuries.

"Don't hurt them!"

"What's going on? Where's Micah?"

"In the tank. They didn't see her." Rebecca threw a nervous glance at Judith, who was whispering something into her terrified captive's ear. "Oh God. Tell her not to hurt him!"

"Who are those people?" Jacob asked. "And why were you talking to them?"

"They're from a refugee center in St. Louis."

"St. Louis? That's almost a hundred miles away."

"They're looking for people like us," Rebecca said, her eyes fixed on Judith. "They want to help. It's safe in St. Louis. It's what we've been looking for!"

"Bullshit," Jacob said. "They're either scouts for Caleb's army or scavengers."

"They aren't scavengers," Rebecca said. "Look at them. They're clean. Their guns are in perfect condition."

"Caleb's people then."

"No! They're wearing regular army fatigues, not black ones. And wouldn't scouts report back when they saw the tank? They'd never show themselves, not when they knew you must be around."

She had a point. That man Judith was whispering sweet nothings to was about to piss himself. He clearly hadn't expected a couple demons to show up.

"All right," Jacob said. "Assuming I don't have Judith slit their throats—which isn't a safe assumption—what should we do?"

"Talk to them!"

Not long ago it would have been impossible to imagine Rebecca in such a wretched state—tears flowing, eyes pleading, trembling from shoulders to toes. She had always been so self-assured, so strong. Now she teetered on the edge of madness. If this didn't go her way, she'd tumble into an abyss there'd be no bringing her back from. Jacob stepped out of the shield, bracing himself for a barrage of verbal abuse. Judith wouldn't like what he was about to tell her to do.

The two captives took up residence in a holding cell at a nearby police station. Rebecca refused to leave them alone with either of the demons, which severely limited the available interrogation tactics. (Jacob had hoped to indulge in a bit of bad cop, *really* bad cop with Judith.) Despite the restrictions, he did his best to find out who the men were and why they had come to Springfield.

He didn't learn a thing. Whenever he approached the men's cell, they pulled pieces of red cloth printed with a black snake from their pockets and thrust them forward like a couple crucifix-wielding priests in an old vampire movie. Rebecca assumed the snake emblem was some sort of military insignia, but Jacob had his doubts. The men appeared to be defending themselves, not presenting identification. Those scraps of cloth carried a warning, one meant for demons.

The prisoners were more than willing to talk to Rebecca though. And what wondrous things they had to say! They spun tales of a fully functional city with a government, a police force, medical facilities, and so much more. St. Louis served as the Midwestern hub of a coordinated recovery effort that would have civilization up and running again in no time.

"What about people who had changed?" Rebecca asked. "People who grew wings, for example."

As it turned out, St. Louis took an enlightened, cautiously compassionate position toward those who had been more dramatically affected by the "event" than others. Abnormal adults were allowed into the city on a case-by-case basis after a probationary period spent in a camp outside of town, provided they had proven themselves well-behaved and amenable to treatment. Changed children were welcome any time if they had parental consent to participate in the treatment program. The men didn't offer much in the way of details about what treatment entailed, but that didn't bother Rebecca. They were soldiers, not doctors. How were they supposed to know how it worked? St. Louis sounded like a dream come true.

Later that day, the group met to discuss their options. Micah refused to go anywhere if it meant being separated from her father and Judith, even temporarily. And she didn't trust human doctors to "treat" a condition she grew more comfortable with by the day. Her strong opposition saved Jacob the trouble of having to shoot Rebecca's dream down himself. Although he had agreed to talk it over, he had no intention of letting Micah disappear into some treatment center while he waited in demon purgatory.

The group voted, and it didn't go Rebecca's way. If St. Louis meant to resurrect the old world, they'd need to do it without the Freemans. Rebecca took the decision better than expected. The only concession she asked for was that the prisoners' lives be spared. She offered to administer tranquilizers to them the following morning, then unlock their cells after they had lost consciousness. That way, the group could leave town unobserved.

Judith vehemently objected. In no uncertain terms, she let Jacob know he'd have to be an idiot to leave anyone behind, especially soldiers who worked for some unknown organization. She was right, of course. It would have been much safer to kill the prisoners, destroy their bodies, and leave town as soon as possible. But they'd do it Rebecca's way, safe or not. Everyone needed to get a little of what they wanted if this group was ever to grow into a team.

A dozen wine bottles sat on the coffee table in front of Jacob. He regarded them with mild annoyance. They wouldn't all fit in the compartment he had been allotted for personal storage in the tank. Maybe he could talk Micah into putting a few bottles with her stuff.

A pop of air and a change in the lighting. From out of nowhere, Judith appeared in midair halfway between the floor and ceiling. She fell in a limp heap, like a bird shot from the sky. Jacob jumped off the couch, sending wine bottles clinking to the floor, and rushed to her side. Her face was slack, and a rope of drool hung from her mouth.

"Bitch…" Judith mumbled, then passed out.

Jacob slapped her across the face. He didn't know what else to do.

Sluggishly, her eyelids pulled hallway open. "I tried…fucking promise."

Two things happened at once: he sensed someone behind him and felt a prick in the side of his neck. He whirled around to find Rebecca backing away, a large hypodermic needle in her hand. Rage flared in Jacob, then drowned in a deluge of sickness. Gasping and choking, he fell to his knees, struck down by his own promise magic.

Rebecca's steely eyes cut right through him. "It's over, Jacob. I'm taking Micah somewhere safe, somewhere she can get help."

A dull, numb sensation radiated from his chest. He fully collapsed, squirming on the floor, overcome with sickness and poison.

"What…"

"What did I do? I injected you with enough animal tranquilizer to kill a horse. I'm sure you'll be fine though."

"Those men, you don't know anything about them."

"I know they're human! Don't you see, I need to get Micah away from things like you before she forgets who she is."

Jacob wanted to talk to Rebecca, make her see reason. He wanted to curse her for betraying him. He wanted to beg her to reconsider. But the only sound that came out of his mouth was a slurred groan.

"Damn you!" she screamed. "I won't sit here and do nothing." She wiped the tears from her eyes. "Don't follow us. Just forget we ever existed."

Everything went black.

Micah's Rules for a Better World

Truth is real. If you tell lies, try to trick people, you make a fake world where you're all alone. No one can help you when it all falls apart. Tell the truth.

Chapter 9

Prelude

Belief is magic. If you want something to be true badly enough, it is. Or at least it feels that way.

Betrayal

Rebecca couldn't see. Bound at the wrists and stuffed into the trunk of a car, she could hardly move. The bag over her head made each breath hot and musty. *What am I going to do?*

She reached into the dark, searching for skin, hair, feathers even, any sign that Micah was there too. Her fingers slid over links of cold metal wrapped around a child's body. Chains. The sound of the engine and the tires on the road kept her from hearing Micah's breathing, hearing if she moaned or whimpered. How much longer would the drugs she had given her last?

The men had said they'd take her somewhere safe. They said Micah would be welcome there even in her current state. Lies!

Dark had fallen long before Rebecca returned to the jail to release the soldiers. The second she walked into the room with Micah sleeping in her arms, the color drained from the men's faces. They didn't see a child in need of their help; they saw a monster. Rebecca should have known something was wrong. How had she been so stupid? Why would those men have reacted that way if they had helped kids like Micah before as they said they had?

Rebecca's hands clenched into balls of rage, her fingernails digging into her palms. She kicked at the inside of the trunk, which accomplished nothing.

The soldiers had bristled with anxiety as they led her to their car. Neither spoke. She assured herself they were just worried about getting out of town before Jacob and Judith woke up. And if they kept casting nervous glances at Micah, who could blame them? There would have been trouble if she woke up too.

They took Rebecca to a beat-up taxicab, its Missouri plates offering a glimmer of reassurance that everything was just as they had said it was. Careful with Micah's strange appendages, she laid her in the back seat. After fussing over the sleeping child, Rebecca took a moment to stretch her shoulder muscles beside the car. Micah didn't weigh much, but it must have been a half mile walk from the jail. Rebecca's breath came easier. She had done it; she had really done it.

Just as the first delicate leaves of hope sprouted, a storm of violence ripped them to shreds. One of the men grabbed her around the waist from behind, forcing the air from her lungs. He wrestled her to the ground. She fought as best she could, but he was much bigger than her and had all the leverage. The pistol she had brought skittered away across the pavement. Handcuffs clamped down on her wrists.

The other man popped the taxi's trunk and pulled out a pile of chains.

Rebecca screamed, her body thrashing. The man on top of her slapped a beefy hand over her mouth. She bit. Cursing, he pulled his wounded hand back. Rebecca braced herself, expecting him to hit her. Instead, he took a black cloth bag from his pocket and slipped it over her head. Everything went dark. Chains jingled. Car doors opened and closed.

Minutes later, the men lifted her from the ground and threw her into the backseat of the car. Micah wasn't there. Rebecca prayed they had left her on the side of the road. Jacob would find her and take her back to Springfield, then...then she would become a monster like him. The totality of Rebecca's failure crushed her. She could say nothing, do nothing, think nothing.

The taxi's engine awakened with a rattling cough. Gravel crunched as the prisoners-turned-kidnappers pulled away from the side of the road. If these men only wanted to save their own skins, why hadn't they simply run away? Why take Rebecca with them? Was she a hostage? She wished some horrid, bloodthirsty thing would swoop down on the taxi and kill them.

"Now *that's* how we do it!" the driver yelled, pounding on the steering wheel for emphasis.

"I don't know about this," the passenger said with a hint of a New York accent that contrasted with his partner's Appalachian drawl.

"Jesus fucking Christ," the driver said. "Luckiest day of our goddamn lives and all you do is bitch and moan."

"Lucky? You call getting caught by gods lucky?"

"We're alive, ain't we? And we got a golden ticket packed in the trunk. I call *that* lucky."

"Yeah, until it wants out of there," the passenger said. "Then we're dead. You realize that, right? Dead."

"No faith. That's your problem, Ron. No faith. Them chains'll hold. They're special made for just this sort of situation."

A tense silence settled between the two men. There was a sharp click, and the passenger, Ron, inhaled deeply. Cigarette smoke filled the car. "What are we going to do with her? The human, I mean?"

"Not what we done last time, if that's what you're thinking," the driver said through cackling laughter.

"Fuck off. That's not what I meant."

"What's the matter? This one too old for you?"

"No," Ron said. "I'll tell you what's the matter. We've got a fucking god in our trunk and you're joking around."

The driver lost it, sending the car into a swerve as he let lose with peels of laughter.

"Hey!" Ron yelled. "Eyes on the road, asshole." He gave his partner a few seconds to settle down. "That lady back there is together with the god. What if she causes trouble later on? I'm thinking maybe we don't bring her back to town."

"You cold-hearted son of a bitch," the driver replied, making it sound like a compliment. "But Captain said to bring back any stragglers with special skills, and she's a doctor. That thing between her and the god has got to be a spell or some such. She'll be right as rain soon as we put some distance between the two of them. Hell, I bet she'll thank us."

"And what makes you so sure it's a spell?" Ron asked, skeptical to the point of derision.

"You ever known a god to accept the company of somebody who *wasn't* under their spell?"

A cold, utterly humorless laugh filled the passenger side of the car. "Yeah, well, I've never heard of the motherfuckers teaming up with each other either. Were you paying attention back there? That guy with the horns, the crazy bitch with a tail, and now a kid with wings—all these gods around and somehow the human gets the better of them all and saves our asses, carrying one of them like a fucking baby. You don't think that's suspicious?"

"Ain't our place to wonder why," the driver said. "All I'm thinking about is the reward we've got coming to us. That sweet little thing back there is our golden ticket, my friend. Golden fuckin' ticket."

Rebecca's paralysis broke. She kicked. She screamed. The men pulled over and threw her into the trunk. How long ago had that been? Impossible to know.

Tortured hours passed as the car moved on unseen roads toward God only knew where. Rebecca cried, she prayed, time and again she cursed herself. Finally, the rumble of the engine cut off. She heard voices outside, a lot of voices. With a click, the trunk popped open. Someone shone a light over her, filling the bag over her head with gray-blue gloom.

"Good Lord almighty," said a man who wasn't either of the ones who had taken her.

"Sir?" a woman asked.

The man sighed. "Can't be helped. That don't make this shit any easier, but it can't be helped. Get 'em out of there."

Rough hands pulled Rebecca from the trunk and set her on her feet outside. Blindly she swung her handcuffed arms like a club.

"Goddamn it!" a male voice roared. "Why aren't her hands secured behind her back?"

"I'd like to see you do any better with somebody biting you," Ron said from somewhere to Rebecca's right.

As the two men argued, a rush of sound swallowed their voices. Shuffling feet, shouts and whispers, engines—too many noises to process. Dozens of people, hundreds maybe, swarmed around Rebecca. Someone grabbed her handcuffs and yanked. "Move it!" a man yelled at her. Unable to do anything but follow, she staggered blindly forward.

After an eternity of stumbling and jostling, the man leading her stopped and pulled the bag off her head. She stood in the middle of a broad road, facing an enormous church. Firelight danced across the building's stone surface, cast from bonfires around its walls and torches set into its facade like blazing eyes. A towering dome rose from the church's midpoint, disappearing into the black sky. Twin spires flanked the dome. From each hung a red banner bearing the snake emblem her captors had shown Jacob in Springfield.

Rebecca stood at the end of a long line of armed soldiers, stretching along the road. At the center of the formation, two men propped up Micah, who was wrapped in chains from her shoulders to her knees. A dirty rag was stuffed in her mouth and secured with a wire wrapped around her head so tightly it cut a ghastly grin into her cheeks. Eyes wide, she stared at the nightmarish scene in utter incomprehension.

More than anything, Rebecca wanted to look away, to see anything except what was there to see. Her fault, all of this.

With a groan, the church's wooden doors swung open. The entire world seemed to hold its breath as a current of nervous energy ran through the line of soldiers. What emerged from the darkened doorway couldn't have been real. There must be a limit to how wrong the world had become. Green-and-black scales glittered in the firelight. Gray hair, filthy and tangled, fell over a human face. Arms, shoulders, and withered breasts. An endless, serpentine body trailing up the stairs behind it, more and more slithering out of the darkened cathedral each second.

No. Impossible.

Rebecca couldn't breathe. Reality itself warped, blurring everything but the thing that moved toward her. Part old woman, part monstrous snake, the beast came to a stop not six feet from her and raised its human section like a cobra preparing to strike. A leather belt wrapped around its body where hips should have been, bones dangling from it on silver chains. Vertebrae, half a jaw, parts of fingers—all children's bones.

As the nightmare grinned in a perversion of friendliness, a forked tongue flickered between its fangs. Yellow eyes regarded Rebecca with detached amusement. "You poor dear," it said, its voice that of a fairy-tale witch. "Just look at the state of you!"

Rebecca's knees buckled. Her pulse hammered at her temples. None of this could be real.

"Don't you worry about a thing," the snake said. "These boys will look after you. Why don't you run along and have yourself a good, long rest? It'll do you a world of good." The thing twisted toward Micah.

Rebecca's voice erupted from deep within her body. "Leave her alone! Do whatever you want with me. Just let her go."

The monster looked back at her. "My goodness! What's got you so worked up? That sweetie over there?"

"Let her go."

"Now, why would I go and do a thing like that? She's the whole reason the boys called me out here. I only stopped to chat with you to be polite."

Rebecca screamed. There weren't words, only a scream.

The snake nodded a farewell and slithered off, its belt of bones rustling.

Interlude

Lamia woke from a dream. It hadn't been hers, of course. The little boy nestled in the coils of her body had made it. And now the poor dear's dreamland had gone dark; he was all used up. She tossed around the idea of taking a bone to remember him by, but decided against it. His dreams had been nice enough, but nothing worth making a fuss over.

Everyone needs a hobby, something to keep their mind occupied as time drifts on by. Some folks took up knitting, gardening, or some such. Lamia didn't care for busywork. Oh, she dabbled in metalwork and had gotten pretty good at it, if she said so herself, but for relaxation nothing beat curling up with a little sweetie and peeking in on a dream.

She could visit anyone's dreams, provided they were sound asleep in her nest—and people in her nest always slept soundly—but she had a taste for children's dreams. Grown-ups' heads were full of doubt and confusion, which muddied up their dreams. Too many ingredients and not enough flavor! Children had simple dreams, pure. Well, most children did at any rate.

From time to time, Lamia dipped her tail into dreamlands that sprung from special people such as herself. If there was one thing to be said for special people, it was that they knew what they wanted. Their dreams burst with flavor, but almost never the kind anyone would care to taste. Blood and guts, greed, and the dirty things people do in the dark. No, thank you! The world outside had plenty of that; Lamia didn't need it in her dreamlands.

But for the most part, she didn't bother with dreamworlds when she dragged a special person into her nest. As soon as they fell asleep, out came the cutting wire. She kept their bones, but the rest of them got tossed out with the trash. Serves them right for making a nuisance of themselves in her city.

That was how she dealt with grown-up special people anyhow, and for the longest time she hadn't know there to be any other kind. That was before Mole Boy.

Back when Lamia lived in her old nest, a cozy spot in the tunnels under the roads, she went into the world above to hunt for children. (Nowadays the boys who looked after her took care of all that.) On her way out one night, she came across Mole Boy fast asleep on her floor. A shiny bauble she had picked up on a lark the last time she had gone hunting rested in his extra-wide paw.

Now, Lamia couldn't abide thievery. What was hers was hers! She fetched the cutting wire straight away and wrapped it around the boy's neck. But as she pulled it tight, something about his pinprick eyes and snub-nosed snout stirred her poor, old heart. Such a precious little face! A boy like that couldn't make one of those nasty dreamworlds other special people made, could he? Seeing as he was already asleep, she supposed there wouldn't be any harm in taking a peek.

And glory be, what lovely things she saw! Mole Boy's dreams were as sweet as any common child's but as vivid as a special person's. All the little sweetie wanted was to burrow into the earth and sleep. He dreamed of sleeping! Sometimes he'd wake up to chase after some shiny treasure or other, but digging and sleeping were his favorite things. And while she visited his dreamland, they were Lamia's favorite things too.

Lazy, carefree nights passed in perfect peace. By the time Lamia pulled away, finally hungry for different dreams, she had long since thrown out any notion of killing Mole Boy. She'd stash him away and visit him whenever she wanted to take it easy for a few days. He was special, so his dreamland would never go dark.

But first she needed to make room for him. Her nest hadn't been built to accommodate guests. She'd be slithering over Mole Boy every time she turned around unless she expanded it. Lamia had never had occasion to change her nest, so she couldn't be blamed for not knowing the whole darn thing would stop working if she tinkered with it. As soon as she took down the back wall to push it farther down the tunnel, the nest's sleeping spell sputtered out like a candle in a strong breeze. By the time she got back to where she had left Mole Boy, he was gone.

After a fair bit of wailing and gnashing of teeth, Lamia resolved to catch every special child she could. Some of them were liable to have dreams as nice as Mole Boy's. She'd build a new nest, one big enough to keep as many children as she wanted. It would be the biggest nest anyone had ever seen! Oh, and she'd stuff it with shiny treasures to attract greedy little things. Mole Boy himself might even come back if the bait in her trap was sweet enough.

It didn't take long to find the perfect place, a mountain of a building chock-full of glittery gold and sparkly stones. Open spaces had always given Lamia the heebie-jeebies, so the prospect of living above ground had her nerves in a tizzy. But something she had read in one of the books cluttering her nest gave her the courage to stick to her plan, a poem about a dream deferred rotting away like old meat. If she put this off, she might never get it done and the idea would eat away at her until kingdom come.

Common folk lived above her tunnels, but she didn't expect any trouble from them. She had never paid them much mind, so they should have no quarrel with her. Oh sure, they got riled up when they caught her snatching a sweetie off the street or stretching up high to pluck one from a bedroom window. Why, a few times they had gone so far as to come after her with guns blazing. (Just what they thought children ought to be doing that was so much more important than keeping an old woman company, Lamia never did figure out.) Nothing like that had happened for weeks though. Water under the bridge.

Still, Lamia and the common folk weren't exactly on speaking terms, so it came as quite the shock when a group of them paid her a social call one night while she worked on her nest. That business with the Owl Man must have given them a change of heart about her.

A couple nights before, sirens started blaring and all around, people took to screaming and running around. The same thing happened whenever someone spotted her taking a sweetie, except she hadn't done anything this time. How was she supposed to concentrate on her work with all this racket?

Aggravated, Lamia swished through the empty streets, looking for whatever had caused such a commotion. She came across a group of common folk hiding inside a wrecked car. A little man with an owl's head stood on the hood, flapping his wings and carrying on. He was so fixed on those poor people in the car that he didn't even hear Lamia creeping up behind him.

Quick as a wink, she wrapped her tail around him and squeezed the air out of his lungs. Before he could use whatever special powers he had, she took her cutting wire from the belt she liked to wear and set about removing his fool head. Once the job was done, she gave the people in the car—who looked more than a little green around the gills—a neighborly wave and went about her business.

She didn't expect anything to come of all that, but then those young men stopped by her nest. She thought they meant to run her out of town, which didn't seem very bright. Common folk weren't known for their smarts though. As it turned out, they wanted to thank her for what she had done. She said it was no trouble at all. The idea of special people prowling around her territory, scaring off all the children, had never sat well with her.

Her visitors asked if it might be all right to send any special people they found snooping around the city her way. That sounded like a fine idea to Lamia. It would save her the trouble of hunting down threats to her supply of children. The men couldn't have been happier. By way of thanks, they said they'd help with some improvements inside her nest and offered to gussy up the outside with torches, banners, and the like. Such nice boys.

To keep her mind off all the sweeties she was missing out on while she toiled away on her nest, Lamia whipped up a batch of the magic metal she had learned to make.

Quite the story there, how someone like her took up metalsmithing of all things. In the early days of Lamia's life, not long after she woke up in the tunnels snuggling up with a dead child already gone to rot, a traveling salesman had come calling, a special person with holes where he ought to have had eyes. This man spun tales of murder, thievery, and all the nasty things that might happen to an old woman living on her own. Scared her something awful! But this man, he had just the thing for a lady with a mind to protect herself. And all Lamia needed to do was give him a few scales and a bottle of venom.

Oh, he went on and on about artifacts and dark magic, but who could keep all that straight? A bunch of mumbo jumbo, if you asked her. And never in her life had Lamia met anyone with such a dull way of speaking. Why, if she spoke that way she wouldn't need a magic nest to put folks to sleep. Anyhow, she gave the man what he wanted, and true to his word he taught her how to make magic metal.

A concoction of steel, bone, and a drop of her own venom—it was just the thing for taking care of any special people who stuck their noses in her business. Her cutting wire was the very first thing she made with magic metal and it had served her well ever since. Of course, her metal had other uses besides killing special people. It worked for catching them too, or at least Lamia reckoned it would. With just a touch, it left them as helpless as babes.

She took a few of the boys down to the workshop in her new nest and showed them the trick of shaping her metal before it cooled. They could make whatever they wanted, as long as they promised to bring her any special children they happened to catch with it. Nothing was likely to come of it, but they had offered to help her with anything she might need, so it didn't hurt to ask.

From there on out, relations with the common folk only got more cordial. Once her nest was finished, they started bringing her their extra children so she didn't need to trouble herself with going out to fetch them. What a nice surprise! The boys even stopped by every so often to clean up any used-up sweeties lying around.

Imagine Lamia's surprise when just a few months later, a crowd of common folk showed up on her doorstep with not one but *two* special children, all wrapped up in her magic metal. Hoping one of the bundles held Mole Boy, she slithered out into the road as fast as her old body would carry her.

But instead of her fuzzy little treasure, she found a couple honest-to-goodness monsters. The first one, a filthy girl with wild hair, growled and thrashed about in spite of the magic chains on her. The second was a boy with a rat's tail who squealed curses at her. They both stank to high heaven. Never in all her nights had Lamia encountered such wretched children. There wasn't anything sweet about them, not a thing. She had half a mind to tell the boys to take them back to wherever they had found them, but she thought that might be rude, considering how many boys had died catching them.

The little beasts were in her nest now, tucked away in dreamlands Lamia didn't have the slightest inclination to visit. Still, it didn't hurt to keep them around in case she changed her mind. She could always take the cutting wire to them if more tasty treats came along.

Lamia hadn't thought special people much cared for each other's company, but going by the way word spread after the boys caught those children for her, she figured they must gossip like a bunch of old hens. Rumors spread far and wide. Some said she murdered her own kind out of sheer meanness; others claimed she had a way to make slaves of them; still others accused her of the worst kinds of indecency with her prisoners. And the fact that she had given common folks tools to do her hunting for her... Goodness, did that ever raise some hackles. For one reason or the other, special people came from far and wide to put an end to her. Not a one made it farther than the entrance to her nest.

Before long, they gave up on the idea of killing her. Instead, every special person for a hundred miles around ran off, children included. How would Lamia find a new a Mole Boy now?

It wasn't in her nature to mope, so she counted her blessings. Her prospects of finding special sweeties might have dwindled, but the boys had brought her so many common children, she could be choosy about which dreamlands she visited each night. Her life wasn't so bad, not so bad at all. She'd be a right fool to complain.

A bell rang, pulling Lamia from her reverie. That would be the boys coming to clean her nest. Such nice boys, so considerate. She stretched, uncoiling herself. The child whose dream had gone dark a while back fell to the ground with a soft rustle. He was skin and bones, the poor dear. As she slithered away from his cell, her mind moved on to happier things, and it was as if the used-up child had never existed.

Not feeling sociable, Lamia retreated to her private rooms while the boys worked. After they had gone, she found a note taped to her door.

"Great Serpent," it read, "Magnificent, Queen of—" She skipped past the foolishness they always wrote before getting to the point. "A god child will be presented outside your nest in four hours' time (6:00 am). We, your humble servants, request your presence so you might receive our offering."

"Oh my!" Lamia gasped. Her lips curled into a delighted smile, revealing sharp fangs.

Chapter 10

Prelude

We worship that which lifts us from the black pit of despair, offers us hope. But what if we can't find hope? What if we can't even imagine it? That's when we fall to our knees and pray to fear itself. And so, our cruelest gods are born—monstrous things that loom just past the limits of imagination, gods to whom only one prayer is possible: *Spare me.*

The Voice of Darkness

A man stood in darkness, his curved horns glowing faintly, as if catching moonlight. But there was no moon. The man and Jacob's prone body at his feet—there was nothing else. Jacob gasped. He couldn't breathe the thick, hot air.

"Pathetic," the man said, his voice an oily sneer.

In a choked whisper, Jacob asked, "Where am I?"

"The same place we always are."

Jacob tried to stand but didn't have the strength. His own weight crushed him. "Help me. I need to…"

"Feeble thing. Stunted. Malformed. A parody of what we might have been." The words fell like stones.

"Let me go," Jacob pleaded. "I have to find them."

"Oh? Have your lambs wandered off? You must be a poor shepherd indeed."

"I..." Jacob's lungs couldn't hold enough air to form words.

"Forget them. Their pitiful bleating has corrupted you, turned you against yourself."

Jacob forced everything he had into a desperate cry. "Let me go!"

"Ah, spirit. If only it weren't so poorly applied."

Exhausted, Jacob lay down and let his eyes close. He had failed. Micah and Rebecca were gone. There wasn't any reason to keep fighting. The world around him became both an ocean and a void, impossibly dense yet nothing at all. He surrendered himself to it, letting it fill the empty spaces in him before pain could settle in. Gentle waves polishing a stone, erasing him.

But as everything else washed away, the strangest thing happened. Something stubbornly solid emerged in the mental place where he often felt the weight of his magical promises. Whatever this thing was, he couldn't surrender it to Darkness, because it wasn't his to give.

Jacob clung to the intrusion, holding it in his mind like a precious memory. He had always thought of the promises as obligations—most obliging others to him, but obligations nonetheless. But this...this resonated with life and potential. If he took it in hand and held fast, anything was possible, anything at all.

"Judith," he whispered. Thoughts of her drifted through his mind: the feel of her body, her smell, the way her eyes burned.

"Ah, yes," the man said. "That vulgar toy you've shackled us to."

Jacob pulled himself up into a kneeling position. He found it easier to breathe now. "She's not a toy."

"What then?"

"My partner."

Cruel, cutting laughter like the torturer's blade peeling skin from a living body. "Such delusions!" the man shouted into the void. "Partner? What a pathetic, bumbling child you are." He paused, considering his next words. "Still, she is lovely, I'll grant you that—an oasis in our desert of deprivation. And yet, despite the risks you've taken in securing her company, we haven't yet enjoyed the pleasure of her flesh. Why is that?"

Jacob climbed to his feet. "I've had enough of this. Let me go."

The man heaved a sigh. "So eager to return to your servitude. This place is ours; you can leave whenever you wish. But before you do, a word of advice: To trifle with desire is to court madness. Take what you want before the wanting of it ruins you."

"And what do I want?"

"The path has always been there. These gifts we have received only clear the way so we can fully explore it. Society, morality, even the memory of such things—all gone. Nothing stands between us and the objects of our desire. You know our nature. Stop resisting it."

"Liar," Jacob said. "I wasn't always like this. Darkness changed me. *You* changed me."

The man laughed again, and once again blades seemed to cut into Jacob's flesh. "A wolf in sheep's clothing is still a wolf, even if the creature has deluded itself into believing otherwise."

"Bullshit," Jacob said. "You're nothing but a parasite. You don't know the first thing about me."

"Listen well," the man said. "Our time grows short. There's danger you refuse to see. Our toy's games have been a sweet torment, but they must not continue. Your desire for her is a festering wound. Don't allow the rot to spread."

"You're asking me to release Judith?"

"What a timid little thing you are." Scorn saturated his voice. "If you turn your back on her now, regret will eat away at you for all your nights. This passion must run its course. You hunger for her, and the time has come to feast."

"You haven't been paying attention, have you? Sleeping with me isn't in her contract."

"The revoltingly lenient terms of your agreement include a leash clause, do they not? Use it. Put enough distance between her and us to make her suffer. When she comes begging for relief, perhaps we'll find her a bit more receptive to our needs."

"You're sick," Jacob said.

"No," the man replied. "Look around, see how the world is. *You* are the disease."

St. Louis

"Wake up!"

Jacob had a vague sensation of motion, like being at the bottom of a deep pool when something upsets the water's surface.

"Wake up!"

A bright ray of pain shot through his body, ripping away the fog that had clouded his mind. Everything became acutely real. Judith's dagger was buried several inches deep in his thigh. She moved the blade from side to side as if trying to scratch an itch located on his femur. Before Jacob could curb the instinctive reaction, he sent her flying across the room. She bounced off a wall and landed in a crouch.

Howling in pain, he sat bolt upright, blood squirting from between the fingers he had pressed to his wounded leg. "What the fuck, Judith?"

She appeared at his side with her healing needles out. "You're lucky promise magic knows when to let me hurt you. We've got to move."

Minutes later the two demons sat in the tank, rumbling toward St. Louis. Neither spoke. They both knew their rescue mission was almost certainly futile. It would be a miracle if anything the captured soldiers had said turned out to be true. More than likely, those men had killed Rebecca at the first opportunity, or taken her back to wherever they really came from, which might be worse. Jacob didn't want to think about what they might do to a little girl with wings.

But he needed to do *something*. The plan was to cross the Mississippi River north of St. Louis in case the bridges that led directly into the city from Illinois were guarded. Downtown seemed as likely a place as any for a camp or a town or whatever the fuck. They'd start the search there. After they hid the tank, they'd proceed on foot, hopefully without alerting the locals. To a couple demons, the element of surprise held more value than whatever protection their noisy hunk of steel offered.

Rebecca's animal tranquilizers had knocked Jacob and Judith out for almost twelve hours. Daylight had come and gone by the time they recovered and made their way to St. Louis in a lumbering machine that topped out at forty miles per hour.

As they approached the Mississippi River, it became apparent their tank wasn't the first machine of war to come through. Instead of abandoned neighborhoods littered with bodies, they found rubble and ruin. The shattered remains of buildings sunk into craters from artillery or bombs. Hundreds of skeletons, picked clean so they shone a ghastly white under the moon, lay all around. By the state of them and the way they were arranged, they had died at the same time, probably in the earliest days of the new world.

After crossing a thankfully unguarded bridge and making their way into the city proper, the demons stashed the tank in a parking garage then set off into the unknown. This part of town had been spared the mass destruction they had seen earlier. It was an old neighborhood of derelict row houses, vacant lots marring the streets like voids in a mouthful of rotting teeth. The place had been mostly abandoned long before the world ended. A heavy stillness hung over the city, which didn't seem right. A city St. Louis's size should have been crawling with crazies this time of night.

By the look of things, there had been an organized effort to defend St. Louis. Barricades and checkpoints blocking intersections, clusters of skeletal remains dressed in military fatigues, bullet casings everywhere—these tired old streets had seen a brutal, street-by-street battle. Many of the dead wore National Guard patches from various Midwestern and Southern states.

An icy dread snaked up Jacob's spine. He took Judith's hand. To his surprise and relief, she didn't pull away. They were in a place of death. The living weren't welcome.

Growing more uneasy by the second, the demons rounded a corner, then stopped short. The road—no, the entire city—had come to an abrupt end. A vast expanse of empty space opened before them, devoid of buildings or even ruins to mark where buildings had once stood, nothing but rubble bulldozed smooth. The blasted landscape could have been the surface of the moon under a dense, black sky.

In the distance, across the sea of dust and stone, an orange glow colored the sky. Shadows of skyscrapers rose above a colossal wall, exposed bones jutting from a corpse. Fires blazed there, a lot of fires.

"What the hell?" Jacob whispered.

"Did this place always have a ditch around it and a huge wall?" Judith asked.

"No... No, it didn't."

The demolition zone stretched as far as he could see to the left and the right. There wasn't time to find a way around. After exchanging a nervous glance, he and Judith pressed on. Uncomfortably exposed on the barren terrain, they broke into a steady jog. Tense seconds shot by like flaming arrows. The wall grew into a hulking mass of concrete and corrugated metal ringed with guard towers. If anyone was on duty in the towers, they failed to notice two figures gliding through the dark.

Minutes later, the demons huddled together at the wall's base. How had such a structure been built after everything fell apart? The implications spun through Jacob's head: construction equipment, engineering expertise, the means to fend off crazies and quite possibly demons. What were he and Judith up against?

He got to work building a ladder of telekinetic objects, two rungs at a time, just like he had done to climb onto the roof of Judith's truck back at the air force base. Judith followed him up until she got close enough to one of the guard towers to teleport into it. After climbing a few more rungs, he scrambled in after her. She stood over a freshly killed soldier who she said she had caught napping, which was a lucky break. The guard tower had an alarm that was presumably supposed to be triggered in this sort of situation.

They climbed down the tower's access ladder to find themselves in a squalid shantytown teeming with filthy, half-starved norms. The place stunk of sewage and rot. It could have been a slum out of a Dickens novel if that slum had recently been ravaged by war. Bonfires lit the streets, serving as communal cooking stations as well as sources of light. Rat and pigeon were on the menu for those lucky enough to have something to eat. Judging by the number of beggars who hovered around each fire, anyone who went to bed with a charred rat in their belly should count their blessings.

Sticking to the shadows, Jacob and Judith made their way through block after block of blighted apartment buildings; shacks cobbled together from salvaged materials; ramshackle, open-air markets; and groups of prostitutes displaying their bodies to anyone who looked their way. Soldiers wearing the now familiar National Guard fatigues patrolled the streets, apparently unconcerned with enforcing any laws or providing for anyone's safety except their own. It seemed nothing short of a riot would motivate them to do a damn thing, which worked out well for the demons infiltrating their city. The less attentive the security, the better.

Jacob paused to look into a burned-out church. A dozen people knelt on the rubble-strewn floor, moaning a wordless hymn to a banner-sized copy of the red and black snake emblem the scouts had carried.

"Somebody's going to see you, stupid," Judith whispered, and dragged him away. They ducked into an alleyway that looked like the scene of a recent explosion.

"Where—"

"Shh!" Judith said, slapping her hand over his mouth. "Listen."

Farther down the alley, a rustling, grunting sound came from behind a dumpster as though a pig had miraculously escaped being eaten and was rooting around back there. Jacob snuck up to the dumpster and peeked behind it. A pudgy soldier with his pants around his ankles lay on top of an emaciated young woman, violently thrusting into her.

Jacob lowered a telekinetic dome over them with the sole purpose of soundproofing the area. He needed information and preferred the conversation that was about to take place not be overheard by passersby.

"They took Micah to the cathedral," Jacob told Judith, who stood guard nearby.

"Nice work, boss. Which way's that?"

"A few blocks south, then west. Can't miss it, supposedly. But first, put this on." He threw her a full skirt he had taken from the woman behind the dumpster.

"Good idea," Judith said as she pulled it over her tail-ready pants. "What did you do with the skank?"

"She's still back there. I told her to keep her mouth shut and stay hidden until morning. She won't cause any trouble."

"What's the word…" Judith mused as she adjusted her skirt. "Pushover? Is that what they used to call people who took dumbass risks so scummy norms could go on with their scummy lives?"

"Something like that. You'll be happy to know her boyfriend is no longer among the living. Look what I found on him." Jacob held up a hooded rain jacket.

"Ready for tomorrow's weather," Judith said. "You'll look like a psycho, but it beats walking around with your horns hanging out."

"Exactly," Jacob said. "Now let's get moving."

The route to the cathedral took them through a much nicer part of town. Electric lights lit clean, tree-lined streets. Stately houses, untouched by the chaos that had consumed the rest of the world, sat behind wrought-iron gates. As the demons moved from shadow to shadow, dodging National Guard patrols, Jacob tried to remember the face of the man he had murdered in that alley. Dozens of people must have died at his hands in battle, but those killings hadn't felt like murder. This last one did.

The soldier had pleaded for his life, kneeling on the ground with his cock dangling below a belly the sweat-stained t-shirt he wore couldn't hope to cover. "Don't do this, man!" he cried. "I won't tell anybody about you. Swear to God!"

Jacob snapped his neck with an invisible hand.

His first unforced kill—the first time he had looked into someone's eyes, known he could spare them, and chosen not to. It seemed like the kind of thing a person ought to remember: first kiss, wedding day, the birth of a child, first murder. Yet all Jacob could recall about the man was that slimy worm of a penis swaying under his hairy gut as he begged and cried. An absurdity, disgusting.

The woman who had witnessed the sordid affair pressed herself against Jacob's invisible wall, hoping his cold eyes would pass her over. Through a mask of cosmetics spread as thickly as frosting on a cake, she peeked out at him—her arms raised to shield herself.

"Hello, little mouse," he said, crouching down in front of her.

She squeaked, which elicited a broad grin shining with malevolence from Jacob.

"I hope that pig of a man wasn't a friend of yours," he continued.

The woman shook her head with such force her whole body thrashed about.

"Good. Now listen closely. Predators are out tonight. If you're a smart mouse, you'll crawl into your hole and keep quiet until morning."

Still holding her arms in front of her face, the woman nodded.

A tugging sensation inside Jacob's head scattered his thoughts. Judith wanted his attention and knew she didn't need to speak to get it. The bond that had formed between her mind and his proved useful in situations like this. He saw her in a pool of shadows across the street, gesturing that it was safe for him to cross.

He gave up on trying to remember the soldier's face. Instead, his family's faces came to him. They were the ones who mattered. He'd murder everyone in this wretched city to find them if that's what it took.

***

An air of foreboding hung over the cathedral. Bonfires raged around a colossal, Romanesque structure of gray stone capped by two steeples and a dome that arched up into the black of night. The building seemed to have been transported from Venice or Rome to middle America. Firelight transformed its intricate stonework into an ever-shifting mosaic of shadow and light, glinting in a rose window set above the doors like a cyclops' eye. Red banners emblazoned with a black snake fluttered from the twin spires framing the cathedral's massive dome.

Soldiers stood guard around the front doors. More walked the building's perimeter and patrolled the road. They were everywhere. The soldiers Jacob and Judith had encountered so far had carried themselves in a lazy, apathetic way, but these appeared poised and alert. Still, a bunch of norms didn't stand a chance against two demons. Jacob was more worried about what they might be guarding.

Until a moment ago, he had clung to the hope that St. Louis was a corrupt version of the refugee center Rebecca had hoped to find. At the top of this dung heap sat a wannabe autocrat with a thing for snakes, or maybe some kind of cult leader, a powerful norm but a norm nonetheless. That idea withered and died as he gaped at the cathedral, looming against a night sky that seemed to embrace it. Despite the bonfires around its base and torches set into its facade, the pools of darkness splashed across the building's face drew the eye—deeper than shadows should be and somehow alive. This building had power.

Crouched beside Jacob behind a bush, Judith cast nervous glances at the cathedral. She sensed it too.

"Okay," he said. "Here's the plan: You teleport to one of those ledges over the guards' heads and scout things out. Maybe you can sneak through a window or something."

If Judith could stare literal daggers, he would have been thoroughly perforated. "First, it's too far. Second, there's no way I'm going in there by myself. Third, fuck you."

"Then what do you suggest? We can't—"

Blinding light flooded their hiding place. From out of nowhere, dozens of soldiers rushed toward them. Spotlights shone from the surrounding rooftops, the backs of trucks parked nearby, on the cathedral itself—all around. An ambush!

With a thunderous boom, the cathedral doors burst open, and an army of norms poured out. Stunned, Jacob froze, mind and body. Something moved behind the soldiers, something that should only exist in stories. A monstrous demon with the torso of an old woman and the body of a serpent emerged from the doorway. Her human section, which she held high, swayed as she slithered down the steps to the road. Under a tangle of white hair, she wore a thin smile.

Neither Jacob nor Judith moved an inch.

"Don't skulk around in the shadows," the serpent called. Her voice carried well, despite its soft, hissing character. "Come out where I can get a good look at you."

Suppressing an urge to flee, Jacob stood.

"What are you doing?" Judith whispered.

"Shut up. They might not know there's two of us. Get out of here."

She disappeared.

Jacob drew a deep, unsteady breath in a futile attempt to calm his nerves, then stepped into the harshly lit road. Unsure what to do next, he took off the rain jacket he had been using to hide his horns and dropped it to the ground.

The serpent squinted at him. "Don't be shy. Come a little closer. I don't bite."

Very much doubting that, Jacob walked up to a line of soldiers standing between him and the old woman. Oddly, each norm held a long spear instead of a gun. Even from a dozen feet away, he felt the other demon's Darkness. Expansive and warm, it wrapped around him like a blanket.

"Ah, that's better," she said. "Does your friend want to join us, or is she feeling shy?"

Jacob didn't answer.

"Don't you worry none, darling," the serpent called past him to the bush where he and Judith had been hiding. "Come out when you're good and ready." She turned her attention back to Jacob. "Now then, who might you be, young man?"

"My name is Jacob."

Her expression shifted to a deranged cousin of delight. "Glory be, he speaks! It never ceases to amaze me how many folks like us don't bother with common courtesy. Of course, a fair number of them don't have mouths fit for making words. Can't hardly blame them for that, I suppose."

"And you are?" Jacob asked.

"Good Lord, where are my manners? They call me Lamia." She held up her hands to stave off any reaction Jacob might have. "I know…I know. That name carries a lot of weight in these parts. Don't you believe a thing you hear about me, not a word of it. A bunch of hooey."

"How did you know we were here?" Jacob asked.

"These boys put all kinds of techie do-dads around my nest." Lamia gestured to indicate that the "boys" she referred to were the stone-faced goons guarding her. "Cameras, motion sensors, night-vision thingies. Who can keep track of it all?"

"And I thought we were being sneaky."

"Oh, darling, don't let it get you down," Lamia said with what sounded like genuine sympathy. "You and your friend did a far sight better than most who come calling."

"A lot of people try to sneak up on you?"

"Not so many nowadays, but they used to come from far and wide to visit old Lamia. Wore me out, truth be told."

While she spoke, Jacob studied the cathedral behind her. It hummed with a Darkness of its own, in harmony with hers. He reached out with his mind, stretching an invisible arm past the line of soldiers to the cathedral's stone steps. As lightly as possible, he tapped the bottom step. The building's Darkness rippled like a pool of water that had been disturbed.

Lamia let out a pointed hiss. She had felt Jacob's probing as though he had touched her own skin. Her eyes narrowed to yellow slits. "Well, aren't you a curious one?" she said, her voice taking on an icy undertone.

"Just admiring the architecture."

"Is that so?" She paused, considering her next words. "How about you tell me why you're here?"

"A woman and a girl were brought here. They're under my protection. Return them to me."

Lamia coiled her body, drawing more of herself from behind to form a twisting mass under her human section, which caused her to grow several feet taller. "I see," she hissed. "And what makes you think I have these sweeties of yours?"

A black, seething rage filled Jacob. His fists clenched, and his gaze became as hard as steel. "I have no patience for games. Being them to me or I'll tear this place to the ground looking for them."

"Watch your tone," Lamia said, her aged voice crackling with anger. "I won't be spoken to that way in my own home."

"I'm done speaking to you. I'll have my family back. And if they've been harmed, I'll spend the rest of my life flaying the flesh from your bones, starting over each time it grows back."

Jacob summoned his powers, ready for anything. He had gotten carried away just now. Threatening the old woman had almost certainly not been the right move. He couldn't take it anymore though. His family had been in danger plenty of times, but they had never been separated like this. Were they even still alive? At least his breakdown of self-restraint had bought Judith time to maneuver. Maybe she had come up with a plan.

Lamia's rising anger cooled. A wide smile broke on her wrinkled face, exposing needle-sharp fangs. "My goodness, what a vicious little man you are. We'll see who gets flayed tonight."

Three pops sounded from different directions. Jacob spun around to see a net of metal chains flying at him. He dodged and stepped into the path of another, which he batted away with a telekinetic hand. A barrier formed an inch in front of his nose. Almost immediately, the third net hit it and fell at his feet.

Lamia slithered around his left flank with a fluid speed he'd never have imagined her capable of. A thrust of his hand shot a bolt of telekinetic energy at her. It grazed the end of her long tail as she changed direction, not even slowing her down.

More pops. Chains rained down on Jacob's position. He moved behind a fresh barrier, then dashed toward a row of office buildings outside the brightly lit battlefield. He needed to get inside. Lamia was over twenty feet long; she wouldn't be able to maneuver in a building that wasn't cathedral size.

Searching for a door to break down, he stepped on one of the metal nets littering the ground. His foot went numb as though he had been injected with a huge dose of Novocain. Jacob lurched forward, then fell to his knees on top of another net. Half his leg was instantly rendered useless. Losing his balance, he collapsed onto yet another net. (The boys had been busy laying out a carpet of the things in his path.) Most of his body went limp as he sprawled, facedown, across a bed of crippling metal.

Pop!

A net landed on his back, completely paralyzing him. Lying helpless, with his face to the ground, he couldn't see well enough to target anything with his powers. A shield? No, he needed to get up, to fight!

Rhythmic scraping sounds behind him signaled Lamia's approach. Her shadow darkened the ground. Then she struck. There was no violence, only a slight prick on the back of his neck, over before he knew it. A cool, numbing sensation spread through Jacob's body. Venom.

Lamia's cooing voice washed over him. "Oh my! There hasn't been that much excitement around here for months. Now why don't we go inside and have a rest? You can tell me all about these missing sweeties of yours."

"What...what is this?" Jacob croaked.

"These?" Lamia rattled the chains on his back. "Handy, aren't they? I make the metal myself, you know. It's a secret recipe. The boys call it hexiron. That's a bit highfalutin for my taste, but they're partial to the name, so it'll have to do."

"Judith..."

"Is that your friend? What a pretty name! I'm sorry, dear, but she can't join us. The boys tell me she fell into one of the traps they put in all the shady spots her kind like to hide. Such good boys. Thought of everything, they have."

Footsteps approached. Two men grabbed the edges of the chains underneath Jacob and pulled him as though he were on a sled. He could see their boots. He'd break their legs... He'd...

His vision dimmed and blurred. A thick fog settled over his senses. Lamia's venom had taken hold.

The soldiers dragged him up the cathedral's steps and through the door. Inside, candlelight bounced and refracted in strange ways. Shadows shifted, forming and dissolving in places they shouldn't be. Patches of light so intense they hurt bloomed then faded into the dark.

Skeletons lined the wall where the stations of the cross used to hang. One had four arms. The next was a giant, ten feet tall at least, with the skull of a horse. A broad shell covered another's back. Each skull hung over its body, separated by a gap maybe six inches wide.

Someone flipped Jacob over and bound his limp arms. Far above, the inside of the cathedral's dome was a golden sky. Angels winked from countless murals. He spun up into the dome, then plunged back down again. The building expanded and contracted around him as though he were trapped in the lung of a great beast. His head swam. Closing his eyes only made it worse—vertigo in the dark.

Then everything was better. Jacob found himself in a good place, a perfect place.

Lurid Dreams

Red neon strips ran along the baseboards of Jacob's bedroom and around each darkened window, providing enough light to see and enough shadow to intrigue. Anything more or less would have ruined the mood. It was just right.

Rebecca lay on the bed wearing only a come-hither expression. She looked good, better than good. He lay down beside her. The clothes he had been wearing a second ago were gone, which was convenient. Rebecca melted into his arms like warm wax. When he entered her, she moaned in a way she had never moaned before, a better way.

After they finished, Jacob lay on glow-in-the-dark sheets, considering staying in bed all night. It would be no problem at all; nothing depended on what he did or didn't do, not a thing. But as tempting as the idea was, he decided to go out. Adventure called! Anything was possible tonight, anything at all.

Leaving a satisfied Rebecca to bask in the neon blush, he hopped out of bed. Without needing to go through the trouble of walking to the bathroom, he found himself taking a shower. Hot with plenty of steam, it was invigorating. After a minute or two, the shower door slid open, and Judith joined him. She was, of course, naked and perfect in every way. Water ran in rivulets over her sylphlike form as she flashed the mischievous smile he loved so much.

Wordlessly, she dropped to her knees and took his cock into her mouth. In slow, languid motions she sucked and licked, all the while gazing up at him with the vacant sensuality of pornography. That was exactly what he wanted to see. With her smoldering eyes fixed on his, she ran a forked tongue up and down his sex.

Dressed, groomed, and ready for whatever life had to offer, Jacob entered the kitchen. Its orange neon strips reminded him of sunshine, but better. A glass and chrome table stood in the middle of the room. Unseen lights embedded in its frame made the entire thing glow blue, a nice contrast to the room's orange hue.

Micah sat at the table eating pancakes with Judith, who looked cute in flannel pajamas. They were chatting about some boy at Micah's school who was always doing ridiculous things, bouts of giggles punctuating the conversation. Rebecca appeared and handed him a cup of coffee. It tasted amazing.

A glance at the clock on the wall reminded him it was time to take Micah to school. It was still dark outside, but why wouldn't it be? It was always dark outside. Jacob held his daughter's hand as they left the house and walked to the sidewalk. He didn't feel sick at all, not the least bit of discomfort. (For a split-second he wondered why he should be sick, but the thought dissolved like salt in water.) With a big smile, Micah jumped into his arms and gave him a hug. Then she spread her wings and flew off into the moonlit sky.

Across the street, the Ghoul pushed a lawnmower over luminescent grass. His little friend, the dead girl, sat slumped in a chair on the porch, looking as fresh and fully fleshed as ever. Jacob waved a neighborly greeting, which the Ghoul returned in kind.

As satisfied as a man could be, Jacob surveyed his neighborhood: glowing, manicured lawns and well-kept houses with neon trim as far as the eye could see. What a fantastic place to live!

A sleek sports car, pearly white, pulled up. Its tinted window rolled down to reveal an attractive Asian woman behind the wheel, the barista from Jacob's favorite coffee shop. He knew she had come to whisk him away to a resort, spa, or some other similarly luxurious place for a full day of sexual exploits. That's what happened when the car pulled up to his house.

Of course, it didn't have to be the barista who picked him up. It could be the cute neighbor who sometimes jogged by, or Judge Cox's daughter, or a girl he had a crush on in college, or that asshole Mike's girlfriend—anyone at all. There was no way to know until that shiny black window rolled down. One thing was certain though: he wouldn't be disappointed.

Jacob said hello to the barista, who responded by licking her cherry-red lips with a narrow, forked tongue. Light at heart and with a spring in his step, he walked around the car to hop into the passenger side.

Then everything went wrong, very wrong. He pulled open the car door but didn't get in. A shadow fell over the world as the moon dimmed. He slumped under the weight of a dull, throbbing ache that uniformly affected his entire body. It was a sensation of acute absence, like the phantom pains people who have lost limbs or organs sometimes feel, except everywhere at once.

"You don't belong here," Jacob said, although he didn't know what he meant.

Leaving the car door hanging open, he turned around and headed back toward his house. The barista followed him with her eyes, her face frozen in a lascivious grin. The short walk felt like trudging through waist-deep mud. He had an overwhelming sense of going the wrong way. The front door was as heavy as lead. Drained and ill at ease, he entered the living room, which had taken on a sickly green glow. What color had it been before? Was there a living room before?

Micah was already back from school, sitting next to her mother on the sofa, dressed for bed with her stuffed lion in her lap. She no longer had wings. In unison, Rebecca and Micah turned expressionless faces to Jacob. For a nightmarish moment, they stared at him like dolls. Then, as if someone had flipped a switch, the light returned to their eyes.

"Daddy!" Micah called. "Can I have a magic show?"

"What?" he asked, bewildered.

"A magic show! With the monkey." She pointed at his right hand.

Jacob looked down and, to his surprise, found himself holding a sock-puppet monkey. Now he could do the magic show! The longer he stayed, the less nauseating this room's green neon became. It was kind of nice actually. He felt silly for getting so worked up before. All he needed to do was see things the right way, and everything would work out. That was the secret to happiness right there: seeing things the right way.

A magic show sounded fun after all. And hadn't he been meaning to make more time for family activities? "Sure, M. Whatever you want."

"Yes!" she exclaimed with a fist pump of victory.

Jacob loved that little gesture. He had worried he'd never see it again. Wait... Why would he think that? Why would he never—

"Ma-gic! Ma-gic! Ma-gic!" Micah chanted.

Jacob got to work levitating the puppet, building platforms for it to rest on, and doing all the things he knew his daughter would enjoy. At some point, a second puppet entered the game, a mean wolf who locked the monkey in an invisible box. Micah stuck her forked tongue out at the wolf when it tried to convince her to root for the bad guys.

Wolf? Hadn't Jacob seen a wolf once, or something like one? The damned thing had nearly killed him. Yeah, he and Judith—

Micah jumped off the sofa and smacked the monkey's invisible box. "He's free! Dad, he's free!"

Jacob released the monkey and made it punch that mean old wolf in the face. Micah fell into an epic giggling fit. Everything was good again. Better than good—perfect. Everything was...

The neon flickered, as if something were wrong with the electricity. Micah's laughter took on shrill, inhuman tones. Pain swirled through Jacob like water running down a drain. The void, that terrible nothingness. A memory formed, then slipped away. He caught only a vague impression: a warm glow in a dark place, someone calling him.

Judith. Somehow this was her fault. He needed to find her. The sock puppet dropped to the floor. Micah fell silent. She and Rebecca watched him walk away, empty smiles fixed on their faces like crude drawings.

He found Judith sitting motionless at the kitchen table, staring at nothing. The room's orange neon had burned out, leaving only the arctic blue emanating from the table. Lighting her face from below, it gave her the pallor of death. She looked washed out, faded. Jacob pushed damp, limp hair away from Judith's face. Her skin was clammy and translucent, her eyes cloudy.

Darkness fell over the Neon Wonderland, the only world Jacob knew. Judith became a black hole, sucking life and color from his world. He didn't want her there. He hated her for being the thing that didn't belong, the thing destroying his...his...

Something clicked in his mind, gears falling into place. *His* world. Not the world, but *his* world. Although he didn't understand what that meant, he knew it was a critical distinction.

Struck by a mad impulse, he leaned forward and kissed Judith's lifeless lips. Like closing one book and opening another, the world changed.

***

Rich, warm oranges and reds against the deepest blacks—the place Jacob found himself in seemed to be lit by unseen flames. He walked through a cavernous space so large there were no walls or ceiling, only a floor of gleaming black tile and impenetrable darkness closing in all around.

Countless tables laden with rolls of fabric surrounded him—every kind of cloth imaginable, so many textures and colors. Human forms stood among the tables. Some struck poses, while others paced in slow circles. All of them were dressed fabulously. None had faces.

He reached out to one of the models, inspecting the lace trim on her blouse. Handmade, delicate, perfect. He smiled. No, not him. Judith smiled. What the—

This couldn't be! Somehow he had entered her mind, or maybe been consumed by it. He'd have screamed if he had a voice of his own.

Everything around him possessed an uncanny quality any physical differences between Judith's means of perception and his couldn't account for. This was more than watching the same show on a different TV. Colors were slightly off in ways that went deeper than simple optics, as though they had always held a soul he had never noticed until it changed. Objects didn't feel the way they should. He wasn't even sure words like "feel" and "see" meant what they used to.

Despite the overwhelming strangeness of his surroundings, Jacob could think more clearly without all that neon around. Strangely familiar images bloomed in his mind like old, faded photographs coming back to life. A girl suffering, brave but a child still. Micah. Judith, beautiful and terrifying, blades in her hands dripping blood. Rebecca's hopeless fight for things forever gone. Yes, there had been another place, neither his world nor this place.

He tried to yell, lash out, do anything to get Judith's attention. She needed to wake up. None of this was real. The world pitched and shifted as though set adrift on stormy waters. Judith's living mannequins fell to the ground, wracked with convulsions.

Then everything changed.

Judith walked down a hallway. A chubby teenage boy wearing only a swimsuit appeared in front of her and shrieked with the voice of an enraged monkey. He thrust out his chest, which made his fat-boy boobs jiggle. She couldn't help but laugh. It was fucking hilarious!

The boy lurched forward and shoved her. Never losing her balance, she whipped her leg out and kicked his knee. He flopped to the floor, crying for his mom.

Judith leaned close and whispered so only he could hear. "Touch me again and I'll break your neck." She lifted her foot and stomped on his other knee, which lay prone in front of him as he cradled the bruised one. Something popped inside it. Blood coursed through her body, driven by the war-drum pounding of her heart. Her breath came in hot bursts. It wasn't fear or anger she felt, but adrenaline-charged excitement.

Time rewound. Back on his feet and uninjured, the boy postured and hooted his animal sounds. This time Judith punched him in the face. His nose became a geyser of blood.

Rewind. She kneed him in the groin, then slammed his head into the wall so hard his skull cracked.

Rewind. She ripped a chunk of flesh from his pimply face with her teeth.

Rewind. She stabbed him to death.

Everything went black, and a new scene appeared. Small now, about Micah's size, Judith sat alone on a merry-go-round at a playground. Other children ran around, but none came near. They were afraid.

A girl with bright red hair and a round, freckled face sat on a bench nearby, reading a teen romance novel. Her drab, ill-fitting dress bunched up around her like a garbage bag. Judith knew this kid from school. Neither of them had any friends, but for different reasons. No one feared the red-haired girl. She was a dumpster other kids poured their hate into, the kid every loser in school could look at and feel better about themselves, the cowering dog anyone could bully. She was prey.

Judith hopped off the merry-go-round and skipped over to the bench. The red-haired girl looked up from her book. Beneath her surprise, a distant hope glittered; maybe a fellow misfit had come to share in her loneliness. Beaming a friendly smile, Judith sat down next to the other girl and scooted in real close. As the red-haired girl opened her mouth to speak, Judith pulled a steak knife from her pocket and poked her in the ribs with it. The tip punctured her dress and pressed into the skin beneath, not hard enough to draw blood but enough for the blade to make its presence known.

The girl froze, her baby-blue eyes wide with terror.

No fight in her, Judith thought, and her smile grew. "Hi! Wanna play?"

Jacob squirmed. This couldn't be a real memory, could it? He tried to look away, but there was nothing else to see. A desperate idea took hold of him. This hot, shadowy world was a closed system of desire and fulfillment, a dream Judith wouldn't want to wake up from. But her dream had a flaw: him. Jacob reached out to his world, the Neon Wonderland. It wasn't a thing, and he wasn't in a place, so he didn't know how to even begin looking for it. Still, he tried.

From some dark recess of his mind, the image of Glinda, the Good Witch of the South, appeared in all her glittery glory. She knew what to do: Just think, *"There's no place like home."* That's exactly what Jacob did. A portal to his fever dream of sex and domestic tranquility opened before him, warped and distorted as though seen through a fisheye lens. The Neon Wonderland pulled at him, eager to welcome him home. It would be so easy to make the pain and confusion go away, all he needed to do—

No! He resisted its siren call. He hadn't opened a door between his world and Judith's to escape; it was a link connecting things never meant to be connected. Jacob stood in a nowhere-space between two realities, a tightrope walker precariously balanced on the bond he and Judith shared. That connection, which had started as a contract then grown into a mystery, was the thing that didn't belong in either world. And if this worked, it would be the thing that destroyed both.

A soul-shaking dissonance filled the entire universe. Clashing perceptions tore at Jacob's mind; things were both one way and another at the same time.

In the shifting shadows of Judith's dream, blue and red neon sputtered to life. Flames licked the cold, hard surfaces of Jacob's fantasy world. Conflicting realities merged like a boiling river pouring onto a glacier. Judith's urgent, visceral need for violence—the hot joy of blood on her hands—meshed with Jacob's constant, gnawing need. Neon lightning streaked across Judith's skies. Faceless mannequins writhed in mute agony.

The beautiful barista prowled Jacob's house, a gleaming blade in each hand. Blood streaked her naked body like war paint.

Micah sat alone in the living room, terrified, clutching a sock-puppet monkey to her chest. Green lights buzzed and popped around her. The front window flickered orange as the yard outside burst into flames. Smoke snaked into the house. Tears streaked down her cheeks.

Teenage Judith in a brazen bikini danced in a hallway lined with red neon. Her cousin, Barry, sat on the floor at her feet, masturbating furiously. She leaned in close, as if to whisper in his ear. With one hand, she undid the clasp on her top; with the other, she slid a blade across his throat. Thick black blood bloomed along its path.

Jacob's dream ripped through Judith's like an iceberg sundering a ship. The dissonance rose to a screeching crescendo. Excruciating.

He clung to his link to Judith. That was real; the screaming chaos around him wasn't. The link would take him home; it had to. He said the word over and over. "Home. Home. Home." If he didn't believe, it wouldn't work. "Home."

Little Judith and the red-haired girl sat on a chrome bench under a neon moon. Judith grabbed the other girl by the hair and pulled her into a forced kiss. With her free hand, she thrust a dagger between her squirming prey's ribs. The girl screamed into her killer's mouth. As she did, Judith ran her perfectly rounded tongue over the red-haired girl's forked one.

Horrified. Thrilled. Part of Jacob recoiled; part cheered.

The cacophony of world grating against world became unbearable. Reality wavered, as though every atom were trying to break free of its bonds and fly off in its own direction.

Then it all stopped. Everything was dark, quiet, and still.

The World That Is

The crucified Christ's alabaster body, larger than any living man, glowed like a moon in the cathedral's candlelight. His benevolent gaze fell on the altar and all that lay before it, including Jacob, coming to the realization that he was still wrapped in paralyzing chains, and a woman with the body of a snake muttering to herself as she murdered Judith.

Bound by chains of her own, Judith lay a dozen feet from Jacob on the other side of the sanctuary—or at least that's what he thought they called this marble platform that elevated the altar above the church's seating area. Lamia's endless body stretched out beyond Judith, her tail disappearing over the edge of the stairs that led down to the pews. Her human section hovered over the younger demon, as though she intended to kiss her. In each hand, she held a wooden rod, handles for a thin wire that stretched between them. The wire wound around Judith's neck, cutting into her as Lamia pulled it tight.

"Poor girl," the old woman cooed. "What has he done to you?"

Helpless, Jacob could do nothing but watch in horror. The chains had paralyzed every muscle in his body except those that moved his eyes. There must be a way out of this. He had to do something. If—

"You..." Lamia's shifted her icy gaze to him. "That little stunt of yours ruined my nest. Stone by stone, I wove power into this place, and you waltz in and wreck it in one night."

Jacob tried to speak, but a length of chain cut through his mouth as a gag.

"And for what?" Lamia asked. "So you can wriggle around like a fish on a hook? Damned fool! You could have faded away in a nice, peaceful dream."

Lightning bolts of panic shot through Jacob's body. With every fiber of his being, he willed the chains off.

"When your turn comes around, I'll take my sweet time," Lamia said. "Yes, I'll take it nice and slow."

He couldn't do anything, nothing at all.

"But first, your pretty friend and I have some unfinished business." She tightened the wire around Judith's neck. "You wrecked her dream too, you know. I've got half a mind to take that blindfold off so you can see the suffering you've brought to the poor dear."

Wet, gurgling, choking sounds, then nothing. Jacob closed his eyes, despair crushing his heart like a vise. Judith, Micah, Rebeca—dead, and it was his fault. How had he let this happen? Why hadn't he—

Wait, what had Lamia just said? Take his blindfold off? He wasn't supposed to be able to see her! Someone had fucked up, and she hadn't yet realized it. A cool wave of calm washed his panic away. He could see, and sight was all he needed. Jacob opened his eyes.

Invisible hands seized the enormous marble crucifix standing behind the altar. Thousands of pounds of stone soared into the air, disappearing into the darkness of the cathedral's dome, then crashed down on Lamia's midsection. Blood and shards of marble exploded across the sanctuary. Lamia shrieked, coiling into a protective ball.

Jacob mentally released what was left of his shattered weapon and grabbed her by the back of the neck, careful not to let her writhe out of his field of vision. With an upward motion, he hoisted her off the ground, her body straightening as more and more of it hung suspended in midair. The part of her he had crushed with the crucifix rose from a puddle of blood. Everything below that point dangled as deadweight from pulverized muscles and an exposed spine.

Jacob split off a portion of his power, grabbed Judith's chains, and dragged her out of harm's way. Bright, arterial blood streaked the white stone along her path. Once she was far enough from the fight, he returned his attention to Lamia. With all his telekinetic strength, he drove the snake head-first into the floor. A sharp crack echoed through the cathedral. Again and again, he lifted her up and slammed her down.

Heart racing, eyes straining to see everything he needed to see, Jacob paused with Lamia's face pressed to the marble. Her thrashing had weakened into a spastic twitch. Blood pooled under her, a stream of it running across the sanctuary to drip down the stairs. Her human arms feebly pushed against the floor, struggling to resist the force pressing down on her. How was she still alive? Her skull should have cracked like an egg. Even demon bones couldn't withstand what he had just done. Or could they?

Jacob's mind whirled. Lamia's spine hadn't broken when the crucifix crushed it. The surrounding flesh had been pulverized, yet the bones of the spine remained intact. Had *he* ever broken a bone? Had Judith? Cuts, bruises, torn muscles, but through all the battles and all the training exercises, neither had broken a bone. And when they had needed to chip his horn to pay the Pale Gentleman in Indianapolis, nothing could break it. What if demon bones *were* unbreakable? It wouldn't be the strangest thing about demon anatomy.

Bones. A memory took shape on the edge of Jacob's mind, floating in the dark, just beyond his reach. The dream prison—no, before that. Skeletons lining the cathedral's walls, demon skeletons, each skull separated from its body.

And his horn...they had broken it. Judith's blade had done the trick. Maybe all it took to separate a demon's head from its body was the right tool. Disappearing knives, for example, or a cutting wire made of magical metal.

The telekinetic hand that held down Lamia's head disappeared. She shot up like an enormous jack-in-the-box dripping gore, which splattered half the cathedral. Her face was a mess of ruined flesh and exposed skull. As quickly as possible, Jacob snatched the cutting wire off the ground and raised it to her throat, holding it by one of its handles. The second half of his power, what he thought of as a hand holding down Lamia's middle, flew up to her neck and grabbed the wire's other handle.

For several nerve-wracking seconds, she was free, looming over Jacob as rigid as stone while he frantically worked with the wire. Her mangled face turned upward to the golden chasm of the dome above. She raised her arms as if offering an anguished prayer.

Jacob executed a series of perilous telekinetic maneuvers, knowing he wouldn't get another chance if the wire slipped from his grasp. Once it looped around Lamia's neck, he held a handle on each invisible hand

and pulled. Cursed metal sliced through skin, muscle, and tendon. The pinched wheeze of strangulation became a wet gurgle as the wire severed her windpipe. Blood poured over her chest, cascading down her body. For a sickening moment, her head lolled around like a tetherball as her spinal cord became the only thing holding it on. She spasmed and convulsed.

With a dull twang, the wire crumpled into a floating ball as the last bit of resistance gave way. Lamia's headless body flopped to the ground, spewing blood across white marble.

It was over.

Reunion

Judith spun slowly in the air as Jacob searched for a place to begin unraveling her chains. Although she didn't move or speak, he knew she was awake. A sense of her consciousness fluttered in his mind, anxious and hyper-alert. He wanted to comfort her, reassure her that they'd be okay, but his own chains still silenced him.

"Get these things off me," she said at last, her voice a strained whisper. "And stay out of my head."

An intolerable amount of time later, his telekinetic fingers finally found a loose end. Struggling to maintain the patience the task required, he twisted his partner this way and that until the last chain fell from her body. Soaked in blood, she dropped into a crouch.

"Hold on," Judith said. "Maybe I can pick at yours with my blades."

They were wound too tightly for that, so she ran off to recruit a norm to help. The chains seemed to only affect demons. Rivers of blood crossed the sanctuary, forming lakes wherever the topography allowed. Thick as sludge, it crept down the stairs at the edge of the marble island. Lamia's corpse, a mountain range curving off into the shadows, sustained the grisly ecosystem. Hopefully it wouldn't occur to Judith to make her assistance conditional on his voiding her contract, because he'd be fucked if it did.

As Jacob attempted yet again to use his telekinesis on parts of himself he couldn't see, Judith burst through the cathedral's main doors with one of

Lamia's guards in tow. The man kicked and screamed, but she held him firmly by the arm. After dragging her captive down the central aisle, she flung him onto the sanctuary.

"Take those chains off him," she ordered.

The man's eyes darted between the bound demon and Lamia's remains. He fell to his knees as though he would beg for mercy, but tried to scurry away instead. Judith grabbed him by the back of the neck and threw him back toward Jacob.

"Last chance, asshole," she said. "Take those chains off or I'll gut you."

"No... This isn't real. It's one of Lamia's dreams. She can't be—"

"Shut your mouth and look at *me*," Judith said slowly, enunciating each syllable. "The only things you need to worry about right now are me and my blades. Nothing else matters. Now, stop crying and take off those chains."

The soldier walked back into Jacob's field of vision like a condemned man stepping to the gallows. Without further comment, he got to work. When the last chain slid off Jacob's legs, he stood up and faced the petrified man. "The girl you people brought here and her mom, are they still alive?"

The man managed a quick nod. "They took the god downstairs. I think that lady, the doctor, is in the offices out back."

"Can you look for Rebecca?" Jacob asked Judith. "Our new friend and I will get Micah."

"Yeah, okay," she said, clearly still rattled. "Send me one of those mind messages if you need help."

After a bit of convincing, the soldier led Jacob down a narrow stairway lit with sconce candles. At the bottom, a wooden door opened into a gloomy space that appeared to be a cross between a medieval dungeon and the isolation ward of a modern penitentiary, capturing the worst aspects of each. A warren of steel corridors barely lit by yet more candles set on small shelves sprawled across the dusty stone of the cathedral's basement. As they moved forward, Jacob and his guide passed dozens of windowless doors of the same steel as the walls.

Jacob paused to open a narrow sliding panel in one of the doors, a feature evidently designed for guards to check on their prisoners. Inside, he saw a barren cell with a pile of blankets in one corner. On the opposite wall, a brightly colored nightlight in the shape of a hot-air balloon shone on the body of a boy no older than seven sprawled out in a puddle of filth. He wasn't breathing. A wave of nausea overcame Jacob. His throat tight and sour, he turned away. Micah couldn't be in a place like this, his brain rejected the idea.

Around the next corner and down another row of cells, they came to a sturdy garage door fitted into a stone wall. The soldier pushed a button, and the door rose with a clatter that echoed through the dungeon. A long tunnel of polished concrete lit by more of Lamia's endless supply of candles, these set in alcoves specially made for them, stretched out before them. At the end, a solitary electric light shone on a giant steel hatch like one might find on a bank vault. Chalk drawings decorated the tunnel walls, depicting scenes of happy children playing with oversized snakes.

When they reached the vault door, Jacob ordered his guide to open it, fully expecting him to not know how to operate the complicated locking mechanism. Instead, the man got right to work. Moments later, the hatch swung open with a whoosh of cool, dry air.

The vault's interior was a well-lit chamber about the size of a two-car garage with stainless steel walls and a gleaming white tile floor. Two solid steel prison-cell doors, one on the right and one on the left, broke up the otherwise featureless space. On shaky legs, the soldier went in, unlocked the door on the right, and pulled it open.

Wary of traps, Jacob peered into the newly opened cell. It took a second for his eyes to adjust to the relative darkness inside. A pile of chains lay on the floor, weakly lit by a nightlight matching the one he had seen in the dead boy's cell. An inner door fashioned from bars stood a few inches inside the one the soldier had opened, blocking his path. Inside, bars lined the walls and ceiling. It might have been an animal pen for a tiger or a bear, but encased in a concrete shell. Jacob reached for the inner door and his hand went numb. Cursed metal!

He rounded on the soldier and grabbed him by the throat. "What is this?" he yelled.

Clawing at the hand crushing his windpipe, the man frantically shook his head.

Jacob released him.

"Please!" the man gasped. "I thought you'd want to look inside first, that's all, make sure it was the right god."

"Idiot. Bring her to me."

The soldier fumbled with the inner door's lock before finally managing to let himself in. A moment later, he dragged the pile of chains out.

Jacob scanned the metal for signs of life, waves of dread lapping his heart. There! A tuft of blonde hair. And along the side...yes, dirty feathers poked through gaps in the chains. "Take those things off her," he said.

Minutes that felt like hours passed as the soldier loosened the chains, which had been carefully wound around Micah. Finally, he uncovered her face. Her expression was one of astonished disbelief mingled with hope. Lazarus must have looked on the world in just that way as he stumbled out of his tomb.

Jacob knelt beside her. "It's me, M. I'm here."

Tears budded at the corners of her eyes, burst, and streamed down her cheeks.

The soldier paused. He needed to touch her to unwind the rest of the chains. With a nod, Jacob gave him permission to continue. Gently, almost reverently, the man turned Micah one way, then another. More chains fell away. The shirt Judith had made for her was a grimy, tattered rag. Bruises blotted her chest and arms. Crumpled and broken, her feathers stuck out in all the wrong directions. She didn't move even after the solider untangled the final chain from her ankles.

"Micah?" Jacob ventured.

She sat up stiffly, cupped her face in her hands, and wept. Heavy, forceful sobs—explosions of horror and relief—shook her small body.

"Are you sure you're all right?" Jacob asked as he led Micah up the stairs to the ground floor.

"I...I don't know. I thought I was dying in there. Sometimes I thought maybe I *was* dead."

"I'm sorry, M. We got here as soon as we could."

"Mom's okay? Where is she?" This was the third time she had asked about Rebecca. It was impossible to tell how much she knew about what her mother had done.

"Don't worry," Jacob said. "The soldiers said she's all right. Judith is looking for her."

Micah nodded.

Jacob paused to glance back down the stairs at her. Tentatively, he asked, "Did any of these people hurt you?" He cast a menacing glare at the guard trudging along behind her. The man withered.

"No...not really. That snake lady talked to me, but I couldn't understand what she said. I was scared, and her voice is weird. When they took me into this church, I got sick. Sort of like when I touch you or Judith, but different. It was like that until a little while before you came."

"This building had magic," Jacob said. "The same kind I have. Judith and I got rid of it."

"Oh," Micah said, not understanding what he meant but in no condition to think about it.

"Do you remember anything else?"

"Yeah," Micah said. "One time, the snake lady lay down next to me and said something about dreams. Not to me though; more like she was talking to herself. When she saw me looking at her, she got confused and left in a hurry. A little while later, some men came and put chains over my head so I couldn't see."

Jacob opened his mouth to speak, but his throat pinched shut, strangling his words. Anger and regret flooded his mind. How had he let this happen to her? A raw croak, heavy with emotion, burst out from deep inside.

"It's okay, Dad," Micah said. "You saved me."

Nothing felt okay to Jacob.

"The Light inside me was talking the whole time," Micah continued. "It said it always knew something like this would happen, that it told me so. But I didn't listen; I just kept saying you'd save us, and you did."

Jacob pushed open the door at the top of the stairs but didn't go through. Micah shouldn't see the mess where Lamia lay. "M," he said. "I want you to close your eyes for a minute. Can you do that?"

"Yeah."

"Good girl. No peeking, okay?"

Usually, Micah would have objected to being treated like a little kid or, at the very least, demanded to know what she wasn't allowed to see. But she didn't this time. Maybe she had already seen too much.

"Hey," Jacob called back to the soldier. "Do you want to gain favor with the new gods?"

"Let me go," the man begged. "I have a kid too."

"We'll see. For now, take that girl's hand and lead her to her mother."

They walked in silence through the cathedral and out a back door. Next to the imposing structure sat a nearly windowless building of gray brick undoubtedly intended to match the cathedral's stone. Inside, they found Rebecca and Judith in the lobby anxiously waiting by the reception desk. When Rebecca saw her daughter, she fell to her knees and let out a tortured wail. A river of misery poured from her as though this broken woman gave voice to the pain of every mother who had lost children to this nightmare.

Micah ran to her and wrapped her in a close embrace, using arms and wings to shield her from a world where cruelty knew no bounds.

Micah's Rules for a Better World

When you're alone and there's nothing but darkness and evil all around, hold on to hope. Nothing can take it from you, but you can lose it. Hold tight.

Chapter 11

Prelude

For better or worse, the world can be remade by simply deciding to remake it.

A Change of Direction

Jacob sat on stone steps that led up to an elegant Victorian townhouse a few blocks from the cathedral. It belonged to a high-ranking member of the St. Louis militia, someone named Captain Marshall.

The captain had introduced himself to Jacob's group earlier that day after being ordered by his superiors to find out what Lamia's killers wanted. Expecting the assignment to be a death sentence, he was immensely relieved to find people with whom he could negotiate. He and Jacob hashed out a quick and dirty agreement in which the group would be permitted to stay in St. Louis while they recuperated, provided they didn't hurt anyone or destroy anything. The city's human authorities had no interest in trying to forcibly remove anyone powerful enough to kill Lamia.

Giddy with relief at having survived the negotiations, Captain Marshall offered Jacob the use of his townhouse. It was by far the nicest place the group had stayed: electricity, running water, even a refrigerator stocked with good beer. *Cold,* good beer.

Relaxed and freshly showered, Jacob felt rejuvenated. His family had been through hell. Damage had been done, the full extent of which would take time to unfold. But they were together—and they hadn't lost anyone.

Judith walked out of the townhouse and sat beside him. Wet from her shower, her hair smelled of lemon and sage. She looked lovely in an oversized t-shirt and pajama pants hastily modified to be tail-friendly. She handed Jacob a bottle of beer and opened another for herself, popping the cap off with her thumb.

"Joining me for a drink?" Jacob asked.

"Yeah. I'll have to piss later, which will be gross, but I feel like getting a buzz on."

"It'll take more than beer."

"Ta-da!" She pulled a flask from a pocket at her hip.

"You're awfully sociable tonight," Jacob said. "Should I be suspicious?"

An enigmatic smile served as Judith's only reply. Any other night, that would have made Jacob *very* suspicious, but not tonight. A comfortable stillness settled between the two demons. Crickets chirped as they always had, unconcerned with the recent changes to the nature of reality.

Jacob took a long swig of beer and leaned back against the steps. "How are they holding up?"

"Washed, fed, and in bed. I didn't think they'd be able to sleep after all that, but they're both out."

"Good."

"So, explain this to me again," Judith said. "Why are we still here?"

"For the children. We're doing it for the children," Jacob replied with a wry smile.

"Those kids under the church?"

"Those are the ones."

"And why do we care about them?" Judith asked.

"Because we're good, decent people."

"Shut up!" She playfully slapped his shoulder. "We're fucking demons. Let the norms take care of the little shits. Tell me what you're really up to."

"I'm curious about something."

"The only thing you are is stupid. Any minute now the locals are going to bust out their pitchforks and come after us. There are thousands of them and they have that weird metal."

"Tens of thousands," Jacob said. "And not one of them will bother us. We'll enjoy a relaxing evening, and tomorrow we'll explore Lamia's dungeon."

"I hope so," Judith said, stretching luxuriously. "I'm done fighting for a while." She finished her beer, tossed the bottle off into the street, and opened her flask. "What's gotten into you anyway? You're usually all cautious and shit. Shouldn't you be the one freaking out about leaving?"

Jacob shrugged. "Maybe our brush with death has left me with a desire to savor every moment life offers."

"About time. Usually you only look like you're having fun when I catch you staring at my tits."

A boyish smile lit Jacob's face. "What can I say? I find your breasts uniquely compelling...in a purely aesthetic way, of course."

Judith laughed, a light musical sound. "You're a pig. How'd you end up with horns instead of a big, ugly snout?"

"Lucky, I guess."

"Seriously, though, what's up? That snake didn't mess up your brain, did she?"

"Nothing like that," Jacob said. "I've just been thinking. We've defeated an army, escaped a magical dream world, and killed a demon-god. Maybe we don't need to scurry around like a bunch of rats looking for a hole to hide in. Maybe we are what everyone else needs to be afraid of. You've been trying to tell me that in various ways, haven't you?"

"Yeah, but—"

"What if all these norms with their magic metal aren't a threat, but an asset? What if we..." Jacob paused a moment to consider his words. "What if we took them?"

"What are we going to do with thousands of norms?"

"You'll see," Jacob said with a devilish grin.

Judith fell silent. He had expected to pique her curiosity, but instead found her staring at the ground, her expression stormy. "What's the matter?" he asked.

"I'll see what happens," she said bitterly. "Whether I want to or not."

"Judith, you don't have to do this with me."

"Yeah I do. Contract, remember?"

Jacob scooted over on the step until his leg was pressed against hers. "I, Jacob Freeman, rescind all your promises. The contract between us is null and void." He turned his head and kissed Judith's cheek.

Time stopped. A tapestry of Darkness manifest between the two demons then unraveled. The few inches of space between their faces echoed with a small but distinct *click*. A great weight lifted from Jacob's heart. He felt lighter than air. Despite the immense danger he had just put himself in, he felt good.

Astounded, Judith's eyes grew as large as moons. "Is it...over?"

"It is. I won't make excuses for what I did to you. You know why I did it, both the reasons I gave you and the ones I'd rather not talk about. You have every right to hate me."

She didn't speak for a long while. A flood of emotions too dense for Jacob to interpret played out across her face. "You're such an asshole," she said at last. "I don't even know what to think."

"I understand."

"Ugh..." She groaned. "Stop worrying about Becky. I won't hurt her. I don't want you and Micah coming after me on some bullshit revenge quest like on the story discs."

Jacob cast her a confused look. "But I didn't—"

"Fuck! I can still hear your thoughts."

Gently, Jacob probed her mind. He felt it too, the connection hadn't dissolved with the contract. To his surprise, he was relieved. Having a little of her in him no longer seemed an intrusion. Her presence comforted him. "Sorry. Maybe it'll go away in time. Or maybe it's a scar of sorts."

Judith thought for a moment. "I can live with it." She stood up and turned toward the townhouse. "I've got some stuff to think about. See you tomorrow."

"You're not leaving?"

Her golden eyes glittered in the moonlight. "No, not tonight."

Captain Marshall's office was a celebration of things Jacob had thought were gone forever: wealth, prestige, influence. Tastefully done without pretension, it exhibited an assured confidence that didn't need to make a spectacle of itself. Not a place for pretenders and their postering, it belonged to someone who breathed privilege the way others breathe common air. Jacob felt right at home.

After browsing the contents of a small but impeccably curated liquor cabinet, he poured himself a neat bourbon and took a seat behind the captain's stately desk. As anticipated, the executive chair was soft, smooth leather and even more comfortable than it looked. Yes, Jacob could get used to this.

There would be no more running, no hiding. Let the faceless fanatic attack St. Louis if he dared. Jacob would be ready.

The Freeman family (plus one) had found a home. Jacob held the idea in his mind, half-expecting its weight to crush him. With the strength of city walls came inflexibility; with comfort, the danger of complacency; so much to gain and so much to lose—everything would change. *Home.* The word settled on him like a crown.

In the morning, he had an appointment with the mayor of St. Louis to discuss the details of their new living arrangement. Did the mayor have leverage Jacob hadn't accounted for? How would Micah and Rebecca react to his unilateral decision to stay in St. Louis? Much was unknown, but one thing was certain: Jacob would get what he wanted.

Those were tomorrow's problems. Tonight, he wanted to lean back in a decadently comfortable chair and enjoy some exceptionally high-quality bourbon. Since nothing in the world could stop him, he meant to do precisely that.

A stylish, mahogany cabinet caught his eye. He got up to investigate and discovered an impressive sound system inside, complete with every imaginable component. A collection of LPs and CDs filled the surrounding shelves. The captain had eclectic tastes in music, encompassing everything from punk to classical. Out of habit, Jacob's eyes gravitated toward rock from the late sixties and early seventies. Although he hadn't been born yet when those albums came out, he had always loved music from that era. It struck him as a dangerous time steeped in the mysteries and horrors of freedom, a dark time in the best sense of the word.

He reached into himself and stroked his personal Darkness. It purred like a kitten.

But this was a night of big ideas and grand gestures; only classical music would do. "Let's see," Jacob said as he scanned the shelves. "Beethoven, Chopin, Debussy..." He skipped to the end of the bottom shelf, which held a selection of the better recordings of Wagner's operas. Now there was a man who would have made a fine demon—all that passion, suffering, and maniacal fury baked into an ego so large reality itself couldn't contain it.

Jacob put on *Das Rheingold*, where the Ring Saga begins, and returned to his chair behind the desk. Relishing the sumptuous leather, he took a sip of bourbon. The music's shimmering harmonies swelled with beauty and promise.

Perfect.

Everything was perfect.

Epilogue

Ribbons of moonlight played across the black ripples and swirls of the Mississippi River. Caleb stood on the riverbank, water lapping his boots. At his feet, a child lay facedown in the muck.

When Caleb had set himself to the task of purging Mother's creation of her malformed and misbegotten children, he hadn't imagined the corruption ran so deep. At every turn he found wastrels and degenerates squandering their gifts on idle pleasure. Such creatures didn't deserve to call themselves Mother's children. They weren't worthy.

The child, a boy who resembled a burrowing animal, had slept through his life. Although he possessed power, he never thought to use it. Even as the lance pierced his body, all he did was weep. Pathetic. How could Mother suffer such an embarrassment to exist? She couldn't. That's why she had laid out this path for Caleb. He alone saw her will.

With a disgusted kick, he pushed the dead boy into deeper water.

"Sir?" a man in black, military fatigues called from behind him.

A servant disturbs me, Caleb thought without turning around. *Why?*

"Uh, yeah. Sorry, sir. A report came in from our agent in St. Louis. Lamia is dead."

Excellent. The servant must know how this came to pass.

"Well, according to the report..." He paused, shifting his weight awkwardly. "It says a man with horns and a woman with a tail killed her."

An old rage gripped Caleb's heart. The usurper. Countless nights had passed since there had been any sign of him. *He can't have gotten far. I will find him. In the name of the Mother of All, I swear it.*

"That's the thing," the man said. "If this report is right, he hasn't left St. Louis."

Caleb considered this for a moment. *The usurper plans to surround himself with walls and servants of his own. Fool.*

Once before, the usurper had goaded Caleb into acting rashly and the price had been great. This was not the time to attack the walled city. Lamia's servants vastly outnumbered his own. Let the usurper sit in his armored cage. When the time came, there would be a reckoning of such significance, Mother herself would surely acknowledge it.

Twisting and turning with the river's whims, the boy floated away from the place he had died. From below, slender arms which glowed like moonbeams given life snaked up around him. The Lady took hold of her fallen child and pulled him into the water's cool embrace. Suspended in murky gloom, she held him to her chest.

"Poor, poor boy," she whispered. "Who could have done this to you?"

Cradling her child, she slowly spiraled down to the riverbed and back up again in an underwater dance. She brought one of his paws, stiff with death, to her lips for a kiss. He had been an offshoot of her own essence. Now he was nothing, the beautiful explosion of life he had been gone forever. The Lady's heart ached.

Sensing her pain, the river nuzzled her cheek. She spoke to it. "Take him to where the Mississippi meets the Ohio, where the silt is soft and deep. Dig a channel and lay him to rest." A swift current took the boy from her. "Sleep well," she called after him.

As the boy faded into the distance, the Lady allowed herself to float, relishing her own buoyancy. With less disruption than an air bubble, her pale body breached the water's surface and lay flat, surrounded by a black halo of undulating hair. High above, the moon traveled its path as impassive as ever.

She rose into the air—higher and higher—until the moon was huge and her land small beneath her. Lights winked along one of the rivers far below. A multitude of living things, both human and not, moved there. One of her children must be involved. She wondered which.

A wispy cloud drifted past, brushing her. She tingled with pleasure at the sudden change in humidity. Droplets of water clung to her skin like lost children finding their mother. In the moonlight, they were tiny pearls.

Overcome by a sudden desire to see *everything*, she shot farther up—a white comet with a long black tail of whipping hair. When the air became too thin to breathe, she stopped and looked again upon her lands. So much life! So much potential! What strange and wonderful things were happening at that very moment?

The music of the Lady's laughter filled the night. Across her lands, her children looked in awe to the sky, Darkness swelling within them.

About the author

J.D. Carmicle is a writer of dark speculative fiction. He currently lives in Cincinnati, where he is busy working on something weird. When not writing, he enjoys spending time with his wonderful family, listening to music, and being tolerated by his two cats.